❧ HIGHLAND WARRIORS ❧

For generations, the Glen of Many Legends has been beset by strife and bloodshed as three Highland clans claim ownership to the land. The warrior chieftains are powerful, noble, and refuse to relinquish their birthright. But three cunning, beautiful lasses are about to band together to bring order and goodwill to their beloved homeland. Yet when the campaign moves from the battlefield to the bed chamber neither laird nor lass will be able to resist the passions unleashed...

PRAISE FOR
SUE-ELLEN WELFONDER

"Few writers can bring history to life like Sue-Ellen Welfonder! For anyone who loves historical fiction, the books in the Highland Warrior trilogy are a true treasure."
—**Heather Graham,** *New York Times*
bestselling author

"With each book Welfonder reinforces her well-deserved reputation as one of the finest writers of S̶

—*RT̶

D1397397

... AND HER NOVELS

A HIGHLANDER'S TEMPTATION

"Sue-Ellen Welfonder has written a wonderful historical romance that will make readers feel as if they have gone back to the past."
> —*Midwest Book Reviews*

"[Welfonder] continues to weave magical tales of redemption, love, and loyalty in glorious, perilous mid-fourteenth-century Scotland."
> —*Booklist*

"4 Stars! A fascinating, intriguing story that will definitely stand the test of time."
> —*RT Book Reviews*

SEDUCING A SCOTTISH BRIDE

"4½ Stars! Welfonder sweeps readers into a tale brimming with witty banter between a feisty heroine and a stalwart hero... The added paranormal elements and sensuality turn this into an intriguing page-turner that fans of Scottish romance will adore."
> —*RT Book Reviews*

"A great paranormal historical romance... Fans will read this in one delightful sitting so set aside the time."
> —*Midwest Book Review*

BRIDE FOR A KNIGHT

"[Welfonder] skillfully draws you into a suspenseful mystery with wonderful atmosphere."
   —*RT Book Reviews*

"Once again, Welfonder's careful scholarship and attention to detail vividly re-create the lusty, brawling days of medieval Scotland with larger-than-life chivalrous heroes and the dainty but spirited maidens."
   —*Booklist*

UNTIL THE KNIGHT COMES

"Welfonder's storytelling skill and medieval scholarship shine in her latest Kintail-based Scottish romance with magical elements."
   —*Booklist*

ONLY FOR A KNIGHT

"4½ Stars! Enthralling... Welfonder brings the Highlands to life with her vibrant characters, impassioned stories, and vivid description."
   —*RT Book Reviews*

WEDDING FOR A KNIGHT

"A very romantic story... extremely sexy. I recommend this book to anyone who loves the era and Scotland."
   —**TheBestReviews.com**

MASTER OF THE HIGHLANDS

"Welfonder does it again, bringing readers another powerful, emotional, highly romantic medieval that steals your heart and keeps you turning the pages."
—*RT Book Reviews*

BRIDE OF THE BEAST

"Larger-than-life characters and a scenic setting... Welfonder pens some steamy scenes."
—*Publishers Weekly*

KNIGHT IN MY BED

"Exciting, action-packed... a strong tale that thoroughly entertains."
—*Midwest Book Review*

DEVIL IN A KILT

"A lovely gem of a book. Wonderful characters and a true sense of place make this a keeper."
—**Patricia Potter, author of *The Heart Queen***

SINS OF A
HIGHLAND DEVIL

BOOKS BY SUE-ELLEN WELFONDER

Devil in a Kilt
Knight in My Bed
Bride of the Beast
Master of the Highlands
Wedding for a Knight
Only for a Knight
Until the Knight Comes
Bride for a Knight
Seducing a Scottish Bride
A Highlander's Temptation
Sins of a Highland Devil

SINS OF A HIGHLAND DEVIL

SUE-ELLEN WELFONDER

FOREVER

NEW YORK   BOSTON

This book is a work of fiction. Names, characters, places, and incidents are the product of the author's imagination or are used fictitiously. Any resemblance to actual events, locales, or persons, living or dead, is coincidental.

Copyright © 2011 by Sue-Ellen Welfonder

Book design by TexTech, Inc.

Forever
Hachette Book Group
237 Park Avenue
New York, NY 10017
Visit our website at www.HachetteBookGroup.com.

Forever is an imprint of Grand Central Publishing. The Forever name and logo is a trademark of Hachette Book Group, Inc.

Printed in the United States of America

First Printing: January 2011

10 9 8 7 6 5 4 3 2 1

In fond memory of Big Boy, a friendly red deer stag who enjoyed greeting visitors at Rannoch Moor's popular Black Mount viewpoint on the A-82 in Glencoe. Tame and trusting, Big Boy delighted travelers from all over the world. He was a highlight of my own drives through this spectacularly beautiful part of the Highlands. And he was the special friend of kindly Earle MacDonald, who was so good to him.

Big Boy's gentle nature brought his sad demise. But he lives on in the hearts of everyone who loved him. He inspired Rannoch, the enchanted stag in this book. Big Boy was even more extraordinary than my fictional Rannoch. I wish he'd also been as immortal.

A thousand blessings on Earle MacDonald of Black Mount, and other dedicated animal lovers everywhere.

Acknowledgment

If it's possible to be born loving a place, I came into this world with *Scotland* engraved on my heart. I visit as often as I can and being there replenishes my soul, filling me with awe and wonder, and always rejuvenating my muse. One of my greatest joys in writing is returning in my mind to the wild landscapes of hill, glen, and moor that inspire me.

When I write, I'm there again, surrounded by rock, wind, heather, and mist. My spirit soars and my office fills with the scents of cold, northern seas, pine and whin, and just the right trace of earthy-rich peat smoke. In those precious moments, the special places that haunt my memory come alive.

My new Highland Warriors trilogy is set in one of those special places. The Glen of Many Legends is fictitious, but its inspiration was one of the most rugged and savagely beautiful areas of the Western Highlands. Known in Gaelic as *Garbh-chriochan*, the "Rough Bounds," this lonesome stretch of dark hills, empty moors, and spectacular coastline, remains one of Scotland's most remote and inaccessible regions. Comprised of several districts, including Ardnamurchan, Moidart, Arisaig, Morar, and Knoydart, this boldly beautiful place is also rich in lore and legend.

Many of the more romantic tales lead to Moidart's Castle Tioram, an ancient stronghold of the Clanranald Macdonalds. Today, Tioram is a picturesque ruin. A place where the distant past feels so close, it's impossible to walk there and not expect to see plaid-draped clansmen rise from the heather, or catch the mournful wail of pipes. It's a place where memories remain and clan pride lingers, inextinguishable.

Tioram inspired Catriona MacDonald's Blackshore Castle. I took the liberty of making Blackshore a Clan Donald stronghold. Blackshore, like Tioram, stands on an island in Loch Moidart. I used a stone causeway to connect the castle to the shore. In reality, a spit of sand provides this access, dependent on tides.

My affection for Clan Donald is deep and I have ancestral ties to the clan. My Hebridean forebears were the Hereditary Keepers of the Records for the MacDonalds, Lords of the Isles. My fondness for MacDonalds made writing this book a special joy.

Several women help me bring my books to life. Roberta M. Brown, my agent and dearest friend. She's my greatest champion. Karen Kosztolnyik, my much-appreciated editor. If I could, I'd give her a medieval strongbox filled with gleaming ambers. She knows why. Special thanks to Celia Johnson, for being so helpful and nice. And an appreciative wave to my copy editor, Anna Maria Piluso, who is so good she makes copy edits a pleasure. Ladies, I'm so grateful.

Endless thanks and love to my very handsome husband, Manfred, who gallantly lets me follow my dreams and always has my back. And my little dog, Em, who is my lodestar. One kiss from him, a single tail wag, and the worst storm evaporates. He's everything to me and there aren't words for how much I love him.

SINS OF A
HIGHLAND DEVIL

The Legacy of the Glen

❖

Deep in the Scottish Highlands, three clans share the Glen of Many Legends. None of them do so gladly. Each clan believes they have sole claim to the fair and fertile vale. Their possessiveness is understandable, because the glen truly is a place like no other. Bards throughout the land will confirm that the Glen of Many Legends is just that: an enchanted place older than time and steeped with more tales and myth than most men can recall.

Kissed by sea and wind, the vale is long and narrow, its shores wild and serrated. Deeply wooded hills edge the glen's heart, while softly blowing mists cloak the lofty peaks that crowd together at its end. Oddly shaped stones dot the lush grass, but the strangeness of the ancient rocks is countered by the heather and whin that bloom so profusely from every patch of black, peaty earth.

No one would deny the glen's beauty.

Yet to some, the Glen of Many Legends is a place of ill fame to be avoided at all costs, especially by the dark of the moon. Strange things have been known to happen there, and wise men tread cautiously when they must pass that way.

But the MacDonalds, Camerons, and Mackintoshes who dwell there appreciate the glen's virtues above frightening tales that may or may not have credence. Good Highlanders all, the clans know that any storyteller of skill is adept at embroidering his yarns.

Highlanders are also a proud and stubborn people. And they're known for their fierce attachment to the land. These traits blaze hotly in the veins of the three clans of the Glen of Many Legends. Over time, their endless struggles to vanquish each other have drenched the glen with blood and sorrow.

Peace in the glen is fragile and rare.

Most times it doesn't exist at all. Yet somehow the clans tolerate each other, however grudgingly.

Now the precarious balance of order is about to be thrown into dispute by the death of a single woman.

A MacDonald by birth, and hereditary heiress to the MacDonalds of the Glen of Many Legends, she was a twice-widowed woman who chose to live out her days in the serenity and solitude of a nunnery.

Sadly, she neglected to set down her last wishes in a will. This oversight would not be so dire if not for the disturbing truths that her first husband had been a Cameron and her second, a Mackintosh.

On her passing, each clan lays claim to the dead woman.

Or, it can be more aptly said, they insist on being her rightful heirs.

Soon land-greed and coveting will once again turn the

glen's sweet grass into a sea of running red and many good men will lose their lives. But even when the last clansman sinks to his knees, his sword sullied and the end near, the real battle is only just beginning.

When it is done, the Glen of Many Legends will be forever changed.

As will the hearts of those who dwell there.

Chapter One

❧

BLACKSHORE CASTLE
THE GLEN OF MANY LEGENDS
AUTUMN 1396

A battle to the death?"

Alasdair MacDonald's deep voice rose to the smoke-blackened rafters of his great hall. Across that crowded space, his sister, Lady Catriona, stood frozen on the threshold. Alasdair's harsh tone held her there, but she did lift a hand to the amber necklace at her throat. A clan heirloom believed to protect and aid MacDonalds, the precious stones warmed beneath her fingers. She fancied they also hummed, though it was difficult to tell with her brother's roar shaking the walls. Other kinsmen were also shouting, but it was Alastair's fury that echoed in her ears.

His ranting hit her like a physical blow.

Her brother was a man whose clear blue eyes always held a spark of humor. And his laughter, so rich and catching, could brighten the darkest winter night, warming the hearts and spirits of everyone around him.

Just now he paced in the middle of his hall, his handsome face twisted in rage. His shoulder-length auburn hair—always his pride—was untidy, looking wildly mussed, as if he'd repeatedly thrust angry fingers through the finely burnished mane.

"Sakes! This is no gesture of goodwill." His voice hardened, thrumming with barely restrained aggression. "Whole clans cut down. Good men murdered—and for naught, as I and my folk see it!"

Everywhere, MacDonalds grumbled and scowled.

Some shook fists in the air, others rattled swords. At least two spat on the rush-strewn floor, and a few had such fire in their eyes it was almost a wonder that the air didn't catch flame.

Only one man stood unaffected.

A stranger. Catriona saw him now because one of her cousins moved and torchlight caught and shone on the man's heavily bejeweled sword belt.

She stared at the newcomer, not caring if her jaw slipped. She did step deeper into the hall's arched entry, though her knees shook badly. She also forgot to shut the heavy oaken door she'd just opened wide. Cold, damp wind blew past her, whipping her hair and gutting candles on a nearby table. A few wall torches hissed and spat, spewing ashes at her, but she hardly noticed.

What was a bit of soot on her skirts when the quiet peace of Blackshore had turned to chaos?

When Alasdair spoke of war?

As chief to their clan, he wasn't a man to use such words lightly. And even if he were, the flush on his face and the fierce set of his jaw revealed that something dire had happened. The stranger—a Lowland noble by his finery—didn't bode well either.

Men of his ilk never came to Blackshore.

The man's haughty stance showed that he wasn't pleased to be here now. And unlike her brother, he'd turned and was looking right at her. His gaze flicked over her, and then he lifted one brow, almost imperceptibly.

His opinion of her was palpable.

The insolence in that slightly arched brow, a galling affront.

Annoyance stopped the knocking of her knees, and she could feel her blood heating, the hot color sweeping up her neck to scald her cheeks.

The man looked amused.

Catriona was sure she'd seen his lips twitch.

Bristling, she pulled off her mud-splattered cloak and tossed it on a trestle bench. She took some satisfaction in seeing the visitor's eyes widen and then narrow critically when he saw that the lower half of her gown was as wet and soiled as her mantle. She had, after all, just run across the narrow stone causeway that connected her clan's isle-girt castle with the loch shore.

She'd raced to beat the tide. But even hurrying as she had, the swift-moving current was faster. She'd been forced to hitch up her skirts and splash through the swirling water, reaching the castle gates just before the causeway slipped beneath the rising sea loch.

It was a mad dash that always exhilarated her. As she did every day, she'd burst into the hall, laughing and with her hair in a wild tangle from the wind. Now she might look a fright, but her elation was gone.

"What's happened?" She hurried forward to clutch

Alasdair's arm, dread churning in her belly. "What's this about clans being cut down? A battle—"

"Not a true battle." Alasdair shot a glance at the Lowlander. "A trial by combat—"

"I see no difference." She raised her chin, not wanting the stranger to see her worry. It was clear he'd brought this madness. That showed in the curl of his lip, a half-sneer that revealed his disdain for Highlanders.

Alasdair noticed, too. She hadn't missed the muscle jerking in his jaw.

She tightened her grip on him. "If men are to die, what matters the name you cast on their blood?"

Behind her, someone closed the hall door. And somewhere in the smoke-hazed shadows, one of her kinsmen snarled a particularly vile curse. Catriona released her brother's arm and reached again for her amber necklace. She twirled its length around her fingers, clutching the polished gems as if they might answer her. Her own special talisman, the ambers often comforted her.

Now they didn't.

Worse, everyone was staring at her. The Lowlander eyed her as if she were the devil's own spawn. He surely saw her fiery-red hair as the brand of a witch. Almost wishing she was—just so she could fire-blast him—she straightened her back and let her eyes blaze. MacDonald pride beat through her, giving her strength and courage.

She turned to Alasdair. "You needn't tell me this has to do with the Camerons or the Mackintoshes. I can smell their taint in the air."

"My sister, Lady Catriona." He addressed the Lowlander, not her. "She sometimes forgets herself."

"I but speak the truth. As for my appearance, I was

enjoying the day's brisk wind—a walk in our hills." She flicked her skirts, righting them. "Had I known we had guests"—she met the man's hooded gaze—"I would have returned before the tide ran."

It was the only explanation he'd get from her.

"Lady." The stranger inclined his head, his dark eyes unblinking. "I greet you."

She refrained from asking *who* greeted her. His rich garments and jewels had already marked him as a fat-pursed, well-positioned noble. Not that such loftiness counted here, deep in the Highlands, where a man's deeds and honor mattered so much more than glitter and gold.

As if he read her mind and knew she was about to say so, her brother cleared his throat. "This, Catriona"—he indicated the Lowlander—"is Sir Walter Lindsay, the King's man. He's brought tidings from court. A writ from the King, expressing his royal will."

Catriona bent a chilly look upon the man. The churning in her stomach became a tight, hard knot.

Somehow she managed to dip in a semblance of a curtsy. "Good sir, welcome to Blackshore Castle." She couldn't bring herself to say *my lord*. "We've never before greeted such a noble guest to our glen."

Sir Walter's brow lifted. He said nothing, but a slight flaring of his nostrils showed he knew she wished she weren't forced to greet him now.

"It is because of the glen that he's here." Alasdair's words made her heart go still. "The King wishes that—"

"What does our glen have to do with the King?" She didn't want to know.

"The crown is greatly interested in this glen, my lady." Sir Walter rested his hand lightly on the sword at his hip.

"Your King would see peace in these hills. He is weary of the endless provocations between your clan and the other two who share this land. I am here to inform you that"—his gaze went to Alasdair—"he orders a trial of combat to ensure his will is met."

"Highland men keep their own peace," someone called from near the hearth.

Other voices rose in agreement, and Catriona's heart leapt. Surely the men of the clan would send Sir Walter on his way, King's courier or not. But Alasdair only strode to the high table and snatched up a rolled parchment, its red wax seals dangling and broken. When he turned back to the hall, his face was darker than ever, the writ clenched in a tight, white-knuckled grip.

"There are many here, Sir Walter, who would say this"—he raised his hand, shaking the scroll—"has too much blood on it to be worth any peace. We of this glen have our own ways of handling trouble. Even so, you'll no' see a single MacDonald refuse the King's challenge." Slapping the scroll back onto the table, he dusted his hands, demonstrably. "No' under the terms set before us."

The kinsman standing closest to Catriona, a young lad built like a steer and with hair as flame-bright as her own, spat onto the floor rushes. "Threatening to banish us from the glen be no terms!"

"They are the King's terms." Sir Walter's voice was impervious. "Be assured the Camerons and the Mackintoshes will receive the same warning."

Catriona heard the terrible words through a buzzing in her ears. Her head was beginning to pound, but she wouldn't show weakness by pressing her hands to her temples. She did flash a glance at her brother. Like every other MacDonald in the hall, he looked ready to whip out his sword and run the King's man through.

If she weren't a woman, she'd pull her own steel.

As it was, she suppressed a shudder and chose her words with care. "I missed the reading of your tidings, Sir Walter." His name tasted like ash on her tongue. "Perhaps you will repeat them for me?

"And"—she tilted her chin—"his reasons for placing us under his vaunted regard?"

"With pleasure, my lady." Sir Walter took her hand, lowering his head over her knuckles in an air kiss that jellied her knees in an icy, unpleasant way. "The King's will is that a trial of combat—a fight to the death—should be held in the glen. King Robert proposes within a fortnight."

He looked into her eyes. "Thirty champions from each of the three clans of the glen must face each other. They shall fight stripped of all but their plaids and armed with swords, dirks, axes. A bow with three arrows per man shall be allowed, and a shield. But no quarter may be given.

"Spectators will attend, and specially dispatched royal guards will assure that no man leaves the field." His gaze narrowed on her, his mien hardening. "At the trial's end, the clan with the most champions standing will be the one who wins your glen."

Catriona went hot and cold. "The Glen of Many Legends already is ours, the MacDonalds'. Robert Bruce granted it to my great-great-grandfather in tribute to our support at Bannockburn. Our men should not have to spill blood for what they fought and won with such honor."

"She speaks the truth, by God!" Alasdair banged his fist on a table. "Would your King see the good King Robert's charter undone?"

"King Robert Stewart would see an end to the strife in his realm." Sir Walter's voice was clipped. "The unrest and lawlessness in these parts—"

"Lawlessness?" Alasdair's face darkened. "What do you, a Lowlander, know of—"

"Do you deny the murders of three Mackintoshes this past summer?" Sir Walter examined his fingernails, flicked a speck of lint from his sleeve. "Innocent men killed in cold blood not far from these very walls?"

"They were stealing our cattle!" The redheaded youth next to Catriona stepped forward. "They chose to stand and face us when we caught them. It was a fair fight, no' murder."

Sir Walter's face remained cold. "Clan Mackintosh made a formal complaint to the court. Their chief informed us they were taking cattle to replace revenue tolls they lost because you menaced and threatened wayfarers trying to use the mountain pass above their stronghold."

"Aye, and what if we did?" Catriona began to shake with fury. "Every time our drovers attempt to use that pass to drive our beasts to the cattle trysts, the Mackintoshes block the way, barring passage to us. Even"—she drew a hot breath—"when we offered them double their toll."

"They cost *us* revenue!" The shout came from the back of the hall. A clansman riled by such absurdity. "They've been blocking that pass to us for years. We tired of it."

"The Mackintoshes are troublemakers." Catriona could scarce speak for anger. "Clan Cameron is worse."

A shiver ripped through her on the name, her heart pumping furiously as the insolent face of the dread clan's chief flashed across her mind. Worse than the devil, James Cameron ridiculed her every time their paths crossed.

There were few men she reviled more. Though just now she'd almost prefer his bold gaze and taunts to Sir Walter's superior stare.

Eyes narrowed, she fixed him with her own frostiest air. "Camerons cannot breathe without spewing insults." She tossed back her hair, knew her face was coloring. "They are an ancient line of Satan-spawned—"

"Ahhh..." Sir Walter spread his hands. "With so many transgressors afoot, you surely see why the King's intervention is necessary?"

"Necessary a pig's eye!" someone yelled near the hearth fire.

Catriona agreed.

Though, with Sir Walter harping on the past summer's squabble with the Mackintoshes, she could imagine that an overblown account of the incident might have reached the King's royal ear.

"Are the Mackintoshes behind this?" She could believe it. The cloven-footed trumpet-blasters wasted no opportunity to shout their claim to the glen. "Did they send another complaint to court? Asking for the crown's interference?"

Sir Walter's mouth jerked, proving they had. "They did send a petition in recent days, yes."

Catriona flushed. "I knew it!"

"They weren't alone. Clan Cameron also sent an appeal, if you'd hear the whole of it." Sir Walter's tone was smooth. The glint in his eye showed that he enjoyed her distress. "Indeed"—he actually smiled—"it surprised us that we did not hear from your brother, considering."

"Considering what?" Catriona's belly clenched again.

Sir Walter's smile vanished. "Perhaps you should ask your brother."

Catriona turned to Alasdair, but when he fisted his hands and his mouth flattened into a hard, tight line, her heart dropped.

Whatever it was that she didn't yet know was grim.

"Lady Edina has passed." Alasdair spoke at last. "She did not leave a testament. Nor, according to the abbess at St. Bride's"—he drew a deep breath—"did she ever make her wishes known to anyone."

Catriona swallowed. Guilt swept her.

She hadn't thought of the old woman in years. She'd been little more than a babe in swaddling when Lady Edina went, by choice, into a Hebridean nunnery. At the time—or so clan elders claimed—she'd desired a life of serenity and solitude behind cloistered walls.

But Edina MacDonald *was* hereditary heiress to the Glen of Many Legends.

She was also twice widowed. Her first husband— Catriona's heart seized with the horror of it—had been a Cameron and her second, a Mackintosh.

And now Lady Edina was dead.

Catriona wheeled to face Sir Walter. "This is the true meaning of your visit. Now that Lady Edina is gone, and without a will, the King means to take our lands."

Again, shouts and curses rose in the hall as MacDonalds everywhere agreed. Men stamped feet and pounded the trestles with their fists. The castle dogs joined in, their barks and howls deafening.

Even Geordie, a half-lamed beast so ancient he rarely barked at all, lent his protest from his tattered plaid bed beside the hearth fire.

Sir Walter stood unmoved. "These lands are the King's, by any right, as even you must know. Be glad he wishes only to bring you peace," he said, his weasel-smooth voice somehow cutting through the din. "When he received petitions from both the Camerons and the Mackintoshes claiming their due as Lady Edina's heirs, he knew strong measures would be needed to settle this glen. He wishes to see these hills held by the clan most worthy."

Alasdair made a sound that could only be called a growl. His face turned purple.

Catriona's ambers blazed against her neck, the stones' pulsing heat warning her of danger. She took a deep breath, drawing herself up until the disturbing prickles receded and her necklace cooled.

"How did the Camerons and Mackintoshes know of Lady Edina's death?" She looked at the Lowlander. "Why weren't we informed, as well?"

"You know better than me how swiftly—or errone-ously—word travels in these parts." Sir Walter shrugged. "Perhaps a missive meant for you went astray? Either way—"

"You mean to see good men slaughtered." Catriona felt bile rise in her throat. "Men who—"

"Men who fight, yes, until only one remains stand-ing." Sir Walter set his hand on his sword again, his fin-gers curling around the hilt. "If they do not"—his voice chilled—"you must face the consequences. Banishment from this glen to parts even wilder. Resettlement, if you will, in places where the crown can make use of men with ready sword arms and women adept at breeding."

The words spoken, he folded his arms. "The choice is yours."

Across the hall, Geordie barked hoarsely.

Out of the corner of her eye, Catriona thought she saw

the dog struggling to rise. She wasn't sure, because the hall was spinning, going black and white before her eyes. Around her, her kinsmen shouted and cursed, the noise hurting her ears. Even more alarming, something whirled and burned inside her. It was a horrible, swelling heat that filled her chest until she couldn't breathe.

Slowly, she felt down and along the folds of her skirts, seeking the lady dirk hidden there. But she caught herself in time, clasping her hands tightly before her just before her fingers closed on the blade.

Ramming a dagger into the King's man would bring even more grief to her clan.

But she *was* tempted.

Fighting the urge, she looked from the Lowlander to Alasdair and back again. "I believe, Sir Walter, that my brother has given you our choice. MacDonalds won't be driven from their land. These hills were our own before ever a Stewart called himself a king. If our men must take up arms to avoid the Stewart wrongfully banishing us from a glen we've held for centuries, so be it."

A curt nod was Sir Walter's reply.

Returning it, Catriona dipped another curtsy and then showed him her back. She needed all her dignity, but she kept her spine straight as she strode to one of the hall's tall, arch-topped windows. Once there, she stared out at the sea loch, not surprised to see its smooth gray surface pitted with a light, drizzly rain. Dark clouds crouched low on the hills, and thin tendrils of mist slid down the braes, sure portents that even more rain was coming.

The Glen of Many Legends was crying.

But she would not.

She wouldn't break even if the Lowland King and his

minions ripped the heart right out of her. Highlanders were the proudest, most stoic of men. And MacDonalds were the best of Highlanders.

So she stepped closer to the window, welcoming the cold, damp air on her cheeks. Countless MacDonald women before her had stood at this same window embrasure. In a fortnight's passing, her brother and cousins would ensure that they would continue to do so in years to come. It was just unthinkable that they were being forced to do so with their lives.

Incomprehensible and—she knew deep inside—quite possibly more than she could bear.

When Geordie bumped her hand, leaning into her and whimpering, she knew she had to try. But even as she dug her fingers into the old dog's shaggy coat, the sea loch and the hills blurred before her. She blinked hard, unable to bring her world back into focus. The stinging heat pricking her eyes only worsened, though she did keep her tears from falling.

On the day of the battle she'd do the same. She'd stand tall and look on with pride, doing her name honor.

Somehow she'd endure.

Whatever it cost her.

Nearly a fortnight later, James Cameron stood atop the battlements of Castle Haven and glared down at the worst folly to ever darken the Glen of Many Legends. Wherever he looked, Lowlanders bustled about the fine vale beneath the castle's proud walls. A different sort than the lofty souls gorging themselves on good Cameron beef in his great hall, these scrambling intruders were workmen. Minions brought along to do the nobles' bidding, whose busy hands erected viewing platforms while their hurrying feet flattened the sweetest grass in the glen.

Already, they'd caused scars.

Deep pits had been gouged into the fertile earth. Ugly black gashes surely meant to hold cook fires. Or—James's throat filled with bile—the bodies of the slain.

On the hills, naked swaths showed where tall Scots pines had been carelessly felled to provide wood. Jagged bits of the living, weeping trees littered the ground.

"Christ God!" James blew out a hot breath, the destruction searing him with an anger so heated he wondered his fury didn't blister the air.

He went taut, his every muscle stiff with rage.

Beside him, his cousin Colin wrapped his hands around his sword belt. "They haven't wasted a breath of time," he vowed, eyeing the stout barricades already marking the battling ground where so many men would die.

A circular enclosure better suited to contain cattle than proud and fearless men.

James narrowed his gaze on the pen, unable to think of it as aught else. "Only witless peacocks wouldn't know that such barricading isn't necessary."

Colin flashed a look at him, one brow raised in scorn. "Perhaps they do not know that Highland men never run from a fight?"

"They shall learn our measure soon enough." James rolled his shoulders, keen to fight now. "Though"—he threw a glance at the men working on the nearest viewing platform—"I might be tempted to flee their hammering!"

Half serious, he resisted the urge to clamp his hands to his ears. But he couldn't keep an outraged snarl from rumbling in his throat. The din was infernal. Any moment his head would burst from the noise. Each echoing *bang* was an ungodly smear on the quiet of the glen, most especially here, in this most beauteous stretch of the Glen of Many Legends.

Equally damning, the MacDonald wench once again stood at the edge of the chaos. On seeing her, he felt an even hotter flare of irritation. He stepped closer to the walling, hoping he erred. Unfortunately, he hadn't. She was truly there, hands on her hips and looking haughty as she glared at the Lowland workmen.

Joining him at the wall, Colin gave a low whistle. "She's Catriona MacDonald, the chief's sister. Word is she's the wildest of that heathenish lot."

"I know who she is." James glared at his cousin, not liking the speculative gleam in his eye. "And she *is* wild— so prickly some say she sleeps in a bed of nettles."

Colin laughed. "She's bonnie all the same."

"So is the deep blue sea until you sink in its depths and drown." James scowled at the lass.

Pure trouble, she'd clearly come to show her wrath. As she'd done every day since the Lowlanders began setting up their gaudy tents and seating. If Colin hadn't noticed her before now, James had. He *always* noticed her, rot his soul. And just now, she was especially hard to miss with the sun picking out the bright copper strands in her hair and her back so straight she might have swallowed a steel rod. And if he didn't want to lose his temper in front of workmen who—he knew—were only following orders, he would've marched down to the field days ago and chased her away.

He'd done so once, running her off Cameron land years ago, when he'd been too young and hotheaded to know better than thrusting his hand into a wasp nest.

She'd stung him badly that day. And the memory still haunted him. At times, sneaking into his dreams and twisting his recollections so that, instead of sprinting away from him, she'd be on her back beneath him, opening her arms in welcome, tempting him to fall upon her and indulge in the basest, most lascivious sins.

Furious that she stirred him even now, he tore his gaze from her and frowned at the long rows of colorful awnings, the triumphal pennons snapping in the wind. The festive display shot seething anger through his veins. Truth be told, if one of the King's worthies appeared on the battlements, he wouldn't be able to restrain himself.

Apparently feeling the same, Colin stepped back a few paces and whipped out his sword, thrusting it high. "Forget the MacDonald wench and her jackal blood. We could"—he made a flourish with the blade—"have done with yon mummery in the old way! Cut down the Lowland bastards and toss them into a loch. We then block every entry into the glen, keep silent, and no one need know they even reached us."

He grinned wickedly, sliced a ringing arc in the cold afternoon air.

James strode forward and grabbed Colin's wrist, stopping his foolery. "The old way ne'er included murdering innocents. The workmen"—he jerked a glance at them—"are naught but lackeys. Their blood on our hands would forever stain our honor. Sir Walter's blood, much as I'd love to spill it, would bring a King's army into the glen. No matter what we did, they'd come. Even if every clan in the Highlands rose with us against them, their number alone would defeat us.

"And"—he released Colin's arm, nodding grimly when

his cousin sheathed the blade—"King Robert would then do more than scatter us. He'd put us to the horn, outlawing us so that we'd lose no' just our land but our very name. A fire-and-sword edict passed quicker than you can blink. That, he would do!"

Colin scowled, flushing red. "Damnation!"

"Aye," James agreed, his own face flaming. "We are damned whate'er. So we do what is left to us. We keep our pride and honor and prove what hard fighters we are. With God's good grace, we shall be victorious."

Colin's chin came up, his eyes glinting. "Perhaps He will bless us now." He flashed a wicked grin and strode for the door arch. "I'm off to the hall to see if God in His greatness might cause Sir Walter to choke on a fish bone. I shall pray on the way."

James's lips twitched. On another day, he would have thrown back his head and laughed. As it was, he watched Colin hasten into the stair tower without another word. Only when his young cousin's footsteps faded did he glance at the heavens and mutter a prayer of his own.

Then he whipped around to toss another glower at Lady Catriona, even though she couldn't see him.

He snorted when he saw her.

She'd edged even closer to one of the viewing platforms, her glare pinned on the workmen. James shuddered just looking at her. He almost felt sorry for the men flamed by her scorching stare. Deepest blue yet piercing as the sun, her eyes could burn holes in a man if he didn't take care.

James knew it well, much to his annoyance.

Fortunately, their paths didn't cross often, but each time they'd had the displeasure, he'd regretted it for days.

Just now, with the wind blowing her skirts and her hair

whipping about her face, he almost felt an odd kinship with her. There was something about the challenging tilt of her chin and the blaze in her eyes that—for one crazy, mad moment—made her not a MacDonald but every Highland woman who'd ever walked the hills.

Almost, he was proud of her.

But *almost* was just that—something that hovered just short of being.

He let his gaze sweep over her one last time, glad that it was so. Catriona MacDonald was the last woman he wished to admire.

Blotting her from his mind, he strode to another part of the battlements, choosing a corner where the sight of her wouldn't spoil his view. Then he braced himself and stared past the fighting ground to the hills beyond, deep blue and silent against the sky. Directly across from him, a sparkling rock-strewn cataract plunged down a narrow gorge cut deep into one of the hills. It was the same vista he enjoyed from his bedchamber window. The sight—as always—took his breath and made his heart squeeze. This day, the falls' beauty also quenched any last shred of sympathy he might have felt for the MacDonald she-wolf.

In Cameron hands since distant times, the glen was his birthright and his joy. Cloud shadows drifted across its length, the gentle play of light and dark bleeding his soul. His eyes misted at the well-loved scene, his throat thickening. He'd always believed his children would one day love the glen with equal fierceness. That they'd carry on tradition, bound to the land and appreciating their heritage, teaching their own offspring to do the same.

Now...

He wrenched his gaze from the glen, fury whipping

through him like a flame to tinder. He should've known better than to come up here. But Colin had wanted to see the workmen's progress. And, truth be told, brisk winds always blew across the ramparts and he'd relished a few moments in the cold, clean air before courtesy demanded he join Sir Walter and his ravenous friends in the hall.

The man's lofty airs and barely veiled insults were more than any man should have to tolerate within his own walls. And watching Lindsay and his henchmen eat their way through Castle Haven's larders—with neither the MacDonalds nor the Mackintoshes helping with the costs—was as galling as it was enlightening.

No matter how the trial of combat ended, the other two clans of the glen would never change their colors.

Most especially the MacDonalds.

The she-wolf's presence on the field vouched for their obstinacy. Just as her flay-a-man stares proved they had a touch of the devil in them.

It was a taint that might serve them well when they soon found themselves in hell.

James's pulse quickened imagining them there.

It was a fine thought.

A well-met fate that sent a surge of satisfaction shooting through him. He could see them landing on Hades' hottest hob or in a deep, icy pit where they could languish for eons, pondering their treacheries.

They deserved no better.

Pity was so many Camerons would be joining them.

Chapter Two

❦

James tossed in his sleep, lost in one of the most heated dreams he'd enjoyed in years. Tantalizing images seared him, scalding his blood with a stirring swirl of lascivious delights. Tempting glimpses of a certain flame-haired siren's lush nakedness as she rode boldly astride him. She held his gaze, her sapphire eyes alight with desire. His own lust sharpened, his pulse quickening to see her need. He reached for her, smoothing his hands along her sleek, fulsome curves, when he became aware of a heavy, cumbersome weight shifting across his lower legs. It was a hot, unyielding burden that had nothing to do with the lithe-limbed beauty whose sinuous movements were so rousing that his heart raced even now.

He came awake at once, glaring into the darkness.

His dog, Hector, shifted again, this time resting his head on James's knee. Ignoring the aged beast, James continued to frown.

Anger suited him.

Had anyone but Hector shattered his pleasure, he'd do more than glower.

Not that his scowls brought back the stormy-eyed Mac-Donald vixen whose voluptuous enticements so enchanted him. She'd vanished like mist before the sun, and the room's emptiness hit him like a physical blow. Quiet lay in the air, and the smell of cold ash pervaded, reminding him that the temptress of his dreams had been no more substantial than the silvery moonlight slipping through the shutter slats.

He blinked, grateful to feel his desire subsiding.

Even so, he felt a strong urge to drive his fist into the pillows. He did allow himself a shudder. Lusting after Catriona MacDonald not only left a sour taste in his mouth, but brought him perilously close to a dark pit of desire that could easily consume him.

Already, he could smell the brimstone. Even taste the sulfurous mist wafting around him. Each curl of drifting foulness reminded him of the folly—and dangers—that awaited chieftains who succumbed to the wiles of temptresses from feuding clans.

The Highlands abounded with tales of the horrors unleashed by ill-fated passions.

Wanting no part of such miseries, he drew a tight, annoyed breath. Then he set his jaw, pushing all thought of his prickly, large-bosomed nemesis from his mind.

Hector gave a grunt of pleasure, blissfully unaware of the turmoil he'd stirred. Clearly content, he settled back to his canine slumber. But the dog's weight increased, causing a welter of fiery, tingly heat to dance up and down James's legs until he felt as if a thousand tiny, sharp-headed needles were pricking his skin. The discomfort chased away any last vestiges of sleep and worsened his mood.

As did the image of Catriona MacDonald when she rose up to vex him anew, whirling—naked and glorious—across his mind's eye as if he hadn't just banished her.

Vibrant as in his dream, she twirled and swayed, her shining red-gold hair tumbling past her shoulders, swinging about her hips.

Her breasts...

"Damnation!" He pushed up on his elbows, his furious gaze snapping to Hector.

The dog opened one eye and met his stare, his canine expression annoyingly innocent.

James peered back, unmoved. He started to scold the dog for climbing into the bed—after all, Hector had his own comfortable blanket before the hearth—but he closed his mouth and simply narrowed his eyes.

Hector was old.

And the chill in the room revealed that the fire had died hours ago.

Hector appreciated the warmth of the bed as much as James did. When the dog rolled onto his side with a long, fluting sigh, giving every indication of returning to the blissful realm of sleep, James almost envied him. He wouldn't mind nestling beneath the covers and finding his way back into his shattered dream.

He'd just paint a different face on a certain flame-haired seductress.

Instead, his night's rest was ruined.

So he extracted his legs from beneath Hector's bulk and climbed from the bed. As it was, he'd planned to rise early. Although he'd intended to do so closer to sunrise and not at this ungodly hour when the moon hadn't even set and the castle was so still.

He'd hoped to slip away in the midst of the morning bustle when no one would bat an eye as he strode through the waking hall.

His kinsmen didn't need to know he meant to visit the Makers of Dreams. Most of his people knew the ancients as Grizel and Gorm, simple herders of sheep and deer. They were famed for making delicious cheese and always offered weary travelers a dipperful of thick, creamy milk. They also lived by the old ways and tended a mysterious cave hidden in a tumbled outcrop of stone.

As Makers of Dreams, the half-mythic couple shared their true purpose only with Cameron clan chiefs, trusting them above all other men. Proud of this privilege, James respected the old pair greatly and was hesitant to prod knowledge from them. For in addition to crafting dreams each night and sending them to those deserving, Grizel and Gorm were also adept givers of prophecies.

But he did feel a need to question them about the trial of combat.

He hoped they'd confirm a Cameron victory.

Now...

He scowled at the silence, sure that every man sleeping below would snap to nosy wakefulness the instant he unlatched his bedchamber door. His footfalls would echo through the dark passage beyond. The sound would swell, filling the stair tower even if he crept along as lightly as a mouse.

It was that quiet.

The shutters were closed against the cold autumn night, but even from across the room he could hear the wind in the pines and the distant rush of the waterfall that spilled down a deep gorge across from his windows.

He also heard Hector shifting on the bed. The ancient beast was a restless sleeper and enjoyed shoving his muzzle in James's goings-on almost as much as some of James's two-legged friends and kinsmen. If a single floorboard creaked, Hector would be scrambling off the bed. He'd then limp across the room to sit before the door, head cocked and eyes hopeful, as he craftily blocked James's exit.

It was a trick that usually worked.

But the way to the high moors where Grizel and Gorm dwelled was too steep and treacherous for an aged dog with hinky hips and unsteady back legs.

So James stepped with caution to the jug and basin on a table near his bed. He poured handfuls of icy water and splashed his face. Then he shoved a quick hand through his hair and dressed even faster, pulling on his plaid as he crossed the room. He slipped away before Hector could protest, and he crept down the stairs, refusing to consider the wisdom of seeking an answer he might prefer not to know.

The Makers of Dreams never lied.

And James didn't get far before his nape began to prickle. He froze where he was, just paces inside the night-darkened hall. The cold, smoke-hazed air felt thick with the sense of an unseen presence. Sure of it, he glanced about as he picked his way forward through the rows of trestle tables. He went slowly, taking care not to disturb the slumbering men sprawled on their pallets.

Nothing moved.

Yet he was certain someone else was awake.

His warrior instinct felt the throb of a heartbeat, stirring the air. There was movement in the hall's shadows, an uncanny sort of shifting. James rubbed his neck, hoping he wasn't sensing the Makers of Dreams. They were said to be everywhere when darkness fell.

They saw everything.

Or so many men believed.

Some even claimed they could see the wind. Or that they knew when the tiniest fish swam across the bottom of the sea. James felt his stomach knot. If the ancients were responsible for the chills nipping at him just now, he only prayed they hadn't also been around during his sensual dream of Catriona MacDonald.

There were some things a man kept to himself.

So he put back his shoulders and crossed the hall, not stopping until he'd opened the door and stepped out into the silver-washed bailey.

The moonlight was brighter than he'd expected, and the courtyard proved as empty as the hall had been packed with sleeping men. Frost glittered on the cobbles and crackled beneath his feet, the noise making him wince. But nothing stirred in the cold, brittle air except the clouds of his own breath.

Even so, he scanned the deeper shadows as he hastened to the postern gate, preferring that little-used door in the curtain wall to the well-guarded main gateway. The half-moon already rode low above the hills. Despite the blue-white light shining down into the bailey, it would soon be morning.

He wasn't going to be the one to break whatever remained of the night's peace.

Or so he thought until he passed through the postern's

narrow opening and spotted a dark shape slip around the far corner of the castle. Clearly a man, the hooded figure crept across the sward, keeping close to the long black line of scaffolding where the Lowlanders were building their viewing platforms.

James stared, his eyes narrowing.

Whoever the man was, he wasn't up to any good.

It was a daily annoyance at Castle Bane that Sir Walter kept his henchmen patrolling the stronghold's perimeters and the edges of the soon-to-be fighting ground. But if this flat-footed craven was one of Sir Walter's guards, he'd be too arrogant to keep to the shadows.

"You—hold there!" James sprinted after the man, one hand gripping his sword hilt as he ran. "Halt, you! You've been seen!"

If the man heard him, he gave no sign.

Castle Haven's guards appeared equally oblivious.

James tossed a glance behind him, but no one burst through the postern door. At this hour, the men on duty would be hunkered around a coal brazier in the gatehouse, keeping warm and awaiting sunrise. Even if they were on the walls, they'd be watching the approach to the main gate on the other side of the castle.

No one could hear his pounding footsteps, or even his shouts.

Furious, he kept running. But the man disappeared into the trees just as James reached the half-built viewing stands.

"Wait!" He ran faster, racing now. But the woods' darkness soon closed around him, making pursuit a folly. Scowling, he took a deep breath of the frosty, pine-scented air. He glanced around but couldn't see anything. Thick mist clung to the trees, shifting around the trunks and curtaining the low-hanging branches. Wishing he could see better, he pressed deeper into the gloom, but the farther he went, the more mist swirled around him.

The dark-cloaked stranger was gone.

"Odin's balls." James loosened his grip on his sword. His pride scalded him. If he'd been two paces quicker or perhaps not yelled a warning—

His heart jumped when a branch snapped somewhere to his right, the sound quickly followed by a light skitter of rolling pebbles.

He swung round, whipping out his sword, and then feeling foolish when nothing but the dark trees and drifting fog stared back at him. Even so, the sensation that he wasn't alone returned. Worse, he now felt as if the woods were creeping in on him.

It was as if the trees had sprung legs and were sneaking closer behind his back, then quickly freezing in place when he glanced at them. Even the mist seemed hell-born, much colder and almost glowing.

He set his jaw, ignoring the strangeness.

He hadn't slept well, after all.

And he'd lived too long in the Glen of Many Legends not to know that, even well rested, a man could chance upon many odd things in these hills he loved so dearly. Trees that stalked men and icy, cloying mist were nothing to some of the tales told late on a cold winter's night at Castle Haven's hearth fire.

He *would* concern himself with the man who'd slipped away from him.

But first he had other business to attend.

So he made for the hill path to the Makers of Dreams.

But before he'd gone three paces, he caught a flash of red in the trees to his right. He turned, his eyes rounding when he found himself staring at the hurrying form of a beautiful flame-haired woman.

And she wasn't just any woman.

Irritation tightened James's chest. He let his gaze sweep her entire fetching length, from her gleaming red-gold hair to the sweet, well-turned ankles that were displayed because she held her skirts hitched high. Ripped straight from his dream, she made the blood roar in his ears.

He blinked, but she didn't go away.

He wasn't dreaming now.

The brazen minx was real, and he'd know her anywhere, even through the mist. No other female would stride so boldly through the chill darkness of the wood. True to her nature, she had a fierce glint in her eye and held her chin tilted with a dash of defiance. Her hair might have been neatly braided when she'd left her own castle walls, but somewhere along the way, the shining tresses had spilled free and now tumbled in wild abandon about her face.

She was magnificent.

And she was definitely Catriona MacDonald.

No doubt making her way to the viewing platforms to blast the Lowlanders with her wicked-eyed stare. She did so every morning, though James was sure he'd never spotted her about quite this early.

That she was here now—at a time when an unknown, dark-cloaked man had been in the wood—proved a damnable complication.

MacDonald or no, she *was* a woman.

James frowned, his fury rising when he couldn't help

but admire the pert sway of her hips as she marched through the trees.

"Damnation." He shoved a hand through his hair, glaring at her retreating back.

She was moving fast.

And he had no choice but to step in and keep her from possible harm.

He started forward before annoyance could override his damnable honor. He had better things to do with his morning than chase after the one female who rode his nerves like a bee beneath his collar. But if she fell to peril and he hadn't stepped in, he'd feel worse. So he quickened his step, not caring if he startled her.

The closer he came to her, the more the air felt oddly charged. He could almost hear the mist crackling around him. For two pins, he'd swear he wasn't cutting through the cold morning, but that he'd plunged into a sea of invisible fire. Each swirl of mist sizzled against his skin, almost searing him. His blood heated, roaring through his veins and pounding in his ears.

And still the vixen hurried on, her raised skirts nearly drawn to her knees. Now he not only had a splendid view of her trim ankles, but also her finely formed calves. When she hopped over a log, lifting those skirts even higher, he saw a great deal more. Enough to darken his mood and send him sprinting forward before she could come across another impediment and taunt him again.

He'd already seen more than was wise of those long, sleek legs.

So he closed the last few paces between them and reached to grab her shoulder. "Catriona Mac—"

"Don't think to touch me!" She whirled around with a

wild toss of hair and skirt, snarling like a she-wolf. He'd
never seen a woman move so quickly. The bright flash of
steel sheathed at her inner thigh stunned him, as did her
quickness to retrieve it. Before he could jump back, she
lunged at him, her eyes burning hotly.

Precise as any man, she sliced his outstretched hand.
Scalding heat and pain and oozing blood filled his palm.
Her blade held high, she danced nimbly just beyond his
reach, her furious gaze pinned on him. "Come a step
closer and I'll cut you where it hurts most."

She shot a glance at the place she meant. "Doubt me at
your own peril."

"Dinnae flatter yourself." Angered beyond measure,
James outmaneuvered her. Catching her wrist, he squeezed
hard so the dirk slipped from her fingers. "I'd sooner roll
naked in stinging nettles than lay a hand on you."

"You already are." She jerked her arm, trying to break
free.

"So I am." He let her struggle. "But you needn't fear for
your virtue. Prickly lasses such as you are no' to my liking."

"That's as well." She couldn't have sounded more con-
temptuous. "Swell-headed, vaunting scoundrels aren't to
mine."

She continued to fight him, and he countered the jab
of her elbows, the kick of her feet. He lost all patience
when her knee slammed his thigh. Hauling her roughly
against his chest, he scowled at her, taking some small
satisfaction in seeing his blood trickling down her arm,
staining her skin with her fool deed.

She followed his gaze, her brows snapping together
when she saw the blood. "I shall scour myself every night
for a fortnight to remove your taint."

James felt a muscle twitch in his jaw. "To think I thought to save you from folly. Now"—he released her, stepping back to wipe his bloodied palm on his plaid—"I wish I'd let you to your own sorry fate."

"What happens to me is none of your concern." She brushed at her skirts, righting them with quick, jerky motions. "You—a Cameron."

"Aye." James inclined his head, proudly. "I am *the* Cameron. And you, lass, needn't straighten your clothes. The time for modesty has passed. Why conceal what I've already seen?"

"Oh!" She glared at him, furious color flashing across her face. "How dare you—"

"I dare much." James placed a deliberate foot on her fallen dagger. "Truth be told, there are many who would say we are now bound, whatever. You've drawn first blood, my lady. Or"—he lifted his hand, casually examining the deep red cut across his palm—"were you no' aware of the consequences of such a brazen act?

"Have you ne'er heard that oaths are sworn on blood?" He met her eyes again, challenging. "Sacred vows so irreversible that doom awaits those who break them?"

"Pah!" She flushed brighter, almost trembling in her anger. "You must think I'm witless. Thon cut has naught to do with such pacts. Nothing binds us except years of feuding and the scorn every MacDonald has for Camerons. Though"—she raised her chin, defiant—"I'll own that if I'd known it was you, I would not have drawn my lady's dirk."

"Indeed?" James lifted a brow. "I'm honored."

"You shouldn't be." She put back her shoulders, ever proud. "I wouldn't have sullied good MacDonald steel with the taint of Cameron blood."

"And if it'd been your blood spilled?" James could hardly speak for fury. He bent to snatch up her dagger, thrusting it beneath his belt. "What then, eh? Did you not think that someone else might have shown less mercy to a knife-wielding she-cat?"

"Mercy?" She fisted her hands on her hips, a hot-eyed Valkyrie in the swirling gray mist. "I neither ask for nor need your mercy. As you saw"—her gaze flicked to his hand—"I can look after myself."

"And pigs roost in trees." James stepped closer, towering over her. He pinned her with his fiercest stare, taking full advantage of his formidable height and size. "You have me, and me alone, to thank that naught worse than hurt pride has befallen you."

She gave him a haughty look. "You are the one bearing a wound."

James set his mouth in a thin, hard line. She was beyond exasperating. Did he not want to risk having to notice—again—how sweet her lush curves felt against him, he'd pull her into his arms and kiss her until she couldn't deny the precarious situation she'd put herself in by marching alone through a dark and danger-filled wood.

He did curl his hands around his sword belt and glower at her.

That, he could do.

"The cut on my hand is a wee scratch." He leaned toward her, so close he caught the gillyflower scent of her wildly tumbling hair. "What could have happened to you would have been a much more grievous injury."

She gave a little shrug, defiant still. "I walk these hills each morn."

"The new day has no' yet broken." James felt an

annoying surge of responsibility for her. She was, after all, on Cameron land. Vulnerable and defenseless, despite her ridiculous and headstrong airs.

He glanced at the sky, so dark and with the moon only now beginning to dip beneath the tops of the inky-black pines. The air was brittle and cold, and the chill mist swirled everywhere, drifting through the trees and curling along the frost-hardened ground.

Catriona didn't seem to notice.

James frowned.

Most females would be shivering beneath the folds of their cloaks. They'd be drawing those mantles closer about themselves. They'd shift their feet, rubbing their arms and blowing on their hands, seeking warmth. In this wood, in the heart of the Glen of Many Legends, they'd also cast cautious glances about them, watching the darkness.

She watched only him.

And she did so in a way that was damned unsettling.

James gave her a hard stare. It was so easy to imagine her as he'd seen her just a short while ago, in the heated depths of his dream. Standing so near to her brought a stirring to his loins, a pestiferous throbbing so annoying it was all he could do not to seize her and give full rein to the maddening heat crawling through him.

Instead, he let his gaze drop to where her cloak outlined the swell of her breasts. Lush, ripe curves he burned to plump and caress. His fingers itched so badly that he balled his hands to tight fists. Other parts of him ached in ways he refused to acknowledge.

She eyed him boldly, the rise and fall of her bosom showing her agitation, fueling his desire. "I know fine how early it is." She lifted her chin, her color rising. "You needn't mind me."

Any other time he would've laughed. *Minding her* was the last thing he'd like to do to her just now.

If she pushed him, he'd heed those urges.

"This is an ungodly hour." He struggled to catch himself. "Goodly womenfolk should yet be abed, no' marching about like she-devils." He spoke more harshly than he would have liked. But her scent, so light yet tantalizing, was irritating the hell out of him.

He looked her up and down, noting the pleasing curve of her hips, his wicked mind imagining the intimate place between her thighs. She didn't flinch, and—something inside him twisted with annoyance—the longer she accepted his brazen perusal, the more he noticed her damnable scent. It wrapped around him, teasing and provoking.

Her eyes glinted in the moonlight, triumphant. Almost as if she knew.

"You call me a she-devil." She spoke the word with relish. "If I were such a creature, I'd fire-blast you, making this a morn you'd never forget."

James almost choked.

She'd already made it a day he'd long remember.

It wasn't often that a woman's mere presence made him feel like a ravening beast. She didn't need fire-blasts. Her scent alone was more than memorable and roused him in ways that weren't good for him.

Allowing himself to wonder if the curls topping her thighs flamed as brightly as the hair on her head disturbed him enough to make him want to break something.

He tightened his grip on his sword belt, furious.

It'd been forever since he'd lain with a woman. Even

so, he'd sooner gorge himself on a trencher piled high with thick black slabs of peat than allow the seductive fragrance wafting from Catriona MacDonald's flaming-red hair make him hot, hard, and aroused.

So he kept his scowl in place and did his best not to inhale. "By rights, lady, it is still night."

"So?" She didn't blink.

She did touch the amber necklace at her throat, letting her fingers glide along the stones in a way surely meant to provoke him.

He frowned at her, refusing to look lower than her chin. "I've ne'er seen you out this early. As a maid of this glen, you—"

"You track my whereabouts?" Her eyes narrowed suspiciously.

"You should know it isn't wise to creep about before the sun rises." He ignored her objection. "There are reasons this vale is called the Glen of Many Legends. And there are truths behind every hair-raising tale.

"Nor"—he caught another whiff of gillyflower—"is it seemly for—"

"MacDonalds don't *creep* anywhere. And you've no right to speak of what is seemly. You forfeited that privilege when you charged up behind me, trying to catch me unawares." She looked him in the eye, daunting. "Until you accosted me, I've never once felt threatened here."

"Perhaps you should be more wary the next time you venture into this wood." James threw a glance at the silent trees. Blackness lurked there, deep and impenetrable. "There are many men about just now. Strangers unused to our Highland ways."

"Then they shouldn't be here."

"But they are. And none of us can say what might push one of them past his limits." He wasn't about to mention the hooded figure. Cameron men didn't frighten women unduly. But she did need a warning.

"You could tempt one of these Lowlanders into villainy." He spoke true, seeing no reason to lie. The proud tilt of her head was proof enough that she knew her worth. Whether she knew what her kind of vital sensuality could do to a man was another matter.

"And you, James Cameron?" Her sapphire eyes burned into him. "Are *you* tempted?"

He snorted, keeping his answer to himself.

But he did let his gaze flick over her again, certain she was disaster walking. Her hair spilled freely now, curling around her face and her shoulders in seductive dishevelment. And her cloak had come undone in their tussle and gaped open, revealing how provocatively her gown's low-cut bodice clung to the round fullness of her breasts. Her ambers gleamed against those luscious swells, and she still toyed with the necklace, letting its golden length slide across her hand, twining it suggestively around her wrist.

Her high color and all those lush, ripe curves would be any man's undoing. But it was her spirit that proved irresistible. He burned for her with a part of himself that had nothing to do with honor or clan loyalties, and everything to do with his maleness. Just the provocative blaze in her eyes took his breath and made him desire her with a fierceness he'd never felt for any woman.

He could take her, quenching his need...

Instead, he straightened his shoulders, incensed that she had such an effect on him.

"Well?" She let the necklace fall. "Have I pushed you past your limits?"

"You test my patience merely being here. This is Cameron land and no place for a MacDonald. Nor are you to my taste—as I've told you." Guilt flayed him on the lie. "I came after you because it is my duty to ensure no ills befall a woman. As chief, especially, I am sworn to defend the weak and—"

"You speak like my brother. He—" she broke off abruptly, her face coloring.

"Your brother is a fool." James meant it. Were Alasdair MacDonald before him now, he'd upbraid him for his light-mindedness. "No chief of merit would allow a woman, much less his sister—"

He stared at her, realization dawning. "He doesn't know, does he? Somehow you've tricked Alasdair, slipping away behind his back to sneak down the glen each morn and glare your venom at the Lowland minions building their viewing platforms and barricades."

"They deserve glares." She bent a heated gaze on him, daring him to disagree.

He didn't, but that wasn't the point.

He took a step toward her. "You spearing them with stares will change nothing. The men of this glen will deal with them, as ever we have done."

"Do as you will." She jammed her hands on her hips. "I say it is the trial by combat that will serve naught. My glares show Sir Walter and his ilk that at least one dweller of this glen despises them."

"I ne'er said they are to my liking. And you"—his voice was steely—"will answer me now. Your brother doesn't know you're here, does he?"

"He knows I've been coming here." Her gaze met and held his, indignant still. "He wasn't pleased, it is true. He ranted, even threatening to set a guard at my bedchamber door. That's why I left Blackshore so early. It was necessary to get away while he slept."

James stared at her, torn between admiring her spirit and being annoyed to discover Alasdair was a better man than he cared to admit.

But the MacDonald chief had made one error he wouldn't have. "Your brother should've made good his threat to have your room guarded."

"He did." She tilted her head as she looked at him. "I persuaded one of the laundresses to distract the man as I slipped away."

James watched something like amusement flicker in her eyes. Somehow, he wasn't surprised. Catriona Mac-Donald might be virtuous—indeed, he was certain of it—but she was anything but innocent.

She *was* a she-devil.

And whether it suited her or not, he was escorting her back to her brother's keep. Now, before the torrid images from his dream could return to torture him. He could see her still, her naked body swathed in moonglow and her glorious breasts swaying with her sinuous movements. Her nipples tight and thrusting, begging for his touch...

James scowled, the breath scorching his lungs. "I'll see you returned to Blackshore." His voice was rough, strained. "Quickly, before you vex even me beyond endurance."

"I can go myself. You needn't—"

"Ah, but I must." He towered over her, the devil in him wakening. "I would have words with your brother. It is in his interest, and my own, that he knows to place a more stalwart guard on your door. One who isn't so easily lured from his duty."

She jerked away when he reached for her. "You wouldn't dare—"

"I dare much, sweet." He was on her in a beat, sliding an arm around her waist and clamping her to his side as he marched her into the trees, leading her in the direction of her brother's stronghold.

"Let me go!" She tried to wriggle free, but he only tightened his grip.

"Och, I'll release you, no worries." He tromped on, not about to risk a glance at her. "You'll be free of me as soon as we reach Blackshore's gate."

Not a moment before. Though he kept that sentiment to himself.

Catriona MacDonald was one dangerous female.

He'd be more than happy to hand her into her brother's care. The only trouble was that some deep and secret part of him wished she'd manage to slip away again. He wouldn't mind enjoying another round of argument with her. Perhaps next time, he'd even kiss her, plundering her lips and scattering her wits, regardless of her name.

For all her evil-tempered fieriness, she *was* magnificent.

And she did tempt him greatly.

Damn the woman, anyway.

Chapter Three

❧

*I*s this true?"

Alasdair MacDonald hooked his thumbs in his sword belt and stared across his solar at Catriona. Not caring for his tone, she resisted the urge to move away from his regard and sweep through the door. She did aim a withering glance at James Cameron, the man responsible for her present quandary. Alasdair didn't even look at the blackguard. Ignoring him, he kept his attention on her, his sharp-eyed gaze flicking over her tangled hair and then dipping to her wet and muddied shoes. When his perusal turned to the blood smears on her gown, she raised her chin. Alasdair's face darkened. Worse, the fierce lowering of his brows as he surveyed her ruined skirts showed that he faulted her for her sullied appearance.

And that was intolerable.

He should have been challenging James—the devil—Cameron for accosting her.

No other man would've dared to haul her into his arms

so roughly. Or seize her at all, truth be told. She bent another chilly gaze on the lout, not surprised by the hard line of his jaw or the glint of arrogance that flared in his dark eyes when he met her stare.

She glared back, furious that the wickedly sensual curve of his mouth made her heart knock against her ribs.

He arched a brow, his insolence chased by a flash of pure masculine triumph as if he knew exactly how much he flustered her.

Knew, and delighted in riling her.

Look away, her good sense warned her. *Don't let him see he affects you.*

But she still felt too raw, too unsettled by the blood thundering in her veins, to tear her gaze from him. She did narrow her eyes in challenge, hoping her own piercing regard would put him at ill ease.

The look he gave her said that was impossible.

Simmering inwardly, she held her ground. And— because she just couldn't help it—she let her gaze settle once again on his sinfully tempting mouth.

She should have lifted her chin higher and straightened her shoulders, showing him how deeply she reviled him. Not gawp at his lips, wondering what his kiss would taste like and recalling the rush of sensations that flooded her when he'd grabbed her with his big hands and pulled her so close to his hard-muscled body.

Even now—and knowing him to be one of the worst scoundrels in the land—she could still feel the brace of his arm around her waist, how his strong fingers had gripped her, the edge of his thumb brushing against the sensitive lower swells of her breasts. His warmth had penetrated the thick folds of his plaid, even burning through her own cloak, to heat her skin with scalding intimacy.

When he'd dragged her through Blackshore's gate and into the bailey, clearly manhandling her, Alasdair should've greeted him with murderous rage.

Instead, her brother had ushered the scoundrel into his great hall, led him past rows of trestle tables filled with startled, swivel-necked kinsmen, and then—Catriona bristled—even escorted him inside the keep's lovely painted solar, where a bountiful table had been laid with sumptuous victuals and libations.

Now, having lost apparent interest in provoking her, James hovered near that well-set table. As she looked on, he helped himself to generous portions of plump smoke-dried herring and fine fresh-baked oatcakes spread thickly with Cook's special herbed cheese.

Catriona watched him eat, noting the relish he put into each bite. Outrage swept her, and she placed her hands on her hips, irritation making her pulse race. She hoped he'd swallow a fish bone. She narrowed her eyes, willing it to happen.

Her anger smoldered and burned, cauldron hot.

Especially when she saw that the welcome offerings included a large platter of honey cakes, each tempting treat dusted with costly sugar. It was clear her brother had taken the famed code of Highland hospitality more than a shade past the expected courtesies.

Just now Alasdair was arching a brow at her. "Well, my sister?"

Catriona raised her chin a fraction, matching his glare. She stepped closer to the hearth fire, secretly annoyed that it burned so brightly. Considering who shared the room with them, she would have preferred cold ash. As things stood, she hoped the dancing flames would pick out every nuance of her dishevelment.

Her rumpled appearance was a badge of honor.

She wore each stain, mud speck, and hair knot with pride.

Alasdair's expression soured as if he'd read her thoughts. "Dinnae test my patience." He folded his arms, waiting. "I'll have your answer."

Catriona didn't flinch. "You can see that I was out."

"That is no' what I asked you." A muscle in his jaw twitched. "Were you caught in the wood at Castle Haven? Did you leave this stronghold, alone and against my wishes? Or"—he flashed a look at James, who stood admiring a vibrantly colored mural of the sea god, Manannan Mac Lir, flying across the foam in *Wave Sweeper,* the deity's self-sailing boat—"do my own eyes and ears deceive me?

"The Camerons may no' be our friends." Alasdair paused, his voice hardening. "But I have ne'er had cause to call their chief a liar."

"And I am one?" Catriona looked him in the eye. "Is that what you're saying?"

"I say you are headstrong and"—her brother sent another glance to the Cameron—"at times, foolish. That is a sad truth and one I am loath to admit, for you are my sister and should stand above such capering. What you did this morn was more than thoughtless. It was dangerous. Do you no' have any regrets or contrition?"

"I do." She let her eyes snap. "I'm pained to see a Cameron whiling in our best solar and"—she flicked her own look at James—"tipping our finest MacDonald ale down his arrogant throat."

"Catriona!" Alasdair's face colored.

James nearly choked. He did set down his cup, returning it to the lavishly decked table, placed so near the painted wake of Manannan's enchanted galley. How Catriona wished those vividly captured waves would burst to life, sending the frothing spume into the solar to swallow the proud Cameron chieftain and carry him out to sea where he could plague her no more.

At the very least, she wouldn't mind seeing the magnificent flowing-bearded, blue-robed god whirl around from his place on the wall and use the pointy end of his trident to jab the Cameron's arse.

Sadly, Manannan chose to ignore her wishes.

Wholly unthreatened, her nemesis merely dragged his sleeve over his mouth. But not before his lips twitched in what could have been the beginning of an amused smile.

The bastard was laughing at her!

Catriona opened her eyes very wide, showing scorn.

Impervious, the lout remained where he was, standing near the table, Manannan towering behind him like a fierce and indignant ally. But unlike the sea god's fixed stare, his gaze slid over her, settling on her face in a way that made her feel disturbingly breathless.

"Be assured, Lady Catriona, that you"—a touch of pride entered his voice—"or anyone of your household would be met with the same deference should you ever appear at Castle Haven's gate.

"Although"—his lips quirked again—"I'll no' deny such amenities would be offered out of a sense of honor and duty and no' because we'd be pleased to greet you."

"And you, sirrah, needn't worry about expending the effort." Catriona glared at him, her entire body flaming.

"I can think of no MacDonald who'd willingly trouble themselves to seek your door."

"If that includes you, my sister, I shall be relieved to know you'll no longer be beating a path across the glen, heading in just that direction." Alasdair poured another measure of ale into James's cup and handed it to him. "Such knowledge will save me from—"

"Spare you what?" Catriona seethed as James accepted the ale. "Setting another keeper on my door? Perhaps two this time? Or will you forgo guardsmen and just bar my door from the outside?"

"That won't be necessary." Alasdair spoke smoothly. "And you will no' be locked in your quarters. You may go wherever you wish so long as you remain within the castle walls. If you attempt to leave, you'll be stopped."

Catriona went to one of the tall window arches, where cold morning sun was just beginning to stream inside. The light danced on the brilliant colors of the wall murals—all fanciful Celtic beasts and pagan deities—and slanted across the sheep-and-deerskin-covered floor, spreading pools of pale, shimmering gold.

Keeping her back to the room, she gazed out at the loch and the wispy haze curling across the glassy black water.

Alasdair was a fool.

Even if she didn't use the causeway to reach the shore, a wean could snatch one of the small, two-oared coracles from the castle's narrow strand and slip silently away before anyone noticed.

She knew how to row such a cockleshell better than most men.

She could swim, too.

More than once, she'd stripped bare and left her clothes

on a rock by the shore, then spent afternoons cleaving the loch's chill waters. Those were hours when she felt as one with the glen's beauty and all that the land meant to her. Naked and with nothing separating her from the past, she liked to imagine she was swimming through the beginning of time or—a little shiver sped down her spine, remembering—perhaps even the distant future. Wherever she fancied herself, the loch always embraced her, as did the enclosing hills, looking on gently. Or so it would seem until her brother's outraged shouts ruined her pleasure.

Those trusted waters would help her now.

Alasdair couldn't hold her captive.

"Put the notion from your head." He appeared at her elbow, proving as so often that he had the power to peer into her thoughts. "You may walk the strand, dinnae fret. But"—his voice hardened—"you'll refrain from taking a boat or trying to swim to land."

She glanced at him. "And why should I?"

He held her gaze. "You will because you're too fond of our kinsmen to be the cause of a single one of them seeking his bed hungry."

"What do you mean?" She flushed, already guessing.

Alasdair rested a hand on the edge of the window arch, his gaze on the loch. "Only that any guard who neglects his duty now knows that his oversight will see him spending time in the dungeon, where he'll sup on such fare as soured ale and moldy bread crusts.

"I think you'll find"—he paused—"that an empty stomach motivates a man even more than the promise of a tumble with a willing laundress."

Catriona's eyes rounded. Her heart sank.

Alasdair was right. She'd sooner eat dust motes and

sip dew off the grass than be responsible for the hardship of a kinsman. The very thought made her stomach knot, taking away all her bluster. She loved her clan—and the glen—more than anything else. Misery was the last thing she'd wish for anyone at Blackshore.

Maili told you. Catriona couldn't believe it. She'd bought the girl's silence with a length of the finest ribbon. She also liked and trusted her.

"The lass didn't betray you." Alasdair answered as if she'd spoken aloud. "She just had the misfortune of entertaining your guard in an antechamber where one of her more ardent admirers chose to spread his pallet. When the man walked in on them, a fight erupted. Their bellowing and crashing about woke the entire stronghold."

Catriona was silent.

Maili was comely and known for being generous with her charms. A tussle such as Alasdair described could easily have happened without Catriona's interference.

"I don't understand." She frowned. "If Maili didn't tell you, then how—"

The truth hit her when she heard the *clack* of James setting down his ale cup. Three long strides brought him across the room, and then he was looming beside Alasdair, his broad shoulders blocking out the brightly painted solar. He stood before her, pinning her with a look that blurred everything else, making her feel as if they were alone.

She swallowed. The room suddenly felt overly warm, much hotter than could be credited to the cheery fire, however well-burning.

James and her brother exchanged a meaningful glance. She didn't need to see more. Especially when the Cameron turned to her, his raven-black hair gleaming in the fire glow and one brow raised appraisingly. His dark gaze held hers, making her shiver and—she was quite sure—even setting the tops of her ears to heating.

"It was you." Her temper came rushing back. "You told Alasdair how I slipped away."

He didn't deny it. "I did naught that he would no' have done for me or"—his deep voice was steady, certain in the truth of his claim—"any other chief with a sister prone to placing herself in harm's way."

Flames shot up Catriona's neck, burning her cheeks.

He hadn't said *errant* sister, but the slur crackled between them, blistering the air.

Alasdair slid a glance at her, his expression showing that he wasn't on her side. Ignoring him, she squared her shoulders and kept her gaze on James.

"You dare much, sir." She used her chilliest tone.

"I thought we'd already established that, my lady?" His words held the faintest trace of amusement. "If you require further proof . . ." He let the words tail off and glanced at Alasdair, who was making a business of smoothing the folds of his plaid.

"Perhaps"—James regarded her levelly—"you'll be less grieved to know that I would have escorted any female out of that wood. My intent was to see you safely returned to your brother's care. No more or no less, I assure you."

"Is that so?"

"It is."

"I see." Catriona brushed at her skirts.

His declaration, surely meant to placate, only vexed her more.

She drew herself up, preparing to say something particularly peppered. It would cut him down a notch to see that he couldn't get the better of her. But then she realized why his words annoyed her so much, and her heart slammed to a halt in her breast.

He didn't remember the last time he'd caught her on Cameron land.

She'd never forgotten.

How she wished she could. Instead, she ignored the fury that always came with the memory. She also damned his dark good looks. Years ago when their paths had first crossed, he'd been a brawny lad, brash and swaggering. Now, as a man, every inch of him offended her. His height and the wide set of his shoulders were an insult.

His *words* made her blood boil.

"I am pleased, sir, that you champion every hapless female who oh-so regrettably sets foot in your wood. Why"—she met his eye, hoping to make him uncomfortable—"you are all chivalry and honor."

Far from looking affronted, his dark eyes crinkled at the corners. "You humble me, my lady."

"I doubt that's possible!" Catriona felt as if her entire body were on fire. She couldn't believe it, but he was actually smiling at her.

Her brother looked livid. "Cat—"

Snatching up her skirts, she swept from the room before he could scold her. Half certain that Alasdair and James would pursue her, she ran along the darkened corridor and raced down the tower stair, taking the tight, winding steps as quickly as she dared. She dashed through the hall, her chin raised against the stares of her kinsmen. Indignation gave her the strength to yank open the heavy hall door as if it weighed nothing. Outside, she flew across the bailey, not stopping until she'd darted past the seaward gate and stood, breathless, on the sliver of shingled strand beneath Blackshore's walls.

She flashed a glance at the top of those walls, not surprised to see her brother's most trusted guardsmen already crowding the battlements. They loomed there like a row of carrion crows, ready to swoop down on her if she so much as sneezed.

Her anger swelled again and she returned their stares, brows arched.

In truth, she couldn't fault them.

They were only following her brother's orders.

So she went to stand at the water's edge. She could still sense the guardsmen's eyes boring into her, but she did her best to blot them from her mind. She needed to watch where she stepped as frost glittered on the stones, making them slippery. The morning was cold, and a sharp wind blew along the loch. She lifted a hand to touch her amber necklace, nestled as always against her skin.

Too bad the ambers offered no solace.

Legend told that the necklace warned of imminent peril.

She stilled her fingers on the stones, waiting for them to warm or quicken. If James Cameron wasn't a danger, she was a barking trout.

But nothing happened.

The ambers remained cool beneath her touch, the polished rounds still as glass. Even so, she didn't doubt that the ambers lived. Their romantic past made it impossible not to trust in their magic.

If the tales were true, the gemstones came from a treasure presented to the clan when a long-ago chieftain returned a land-trapped selkie ancestress to the sea.

Manannan Mac Lir, god of sea and wind, was said to have ridden his great steed, Embarr of the Flowing Mane, to Blackshore's gate, allowing no other to deliver the gift.

Some claimed the gemstones were part of a stash of Viking plunder. Prized ambers stolen from distant Jutland in the north, where the golden stones were said to litter the coast. Those clansmen who supported this tale swore that Norse raiders buried the amber on MacDonald shores, where, in the fullness of time, a lucky forebear stumbled across the hoard while gathering winkles at low tide.

Catriona preferred the Manannan legend.

Whatever she believed, the stones weren't speaking to her now. Frowning, she let the beads run through her fingers, but their glide across her wrist reminded her of James's hands on her and how her entire body had tingled with startling female awareness.

That same prickling, steal-her-breath sensation had seized her years ago, the first time he'd grabbed her so rudely. Even if he'd forgotten, the memory was forever branded on her mind. She'd only wanted to sneak a glimpse at Grizel and Gorm, the half-mythic ancients everyone knew dwelled on the high moors above the Cameron stronghold. The pair were said to have a magical white stag, *Laoigh Feigh Ban*, that they called Rannoch. She'd hoped to see the creature. But James had intercepted her, thwarting her chances.

Then, as this morn, she'd been sure he'd meant to kiss her. And each time, she'd almost wished he would. There was something wickedly exciting about his devilish handsomeness and those dark, flashing eyes. Yet in the wood earlier—and during their tangle years before—he'd only held her fast and pinned her with a mocking glare.

Most galling, she was sure he'd also laughed at her.

She hadn't missed how his lips had twitched in Alasdair's solar when she'd fixed him with her own stare, declaring he was full of chivalry and honor.

He'd howled with laughter the other time, up on the high moorland.

But it wasn't the memory of his youthful mirth that stayed with her, haunting her all these years. It was—and she hated him for this—how his dashing looks and boldness made every other lad who'd paid court to her seem pale and lifeless beside him.

That long-ago day, she'd let her eyes blaze at him, determined to prove her own bravery and daring.

The years fell away, and she recalled their meeting. It might have been long ago, but it felt like yesterday. Confronted by a young James Cameron, she'd flipped back her hair, her gaze one of challenge.

He only cocked a brow, unimpressed.

"Fire in your eye will serve you naught in these parts, lassie." His strong grip on her arms felt dangerous, making her believe him. "This is Cameron land, and you"—his dark gaze flicked over her, then locked with her own—"as a MacDonald are no' welcome here."

"I know that." She met his stare, hotly. "It's not you that I came to see. I wanted—"

"You wished to see the Makers of Dreams, I know." He was already shepherding her down through the heather, away from the high moors where she'd been heading. "I have ears, see you? I heard well what you told me. But I'm here to tell you, it was a mistake to come here.

"Grizel and Gorm speak only with Camerons." He

flashed a grin at her. It was full of malice. "They stay hidden to everyone else. But if you did find them, be warned that they turn anyone in our disfavor into toads. All it takes is a word cast to the wind and your fate would be sealed. You could then spend eternity in Cameron territory, hopping about on four slimy, wart-covered legs."

"Pah! I do not believe a word." Catriona tried to jerk free, but her efforts only made him grip her arm more tightly. "You're just trying to scare me."

He stopped, swinging her around to face him. "Aye, well. If you're no' bothered about being spelled into a toad, perhaps you'll think deeper on what might happen if one of the dreagans gets you?" His gaze slid meaningfully to the bottom of the hill where thick mist filled the heart of the glen. It was there, she knew, where strange rock formations were said to be sleeping dragons.

She followed his gaze but clamped her lips, not deigning him an answer.

But his mention of the dreagans did send shivers along her nerves. More than a few of the MacDonald elders claimed the beasts were real.

James gave her a very direct look, his face bitter earnest. "I cannae say for sure, but I've heard thon dreagans relish fiery-haired maids. Belike someone also said they're especially fond of MacDonalds.

"Word is"—he leaned close, so near that his warm breath brushed her cheek—"they eat a body whole, cracking the bones with glee and lapping up the blood for sauce."

"Fie on you for telling such lies. Why, you're..." She glared at him, temper taking her breath.

"*I'm much worse than a dreagan.*" He sounded proud of his claim. "*You'll have to take your chances with the fire-breathing beasties. But if e'er I catch you on Cameron ground again, you'll wish yourself in their clutches and no' in mine, that I say you!*"

"*Oh?*" She felt herself flushing. "*What would you do, other than spout tall tales?*"

"*I'm thinking I'd best no' tell you.*" He released her then and tossed his plaid over shoulders that already hinted at how broad they'd be in manhood.

"*And I'm thinking I don't care to know.*" Catriona brushed at her skirts, vigorously.

"*Then be off with you, Catriona MacDonald, before I do tell you.*" He stepped close again and gave her a look that squeezed her chest tighter than his hands had gripped her arms. It was a hot, entirely unpleasant sensation that made it hard to breathe and filled her with such a floodtide of fizzy prickles that her knees wobbled.

"*Better yet, perhaps I should show you…*" He reached for her then, his dark eyes glinting, but she whirled and ran from him.

She tore through the glen on winged feet, not risking a backward glance until Blackshore's walls rose before her. Only then did she stop hearing the echo of his laughter in her ears. It was as she'd leaned, panting, against the curtain wall, that she'd realized why she'd run so hard.

It hadn't been because of his foolish talk of Old Ones who would transform her into a toad or even his warning about the dreagans and their appetite for MacDonalds.

It was the wave of giddiness that swept her when he'd stepped so close and threatened to kiss her.

That was what he'd meant.

She'd known it with a certainty beyond her years.

Just as she'd known she'd thrill to his embrace. He'd stirred irresistible desires and longings in her, initiating her in a woman's passion. And considering he was who he was, that was a terrible thing.

For the sad truth was, she'd run from her family's wrath, not James Cameron's kisses.

She'd wanted those.

But she didn't want them now.

Far from it, she blinked away the memory.

Unfortunately, that didn't stop her pulse from racing with annoyance as she stared across the loch. Morning sun struggled through the clouds, making the water dance and shimmer. Her necklace also shimmied. Or rather, she fancied she'd felt a slight trembling deep inside the stones. She frowned and reached up to clasp them between her fingers, running her thumb across each stone.

They weren't humming.

But she did hear the crunch of footsteps on stone. The sound came from behind her, near the seaward gate. Her breath caught, and she knew even as she turned around that James would be there.

And he was.

He'd taken a few steps onto the strand and stood in all his vaunting glory, the wind tugging at his plaid and riffling his hair. He was looking right at her, an unmistakable glint of amusement in his dark gaze. Something else was there, too. An indefinable something that made her feel slightly faint, even breathless. Not wanting him to guess, she narrowed her eyes, giving him her own coldest stare. In response, he flashed just the kind of smile that reminded her why he was so powerfully attractive. He made no attempt to come closer, but that didn't matter.

He could be on the moon and she'd still feel as if he were right before her, banishing the world around them and making her heart hammer wildly.

She resented how his tall, broad-shouldered presence seemed to claim the little boat strand, almost as if he owned the very air around them. He did cause a flurry of shivers to ripple through her, and she straightened her back, hoping he couldn't tell.

"Lady Catriona." His smile deepened, turning devilish.

"You..." She took several steps closer to him, then stopped when she realized she'd moved. "You shouldn't be here with me—" She started to tell him to leave but broke off when he raised a hand.

"I am no' with you, regrettably." His meaning brought a flush to her face. "If I were"—he gave her a look that made her feel naked—"rest assured you'd no' be spluttering like an angry hen. You'd be purring in sweet female contentment. As things are—"

"There are no *things* between us." Catriona felt hot color rush onto her cheeks. "You are arrogance walking!"

"I have been called worse. Though"—he glanced at the guards lining the wall-walk above them, then back to her—"no' usually when I am trying to be honorable. Do you truly believe I'd offend your brother's hospitality by compromising his sister beneath his very nose?"

Catriona couldn't respond. She believed every wicked tale she'd ever heard about him. Most especially the wilder stories that claimed he kept scores of women trapped in the impenetrable fastnesses of Rannoch Moor and visited them regularly, forcing them to satisfy his basest cravings. She shivered, just imagining. Yet everything female inside her whirled in hot tumult, and she was sure that if she opened her mouth, all the sordid images conjured by his words would come spilling out to shame her.

Purring in sweet contentment…

She bristled.

She'd known for years what his touch could do to a woman. At least, she knew what he did to her. How she wished she didn't, for she'd be long wed and bouncing bairns on her knee if her secret obsession with him hadn't made all her suitors seem like toads.

She also knew he spoke the truth.

He was too proud to mar his lairdly reputation by breaching Highland hospitality codes. She could prance naked before him and he wouldn't look at her—save with scorn—so long as she performed such a spectacle beneath Alasdair's roof.

"I see you agree." He spoke at last, sounding satisfied.

"I said nothing."

"But you're eager to know why I'm here."

She tucked a curl behind her ear, feigning indifference. "I'm sure you're about to tell me."

"I wanted to leave you with a warning." He looked across the loch to the distant hills. "Know that if I find you on Cameron land again, alone and without your brother's knowledge, I will no' be as gallant as I was this morn.

"Indeed"—his dark gaze fixed on her—"I will make good my threat from the last time."

Catriona's eyes widened. "I can't imagine what you mean."

She knew exactly what he meant.

And the words made her light-headed. Shimmering desire warmed her, and she was sharply aware of him coming across the strand toward her, his strides predatory.

"That's right, Catriona." He spoke when he reached her, his voice intimately low. "I will prove to you that my kisses will scorch you far worse than any dreagan's fire-breath. They'd brand you forever.

"So"—he cupped her chin, his touch searing her—"if you'll no' be wishing to taste them, take heed and keep to the safety of your lady's bower."

Catriona stood still, sure the air between them was about to burst into flame. But before she could regain her composure, he leaned in, bringing his face dangerously close to hers.

"See you, sweet"—he gave her a look that made her hot all over—"you rouse me even when I'm not holding you crushed against me. Dinnae make me show you what'll happen if you tempt me into kissing you."

Catriona's heart flipped. Her knees began to tremble, badly. "I—"

"You've been warned, lass." He tightened his grip on her chin and stared down at her, his eyes fierce. Then he turned and strode back across the little strand, disappearing through the seaward gate.

Catriona stared at the empty archway, unable to breathe. The force of her feelings—*her surprise*—shook her to the core. She pressed a hand to her breast, letting her fingers clasp her amber necklace, needing the familiar comfort she took in the gemstones.

He hadn't forgotten their long-ago meeting, high on the moors.

And his agitation could only mean that the encounter

haunted him in the same way it'd stayed with her. He wanted her—at least, carnally.

She'd seen the lust in his eyes, heard it in his voice.

It was a revelation that thrilled her to her toes. Even though she did despise him and knew well that he surely didn't favor her. Yet there *was* passion between them. The only trouble was that she didn't know where such desire might lead. Whatever path she chose was fraught with danger.

Any kisses from James wouldn't just brand her.

They'd be incinerating.

And forbidden.

Alasdair might even punish her by seeing her wed to some bleary-eyed, age-palsied laird who couldn't keep his dribble from his beard.

Of late, he'd hinted at the possibility.

If—she shuddered—she dared once again to decline a viable bid for her hand.

But she burned too hotly for James to care. Nor was she known for backing away from a challenge. She certainly couldn't resist one that made her feel all warm, melting, and tingly. James did that to her, and more. Even now, annoyed with him as she was, her stomach fluttered deliciously and her knees were so weak she could hardly stand.

If he kissed her…

And, o-o-oh, she wanted his kisses.

One would do, just to satisfy her curiosity and let her explore the tumultuous emotions and exciting sensations he stirred inside her.

She turned back to the loch, smiling for the first time in days. She'd take his own words and make him regret tossing down such a tantalizing gauntlet. She *would* tempt him into kissing her. A plan to do so was already forming in her mind. And the possibilities sent shivers of anticipation rippling all through her.

One little kiss should be easy to provoke.

Afterward, she might feel shaken to the soul, perhaps even worse than sinful. But she would have tasted a wee bit of sparkling bliss.

And—she shook back her hair, her heart pounding— she wasn't going to let anyone take that from her.

Chapter Four

❧

James strode purposely across Blackshore's bailey, careful to keep his face as hard-set as possible. If he looked fierce, the long-nosed guards watching him wouldn't suspect how tempted he was to march back to the boat strand, toss Catriona over his shoulder, and carry her away with him. But first, he'd seize her and kiss the wicked breath from her for pushing him to his limits.

Instead, he quickened his pace and made for the gatehouse, eager to be gone.

He could make his head ache on his own, without the help of a firebrand more vexatious and—a plague on her—so scintillating, he wondered she didn't burn the clothes right off her lushly curved body.

If he didn't soon put Blackshore behind him, he'd do the deed himself. The rapid beat of his heart proved how much he'd enjoy ripping each shred of cloth from her until the entire well-made length of her stood naked before him, vulnerable and enticing.

The trouble was he had no wish to add to his already long list of sins by stripping the gently born sister of one of his worst foes.

He *was* of a mind to be wary.

He'd been shown hospitality, but he was still on enemy ground and couldn't discount an attack from nowhere. MacDonalds were known for their hotheadedness. And not all of them were as courteous as Alasdair, even if his openhandedness had more to do with the circumstances of James's visit than any desire to be welcoming.

Alasdair wouldn't taint his name by not adhering to the Highland tradition of greeting all guests warmly, regardless of their name.

In another time and place, Alasdair would show his blood. Everyone knew MacDonalds were masters at ambush. They flitted like shadows from darkness to launch assaults and then melted into the mist before a man knew what— or who—had struck him a fatal blow.

James scowled, sure of that truth.

It was just a pity that the threat of a quick dirk in the ribs wasn't the reason for his frown.

That honor fell to a lusciously rousing hellcat named Catriona.

Overwhelmed by the urge to touch and taste her, he tightened his fists as he neared the gate. The brazen minx stirred him in ways he couldn't ignore. And—damn her snapping sapphire eyes—he found her most appealing when she was at her lively, high-spirited worst.

There was vibrancy in every mouthwatering, sweetly turned curve of her, and it galled him that he noticed. He'd come very close to ravishing her on the little sliver of a boat strand. And if he had, his plundering of her would've been rough and savage. He wasn't a man to hold back in a fury. And his rage at her—and himself because he wanted her—roiled like a storm inside him.

Hot, thunderous, and barely controlled.

His blood seethed and his head would surely split any moment. Praise God he had the will to ignore the persistent pounding elsewhere.

A pity he couldn't banish it.

But it'd been so long since he'd slaked his need with a woman, and—he loathed admitting the truth—the sharp-tongued, dagger-carrying hellion tempted him more than any female he'd ever known.

Grimacing, he stalked on, keeping an angry eye on the gate before him.

Already standing wide, no doubt in anticipation of his departure, the gate gave a fine view of Loch Moidart. Mist still floated across the water, and he caught the strong scent of the nearby sea. The air also held traces of drying fish and seaweed, the unsavory smells lending just enough nose-wrinkling piquancy to suit his mood.

Catriona wasn't the only reason for his ire.

Blackshore's courtyard minded him too much of his bailey at Castle Haven. Even the smoke rising from the tower chimneys and the yellow glint of torchlight in the turret windows struck him as an affront.

The similarity almost made him choke.

He'd rather have found black, foul-reeking weeds growing between the courtyard cobbles and a gaggle of hunch-backed, wart-nosed crones cackling in a corner, their glowing-eyed, hissing and spitting felines winding about their mistresses' spindly legs. At the very least, the arched pend leading through the gatehouse could've been hung with the winged bodies of a few bats.

A cauldron filled with a steaming blood-red brew would have been a nice touch.

As things stood...

Men bustled everywhere, a handful of dogs bounded over to run circles around him, and several strapping lads were pulling carts piled high with cut wood and peats toward the shadowed entrance to the kitchens. A chill wind came from that direction, bringing a waft of woodsmoke and savory stew, making his mouth water.

But the keep's homey appearance was deceptive.

Several guards leaned against the tower wall, watching his progress with sullen eyes. Others paced the battlements, where the MacDonald banner snapped in the wind and morning sun glinted on well-polished helms and mail. Each garrison man bristled with arms, and James knew by the sour glances aimed his way that they'd love nothing better than to give him a taste of their steel.

"Is it true you once tossed your sword higher than the clouds?" came a small boy's voice behind him.

"Ho, there!" James swung around, nearly colliding with a skinny, tousle-haired lad. The boy stood less than a pace away, his thin arms clutching a creel of onions—a basket almost bigger than himself—as he peered up at James with round, wondering eyes.

The boy edged closer, the reek of onions with him. "The storytellers say you caught the blade when it fell."

Before James could respond, an older lad, equally dirt-smeared and scruffy, sauntered over to them. "He caught an *angel,* you nit-head." Thumping the younger boy's shoulder, the second lad puffed his chest. "The sword went as high as heaven, where the blade snagged the skirts of the angel, pulling her down to earth. But as soon as she landed in his arms, she was an angel no more!"

"There's no' a word of truth in that." James eyed the older boy sternly. He'd savored the pleasures of more angels than he could recall, but not a one of them had been of the heavenly variety.

And he wasn't sinner enough to soil the ears of wee laddies with his amorous adventures.

"Then you cannae toss your sword so high?" The younger boy's face fell.

His friend cuffed him. "You are a daftie. He means he didn't tumble an angel."

"Tumble?" The younger boy's brow furrowed.

The older lad smirked. "It's what—"

"See here." James drew his sword and held her at arm's length, his attention on the smaller boy, whose eyes were again wide. "You're both too young to think of swords or"—he shot a warning look at the older lad— "heavenly beings. Though if your chief will let me, I'll return one day and show you how to do this."

He tossed the blade in the air, secretly pleased by the boys' gasps as the sword arced high and then spun, turning brightly before racing down to land, almost magically, in his outstretched hand.

"Now run along and remember"—James slid the blade back into his scabbard—"this isn't the time to fash yourselves o'er swords taller than you are. The day will come sooner than you think."

James watched them go, then threw a quick glance across the bailey to the postern gate. The devil inside him made him wish Catriona might have left the boat strand and seen his sword toss.

He was rather proud of his flourish.

But she was nowhere in view, though when he turned to leave, a door opened in the thickness of the curtain walling near the castle gate. An ancient stiff-legged dog appeared, followed by Alasdair. The other chieftain did his fierce reputation justice, with his plaid thrown proudly over one shoulder and his sword belted low at his hip. He wore a different blade than in his solar. This one had a large amber stone gracing its pommel and other, smaller ambers glittering from the elaborately tooled scabbard.

"A word, Cameron!" Alasdair started toward him, matching his pace to the hinky-hipped gait of his dog. "I'll no' keep you long."

James waited, his rival's approach minding him of his own aged beast, Hector.

He, too, needed twice as long to make his late-night castle rounds in recent years because Hector insisted on shuffling along with him. There were times when he even carried Hector for the last few turns of the stairs to his bedchamber, saving the dog his dignity rather than let him stumble just before they finished their patrol. Something told him that the MacDonald followed a similar routine.

James frowned, not wanting to feel sympathy with his foe.

Or even Alasdair's dog.

But when the other chief reached him and the dog plopped onto his bony haunches, James couldn't muster the stern look he'd intended to turn on his rival. The younger dogs tailing him bolted away and nosed Alasdair until he pulled a leather pouch from his plaid and gave each dog, including the old one, a twisted length of dried meat.

"You wish to speak of the trial by combat?" James guessed at Alasdair's reason for hailing him. "No good will come of it, I vow."

"You're well prepared. That was no mean feat with your blade just now. Though"—Alasdair grinned—"I'll still cut you till your bones show."

James returned the smile but pulled back his plaid to display his sword. "You can try. Many men have done, and now lie sleeping beneath the heather."

"I'll keep using my bed, be warned." Alasdair didn't sound concerned. "And I didn't stop you to speak of the battle." His gaze flicked across the bailey to the seaward gate. "There's a matter I didn't wish to broach before my sister. Even in the best of times, she can be—"

"Your sister is—" James broke off, heat flashing up the back of his neck. Had he truly been about to declare that she was the most vibrant, desirable creature he'd ever encountered?

He cleared his throat. "She . . ."

"She is herself!" Alasdair sounded proud, for all that James was sure his words weren't meant to flatter. "And she can vex even those of us who love her well. She also turns heads. She does so effortlessly, rousing passion in all men with red blood in their veins."

James looked at him sharply. "Surely you dinnae think that I—"

"Misused her?" Alasdair put the outrageous notion to words. "God be good, I meant none the like. I may no' care for you claiming a goodly portion of my glen, but I'll no' be laying such sins at your feet, whatever."

James blinked, only mildly relieved.

He shifted uncomfortably, certain that his every lustful thought about Catriona was stamped on his forehead, red and glowing like a brand.

"Aye, well." He brushed at his plaid. "A man would have to be blind no' to see her charms."

"True enough." Alasdair reached down to stroke his dog's ears. "What I'd know from you"—he met James's eye, his gaze piercing—"is why you accompanied her here?"

"No' to salt your tail, I assure you." James didn't waste words. "And however fetching she is, it wasn't because of her charming company."

"That I can believe." Alasdair's lips twitched. "Yet I'm also sure there was cause beyond your chiefly concern for womenfolk lost in your wood. And"—a thread of steel entered his voice—"I'm for thinking that reason is one I should be hearing."

"I was concerned for her." James's mind worked furiously. "She—"

Alasdair harrumphed. "She knows the glen. She could've found her way home."

"It was still dark, the mist thick." James rubbed the back of his neck. "No fine day for a young lass to traipse about the glen whether she—"

"You're tying your tongue in knots." Alasdair's blue eyes glinted. "Her tender age didn't stop you from chasing her from your land with tales of dreagans years ago. As I recall"—he folded his arms—"you taunted her, claiming the fire-breathing beasties eat MacDonalds? She arrived here in a terrible state, having raced through the whole of the glen, alone and frightened."

James bit his tongue. He was sure nothing had ever scared Catriona in her life.

Not even dreagans.

Even so, he had treated her abominably.

"I was a lad." He quashed a surge of guilt. "That was a foolhardy cantrip, no more. Now I place more value on honor than youthful pranks and devilry."

"Indeed." Alasdair looked skeptical.

"So I said, aye." James wasn't inclined to say more. And all the shrewd glints in Alasdair's eyes weren't going to persuade him. The lout should be grateful his sister was beneath his roof, safe and sound.

That was enough.

He'd taken Catriona under his arm when she could've been in grave danger. It was an act of chivalry any Highlander would tender, regardless of the woman's name. Such was the way of the hills, and that had been so since distant times. Trusting an enemy chief with suspicions he couldn't even pinpoint was another matter entirely.

Alasdair was astute enough to now keep a firmer grip on his sister.

James's duties were elsewhere.

And Alasdair was still looking at him, his gaze boring deep. "Then it was only your sense of honor that caused you to stay with her?"

James shoved a hand through his hair and blew out a breath. "Damnation..." He strode a few paces and turned, wondering why he felt so compelled to share his concerns with a man who was more than a thorn in his side. There was clearly an odd taint in the cold, damp air hovering over Blackshore that was addling his wits.

He was sure of it when something bumped his leg and he looked down to see Alasdair's dog leaning into him. He knew then that he couldn't lie. The motley-coated beast was peering up at him, his scraggly tail swishing and his rheumy eyes full of trust.

James bit back a curse.

"There was another reason, aye." He ignored the dog and glared at Alasdair. "Though the saints know why I'm telling you. It was no more than a feeling."

A look of satisfaction flashed across Alasdair's face. "So it is as I thought? You perceived Catriona in some kind of peril?"

James nodded. "It seemed so at the time, aye."

He frowned at the morning sky. Thick clouds were drifting across the sun, and the darkness they brought suited his mood. The air had also turned colder, the wind more biting. Any moment he expected icy rain to pelt down, and that, too, would be fitting.

Such tidings as he was about to share shouldn't be spoken on a bright sun-filled day.

Beside him, the old dog pressed harder against his leg, this time even thrusting his cold, wet nose into James's hand. The trembles in the beast's hips made James set his jaw. A soul could believe Alasdair used his aged companion as a secret weapon.

"Is your dog e'er so friendly to your foes?" James tried to sound unmoved. "Does he ne'er bark when an enemy approaches?"

"Geordie sees himself of an age where he expects everyone to treat him kindly." Alasdair's voice held a softness that irked James. His own heart, too, warmed when he spoke of Hector. "As for barking..." Alasdair looked at the dog. "Geordie rarely makes a sound. I sometimes think his years have stilled his voice."

That did it.

James scowled his fiercest glower of the day.

It was beyond tolerating that he'd felt such a pang over a MacDonald dog.

Eager to be on his way, he began pacing. "Whether you believe me or nae, I would have seen your sister returned safely to you this morn. But had I no' seen what I did just before I spotted her, I'd have escorted her only to the fringes of your territory and then gone about my business."

"Was it Sir Walter, the King's man?" Alasdair fell into step beside him. Geordie hobbled along at their heels, following at a slower pace. "I didn't care for the way he looked at Catriona when he visited us."

"It could have been him. I'm sure the man I saw was a Lowlander. But he wore a hooded cloak, and—"

"Did he approach Catriona?"

"Nae." James glanced at Alasdair. "He had no chance because I chased him."

Before Alasdair could question him, James recounted his morn. He started with the strange chills he'd felt in his hall, then the figure near the barricades of the fighting ground, and ending with how he'd pursued the man. He left out no detail, even mentioning his annoyance at Catriona marching so boldly through his wood.

Finished, he folded his arms. "Now you see why I brought her here."

"I would ken who was hiding behind that cloak." Alasdair rubbed his chin. "Something tells me he might have more evil on his mind than seizing one of our womenfolk."

"I agree." James was sure of it. "The man gives me shivers like a thousand ants crawling up and down my spine."

Alasdair nodded. "I doubt Sir Walter would soil his own hands, but who knows what—"

"There are some at Castle Haven who would have done with the lot of them in the old way." James secretly admired his cousin Colin's fervor. Even his younger brother, Hugh, the clan's soft-spoken bard, had raised his voice in favor of such action. "They talk of dirking the Lowlanders in their sleep and sinking the bodies in a bog or"—he glanced at the loch—"some other place where they'd ne'er be found."

"They are men after my own heart." Alasdair raised a balled fist. "In the old days, Clan Donald would be the first to rally with you. As is"—he sobered, watching a red-cheeked, big-boned woman hasten past, carrying a basket of herring—"the King has turned us into little more than grains caught beneath a quernstone.

"Too many innocents would suffer if we used the stratagems of our grandfathers to rid ourselves of this folly." Alasdair's voice was grim. "I'll no' see good lives ruined for a taste of triumph that would prove hollow."

James agreed. "The King is so sure we'll refuse to fight that he's gathering a fleet to convey us to the Isle of Lewis." He shuddered, certain there was no more distant or benighted place. "Sir Walter's men have been placing bets. They wager on which one of us will break the King's command, giving him cause to banish us."

"Then we shall have to show them our strength, whatever the cost."

"That is the way of it." James nodded.

He only hoped the trial by combat would be the end of

Lowland interference in their glen. Machinations that he suspected had little to do with King Robert's wish to see peace between the clans.

It was a notion he couldn't shake.

He could almost smell the perfidy.

But before he could say so, Alasdair stepped forward and gripped his hand and forearm. "You ken"—his voice was gruff, his gaze direct—"when next we meet, there'll be no cordiality between us. My sword will be sharpened, and I intend to use it well."

James grasped Alasdair's hand with equal firmness. "I would wish nothing less. God be with us both."

"Can I lend you a horse?" Alasdair glanced across the bailey to the stables. "A token thanks for your trouble with Catriona."

"She was no bother." James hoped his tone didn't reveal the lie.

Shepherding a she-devil through the glen would have been easier.

Yet he'd relished every step of the way.

He turned on his heel, making for the gate before Alasdair guessed the truth.

"A pity you're a Cameron!" Alasdair's hail stopped him just as he was about to stride into the shadowed arch of the gatehouse pend.

James looked back. "How so? I wear my name with pride and would sooner grow horns than carry another."

"Simply that"—Alasdair set his hands on his hips—"were you of any other blood I might be calling on you to offer my sister as a bride."

"I'd have to pass." James grinned to soften his words. "I prefer my women docile and less quick to wield a blade." He glanced at the red slash across his hand. "Your sister might take my breath, I'll admit, but I'm no' the man for her.

"No' by any name, I say you." He gave a small bow and disappeared into the gatehouse. Regrettably, he didn't leave fast enough to miss the bemusement that flashed across Alasdair's face.

The bastard knew he fancied Catriona.

Even more annoying were the meaningful glances that passed between the MacDonald guards as he strode past them and out into the brisk autumn air. God help him if they knew their mistress had bewitched him.

Their smirks said they did.

Wishing he'd stayed abed that morn, he ignored their goggling and marched across the narrow stone causeway back to the mainland. Unfortunately, the tide was rushing in and the slippery, moss-grown stones were already several inches under water. And—he really resented this— the waves sloshing across his feet didn't help him to depart with dignity.

He looked a fool and knew it.

The soggy *squish-squishing* of his shoes and the way the bottom of his plaid was beginning to dampen and cling to his legs told him that much.

Furious, he set his lips in a tight, angry line and stomped on, unpleasantly aware of the stares of the guardsmen watching him go.

They were laughing at him.

And—he quickened his step—he wouldn't give them the satisfaction of seeing that he knew.

But when he reached the end of their foul, half-useless causeway, the devil took him. His back almost burned from the scorching heat of their stares, so, unable to help himself, he set his hand on his sword and whirled to send them a parting glare.

Instead, the glower slid from his face.

It hadn't been the guardsmen watching his progress across the causeway. The battlements were empty, and the closed gate hid whatever men might yet lurk within the stronghold's entrance tower.

He'd felt Catriona's stare.

She still stood on the boat strand, her gaze pinned on him, unwaveringly. Wind tugged at her skirts and whipped her hair, the sight of her taking his breath and making his heart pound hard and slow.

The same cold wind tossed his own hair and tore at his clothes, giving a strange intimacy to the moment. Almost as if they were alone, the only two people in all these great hills. They locked gazes, the air seeming to crackle between them until James was sure that if he reached out a hand, he'd be able to touch her.

Frowning, he clenched his fists and kept his arms at his sides. But he felt her all the same. The longer their stares held, the more he remembered the supple warmth of her against him as they'd crossed the glen. He recalled, too, how the light, fresh scent of her—*gillyflowers?*—had almost made him dizzy. And how she'd challenged him with those dazzling sapphire eyes, rendering him helpless and unable to think of aught but having her naked beneath him…

There, exactly where he wanted her now.

Until a particularly roguish wave smacked into the rocks near where he stood, dousing him head to toe with cold, briny water.

"Damn it all to hell!" He shook back his hair and knuckled his eyes.

When he looked again, Catriona was gone.

Even so, he scowled darkly at the spot where she'd stood.

He wouldn't be surprised if she was watching him still, peeking at him through some nefarious hidey-hole in Blackstone's curtain walling.

Such would be like her.

Sure of it, he whirled around and began the long trek back to his corner of the glen. If he hurried, he could still pay a call on the Makers of Dreams before the afternoon gloom drew in, making the steep and rocky path to their high moor too treacherous even for one well-used to the journey.

But first he had to put Catriona from his mind.

To that end, he cast one last look at the deserted strand. Hoping that she *was* watching him from some unseen spy hole—just so she'd see how swiftly he'd forgotten her— he quickened his step, doing his best to stride manfully despite the wet clamminess of his plaid and the annoying *squish-squashing* of his shoes.

He was certain he could feel her stare, and the knowledge buoyed him.

His brisk pace would annoy her.

And if she was offended, she might keep well away from him in the future.

A man could hope.

Not that he'd find it difficult to resist her. He'd ignored the charms of many women when an attraction proved ill-advised. And for all her beauty and spirit, Catriona was no different from other females.

No different at all.

He knew that beyond a doubt.

It was just a pity that his heart disagreed.

Chapter Five

❖

Hours later, James stood near one of the corries high above Castle Haven and knew again that he shouldn't have left his bed that morn. Cloud and mist swirled around him, biting wind chilled him, and he couldn't shake the feeling that the soaring, rock-faced walls of the gorge were closing in on him. Frowning, he peered into the abyss. Deep, narrow, and treacherous, the boulder-strewn defile should've opened into the vast stretch of heathery gloom that was the almost inaccessible world of the Makers of Dreams.

Instead, the far end of the ravine tailed away into an impenetrable tumble of jagged, ageless stone.

He scrunched his eyes, hoping he'd missed something. That shadows or mist somehow hid a gap through the rocks. But there was none. Not even a crack wide enough to provide wriggle room to a half-starved mouse.

A flea wouldn't fare better.

He stepped closer to the edge of the ravine and scowled at the spill of rocks. He'd rarely seen a more impassable barrier. If he were a fearful man, he'd suspect that ill luck was following him like a curse. Why else would he not be able to put the MacDonald she-devil from his mind? Even now, with much more serious matters plaguing him, he couldn't stop wanting to strip off her clothes and drag his hands over every voluptuous inch of her. His desire to *kiss* those inches was worse. He especially ached to taste her darker, most mysterious places. It was a raging, inexorable need that heated him and made his heart pound as hard as if he'd just tossed aside every fool boulder blocking his path.

As it was, he glared at the rocks and took a deep breath of the cold, stone air.

Even so...

Disappointment cut like the sharp edge of a sword.

Not wanting to admit defeat, he braced his arm on an outcrop of quartz-shot granite and looked back over the trackless ground he'd covered to reach these heights. He'd been so sure that he'd headed in the right direction, confident that each corrie—this was the fourth to defeat him—was the one that accessed Gorm and Grizel's high moorland.

But he'd erred.

He had yet to find the hidden pass.

And the towering outcrop beside him was just that: a jumble of broken stone and not, as he'd hoped, the monolith known as the Bowing Stone. That hoary monument where, in ancient days, pagan men had circled three times and then dropped to one knee, begging good fortune and an abundant harvest. Men no longer sought the mercy of the Old Ones for a bountiful crop, but the Bowing Stone remained the only true marker for those seeking counsel with the Makers of Dreams.

Those of Cameron blood.

If one such reached the Bowing Stone, the path to the half-mythic pair stood open.

Unfortunately, the standing stone and even the corrie could shift location, depending on Gorm and Grizel's willingness to welcome visitors to their enchanted realm. Strange mists often appeared out of nowhere, sent by the ancients to guard their privacy when they wished to be left alone.

Such were the ways of Highland magic.

And it would seem he was presently out of favor with those who wielded such powers.

It also seemed he'd been followed.

Not trusting his eyes, he peered through the mist at the slender, dark-haired figure slipping through the sea of rock and heather below him. A beautiful maid, she stepped lightly, her raven tresses streaming behind her like a glistening river of blackest silk. She didn't wear a cloak, and her gown floated about her like a thin gossamer cloud.

James narrowed his gaze on the girl, all thoughts of the Makers of Dreams vanishing as he watched her move past a cluster of bog myrtle and yellow-blooming whin. Mist cloaked her, making it difficult to see her face, but he still recognized her.

She was Isobel.

His sister.

Pushing away from the outcrop, he scanned the dense heather and jumbled rocks surrounding her. She wasn't too far from a stretch of birch and rowans where anyone could lurk in shadow. Almost as close was a steeply rising knoll covered with tall Caledonian pines, their massive girth and dark, twisted limbs offering an even better hiding place.

A prickling at his nape told him someone else agreed.

He might not see anyone, but he could feel the menace of another man's presence. And he knew the varlet's gaze was on Isobel.

"Damnation!" He sprinted down the hill, leaping over rocks and plunging through heather and bracken, trying all the while not to lose sight of his sister.

He saw no one else.

But he was sure someone was watching him.

Worse, he was now certain—well, almost—that the stare he felt wasn't from anyone this side of the living. Dreagans came to mind. But he pushed the notion aside, furious he'd considered the beasties.

There was no such thing as a dreagan.

But it would seem the glen was turning into a haven for errant sisters.

Even so, dread clawed at him. And it grew with every beat of his heart. His blood was freezing, cold chills turning his skin to ice.

"Isobel!" He ran faster, his feet sliding on the slick, boggy ground. "I'm no' fashed!" he yelled, hoping she couldn't tell he was seething. "Wait, lass! Where are you going?"

She did stop then, turning to face him through the icy gray fog stretching between them. At a distance, her face looked pale and cold, and although he couldn't tell for sure, he had the impression her eyes were huge and filled with sadness. Even the mist around her seemed to darken as their gazes met and held. Wind whipped the glossy black strands of her hair across her face, but rather than brush them aside, she lifted an arm to point at him.

He kept on, and then cursed when his foot slammed into a rock he hadn't seen. He shot a glare at the offending boulder, craftily hidden in a clump of heather. When he glanced up again, Isobel was darting behind a rowan tree that glowed with berries as red as blood.

"Foolish chit!" He limped to a halt, glowering at the rowan.

His foot throbbed maddeningly. He could feel it swelling inside his shoe, and he winced at the tongues of flame shooting up his leg.

He suspected he'd broken a toe.

And if he had—he gritted his teeth, determined to ignore the fiery pain—he'd place the blame on Isobel. No matter that she was the last person he'd expect to behave so strangely. His sister was the heart of Clan Cameron. She soothed all ills and always kept a cool and gracious mien. Just now he didn't know her. And although he loved her dearly—and never in all their days had ever once spoken harshly to her—he was soon going to give her a scolding that would set her ears to ringing for a hundred years.

He might even follow his advice to Alasdair and lock her in her bedchamber.

At the least, it would be a long time before he trusted her again.

She was worse than Catriona.

Flitting about in the coldest, darkest part of the glen where even he took care to tread with caution. And—he could scarce believe what he'd seen—she'd worn such thin-soled slippers that her feet would have frozen even if she'd been standing before a roaring fire in the great hall.

Down there, on the chill and boggy ground—

"Guidsakes!" His eyes flew wide when she reappeared from behind the red-berried rowan and he could see the whole of the moor right through her.

He blinked, sure he was mistaken.

Sadly, he wasn't.

The world tilted beneath his feet and blood roared in his ears as the see-through beauty drifted to the rocky edge of a burn. Clearly not Isobel, she wrapped her arms around her waist, hugging her middle as she peered down into the stream's rushing waters.

Then she was gone, vanishing as if she'd never been there.

"Guidsakes!" James stared, flushing hot and cold.

He tried to breathe and couldn't.

He'd been raised on tall tales about the ghosts said to walk the Glen of Many Legends. His path hadn't crossed one until this moment. He'd never truly believed the stories, had even laughed at those who did. But he couldn't deny what he'd seen, and there could be just one explanation for the mysterious raven-haired beauty.

She could only be Lady Scandia Cameron, a clan ancestress from distant times. She was named after the northern homeland of her Viking mother, a woman given as a war prize to a long-forgotten Cameron champion. Scandia remained in clan memory because she haunted Castle Haven.

When the bards sang of her, their eyes always lit on Isobel, for—although no one could say for sure—it was believed that Scandia had been a great beauty with the same creamy alabaster skin and silky raven's-wing tresses. But that was long ago and mattered no more.

Now she was a gray lady.

And her appearance foretold doom.

The problem was James wanted nothing to do with disaster. His only concern was the well doing of kith and kin and seeing his clan stride triumphantly from the King's fast-approaching trial by combat.

He also needed to banish his lust for a headstrong,

flame-haired hellion who could shatter his world with the crook of a finger.

Nothing else was of consequence.

Certainly not a see-through woman who'd lived hundreds of years before. She might be known as "the Doom of the Camerons," but it remained beneath his dignity to show how deeply her appearance beset him.

It was maddening enough that his toes ached so badly he couldn't walk without favoring his foot.

And it was a greater annoyance that even after Scandia's departure, he couldn't shake the feeling that something wasn't right. There was a curious shivering in the air that persisted in raising the hairs on his nape. Some dim unseen presence, watching him still.

Sure of it, he summoned his fiercest mien and gave the burn a hard stare. Just in case Scandia yet lingered there, eager to plague him.

He wanted nothing to do with her and hoped his scowl made that clear.

Blessedly, she didn't reappear. Though there was—his heart jumped—the unmistakable patter of cloven hooves on the stony ridge behind him.

He whirled, spotting the deer at once.

The herd was in full view, a good number of hinds and at least six young stags, each one proudly carrying wide-spanned antlers of no less than eight points. James tipped his head back, watching them. They moved carefully, their red-brown coats gleaming softly through the mist as they picked their way along the edge of the high corrie where he'd stood such a short time ago.

Only now the ravine looked different, and the mist hovering over the jagged rocks held an eerie luminance that wasn't there before. Thick and shimmering, the fog poured through the corrie like a rolling sea, glowing from within as if lit by the flames of a thousand candles.

James stared, spellbound.

A strong wind rushed down off the hill then, circling him and filling his lungs with cold, damp air and the scent of dark, ancient magic. High above him, through layers of shifting, glittery mist, he saw the deer herd freeze and then turn as one to bound away, leaping over a river of stones that sparkled like stars.

And as soon as the last deer bolted out of sight and the clatter of hooves could be heard no more, the very mist drew breath, glimmering brightly before the curtains of fog rolled back to reveal a single standing stone spearing toward the heavens. Shining with the luster of costliest pearls, the monolith hummed, its music soft, old, and sweet, strumming the air.

The stone was covered with beautifully carved runes, curving and fluid, as if each hoary line and symbol beat in rhythm with the living rock.

It was the Bowing Stone.

And beside the monolith stood a magnificent white stag, his peaty-brown eyes all-seeing and wise, and fixed steadily on James.

Laoigh Feigh Ban.

He was the Makers of Dreams' pet deer. Called Rannoch, after the vast moorland said to be his true home, he was an enchanted creature, possessing untold powers. Clan bards swore his age rivaled that of his venerable masters, Gorm and Grizel, who made no secret that they'd lived since before time was counted.

Few men had ever seen Rannoch.

Even James had glimpsed him only on rare occasions. Most recently, when he, Colin, and several other trusted men brought Gorm and Grizel their winter supply of cut wood and peats, an important gift to the ancients who, all knew, kept benevolent watch on the glen.

Then, as now, Rannoch had turned his velvety gaze on James, making him feel as if all creatures, large and small, ever to walk the earth, were looking at him through the stag's kind and gentle eyes.

James started forward. The wind roared, swooping down from the heights once more, this time bringing the sparkling mist to whirl and spin around him. He kept on, ignoring the pain in his leg and making for the steep path back up to the corrie, to Rannoch and the Bowing Stone. But then his knee buckled and he stumbled on the slick, wet ground.

"Damnation!" He righted himself and hurried on, determined not to falter again.

Rannoch watched him with interest, edging forward to peer down at him from where—James was certain—he'd braced his arm against the jagged outcrop. But now the jumble of stone was no longer there.

The Bowing Stone had taken its place.

And although Rannoch stood only a few paces from the monolith, still so high up on the mist-draped hill, James could see the magical beast as clearly as if he were right in front of him.

Indeed—his breath caught and his eyes rounded—the *Laoigh Feigh Ban* was closer than a hand's breadth. Man and stag stood face-to-face. So near that Rannoch's nose almost bumped James. He could even see how the stag's perked ears quivered with curiosity.

James closed his eyes and shook his head, certain he

hadn't moved. His foot hurt too badly for him to have reached the corrie so quickly.

But when he looked again, that's where he was.

Rannoch was there, as well, eyeing him with a look that held more intelligence than some men's.

And somewhere close by, something—perhaps a woman's skirts?—rustled lightly and an amused-sounding cackle filled the air.

"Begad!" James jumped as the world blurred, dipping and slanting, then turning brilliant white, the starlike flickers of light he'd noticed in the mist, now blazing like a sea of dazzling suns.

"Holy saints!" He reeled, his injured foot sliding dangerously on a peat slick. He thrust out his arms, wheeling them for balance when a quick grip caught his wrist, preventing his fall.

"There be no holy men here," trilled a reedy, old woman voice, "though we do hold them in esteem, whatever!"

"Grizel!" James drew himself up, brushing at his plaid.

"That's myself, true enough." The tiny black-garbed woman peered up at him, looking proud. "I've been the same for"—her wizened face wreathed in a smile—"ach! Who is to say how many years?"

James glanced at her, noting the freshening scent of cinnamon wafting from her dark woolen cloak and how carefully she'd looped her scraggly white braids on either side of her head. Her wrinkled cheeks held a hint of rose, thanks to the day's chill. And, as always, she wore a half-moon brooch of beaten silver and had taken care that her small black boots were spotlessly clean.

As a cailleach of the highest order, she took pride in her appearance.

James suppressed a smile. He also pretended to peruse her more critically. "Ach, Grizel." He laid on a tone of appreciation. "'Tis true that you dinnae look a day more than eighty summers."

She preened. "Some do be saying the like. Though"—she eyed him shrewdly—"I know fine that you're not here to ply me with sweet words."

"That is so." He nodded. He'd enjoyed bantering with her. But at the moment he had more important things on his mind than stoking the crone's vanity.

He hooked his thumbs in his sword belt, hoping to uphold his own image.

"How did I get here?" He needed to know, seeing as they were at the far side of the corrie. The opposite end from where Rannoch now grazed beside the Bowing Stone. "I was down near the rowans, at the burn and—"

"Ach!" Grizel's blue eyes twinkled. "That's where you were, right enough. But here's where you are now, eh? And I'll tell you this"—her thin chest puffed—"you didn't climb the hill on thon aching foot."

"I didn't think so." James folded his arms, trying to look stern. "It wouldn't be yon mist—" He broke off when she wriggled her fingers and the glittering mass quivered and spun away over the edge of the corrie. Only a few twirling sparkles remained and then they, too, winked out, leaving no trace of the luminous fog.

James cleared his throat, frowning. "I would have preferred—"

"Pah!" Grizel set her hands on her hips. "What, then? Would you rather have tromped up here on your own, with two broken toes?"

"My toes aren't broken." James was sure they were.

"Say you." Grizel wasn't fooled.

It was also clear that she'd used her craft to do more than whisk him into her midst. A glance showed that the spill of rock that had blocked the corrie no longer proved an obstacle. Now there was a narrow gap where the ravine ended, a dark passage through stone, just large enough for a man.

Beyond that the heather-rich ground swept away and upward, widening into a rolling moor of finest grazing, bounded by the daunting heights of some of the most steep-sided, jagged peaks in the land.

This was the heart of the Glen of Many Legends.

And—James knew well—no mortal man could call this stirring place his own.

A light touch to his elbow made that clear. "Are you for having me rid you of those aching toes now, or"—she darted a glance across the moor to a low, white-walled cottage tucked snugly between a tangle of boulders at the base of a particularly steep cliff—"will you be wanting a wee bit of nourishment before—"

"I'll be keeping my toes and the pain." James was sure she didn't mean she might banish his digits, but he didn't want to take any chances.

Wise women such as Grizel sometimes took a visitor's wishes too earnestly and—he swallowed—worked spells that wrought all sorts of havoc.

So it paid to speak plainly.

It was also in his best interest not to set foot inside the home she shared with her partner, Gorm. Known as *Tigh-na-Craig*—"House on the Rock"—the earthy-sweet peat smoke that permeated the thatched cottage was said to be so soothing it could lull susceptible visitors into a doze that could last a thousand years.

Longer if a soul was unlucky.

James tried not to shudder.

Grizel stepped closer. "This day has seen me busy." Her gaze flitted again to the cottage. "I've set out some fine cheese, made from the milk of my best hinds, and"— she laid a knotty-knuckled hand on his arm, the glint in her eyes showing that she'd read his thoughts—"fresh-baked oatcakes, hot off the toasting stone.

"There's even a thick meat broth bubbling over the fire." She peered up at him, her voice crooning. "A fat capon, well larded and savory—"

"Nae." James broke away before her words could spell him to her cottage with its softly glowing peat fire and tantalizing smell of food. "I'm no' hungry," he lied, his stomach rumbling loudly.

"Och! I do be sorry to hear that, I am." She didn't sound grieved at all.

But her voice did come from at least twenty paces behind him.

James froze, balling his fists.

He'd been marching through knee-high heather and grass, making for Tigh-na-Craig, as had undoubtedly been Grizel's nefarious plan.

He swung around to glare at her. "You tricked me."

"And if I did?" She glanced at his foot. "Be you still in pain?"

He wasn't.

James pressed his lips together, not wanting to admit that his toes felt good as new.

"I see you aren't!" She had the cheek to look mightily pleased.

James frowned, stubborn.

Grizel didn't seem affronted. "I've been healing worse than broken toes since before the first sprig o' heather bloomed in these hills." She came forward to poke him with a slightly crooked finger. "That be long enough to know that some men would sooner choke to death than admit they've got a bone in their throat."

"Ah, well..." James pulled a hand over his chin. "The pain has gone, aye. And"—he glanced at the deer herd, now nibbling grass along the edge of a black-watered lochan—"I do thank you."

"It was Rannoch what told me you were in need." Grizel sent an affectionate glance to the white stag. He stood apart from the other beasts, his proud head held high and his uncanny gaze fixed on them.

"Did he tell you my foot was aching?" James felt foolish discussing a deer with such capabilities. But he knew better than to doubt the cailleach. "Or did he...Rannoch... reveal the true reason I came to see you?"

He just hoped she and Gorm would give him the answer he sought without too much ceremony.

She might have cured his throbbing toes, and he did feel obliged to her, but it was late. He'd hoped to be back at Castle Haven by noon. Now—he could scarce believe how swiftly the day had vanished—the gloaming was slipping across the land, darkening the moor.

"She's a great beauty, eh?" Grizel was eyeing him, looking purposeful.

"Who?" James felt the back of his neck heat.

"Why"—she didn't even blink—"she who you saw this day."

"What makes you think I saw a woman?"

"Hah!" Grizel gave a cackle that would have curled

the hair of a lesser man. "She cares for you, that one. I do be speaking of the maid with the shining tresses."

"Humph." James felt a spurt of irritation.

Grizel was baiting him. Catriona and Scandia both had shining tresses. But he knew from experience that it'd be pointless to try and prise a more direct explanation from the crone.

She enjoyed riddles.

James couldn't abide them.

"Is Gorm in his cave?" He looked past Grizel to a cleft in one of the hills. It was there that Gorm spent his days, peering into a smooth-surfaced pool in the floor of the cave. Said to be bottomless, the pool reflected every thought and deed in the world since time beginning. And, some claimed, beyond earth's end.

Every evening before sundown, Gorm gathered hand-fuls of these truths and formed them into dreams. These he took with him to the front of the cave, releasing them to the night wind, which bore them to those deserving.

James shuddered.

He knew the old man carried his tidings in both hands, his right hand clutching the good and true dreams, while he used the left one to deliver nightmares and false omens meant only to deceive.

The bards swore Gorm never erred.

His credo was simple.

Those pure of heart needn't fear him. Others...

James swallowed, his every sin flashing across his mind. He was especially aware of how he could still feel Catriona's warm, supple body pressed to his side. How he'd burned with desire for her. He did now, fevering to taste the soft ripeness of her lips. Need rode him hard, making him ache to drink in her sweetness. He drew a tight breath, certain his lust stood all over him, blazing like a beacon.

And now that he was here, so close to Gorm and his Pool of Truth, he was no longer sure he wanted to hear what the ancient might tell him.

"Gorm is there, aye." Grizel spoke at last, sounding a bit miffed. "There be no day what passes when he isn't up at thon cave."

She leaned close, eyeing him sharply. "You've no need to see him. There's naught he can say that I don't know myself, mayhap better."

"To be sure, and I respect your wisdom." James kept his voice firm. "But I'll no' be offending Gorm by leaving here without conferring with him, as well. Therefore"— he held Grizel's bright gaze—"I will be making the journey up to his cave."

"So be it." She turned then and struck out across the moor, taking a narrow path that had suddenly opened between the windblown grass and heather. "But keep close, for the way there changes more swiftly than the climb to the Bowing Stone and its corrie."

Moving swiftly, she led him toward the steep rise, where the cave's black-jawed opening grew more ominous the closer they came. Jagged rocks guarded either side of the entrance, and any moment he expected the boulders to rear up as scaly-backed, fire-breathing dreagans.

But as they neared the cave, it was only Gorm who stepped from the darkness to greet them.

A small, slightly bent man with a whirr of iron-gray hair and a particularly fine beard that reached to his knees, he hobbled forward on short bandy legs, his elfin face lit with a smile.

"It's yourself, young James!" He beamed welcome from warm, intelligent eyes. "I know why you're here and can put your mind to rest."

Relief flooded James. "Clan Cameron will be victorious? The King will honor—"

"The King will be just, sure as I'm standing here. But..." Gorm closed his eyes, drawing a long breath. "You know fine I cannot tell you more. To do so would break faith with the Old Ones who've asked me to guard this sacred place.

"Truth to tell"—he opened his eyes, and James saw a flicker of sadness in the clear blue depths—"they'd poison the waters of the Pool of Truth and cause it to overflow, flooding this high moor and, belike, the whole of the glen. The deluge would be unending, not stopping until a vast loch covered every stone and no living creature, man or beast, could ever call this land home again."

"Pah!" Grizel kicked a pebble with her tiny black-shod foot.

Gorm gave her a look, undaunted.

James felt the blood rush in his ears, a dull roar that crushed his hopes. His gut twisted, and a scalding heat filled his chest, making it hard to breathe. When he then noticed Gorm's hands—both clasped loosely before him—he knew real dread.

Whatever truth the Maker of Dreams had seen, it held both good and evil.

Through Gorm's fingers, James could see tiny bursts of brilliant blue-white flames and dark, pulsing shadows, blacker than the coldest night.

"Is the answer there?" He couldn't look away from Gorm's joined hands.

"So it is, aye." The ancient nodded. "I have seen a truth that belongs to many men. You and your warriors will not stand alone on the field that day. Others will be there, too. Champions who fight and"—his eyes met James's, piercing—"those who simply watch.

"I have seen into the hearts of all these souls." He paused, flinging up his hands so that the swirls of light and darkness were caught by the wind and swept away. "It is your mingled fates, and the outcome you share, that I brought from the cave."

"And that you've now released." James couldn't keep the bitterness from his voice.

"I could do naught else." Gorm took a step toward him, his beard fluttering in the wind. "Such is the truth I've seen, and no power on earth, not even my own, can change the events about to unfold."

James cocked a brow. "Yet you say my mind should be eased?"

"I've been given a message to lighten your heart." Gorm's ancient voice rang deep, bold, and powerful. "Men cannot alter their destiny, but they can choose how they master what comes. The words I have for you are ones the gods allow me to share. No more, no less. If you are wise, their portent should please you."

"Then tell him." Grizel jabbed him with a bony elbow.

Gorm kept his dignity. "I have seen"—he stepped aside to make room for Rannoch when he clattered up to the cave, joining them— "that peace will be had when innocents pay the price of blood and gold covers the glen."

James stared at him. "That's a riddle. It makes no sense."

"It is what will be."

"And if I ignore it?"

"You can, to be sure." Gorm took a slow breath. "But doing so will not change the prophecy."

"It's a prophecy?" James felt as if icy mists were swirling around him, dark and terrible.

"It is the truth." Gorm's words came from far away, an echo beneath the rushing wind.

James frowned and clutched his plaid, the wind buffeting him. He struggled, staggering against the lashing gale and furious because he wanted to tell Gorm—and Grizel and their nosy white stag—that he didn't care for their truths, by any name.

But when the wind died, he was no longer with the ancients at their cave. He was back at the corrie, his arm braced against the outcrop that—his eyes rounded—was no longer the shining, rune-carved Bowing Stone, but a jumble of towering, weathered stone.

And the end of the ravine once again tailed away into nothingness. The gap he'd passed through was no more.

Not that it mattered.

He knew where he'd been and what he'd heard.

He just didn't like it.

And he'd be damned if he was going to accept a fate that didn't please him. So he squared his shoulders, set his jaw, and started down the hill.

He had much to do.

Chapter Six

❧

"Lady—you'll catch your death in that draught."

Maili, Blackshore's laundress and Catriona's friend, swept up to the window in a cloud of musky perfume and swirled a shawl around Catriona's shoulders. In a flash, two small dogs flew off Catriona's bed and sped across the room, barking madly. They leapt at Maili, hurling themselves against her legs as if she had something dire in mind rather than seeing to her mistress's comfort.

"Birkie, Beadle"—Catriona spoke sharply to the yapping dogs—"be still. Maili isn't hurting me."

"That be true." Maili stood back and yanked her skirts aside, away from the jumping beasties. She was a plump maid with bouncing dark curls, a generous bosom, and merry brown eyes. "But they're only trying to protect you, as am I. The wind is cold and—"

"Brisk air is good for the lungs." Catriona smoothed the shawl in place all the same. "And I'm not in need of protection. It's our men who are in danger."

"Men have swords." Maili flounced onto one of the window embrasure's cushioned benches. "Two kinds, praise God. And most of them"—she crossed her legs, swinging one foot—"wield both weapons with mastery."

"Pah." Catriona's gaze went to the black clouds racing in from the sea, then back to Maili. "If they knew what they were about, the King's men wouldn't be in the glen, fouling good Highland air."

She ignored the rest of her friend's comment.

Maili couldn't breathe without swooning over men's amatory skills. Catriona understood—especially since she'd felt the hard press of James's powerful body against hers when he'd hurried her through the glen, how he'd almost kissed her on the boat strand, his breath teasing her skin and the heat in his eyes making her tingle—but unlike Maili, she lacked experience in such delights.

And she was interested in only one man.

Her heart beat for James Cameron alone, even if her position as Lady of Blackshore made him the least suitable contender for her affections.

Her feelings for him were a plague she'd always managed to suppress until their fiery encounter in the wood. Now tinder had been thrown onto the flames, and she feared she'd never be the same again.

She did lean down to scratch Birkie and Beadle behind the ears, and then straightened when they dashed across the room and leapt back onto the bed.

As soon as they settled, she turned again to the window. She *liked* the cold rain just beginning to spit down from the heavens, and the lashing wind suited her mood. If James wasn't going to return and darken Blackshore's gate, she wouldn't mind him receiving a drenching on his journey back to Castle Haven.

A dousing from above to match the wet and soggy feet he'd earned when he'd stomped across Blackshore's causeway as the tide raced in.

Had he returned as any sensible man would've done, given the wild and roiling skies, he could've spent the evening in a chair by the hearth, his belly full, sipping ale, and—she was quite sure—proving to her that his kisses were hotter than dreagan fire.

As it was...

He'd preferred to stalk off into the gloaming.

She bristled, his ability to ignore her twisting like a knife in her gut. Her *worry* about him—there wasn't a MacDonald born who wasn't a wizard with a sword, after all—tightened her chest, almost suffocating her.

The intensity of her concern was galling.

She should hate him.

Instead, just the thought of him made her pulse quicken and her heart pound as whirls of deliciously heated prickles spilled through her, until she was left wanting him more badly than ever before.

If he fell at the trial by combat, she'd never recover.

There had to be something she could do. Indeed, she *would* do something if only Alasdair weren't treating her as if she'd lost her wits.

She glanced at Maili, bristling. "The men should be locked in their bedchambers, not me."

"But you aren't, my lady." Maili's dark eyes met hers. "You're free to roam anywhere—"

"Anywhere within Blackshore's walls, which is the same as being trapped in my room." Catriona fumed inwardly, a wild and wicked part of her rebelling against her brother's foolery. "I'd wager my toes that James Cameron hasn't forbid his sister from leaving Castle Haven."

"Lady Isobel isn't you." Maili tucked her feet up under her on the window bench. "Word is she's quiet and biddable. She's not one to stir trouble."

Catriona turned back to the window. A thick wall of mist was beginning to slide across the loch, blanketing the far shore and the hills beyond. "I don't stir trouble."

"Mischief, then."

"That neither."

"There are some who'd argue that you do."

"Then they aren't harangued by overprotective brothers who sometimes can't be suffered without a touch of trickery." Catriona took a deep breath, remembering Alasdair's most recent sampling of good intentions. He'd proposed she wed a deep-pursed, generously landed laird who—for once—had been only a few years older than herself, but whose face had been marred by bulging, fishlike eyes.

The man had also possessed the annoying habit of slurping when he tipped back his ale.

Catriona shuddered. "I promise you, any woman would stoop to *mischief* if the need arose." She shot a look at Maili. "Including Isobel Cameron, I'm sure. Indeed, I should like to meet her. I've no doubt that she's just as troubled by King Robert's writ as I am."

On the bed, Birkie and Beadle barked agreement.

Maili twirled a glossy brown curl around her fingers. "I'm thinking it's Lady Isobel's brother you're twitching to see again."

"I'm not twitching." Catriona smoothed the folds in her skirts.

Maili's eyes lit with laughter. "If you say..."

"I do."

"But you wouldn't mind a meeting with James...I mean, his sister?"

"I—" Catriona bit off her protest. She did want to see James again, and she would like to meet Isobel, but she didn't care for Maili's amusement.

Unfortunately, she could still feel James's hands on her. The memory made her breathless. And she couldn't stop hearing his rich, deep voice threatening her with kisses. She shivered, grudgingly aware that he not only filled her with excitement and longing, but also stirred her in ways that mattered more than Maili's teasing.

She inhaled slowly. "It might be good to see them." Something close to a smile tugged at her lips before she could catch herself. "Times of strife do require us to make sacrifices."

"To be sure." Maili pulled a tasseled cushion onto her lap. "And when the day comes"—she leaned forward, her face lighting with the charm that won so many manly hearts—"it won't hurt to flutter your eyelashes and thrust your bosom beneath James Cameron's nose."

"Maili!" Catriona flushed. "The devil will take you for such wickedness."

"I wish he would, my lady." Maili sighed and leaned back against the wall. "Trouble is I'm quite sure he has his eye on you."

Days later, James stood at the arched window of his bedchamber and stared out at the rain-drenched night. Thick clouds blotted the stars, and there was no moon to edge the hills in silver. Somewhere in the distance, thunder rumbled, low and ominous. And the wind blew steadily, racing in from the west and bringing the faint tang of the sea. He listened to the keening, appreciative.

He wouldn't have minded a howling gale.

He did crack the shutters, welcoming the hiss of rain on stone and the bracing chill of cold, damp air.

Clan tongue-waggers claimed he'd drawn his first breath on such a night. A black e'en of roaring wind and darkness, the glen cloaked in gloom. He couldn't remember, but those who had cause to know swore that it'd been so cold that the hearth fires froze and icy rain hammered the tower with such ferocity that some feared that Castle Haven wouldn't be standing in the morning.

But it was, of course.

And to this day, such raw, untamed weather quickened his blood. This night was no different. He just wished he could also rejoice in the words that kept ringing in his ears. Or feign indifference as he was presently ignoring the gnawing hunger in his belly.

A pity he could do neither.

And although he knew fine why his stomach rumbled—he had hardly eaten in two days—he couldn't make sense of Gorm's prophecy.

Innocents paying the price of blood.

Gold covering the glen.

Frowning, he splayed his hands against the icy stone of the window splay. The Makers of Dreams and their truths weren't the only thing plaguing him. He couldn't put Catriona from his mind, either. And that vexed him even more than his inability to decipher Gorm's words.

It was maddening.

Each time he tried not to think of her, his desire for

her only flamed hotter. She was worse than a pebble in his shoe. She was prickly, proud, and utterly infuriating. A proper pest, the likes of which he'd never encountered. He didn't need her slipping into his thoughts, banishing his logic and every whit of his sense.

Yet even now he could feel the awareness crackling in the air between them. Inside him, heat stirred and simmered, sharp and intense. She made him feel like a caged animal, straining for release. Just the whisper of her name sent jolts of lust spearing through him, straight to his loins. And that was an annoyance that frayed his temper and put a sour taste in his mouth.

He couldn't believe he'd threatened to kiss her.

Cold, bitter fury swept him, minding him of his folly.

She'd accepted his challenge. He'd seen that in her eyes, even if she hadn't said as much in words. He didn't know how she'd do it, but he was sure she meant to tempt him beyond restraint.

Catriona was capable of robbing a man of reason. If ever he took her, he'd be lost in her spell.

His sudden urge to slam his fist into the wall said he already was.

And that annoyed him more than anything.

She was a MacDonald, by God.

Before a few more suns could rise, he might prove to be the man who'd end her brother's life. And if the gods were kind to Camerons, his steel would cut down a goodly number of their kinsmen along with Alasdair.

Why that notion suddenly felt like a score of iron-shod fists beating down on his head and pummeling his chest was beyond him. It was a mystery that put a cold, hard knot in the pit of his belly.

Especially when he knew Alasdair would run him through with his own blade, given the chance.

The bastard had said as much.

Even so, James dragged a hand through his hair, furious.

He should be pacing around the room—he thought better when moving—but each time he started stomping about, Hector struggled to his feet and came to trail after him. The old dog only retreated to his pallet by the fire when James stopped to stand before the window.

If he didn't move, Hector allowed himself to rest.

He glanced at the dog, relieved to see he was now sleeping soundly.

He hadn't slept in days.

Not well, anyway.

But—at last—a plan was forming in his mind. Hadn't Gorm said that "while a destiny might be writ in stone, a man could decide how he wished to meet it"?

And he wished for Clan Cameron to be victorious.

So it was with a mounting sense of hope that he carefully latched the shutters. He listened for Hector to stir, but the dog's snores proved that the sound hadn't disturbed him. Relieved, James crossed the room to a large chest at the foot of his bed.

A sturdy iron-banded coffer of heavy, age-blackened oak, the chest held something that just might be the answer to his problems.

Hoping he was right, he slid another look at Hector and then knelt to retrieve a key from beneath his bed's mattress. After slipping the key into the lock, he undid the strongbox's rusty hasps and opened the lid.

Puffs of dust swirled up to tickle his nose, the musty

smell of time and ancient glories almost making him sneeze. But he stifled the urge and was just reaching into the coffer to lift out his treasure when the door opened behind him and a blaze of torchlight flooded the room.

"James..." His sister's voice rose above a rustle of movement.

"Ho, cousin!" Colin's greeting boomed. "Praying, are you, what?"

"Sakes!" James jumped up, whirling to find Isobel and Colin in the doorway. He glared at them, ignoring his cousin's fool query. The lout held a torch flaming bright enough to rival a balefire, and his sister clutched a tray of food, the tantalizing aroma of roasted meat and hot, fresh-baked bread making his mouth water.

The delicious food smells filled the air, almost overwhelming.

James's stomach gurgled loudly.

Across the room, Hector's eyes popped opened. With the fierce determination of a dog hoping for a tidbit, he pushed to his feet and shuffled across the floor rushes, plopping onto his haunches before the door. He lifted his head, fixing Isobel with an unblinking stare, his great bulk blocking entry to the bedchamber.

"We brought this for you." Looking poised as always, Isobel lifted the tray higher, out of Hector's reach. "As you refuse to join us in the hall, we thought you might as well dine here again.

"But"—she flashed a look at Colin—"we'll wait while you eat this time." She narrowed her gaze as she spoke, her fierce look of disapproval making clear that she knew he'd give more than half the food to Hector if she didn't keep her hawk eyes on him.

That was, after all, what he'd done with every other meal that'd been left outside his door since he'd returned from the Makers of Dreams.

"See here, James." Colin set his torch in an iron ring on the wall and stepped around Hector. "You cannae go on no' eating. Word is that the King's entourage is less than a day's ride from the glen. The trial by combat will begin when he arrives. You'll need your strength—"

"Think you I've lost it?" James snatched the food tray from Isobel with lightning speed and plunked the victuals down before Hector. "If so, you err."

He grinned, triumphantly. "Or"—he stepped back, dusting his hands—"will you say otherwise?"

"I say tossing meat to a dog is a far cry from crossing swords with MacDonalds and Mackintoshes." Colin gave him a look as dark as Isobel's. "I'll no' be denying Hector his due"—he glanced at the dog, who was enthusiastically devouring a choice beef rib—"but I'll see you filling your belly if I must force the food down your throat. You've been hiding up here for nigh onto three days, and—"

"I've been thinking." James matched his cousin's stare, belligerent.

"No, you've been brooding." Isobel set her hands on her hips and gave him a look so fierce that his head started to pound.

"Have a care, lass. I'm no' in a mood to be pestered." He turned an equally fearsome stare on her, but she didn't flinch. He wouldn't have believed it, but he could almost see steel gleaming in her spine.

As if she knew—and was pleased he'd noticed—she inclined her head, infinitesimally. He was sure she'd done so to annoy him. So he swatted at a fold of his plaid, pretending he hadn't seen.

Not to be deterred, she gave him her most disarming smile. "I'm here because I do care."

"Humph." James clenched his jaw.

Had he truly thought of her as biddable? A mild-spoken, acquiescent sister he could soon offer to a well-suited, allied laird as a fine, conformable wife?

At the moment, she struck him as bold and brazen as Catriona.

Worse, in the blaze of light cast by Colin's damty torch, she minded him so much of Scandia that he was sure he'd splutter if he dared to argue with her. She stood tall and held herself erect, pride and willfulness shining all over her like a flaming beacon.

She lifted her chin then and her braided hair slid over one shoulder, the strands shimmering like a ribbon of blue-black silk. James blinked, feeling whisked back to the mist-hung moor and a certain burn side, hemmed by a cluster of red-berried rowan trees.

Isobel truly did look like their beautiful spectral ancestress.

James scowled at her, wishing he hadn't noticed.

"Brooding," she said again, sailing past him to claim one of the chairs before the fire. She sat very straight and folded her hands in her lap. "That's what you've been about, and we all know—"

"God be good!" He wasn't fooled by her demure attitude. "What you know is that I've been up here and"—he narrowed his eyes—"that I wished to be left alone. To think, not brood, on the weal and honor of the clan.

"That is what has occupied me, whatever." He spoke with all the lairdly authority in him.

Colin snorted. "So you say."

"I just did, aye." James wasn't giving an inch.

Especially when he knew his cousin and his sister were right.

His thoughts *had* slipped to other concerns. But now he'd caught himself, pushing the matter of Catriona firmly from his mind. Although...

Isobel's delicately arched brow and the faint, quizzical smile playing about her lips didn't help him pretend that his life wasn't being overrun by a pack of scheming, bolder-than-brass Valkyries.

Even *ghostly* females were after him, it seemed.

And he was having none of it.

He did shoot an angry look at Colin, who'd gone to stand beside the bedside table—*James's bedside table*—and was presently pouring himself a generous measure of finest Gascon wine. The lout had also imbibed the last few sugared almonds and honey-stuffed dates that had been left on a tray for James's own delectation.

He had a sweet tooth, as did many Highlanders. The treats were all he'd been allowing himself to enjoy these last few hungering days.

Now his cousin had eaten them.

James fisted his hands. His rising hopes of moments before were spiraling away before his nose, dwindling rapidly to a mean rumbling somewhere in his empty stomach.

He cleared his throat, his gaze on Colin, the sweet-thief. "If you must know, you sticky-fingered buzzard, my time up here hasn't been wasted. Solitude is good for the soul." He clasped his hands behind him, began walking slowly toward his cousin. "Wits are as crucial to winning a battle as broadswords and cold steel.

"This e'en"—he lunged to snatch the wine jug from Colin's hand, returning it to the table before the loon could refill his cup—"we rally the clan. I have something that will stir—"

"They're roused already, though no' in a way that'll please you." Colin grabbed the ewer and splashed wine into his cup, tipping back the contents before James could object. "Some of the men are angry, now that the King and his entourage are so near."

He dragged a hand over his mouth, leaning close. "They're riled, James. They say we've waited too long, and wrongly. They're growling that we should've seen to the Lowlanders in the old way."

"Then they're fools." James spoke in a low, hard voice. "They know what happens if a Highlander even looks cross-eyed at the King. To openly defy him, ignoring his writ and having done with his men..." He let the words tail off, shaking his head. "I say you, our men know better."

Colin held up his hands. "I only repeat the grumbles in the hall."

James looked at him, a ghastly notion prickling his nape. "Then some flat-footed troublemaker has slipped into their ranks, spreading doubts and lies."

Something golden caught his eye then. A drop of honey on the table, all that remained of his special stuffed dates. At once, the image of Alasdair MacDonald's magnificent sword rose before him, the amber pommel stone shining brightly, just as it'd done in the bailey at Blackshore.

The speck of honey glistened in the firelight, almost winking at him.

His mind raced, whirling with possibilities.

If Alasdair had sent someone, perhaps in a guise, to mingle with James's men, dropping a poisoned hint here, a goading word there...

But the thought vanished as quickly as it'd come.

Alasdair would challenge him openly, he was sure.

Much as it irked him to credit the bastard with even a smidgen of honor. Worse, the lout's penchant for valor left James little choice but to show him equal gallantry. Anything else would shame him as chief and discredit the good Cameron name.

Yet he had a terrible suspicion that when he next came face-to-face with the loon's delectable sister, honor and all its attendant qualities would be the last thing on his mind.

The silken swells of her breasts and her sweetly rounded hips would bring out the devil in him. His need to get his hands on her, to taste her ripe, dusky nipples, would see him pulling her into his arms and dragging her straight into hell's most wicked fires.

And no power on earth would stop him.

Her brother be damned.

Chapter Seven

❖

Before James's head could begin to pound, he pushed all thought of Catriona from his mind. He especially tried not to dwell on the curve of her breasts or the darker delights hidden beneath her skirts. Here in his own privy quarters, it was so easy to imagine carrying her to his bed and divesting her of those meddlesome skirts and everything else that kept her beauty from view. For such a pestiferous plague of a female, she possessed more feminine charms than any woman he'd ever known. Her wiles were boundless. And if he meant to think clearly, he needed to stop lusting after her. Doing so only made him the more furious.

His inability to stop worrying about her riled him in a worse way.

She might be her brother's responsibility, but somehow he doubted Alasdair recognized how much trouble she could stir with her passionate, headstrong ways. And much as he resented his fool urge to protect her, his fingers still itched to shake sense into her.

Even more vexing was that he admired her spirit.

And it was that *admiration* that sent heat crawling up his neck and twisted his innards to knots.

He frowned, not wishing to examine the feeling too closely. He did pull a hand down over his chin and tried again to blot her from his thoughts.

Forgetting her brother proved easier, but other irritations still nagged at him.

And he wouldn't have any peace until he voiced them.

Angry, he glared again at the drop of honey on the table, evidence of how swiftly his cousin had devoured his special stuffed dates.

There were others—men not near as close to him as Colin, or as noble as Alasdair—who'd take more from him than his favorite sweetmeats.

Sure of it, he reached to swipe away the honey-dollop with his thumb. "Tell me"—he turned to face Colin—"have any Mackintoshes been seen skulking about in these parts?"

Those sniveling, mealy-mouthed cravens, he *could* see stooping to such trickery. The cloaked figure in the wood could've been one of their ilk and not, as he'd guessed, a Lowlander.

The chills creeping up and down his spine told him anything was possible.

"Well?" He arched a brow, waiting.

"Word is"—Colin rubbed the back of his neck—"their chief, Kendrew, has every man at Castle Nought training in the lists. Some say he's even barred the gate with a chain, just so nary a man can escape if his sword arm tires. He wants victory, that one."

"Bah!" James almost choked. "The Mackintoshes are

naught but a pack of shrieking women. If Kendrew locked his gate with a chain, I'm for thinking he did so to keep out the dreagans thon clan fears so greatly. No' to keep his soft-sworded, scared-of-their-own-shadow warriors inside.

"Or"—he really liked this idea—"to keep the loons from tumbling down the cliff some horned and furry he-goat Mackintosh forebear was fool enough to choose as a site for their wretched stronghold."

"I've heard the odd stone formations around Castle Nought do turn into dreagans at night." Isobel spoke from her chair by the fire. "And some say they built where they did, with the walls of their keep rising so seamlessly from the cliffs, so that they can best guard the high mountain pass above their keep." She smoothed her skirts. "Indeed, as we've never succeeded in using the pass without grief, perhaps they aren't such dafties, after all?"

James's eyes rounded. He was sure he could feel steam shooting out his ears.

"Since when have you become a champion for that ill-famed race of cloven-footed rock climbers?" He glared at her. "And there's no such thing as a dreagan. There aren't any such beasts hereabouts. And"—he leaned toward her, hoping he looked menacing—"you'll no' be seeing any in the benighted corner of the glen claimed by Kendrew Mackintosh and his flock of whiny women."

"Cook says he saw one once." Her voice was smug.

"Then he was either drunk or dreaming." James folded his arms. Any moment his head was going to burst. His temples were pounding with a vengeance.

"Ah, well." Isobel smiled sweetly. "You will have the right of it. The dreagans said to lurk near Castle Nought are surely no more real than our own Lady Scandia, Doom of the Camerons."

She gave a delicate shiver. "I can't recall having ever glimpsed her, either."

"Be glad you haven't." He blurted the words before he could stop himself.

"You've seen her?" Colin's eyes bulged, his brows hovering near his hairline. *"The ghost?"*

"Nae, I haven't." James felt heat flood his face. "Bogles are the same bog mist as dreagans. Castle Haven's gray lady is nothing but—" He stopped when a blast of cold, wet wind blew open the shutters and gusted into the room, flapping tapestries and guttering candles. Colin's hand torch went out with a great belching of smoke and ash. The sparks floated through the air, glowing and hissing.

Everyone stared.

Hector began to howl.

"Good lad. It's only the wind." James reached down to pat the dog's bony shoulders and then strode across the room to close the shutters.

He was just relatching them when a loud bang sounded behind him. The noise was suspiciously like the slamming of his strongbox lid.

"Hah!" Colin's voice rose above the echoes of the crash. "I should have known."

James stood frozen, his hands on the icy-wet iron of the shutter latch. His bed, a massive four-postered monstrosity, sheltered the chest from wind. The lid couldn't slam shut on its own.

He'd braced it open.

Unless...

Whirling around, he saw Colin and Isobel staring at

the coffer. But it wasn't the iron-bound strongbox that had their jaws dropping.

It was the length of red and gold silk spilling out from beneath the chest's now-closed lid to pool on the rush-strewn floor.

The clan banner.

An ancient standard, its silken red furls decorated with gleaming yellow bars and, at its heart, emblazoned with the embroidered likeness of a snarling black dog.

Known as the Banner of the Wind, it was the clan's most prized possession.

In the darkest days of clan legend, when Ottar the Fire-worshipper and his warriors had searched along coasts and throughout the hills for a meet place to gather food, breed, and build a dwelling place, they'd used the proud standard to help them make the decision.

And now the glorious banner lay tangled on the floor rushes.

The rushes might be fresh and strewn with dried heather and sweet-smelling herbs, but the floor was still an unworthy resting place for the relic.

And the chest's heavy, humpbacked lid was crushing stitches that had been sewn hundreds of years before, in the very morning of the world.

"Damnation!" James sprinted across the room, raising the lid before the weight of iron and wood could damage the precious cloth.

He scooped the treasure off the floor and into his arms. His heart raced, the old tales swirling in his blood, quickening his pulse. For tradition held that, during his quest for land, Ottar the Fire-worshipper dreamed that the gods would wrest the banner from the hands of their standard bearer so that wind could carry the banner away, planting its pole in the spot where the great Clan Cameron was destined to build their home.

And so it had been.

James clutched the banner to his chest, his gaze sliding to where Colin and Isobel stood watching him, each with wide, round eyes.

Any other time, the fabled Banner of the Wind would fill him with clan pride and exaltation. But now the relic lifted every fine hair on his body, including some hairs he didn't know he had.

Because of its great age, the standard was kept in a soft linen pouch. And that cloth bag was then tucked inside a protective wrapping of oiled sheepskin. James's strong-box was the treasure's final defense, and—he was sure— he'd only just thrust his hands inside the chest when Colin and Isobel stormed into the room.

He hadn't removed the banner.

And wondering who might have done so—especially moments after Isobel had uttered Scandia's name—turned his knees to jelly.

"So you *were* seeking divine aid." Colin appeared at his elbow.

"I was not." James began folding the banner, not trusting himself to meet his cousin's eye lest the long-nose see that he'd lied.

He did hope to use the standard's rallying power.

But he wasn't of a mood to hear Colin's hooting if he admitted that it wasn't any divine power he was counting on. He was putting his faith in the old gods who'd led Ottar the Fire-worshipper to the beloved clan lands where Castle Haven stood this day.

Those were the powers he wanted at his side.

Hoping they'd guide him, as well, he tucked the folded banner beneath his arm. "I told you what I intend to do this e'en." He turned, meeting Colin's gaze. "If you have wax in your ears or have forgotten already"—he laid a hand over the bundle of gleaming red-and-yellow silk—"I mean to take this down to the great hall and—"

"He's going to use the Banner of the Wind to talk sense into our kinsmen." Isobel's face lit with pride. "I want to be there to hear him."

"Then come." James started forward, a thrill already coursing through him as the Banner of the Wind began to weave its ancient magic.

He was out the door and halfway to the stair tower when he heard Colin's muttering and knew his cousin and his sister were hurrying after him. He also caught the slower *clack-clackety-clack* of Hector's toenails on the cold stone floor of the corridor, proving that the dog didn't want to miss the excitement.

And if he'd looked over his shoulder—which, fortunately, he didn't—he might have seen a fourth figure hastening along in their wake.

A slender, dark-haired figure, graceful and lovely, and whose lightly slippered feet didn't touch the floor.

Scandia, Doom of the Camerons, was just as eager as everyone else to hear what James had to say.

Her life, as it were, might depend on it.

Shimmying with anticipation, Lady Scandia, Doom of the Camerons, let herself whoosh past the little party and paused by the arched entrance to the great hall. She tried to stand still but found it so difficult. Such was the nature of her ghostly state that she sometimes quivered when excited. So she did her best not to flutter and peered back down the corridor. Soon, James and the others would catch up with her. And she couldn't wait to see what would then transpire.

There was already a stir in the hall.

Grumbles, mutterings, and dark looks the likes of which she hadn't seen since her own day. And as those troubles had led to such disaster—her own sad demise—much depended on how James handled the brewing dissent.

That he'd fetched the Banner of the Wind said he meant action.

He was prepared.

But—she cast a glance into the crowded, smoke-hazed hall—certain unexpected matters would still surprise him.

Unfortunately, one problem wouldn't catch him unawares. Sir Walter must have ears as sharp as Scandia's own, because he stalked from the shadows the moment James and his entourage burst into view.

"Cameron! I greet you!" He planted himself in front of James, clearly bent on causing havoc. "We've wondered when you'd leave your bed. Indeed"—he surveyed James from cold, dark eyes—"I was almost of a mind to send someone to tell you there is no need to join us."

He flicked a speck of lint off his sleeve. "If the snarling of your men is any indication, they'd rather toss your King and his Lowland *rabble* into a bog before they'll take to the field in a fair trial by combat.

"And if they stoop to such villainy"—he met James's gaze again, his own triumphant—"the lot of you will be packed off to the Isle of Lewis before—"

"Say you, Sir Walter. I say you err." James spoke so

resolutely, and his eyes glinted so dangerously, that Scandia shimmied almost uncontrollably.

She drifted closer to the two men, careful to keep one hand pressed to her breast to still the rapid beating of her heart. She'd taken measures to stay unseen, but there was always a risk someone might note a flurry in the air if she failed to contain her glee.

The dog, Hector, was already eyeing her curiously.

It wouldn't do if the others noticed he'd seen something unusual and became distracted.

The young laird, especially, would need all his wits presently.

So Scandia took a deep breath and stood patiently, hovering as unobtrusively as she could. She also bit her lip, some of her elation dimming because this was—or once had been—her beloved home. It grieved her to float through its walls as *something unusual*.

But there could be no changing what she was, so she let her own Cameron pride sweep her and turned her attention back to young James.

"Truth to tell…" James now stood toe to toe with the Lowlander. "You mistake on two counts. One, Cameron men ne'er take to their beds lest they have a warm and comely reason for doing so."

"That's the way of it, by God!" Colin swaggered up to them, his tone daring Sir Walter to argue. "Though I'll add we like those *reasons* well made and"—he sketched a shapely form in the air—"eager to please."

The nobleman glowered at him, his mouth thinning. His narrow, hawkish face soured as if he'd smelled something unpleasant.

It was all Scandia could do not to giggle. But, she

remembered with sorrow, it'd been so long since she'd laughed. She wasn't sure she still knew how.

She did allow herself a quick twirl.

It did her heart good to see two braw Cameron warriors at their magnificent best. With their colorful plaids slung boldly over their shoulders, swords at their hips, and fire in their eyes they were simply glorious.

Indignation suited them.

Sir Walter's pinch-faced umbrage only made him look like an irate vole. "A man's prowess in bed says nothing of his valor in the field." His sneer darkened the air, spoiling Scandia's brief pleasure. Hector's hackles rose as the dog took a step toward him, growling.

"There will be no room for beasts on board the King's galleys." Sir Walter spoke with relish, his voice ringing. "They shall be dealt with before you leave, each mangy cur banished like so much windblown smoke. The whelps, too, make no mistake."

Hector showed yellow teeth, his snarls low in his throat now.

Sir Walter raised a hand, snapping his fingers. "So quickly, and they're gone."

James put back his shoulders, his eyes narrowing. "Have a care when you speak of our animals, Lindsay. Their lives are more dear to us than"—he paused, letting his gaze rake the Lowlander—"some who go on two feet."

He cocked a meaningful brow then, all cordiality.

"No' that you need trouble yourself." His tone said the opposite. "Though . . ." He shifted the bundle of silk in his arms. "Perhaps you should hear our war cry. It is *Chlanna nan con thigibh a so's gheibh sibh feoil* and means, 'Sons of the hounds, come here and get flesh.'"

"That's heathen babble." Sir Walter didn't bother to hide his scorn.

"Nae, good sir." James's voice hardened. "It is a warning to all who vex us that we feed the flesh of our enemies to our dogs."

Scandia almost spun in a circle at his daring. She did shimmer brightly, ripples of pleasure tingling clear down to her toes.

Sir Walter clamped his jaw. His face took on a purplish hue.

Lady Isobel, who reminded Scandia so much of herself, turned quickly aside, touching her fingers to her lips to smother a smile.

"Further"—James placed a hand on Hector's gray-tufted head when the dog came to lean against his legs— "the only souls, man or beast, that you'll see leaving here will be your own. After we of this glen do what we must to meet our sovereign's wishes. Highlandmen are aye loyal. We are so to our King and to our land.

"Be assured I speak as well for Alasdair MacDonald and Kendrew Mackintosh." He sounded so certain, his words making Scandia glide nearer. "They, too, would sooner draw their last breath, dying here of a sword-drink, than face a life beyond these hills."

Scandia shivered, for she knew he spoke true.

"And that, Sir Walter"—he paused, his dark eyes glittering fiercely in the dimness—"is what you and those like you e'er forget. To a Highlander, there is no life away from our home glen. There is only nothingness and sorrow that would kill us more surely and in a much more painful way than any bite of steel."

"Then you're all heroic fools." Sir Walter was vehement.

He slid a glance over his shoulder at the noisy hall. The trestle benches were crowded, the aisles thronged with milling clansmen and scrounging dogs. Everywhere heads swiveled and turned as men stared, many arguing. Some pounded the tables with balled fists, while others simply ate or quaffed their ale, grim-faced.

One sat apart at the high table, his expression even more stony than the others'.

And with good reason.

Scandia bit her lip, waiting.

Sir Walter turned back to James, looking annoyed. His ire set another whirl of icy air whipping around the great arched entry. And although no one else noticed, the frigid gust caught Scandia's wispy form, casting her into the deeper shadows. When the wind settled, she shook out her filmy skirts and brushed at her sleeves. She also combed her fingers through her hair, trying to tidy the mussed strands.

Not that anyone could see her, but still...

Her composure regained, she turned again to James and his foe. Sir Walter had retreated and now stood on the far side of the entry, near to the hall. He'd curled his hands around his gem-encrusted sword belt and had swelled his chest to an unlikely degree. Looking much like a puffed-up peacock, he fixed James with an arrogant stare.

James glared back at him, his grip on the Banner of the Wind, white-knuckled.

"You're all tartan-draped madmen." Sir Walter spoke down his nose, the words edged with disdain. "Heathery hills, glens, and sword-drinks! Even the MacDonald speaks the same fiery nonsense. Though how the man"— he threw another significant look at the chaos behind him—"can sit at your table, eating your meat and drinking your wine, when the two of you—"

"Alasdair?" James stared at him, his brows arching. "He is here?"

"Him, and no other." Sir Walter stepped aside with a flourish, giving James an unobstructed view of the torch-lit hall. "Or is the flame-haired man at your high table an imposter?"

James scanned the hall, his eyes widening when he spotted the other chieftain. "It is him, by God! And he'll have no good reason for being here."

But even as he said the words, his gaze snapped away from Alasdair.

His entire focus belonged to the flame-haired woman sitting next to the rival chieftain. She inclined her head ever so slightly, a faint smile touching her lips. Something flickered in her eyes, almost a challenge. When her gaze met and held James's, Scandia was sure tiny sparks ignited between them. Even across the vastness of the hall.

She felt them like tiny pinpricks of fire in the soft haze that always surrounded her.

The maid took James's breath.

Scandia had never seen him make such moony eyes at any female.

Which, given the maid's vibrant beauty, was more than understandable. Scandia eyed the girl critically, noting her charms. Torchlight fell across her face, calling attention to her creamy, flawless skin and burnishing her red-gold braids. Thick and glossy, the plaits fell to her hips. Her eyes sparkled like sapphires. And although she'd draped a tartan shawl around her shoulders, its folds only emphasized the fine swell of her breasts.

She was undoubtedly a lady, but one who knew her worth and was aware of how easily she could tempt a man with her high good looks and provocative glances.

In life—her real, earthly one—Scandia would have prickled with envy.

Poor James didn't stand a chance.

Scandia fluttered nearer to him, concerned. Her sharp ghostly senses picked up the rush of his blood, the loud thundering of his heart.

Her own began to beat wildly, the excitement almost too much for her.

She looked at James and wondered what he'd do. He had yet to wrench his gaze from the young woman. He'd clearly forgotten everything else around him. He stood frozen, his jaw clenched and his handsome face flushed as he gripped the clan banner like a shield.

"What's the meaning of this?" He whirled to Colin and Isobel, looking so angry that Scandia felt his shock as powerfully as if it were her own.

His sister spoke first. "We did mean to warn you. That's why we brought your dinner ourselves, rather than send one of the kitchen lads. We—"

But he was already pushing past them, elbowing his way through the crowd, his strides long and purposeful. Men leapt out of his way, and dogs scurried beneath tables. He looked that fierce, his face dark as thunder, a deep furrow digging into his brow.

"Ho, James—wait!" Colin shot after him. Isobel sped hard on his heels, hitching her skirts as she ran. "I swear we were going to tell you, but—" The rest was lost in the din, the shouts and raised voices.

Not that it mattered.

At least it didn't to the Doom of the Camerons. She'd learned long ago that words could be so hollow. Her lessons had been bitter, but through them, she'd grown wise.

What counted was what was.

And watching James march up to the high table—and the proud young woman who sat there, her sapphire gaze locked with his—Scandia knew much more than Colin's blundering cries could have told her.

Young James burned to do one of two things: wring the lovely Lady Catriona's neck or haul her into his arms and kiss her, soundly.

Scandia pressed a hand to her heart, certain she knew what his choice would be.

She understood passion, after all.

Even if there were some who thought otherwise.

Chapter Eight

❧

MacDonald! I welcome you." James strode onto the dais, his gaze on Alasdair. The lout's sister tilted her cheek as if she expected him to lean across the high table and greet her with a kiss. When he didn't, she gave a light shrug he was sure no one else saw and began running the tip of one finger around the edge of her wine cup.

James tried to ignore the provocation.

Unfortunately, he couldn't.

"Lady Catriona." He inclined his head. Then, before she could make another taunting circle around the cup's rim, he narrowed his eyes at her and seized her hand, kissing her fingers.

He nipped the edge of her thumb, regretting his boldness at once because she tasted fresh as rain. Her skin proved cool, smooth, and silken, minding him of soft spring meadows, shimmering beneath a morning sun.

He released her at once, the blood pounding in his ears.

"My lord." She met his gaze directly.

"Lady"—James's heart drummed against his ribs—"you do me honor."

She'd bring him to his knees, was her plan.

He knew that as sure as the sun would rise on the morrow.

Above all, he hoped she couldn't tell that the whole of his body tensed from having savored the taste of her. He wanted more and now might never be rid of his lust for her. His teeth even hurt from how hard he'd clamped his jaw, but he suppressed the discomfort as best he could and determined to keep his attention on Alasdair.

Turning to him, James pretended the air wasn't laced with the scent of gillyflowers.

"MacDonald—this is a surprise." He couldn't believe his voice wasn't choked. His pulse raced, and he'd swear the feel of Catriona's delicate flesh was branded on his tongue. "I didn't think to greet you in my hall so soon."

Alasdair set down his meat knife. "I am no less amazed, whatever."

"Did you come to discuss the King's challenge?" James spoke so that everyone in the hall could hear. "If so"—he flashed a glance to Sir Walter and his henchmen—"I'll say you the same as I did at Blackshore. I'd sooner see the glen dunged by Lowland blood than yours. As is—"

"You'll cut me to pieces before I can think where to make my first slice into you?" Alasdair arched a convivial brow. "It'll be a good, hard fight, I warn you."

James watched the annoying bugger help himself to an oatcake. "I didn't ask your counsel. What I'd know is why you're here."

He didn't need to know how Catriona's shawl mysteriously

slipped down one shoulder to reveal a tantalizing glimpse of her creamy, well-rounded bosom.

That was obvious.

The she-demon meant to taunt him, and he could already feel her talons sinking into him.

He wrenched his gaze from her before she maddened him into showing her what happened to innocent maids who marched onto such thin ice. The coldest pit of hell awaited, and he burned to teach her not to tempt the devil.

Instead, he drew a tight breath and flicked a glance over the sumptuous spread of victuals that had been provided for his unexpected guests. Platters of roasted meats, cold sliced capon, and wedges of cheese showed that Camerons never stint. Oatcakes, fresh-churned butter, and a jar of heather honey rounded up the offerings. A tray piled high with Cook's cream-filled pastries and a dish of sugared almonds ensured that all comforts had been met.

Even the MacDonald escort, a small number of men eating with gusto at a nearby long table, appeared to have no reason for complaint. Far from it, they'd been presented a repast worthy of kings.

Cook had done the clan proud.

"We've been treated well, as you see." Alasdair gestured to the savories, as if he'd read James's mind. "Though, like you, I ne'er thought"—his voice took on a tone of lairdly commiseration—"to find myself supping at your table this e'en. But—"

"We had to call here." Catriona raised her wine cup to her lips, sipping determinedly.

"Say you?" James eyed her sharply.

She didn't turn a hair. "My dog went missing, and we thought he might've come this way."

"Your dog?" James blinked.

She nodded. "A wee brown-and-white male." She spread her hands to indicate the dog's small size. "He's young and must be lost."

James didn't believe a word.

She'd come to return the gauntlet he'd tossed at her. And she was brazen enough to know he'd be only too happy to make good on his threat to ravish her. She might be a maid—he didn't doubt her purity—but she understood how to use her desirability to dazzle him.

Proving his suspicions, she lifted a hand to her amber necklace. The bit of frippery rested much too near the lush swells of her breasts, and seeing her trace her fingers so lightly along the gleaming gemstones pushed him close to his manly limits.

Especially when she flicked one of her glossy red braids over her shoulder. A siren's trick designed to send her shawl dipping a tad deeper, offering him an even better view of her low-cut bodice.

Worse, the glow from a candelabrum set near her trencher revealed the top crescents of her nipples just peeking above the silk of her gown. It was only the slightest hint of taut, dusky-rose flesh, but enough to tighten his chest and send whorls of heat pouring into his loins.

She smiled and took a deep breath, her inhale revealing just a bit more. James stared, cold sweat breaking on his brow as the lusciously crinkled rims winked at him, then slipped back inside her bodice as she exhaled.

He swallowed, hoping no one else had seen.

His brother, Hugh, clan bard and general fool, did notice. Gawping at her from the end of the high table, the oversized lummox looked as if his brows would soon vanish into his hairline.

"Hugh's besotted." Colin bumped against James, leaning in to speak low, as he and Isobel arrived on the dais. "Word is"—he sounded amused—"he even slipped into the kitchens and raided your supply of honey-stuffed dates, giving her a dishful in welcome."

"He speaks true, I was there." Isobel smiled as she sailed past, heading for her place at the high table. "She thanked Hugh profusely, calling him a gallant."

Hector clattered up then, slinking past James to duck beneath the table and flop down—it could only be assumed—very near to the MacDonalds' feet.

James frowned. It wouldn't surprise him if the disloyal beast licked Lady Catriona's ankles.

He would, and the knowledge scalded him.

Furious, he tightened his grip on the Banner of the Wind. Never had a maid turned him inside out with such ease. He'd only flicked her thumb with his tongue and caught the merest hint of her nipples, and he ached to drown in the feel, taste, and scent of her. She'd stirred such a fever in him that he didn't trust himself to speak.

Alasdair showed no such reticence. "My regrets, Cameron, that we've disrupted your peace. We'll be on our way in the morning. My sister told you why we came. She thought she saw one of our younger hounds trail after you when you left us. It would seem she erred." He shot a glance at his sister. "The dog isn't here."

"I could've told you that." James tried not to show his irritation when Hector's tail began to wag beneath the table.

"The whelp is a favorite of Catriona's. We spent days

searching around Blackshore, but couldn't find him. So we thought—"

"He followed me?" James knew better.

"It was a hope, aye." Alasdair nodded, clearly duped.

Catriona sipped her wine, all innocence.

James wondered what spells she'd worked to trick Alasdair again. "No such animal trailed me. Though I'll suggest you make a more thorough search on your return to Blackshore. If the dog is young"—he suspected there wasn't a lost dog at all—"he might have taken a fright to something and hied himself beneath a bed."

That was the closest he'd come to bursting Catriona's ploy.

He did fix her with an I-know-what-you're-about stare.

Looking at her crossly was safer than letting her guess that her campaign to see him again filled him with ridiculous pleasure. It was a giddy, unwanted elation that flared in some dark, unnamed place deep inside him. And—the worrisome feeling warmed and spread—it was a sensation entirely different than his urge to see more of her nipples.

He hoped it wasn't his heart.

"You could be right." She was watching him over her wine cup's rim. "Perhaps we'll find Beadle in my—"

"Beadle?" Alasdair's eyes widened. "I thought we were searching for Birkie?"

"Did I say Beadle?" Catriona didn't blink. "I did mean Birkie."

Isobel hid a smile behind a cough. Colin leaned forward to peer at them, watching James much too closely. And—this could mean no good—the rest of the hall fell silent. Even Sir Walter and his men had stopped eating to crane their necks toward the dais.

"I'm good with dogs." Hugh half stood from his chair. "If anyone can find Birkie, I—"

"You're needed in your turret, taking up your quill to record the trials we're facing these days." James glared at Hugh until he lowered his big, thickset body into his seat. "There are others who can be of service to Lady Catriona."

Hugh glowered back at him, looking mutinous.

James tucked the Banner of the Wind more securely beneath his arm and stalked to the hearth at the rear of the dais. Someone had tossed several fat logs onto the fire, causing it to blaze. No doubt some loon who felt that the softly smoldering peats they usually burned wouldn't keep Catriona sufficiently warm.

Peats *glow*, after all.

Cut wood…

He scowled at the roaring fire. The dancing flames offended him. Log fires were for Lowland Scots and the English. All those too thin-skinned to suffer the cold, black nights of Highland winter.

He preferred peat.

"Damnation!" He jigged when one of the fire logs popped, sending out a spray of orange-red sparks. Holding the Banner of the Wind aloft with one hand, he used the other to swat at the swirling cinders.

A chorus of hoots came from the hall. But when he whipped around and swept the fools with a glare, their chortles died away. Satisfied, he placed the banner on a coffer and then marched over to the ewer and basin on the ledge of a window embrasure. He splashed water into the bowl and washed the soot from his hands.

He ignored the ash on his legs.

He'd bathe later.

Now he needed to figure out how to rouse his men with Alasdair present. He'd meant to use the clan's long-standing feud with MacDonalds and Mackintoshes to fire their blood. But so long as MacDonalds whiled beneath his roof, courtesy demanded he not slur their name.

As did his honor.

Frustrated, he snatched a length of folded linen off the embrasure's stone ledge and wiped his hands. Moonlight slanted through the alcove's window slit, spilling across the bowl of water. Its surface glistened like smooth, dark glass. Or—his nape prickled—like his sister's and Scandia's shining raven tresses.

Two women who both, in their own time, loved the glen fiercely.

Catriona shared that passion. She carried her love for the glen inside her as a burning, living flame. It plagued him to admit it, but he knew she stood in as much awe of their hills and moors as he did. This wild and beautiful place meant everything to her. She'd cling to the last rock in the glen, gripping so tight her fingers bled, before she'd let anyone, even a king, tear her away.

He sensed that devotion in her, blazing bright with every beat of her heart. He also felt her looking at him. It was like a physical touch. And he didn't need to turn around to know her gaze was sweeping over him, moving from his hair to his shoulders and lower.

She lingered around his hips, his buttocks. Praise God, he wasn't facing her. Even so, the assessment in her stare made heat pulse inside him.

He took a deep breath, squeezing his hands to fists.

Behind him, the hall was silent. His men would have

recognized Ottar's banner by now. They'd be staring at its glory, the silken folds gleaming so proudly on the coffer by the wall. Stone laid by the Fire-worshipper's own hands. Or so the legend-tellers claimed, boasting that the mighty half-Viking war-leader had taken pride in toiling alongside his men as they'd raised the stronghold.

James drew another tight breath, willing himself to think of Ottar and his banner rather than the enemy vixen sitting at his high table, making him burn to feel her skin against his. How he was consumed by an agonizing desire to plunder her mouth with his tongue, to kiss her for hours, and everywhere.

Steeling himself against her, he stepped deeper into the embrasure, welcoming the cold, damp air until the ancient pride surged through him, gripping him more powerfully than if an iron fist squeezed his heart. Outside, the night wind whistled and moaned, rushing through the trees and sending dead leaves rattling across the bailey. To a fanciful mind, the skitter of leaves could almost be the metallic clink of mail, the clanking of long-ago swords, as Ottar and his men ran through the glen, chasing their windblown banner, their hearts bursting with exultation when the standard's pole plunged into rich, peaty earth.

He could almost feel their glee, hear their triumphant whoops.

They were that real, that close...

Then, somewhere in the depth of the hall, someone shouted for more ale. Other cries followed, breaking the strange silence. Chaos returned. And Ottar the Fire-worshipper and his mail-draped pagan followers vanished into the cold darkness whence they'd come.

But rain still battered the tower's thick stone walls and

drummed on the roof. The wind wailed louder than ever. And beneath the storm's fury came the familiar roar of the cataracts that plunged down the gorge in the hillside nearest Castle Haven's curtain wall.

It was a night like every other.

A night of sounds—*Highland sounds*—that might be similar on the distant Isle of Lewis. But that couldn't ever fill him with the same love, pride, and sense of oneness that beat through him now.

He closed his eyes, his heart thundering.

Ottar the Fire-worshipper might be gone, but *he* was here.

Something inside him cracked and split, flooding him with a white-hot determination such as he'd never known. Highlanders and their land were inseparable. His bond with these hills was deep, powerful, and impossible to sever. The Glen of Many Legends was more than just his home.

It was his soul.

And he'd face down the Dark One himself before he'd allow even a single kinsmen—or a MacDonald or Mackintosh—to do anything that might give the King reason to enforce his threat to transport them.

Not that any of them would go.

They'd sooner fall on their swords and spare themselves the agony.

He meant to see that such a tragedy never happened.

So he retrieved the Banner of the Wind, taking the relic to the edge of the dais, where he unfurled the precious red-and-yellow standard with a flourish.

He flashed a glance at Catriona. She looked like a Valkyrie with the torchlight shining on her garnet-red hair and casting shadows across her proud face and magnificent breasts. Her gaze met and locked with his, and she raised her chin, challenging him.

Then a smile lifted the corner of her mouth, and in that moment, she was no longer the enemy. She was a woman of the glen, showing support. But it was a tenuous bond that could only be fleeting.

So James turned back to the hall, not wanting to see the passion fade from her eyes or the prideful smile slip from her lips.

"Camerons! Kinsmen, friends, and guests—hear me!" He held the banner high, half of the rippling silk slipping down his arm. "Behold our Banner of the Wind! The clan's most ancient and worthy relic, carried by our great forebear, Ottar the Fire-worshipper, when he—"

"*Ottar! Ottar!*" Loud cheers interrupted him, voices rising as the din grew deafening.

Everywhere men pounded fists on tables and stomped their feet. Some leapt onto the trestle benches, whipping out their swords and waving them above their heads. The shouts echoed to the rafters, calls for Lowland blood mixed in with the repeated Cameron slogan.

"*Chlanna nan con thigibh a so's gheibh sibh feoil!*"

"Sons of the hounds, come here and get flesh!"

The cries shook the walls and filled the air. Sir Walter and his men strode from the hall, their noses high. Glad to see their backs, James gathered the banner as the clan rallied. He smoothed his hand down over the ancient rippling silk, using the ruckus to drape the precious relic over his laird's chair. He took care to ensure that the banner's snarling dog was prominently displayed, the exquisitely stitched beast making his heart pound and inflaming his blood. As he hoped the sight would do for his warriors.

Certain it would, he crossed his arms and waited for the commotion to settle. When it did, he hoped his words wouldn't dampen his men's enthusiasm.

He also risked a look at Alasdair.

The fate of them all might depend on the other chieftain's reaction.

"Cameron is a man after my own heart." Alasdair's voice held a mix of admiration and annoyance. "He has a good tongue in his head, for all his tainted blood. A pity he's no' a MacDonald."

"Shhh!" Catriona almost choked on a sugared almond. "We're at his high table, if you've forgotten. Even in this din, words carry." She reached out, pinching his arm. "Someone might hear you."

She glanced at Isobel, hoping she especially hadn't heard. Thankfully, her back was turned. Catriona felt a catch in her breast, looking at her. Were their clans not feuding, she wouldn't mind being Isobel's friend. It hadn't taken long to discover they were very much alike. She'd come here expecting to admire James's sister, but she'd been surprised to find she also liked her.

And she'd find ways to make Alasdair sorry if he offended her.

"Have a care, please." She released his arm. "This isn't Blackshore."

"I know fine where we are." Alasdair leaned close, a dangerous glint in his eye. "Be glad I was speaking of himself and no' you. Were I to say what I think of your trickery with Beadle, Birkie, or whichever dog you claimed went missing, you'd have more cause to flush than hearing me say I wish Cameron were of our own noble stock.

"You'd best hope Birkie is at Blackshore when we return." He gave her a hard look. "Otherwise—"

"He's in my bedchamber." Catriona brushed a bit of sugar off her sleeve. "Maili's seeing to him."

Alasdair snorted. "I thought as much."

Ignoring him, Catriona peered past him at James. He stood beside his laird's chair and looked so tall and proud, so perilously tempting, that her heart hurt. If it weren't for her wicked streak, she'd push back from his table and flee the hall. No good could come of hanging her heart on the chief of a rival clan. Worse things would result from indulging her longing for him.

But she'd endured those yearnings for too many years, and now that'd she'd been in his arms—even if he hadn't held her in passion—she couldn't help but want more, regardless of the consequences.

She'd rather be wicked than good.

How could she resist when firelight danced across the wall behind James, so that he looked as if he towered at the rim of hell? His standard gleamed brightly, its silken length almost seeming alive, as if the banner preened beneath the clan's adulation.

The fierce-looking dog at the standard's center appeared even more real. Glistening black threads spun his fur, embroidered hackles that seemed to rise as the stitched beast turned glowing, accusatory eyes on her. Almost as if the banner mascot were chiding her for hoping to steal a kiss from his master.

She sat up straighter, refusing to feel guilty.

She did feel brazen. But it was a delicious kind of daring. And one that wasn't going to go away until James's arms went around her and she could revel in the searing-hot brand of his kiss. He'd sworn they'd be savage, and the thought ignited tingling awareness inside her. Sensations she'd enjoy if Alasdair weren't being such an ox, purposely leaning forward to block her view of James.

"How did you plan to explain Birkie's presence in your room?" Alasdair's gaze was implacable.

Catriona popped a sugared almond into her mouth, chewing deliberately.

When she reached for another, he shot out a hand to seize her wrist. "Well?"

"Bog mist."

Alasdair's eyes rounded. "You've run mad."

"Pah." She jerked her arm from his grasp. "There was a thick mist when James left Blackshore. I could've mistaken a swirl of fog for a small, wayward dog."

She rubbed her sleeve, smoothing the crease he'd made. "When James headed into the hills, I thought I saw an animal trailing him. *Laoigh Feigh Ban.* The magical white stag his clan calls Rannoch. But when I looked again, it was only a patch of blowing mist that seemed to be chasing after him."

"As you are doing now."

"So you say."

"So I know. And I'd hear why you went to such lengths to see him again?"

"I wanted to come to Castle Haven." Catriona sat up straighter. She refused to discuss the seductive attraction James held for her. "Everyone knows the King's arrival is imminent. I thought to catch a glimpse of him."

Alasdair snorted. "You'd sooner scatter stinging nettles in the King's bed than swoon in adulation when he and his entourage clatter past."

Catriona said nothing. She *had* hoped to see the King. But she'd intended to glare at the royal party, not fall into a flutter.

The look in Alasdair's eye said he knew.

But before he could say so, a burst of foot stomping and whoops swept the hall.

"Camerons!" James' voice rose above the chaos. "Hear me, you who carry the blood of Ottar. And you, men of the glen, but of your own proud lineage." He threw a glance at Alasdair, then the MacDonald guards, crowding a long table near the dais. "I know of your bellyaching, how some of you burn to have done with our woes. And I challenge you to think well before you yield to the glories of the old ways."

A low rumbling of dissent rolled through the hall.

James gave his men a stiff nod. "Hear me now and I'll show you the foolery of such notions."

"How so?" A large-bellied, bearded man jumped to his feet. "Would you see us turn from snarling dogs to whipped curs, howling in the wilderness?"

James met the man's angry stare. "Since when would any Cameron even consider being mistaken for a whipped cur? The men I know and respect as fellow kinsmen would ne'er make such an error."

"Hah!" Alasdair reached for his wine cup. "Did I no' say he has a fine tongue?"

Catriona glanced at her brother and wasn't surprised to see a faint smile tugging at the corner of his lips as he sipped his wine. It pained her to know his sympathy would turn to scowls if he knew her feelings.

James's voice boomed on. "Fire and sword might've served Ottar the Fire-worshipper, but his day is gone.

Such flourishes now, and against the King's own men, will bring none of the splendor of yore."

Someone slapped a table. "He speaks true!"

"Any such actions"—James fisted his hands on his hips and raked the hall, his dark eyes glittering—"would make our days here as fleeting as moonlight on water."

"Hear him!" The cry whipped around the hall, growing louder as more men joined in.

"Armies of Lowland knights and fighters would pour north from their burghs and towns." James was shouting now, his words echoing in the smoke-hazed hall. "They'd come in droves to avenge the men you'd like to dirk and pitch over cliffs or into bogs. They'd flood the glen, more men than if all the Highland clans banded together. As one, they'd scourge our hills, giving no quarter until even the last suckling bairn lies dead in the heather!

"If any of you think we'd meet a kinder fate on the Isle of Lewis"—his voice chilled—"be assured there isn't a poet living who could do justice to the trials we'd suffer there. And it wouldn't be the cold darkness of a Hebridean winter that would freeze our hearts."

A chorus of *ayes* surged through the throng.

When James spoke again, the air rang with his words. "Lewis and its black nights can have nothing on us. Few men are more winter-hardy than we of this lonely and windswept glen. We thrive in ice-rain and beneath cold, stone-gray skies. Shrieking gales are music to our souls, and ne'er do our hearts sing louder than on the stormiest days!"

The men in the hall went wild. The ruckus swelled to a great roar, the clamor reaching deafening proportions. Castle Haven's dogs raced everywhere, streaking through the aisles and around the crowded tables, their shrill barks lending to the confusion.

James folded his arms, waiting.

From the corner of her eye, Catriona saw Alasdair clench his hand and pound the table, keeping rhythm with their fist-banging tablemates.

"Nor"—James lifted his voice—"would our souls be ripped by the men we'd lose when we'd take arms against any Lewismen of rank and wealth, seizing their goods and lands, in the name of our King!

"To be sure, we'd grieve the loss of braw kinsmen. But warriors ne'er draw steel without knowing they might no' live to greet the morrow."

He pulled a small leather pouch from beneath his plaid, carefully untying the drawstring before he raised his arm, displaying the little bag. "This, my friends"—he dangled the pouch from his fingers—"would be the greater tragedy. Placing such valiant souls to rest in strange, unloved soil, not their own."

Upending the bag, he let the rich peat-black earth pour onto his palm. As the hall fell silent, he closed his fingers around the peat and thrust his fist in the air.

"Men will soon die so that those of us remaining must ne'er set our feet on distant soil. On that day our swords will spare no one. Our foes will wield their blades with equal purpose, and rightly." He glanced at Catriona, his face dark and unreadable. "For we'll all be fighting so that none of us must e'er turn our backs on the only sustenance that nurtures us, heart, body, and soul."

"Ottar! Ottar!" Men cheered, many jumping to their feet.

James clutched his fist to his chest, thumping his heart,

roughly. "We *are* this glen we've called our own since before time counting. We're hewn from the rock of these hills, taking our strength from the land. Just as we breathe life into the very wind here, each blade of grass and sprig of heather. The glen would be a different place without us, empty and desolate and weeping."

Catriona's heart swelled. A fierce heat burned at the back of her throat, but she kept her chin lifted and swallowed against the discomfort. She doubted James would glance at her again, but if he did, she didn't want him to see how much his fervor moved her.

He was still speaking, his voice rising on each word. "...as we would weep inconsolably if we were to be torn from this place where we belong."

Then he lowered his arm, letting the soil spill from his hand. "So I challenge you, men of my race. In the name of Ottar and before the Banner of the Wind, live by the honor that was breathed into you at birth.

"If you cannot"—he whipped out his sword, offering it hilt first to any takers—"run me through now because I have failed as a chieftain."

Silence descended, not a single man moving.

"Here is the way of it, by God!" The big-bellied kinsman who'd argued earlier shouldered his way through the hall to clamber onto the dais. "We have honor!" He grabbed the sword and flipped it, pressing the hilt into James's hands. "I'll be the first to break the head of any who dares to sully our good name."

James nodded and sheathed his steel. Then he clapped the man on the shoulder, turned, and strode from the dais. He moved through the throng, clearly intending to have a word with every man.

Magnificent, isn't he? Isobel put a light hand on Catriona's arm, her soft voice clear despite the tumult in the hall.

Catriona glanced at her, certain she hadn't noticed her slipping into the seat beside her. But she was there now, smiling as she watched James wind through the cheering crowd. His dog, Hector, was at his side. The aging beast trailed along with his stiff-legged gait, stopping now and again to raise his head, importantly. The dog looked proud—and so dear, with one ear tucked inside out—that Catriona's heart tumbled in her chest.

She liked the dog.

He'd spent much of the evening beneath the table, his great bulk resting on her feet. She'd welcomed his warmth. And she would've appreciated that comfort now. Shivering, for a cold draught stirred out of nowhere, she turned to see if someone had opened a shutter.

No one had.

But her jaw slipped when she spied Isobel sitting at the other end of the high table, speaking with her brother Hugh. Catriona's blood chilled, for the raven-haired beauty appeared quite settled. As if she hadn't left her accustomed place in hours.

Yet a moment ago, she'd rested her hand on Catriona's arm.

And she'd spoken...

Catriona's heart began a wild, hard knocking as she spun around to see if the seat next to her was occupied.

It wasn't.

Indeed, it wasn't there at all.

Hers was the last chair at the table. And nothing stirred beside her except a breath of icy air.

Chapter Nine

✤

Y ou're heading in the wrong direction, my lady."

Catriona froze near the arched door to a darkened antechamber. But instead of peering into the room's shadowed depths, she looked up to find Colin stepping before her, blocking her path.

"Am I?" She held his gaze, refusing to squirm. The amusement in his eyes made it clear that he knew she was aware that this corner of Castle Haven's great hall wasn't anywhere near the necessary place she'd used as her excuse to leave the high table.

"The place you seek is yon, inside the main stair tower." He tipped his head toward the other side of the hall. Or"—he smiled, dimples flashing—"were you searching for something else?"

"I must've gone the wrong way." Catriona itched to whisk past him, continuing on her business. Nor did she wish to respond to his question.

His words were too smooth, his deep voice richly timbred and teasing.

He looked down at her, his silky blue-black hair—so like James's—skimming his shoulders, his mouth still curved in a wicked smile. Which wasn't surprising, as Colin Cameron was known as a rogue of supposedly insatiable sensual appetite, rumored so skilled at seduction that he could charm the blush from autumn leaves.

But his dark good looks and dashing airs only struck her as a pale reflection of James.

And thinking of *him* brought a fresh rush of hot color to her face.

Never had a man affected her so strongly.

She slid a quick glance at the hall, her gaze immediately drawn to him. His long, confident strides were taking him toward the massive double-arched hearth as he made his way through the throng. Men crowded him, talking and laughing, their bearded faces shining with pride. James's power and strength glowed like a flame inside him as he accepted the back slaps and good words of his clan.

Catriona shivered beneath her shawl, but not from the cold. Her attraction to him flared like a fever in her veins and made her heart trip, beating much too light and fast than was good for her.

She took a deep, calming breath and turned back to his cousin. "There's quite a stir in your hall this night. The ruckus must've caused me to take a wrong turn."

Colin looked bemused. "A simple enough mistake, to be sure."

"Ummm." She gave a noncommittal half shrug. She'd known exactly where she was going. Or, better said, what she'd been doing.

Her error had been leaving her seat.

She should've known she wouldn't find a comely, raven-haired woman who bore a striking resemblance to Isobel. No such soul existed. And she'd felt foolish for attempting to spot one even before she'd started her surreptitious, peek-into-every-corner circuit of the great hall.

But she'd had to try.

The alternative—that she'd been visited by a *bogle*—was something she didn't want to consider. Not that she had anything against ghosts. She didn't. Nor would she be surprised if the soft-voiced lovely had been one. Everyone born and bred in these hills knew better than to doubt the existence of spirits, haints, and their like.

She just didn't care to meet a Cameron ghost.

Along with believing in the old gods, monsters, and other magical creatures, Highlanders held grudges.

It wasn't that she feared tangling with an angry, long-dead Cameron. She just didn't want to attract the attentions of one and have her night rest disrupted if such a being sought to pester her.

She did enjoy her sleep.

What she didn't like was the way Colin's eyes glinted as he watched her.

Something told her he was as perceptive as her all-seeing brother.

Worse, she saw now that he held the Banner of the Wind looped over one arm. The silky folds dipped halfway down his side, revealing the head and shoulders of the standard's magnificent black dog centerpiece. In the flickering glow of the brazier—and so close before her—the embroidered beast's snarl appeared more ferocious than when James unfurled the banner on the dais.

She drew herself up, trying not to notice.

She did feel a spurt of annoyance that a few cleverly plied wisps of thread could breathe such vivid life into a beast of cloth.

I mended the rip beneath his eye...

Catriona gasped. The softly spoken words hushed past her ear, so close. She glanced behind her but saw nothing except a faint luminance near a shuttered window set deep into the hall's smoke-darkened wall. Cold, silvery light that was surely moonglow slipping in through the shutter slats.

When she looked again, it was gone.

Colin hadn't budged.

"The beast looks real, eh?" He grinned, stroking the dog's silken withers. "There are some who believe he is. They say that, at times, he can be seen prowling through the keep or..."

"Visitors awake to find him standing at the foot of their bed. See you"—he leaned close, his eyes glittering— "Skald, for that is his name, doesn't care for strangers."

"Then I'll be on my way before my presence annoys him." Catriona smiled. She didn't comment on the appropriateness of the Norse word for a court poet as the name for a beast associated with such tall tales.

"Before I go..." She hesitated. "Does Skald have a stitched tear beneath his eye?"

Colin's smugness vanished. "How would you know of the mend? The banner's been locked in a chest in James's bedchamber for years. There are men who ne'er set eyes upon the standard until this night.

"There is"—he glanced down at the reams of silk draped over his arm—"a small repair beneath Skald's left eye. The tear happened centuries ago and, according to clan tradition, the damage was stitched by Ottar the Fire-worshipper's wife, the lady Astrid."

Pah!

A blast of cold air swept in through the shutter slats, swirling around them. The coals in the brazier snapped and hissed, the chill wind even guttering several candles on a nearby table. Gooseflesh rose on Catriona's nape and shivered along her arms. She could almost see the raven-haired beauty shimmering beside her, indignant.

For sure, she'd heard her.

Colin didn't seem to have noticed. "See here." He lifted a handful of silk, indicating Skald's jewel-like eye. "The repair is so finely stitched it's nigh impossible to tell the banner was e'er torn."

He frowned. "You couldn't have known."

"I have good eyes." Catriona smiled.

The icy draught rippled the air, fluttering her shawl until she felt a light touch on her arm as frosty fingertips brushed her sleeve, seeking attention.

Those stitches are so tiny because my skilled needle plied them.

Lady Astrid had naught to do with the repair.

'Twas my hand...

Catriona started. The words rang in her ears, hushed but unmistakable.

She recognized the voice.

And as the cold air hovered at her side, chilling her so thoroughly she'd soon be coated in ice, she also knew what she had to say.

She took a deep breath. "I heard about the tear, some-where." She scrambled for an explanation. "A bard or a wandering friar, I can't recall. But I do remember someone other than Lady Astrid being praised for mending the banner so beautifully."

Colin blinked. "Any Cameron will say otherwise. Lady Astrid was renowned for her stitchwork and is believed to have worked on many of the castle's finest wall hangings. Though it scarce matters after all this time."

He looked at her, the twinkle in his eye belying his earnest tone. "What I'm concerned about is that James will have my head on a pike if I don't see the banner safely back into its strongbox.

"May I escort you to the stair tower on my way to his chamber?" He held out his arm, grinning. "Skald is less likely to leap from the banner and pounce on you if I'm at your side."

"I'm sure he's vicious." Catriona glanced at the silken beast. "But I'll take my chances."

She knew who'd *pounce* as soon as they stepped into the dim passage.

It wouldn't be an embroidered dog.

And wasn't she running after trouble by wishing that it wasn't Colin who was so eager to slip away into the shadows with her?

Had James been the one to offer his arm, she wouldn't have refused.

She'd have grabbed his hand and pulled him straight into the darkness.

…at times, he can be seen prowling through the keep or…

Colin's words taunted Catriona as she hurried along the passage to the main stair tower. She already regretted taking this route. The poorly lit corridor did skirt the hall,

shielding her from curious glances. But it was also filled
with the skitter of tiny creatures flitting across the stone-
flagged floor. Equally unsettling, the shadows felt heavy
with unseen menace.

Sure of it, she quickened her step.

Squeak!

"Agh!" She jumped as high-pitched chittering revealed
the nature of the wee beasties scurrying about in the darkness. She glanced over her shoulder, seeing nothing.
But she did touch a hand to her amber necklace, taking
strength from the polished stones.

She didn't fear mice. Her concern was not to step on
one, hurting him.

But if anything besides mice stirred here, the ambers
would protect her. The gemstones guarded MacDonald
women all down the ages. Even so, she wished she'd again
slipped along the edge of the crowded hall. The cold, dank
corridor held some of the deepest shadows she'd ever seen.
Quite a few of the torches had burned out. And those yet
flickering gave off little more than smoky, feeble light.

An unpleasant haze that smelled almost sulfuric.

Wishing she hadn't noticed, she drew her shawl closer
about her shoulders.

Her footsteps echoed in the gloom, the eeriness making the possibility of Skald lurking in the darkness all too
believable. Every few steps, she caught rustlings behind
her, or somewhere. It was difficult to tell. But the stirrings
sounded larger than mice.

And ominous enough to make her curl her fingers
around her ambers. A tiny pulsing came from deep inside
them, each stone warming against her skin.

Her heart began to gallop.

This wasn't the time for the stones to alert her of imminent danger.

Yet the ambers almost scorched her fingers, their heat burning her neck. Clan tradition forbade her to let go of the waking stones. To do so before the necklace cooled of its own will brought misfortune.

She did look back to the entrance to the passage, a hidden door Colin had revealed by pulling back a rather splendid wall tapestry. He'd promised the secret corridor would allow her to quickly reach the stair tower.

Except...

She felt as if she'd been marching for hours.

Tamping down her ill ease, she hurried on. Then—

The ambers cooled abruptly, slipping like water from her fingers as an icy draught blew along the passage, whipping her skirts. Chills sped along her nerves, her heart pounding, when something large and black rushed across the darkness ahead of her.

It might have been Skald.

She could almost hear his growl beneath the whistle of the wind.

Hoping she was wrong, she hitched her skirts and stepped faster until she reached the vaulted dimness of the main stair tower.

There, she drew to a sudden halt.

A huge shape, dark and threatening, loomed in the entry to the curving stair. And it wasn't Skald, the snarling banner beast.

It was the devil.

James Cameron.

And he looked so shockingly handsome she nearly swooned.

She did stare, her heart flipping. *"You."*

"Aye." Amusement flashed in his eyes. "I'm myself, true enough."

He slid his gaze over her in a slow, daring manner and she took a step backward, knowing he was so much more than just himself.

He was irresistible.

And being alone with him in this empty corner of his castle was dangerous. Torchlight fell across his raven hair but cast shadows over the proud lines of his face. The contrast suited him, making him look like he stood on the edge of light and darkness. He was a fallen angel come to tempt her. And she wanted to succumb. She drew a breath, sure she'd never seen a more beautiful man. Pure masculine power rolled off every inch of him, and his tall, broad-shouldered presence made her hot and shivery.

His magnificence overwhelmed her, sending desire racing through her.

"What are you doing here?" She held his gaze, quivers of sensation making her tremble. "You were in the hall, with your men."

"So I was." He pushed away from the wall he'd been leaning against, the move predatory. "And now I'm here."

"Aren't you needed elsewhere?" She lifted her chin, her physical awareness of him so strong that if she didn't feign a bit of coolness, she'd cut out her heart and offer it to him on her outstretched hands. But his scent—dark, heady, and oh-so-rousing—drifted to her across the space between them, teasing her senses.

She felt dizzy, lightheaded with the need for him to come closer. "I—" She had trouble speaking, tingling anticipation flooding her when his gaze dropped to her lips. "I thought you'd be in the hall until the small hours."

"You thought wrong." He took a step forward, his eyes not leaving her face. "We have unfinished business. Or"—his voice deepened—"have you forgotten?"

"You know I haven't." A hundred reasons to turn and run swept through her mind. She ignored each one. She wanted him too badly, had waited too many years for this stolen, forbidden moment.

"A pity your wits are so sharp, my lady." His tone was seductive, the words caressing her. "I'd hoped to enjoy reminding you."

"Perhaps there is a bit I don't recall?" She couldn't believe her daring. But he'd whirled her into a place she didn't know, where her heart thumped crazily and all she could think of was the emotion rising inside her. It felt so right, so thrilling to be alone with him.

Heat swept her, and flutters teased the lowest part of her belly, exciting her. It was a sinfully wicked sensation. A pleasurable feeling she knew was pure womanly desire, brazen and carnal. An acknowledgment that made her pulse race all the faster, beating so rapidly in her throat that it was difficult to breathe.

But she kept her chin raised, unable to look away from him.

Moving proved impossible.

She tried—she wanted to close the distance between them, stir him into kissing her—but nothing happened. Her legs seemed incapable of doing what she wanted. Even her arms wouldn't cooperate, staying at her sides, her fingers frozen into the folds of her skirts.

Her inability to move made her wonder if he *was* the devil.

The fierce pull of attraction she felt for him hinted at such powers. And with his dark, flashing eyes and his glistening black hair unbound and wild about his shoulders, he could pass for the hell-fiend. He was certainly watching her as if he were. How else could he make her feel as if no one else in the world existed for him?

Or that nothing mattered except the raw desire he roused in her.

She frowned, not wanting to admit that so much more did matter. The truth was, he melted her heart along with her capitulating, not-to-be-mentioned feminine parts.

A corner of his mouth lifted as if he knew.

It was a slow, devastating kind of smile. A look that was full of heat, triumph, and seduction. But his eyes also held a challenge. And seeing it broke the sensual spell he'd wrapped around her.

Catriona accepted the dare. "Colin told you where I was, didn't he?" She set her hands on her hips. "He said you could catch me—"

"Devil take Colin!" He advanced on her, his smile gone now. "It scarce matters how I knew you were here, flitting through a passage no one but a Cameron should know exists. You desired to be caught." He looked down at her, his eyes glittering in the darkness. "That's why you came here. Or will you be denying it?"

Catriona felt her face flood with hot color. "I came here to—" She broke off when Hector hobbled out of the shadows, his scraggly tail wagging.

When the dog—who could never have been the fast-moving blur of blackness she'd seen shoot across the passage—came over to stand beside them, she knew it would be difficult to remain belligerent.

The beast had spent hours resting his bulk across her feet, after all.

He'd even licked her ankles.

Now, as he settled his bony haunches on the cold stone floor with a deep canine sigh, she knew she was in trouble. Especially when Hector's trusting gaze moved from her to his master, then back to her again. The hopefulness on his aged, white-muzzled face split her heart.

"You needn't tell me why you're here." James stepped closer, taking her by the shoulders. "We both know the reason. It had naught to do with a wee lost dog named"—he pretended to consider—"Birkie, I believe? If he even exists?" He arched a brow, waiting.

"Birkie is real enough."

"The mite is no' missing, is he?"

"Nae." Catriona shook her head, trying not to notice Hector peering up at her so steadily. "Birkie is in the antechamber of my quarters at Blackshore," she admitted, certain Hector knew they were speaking of another dog. "Beadle, his brother, is with him, and one of our laundresses, Maili, will be looking after them."

"Ahhh…" Something very close to a smile flickered across James's face. "Then I was correct in being flattered that you troubled yourself to come here."

"I do not understand your meaning." She knew exactly what he meant.

"Then you do need reminding." His smile flashing dangerously again, he slid his hands from her shoulders down to her arms, gripping tight. "You came to see me. You knew that, once here, arriving so late in the day and on such a noble mission, I'd be honor-bound to offer you and your entourage accommodation. You hoped to claim the kiss I swore to give you if ever I saw you on my land again."

Catriona tossed her head. "Your opinion of yourself is grand."

He looked amused. "With good reason, as I'll show you."

Eyeing her up and down, his gaze heated as it lingered on her amber necklace. Though—a thrill shot through her—she was sure he was assessing the swell of her breasts rather than the gemstones.

She should be scandalized.

Instead she felt breathless. Under his perusal, her breasts went full and heavy, her nipples tightening with prickling, needful sensations she'd never dreamed. She tilted up her chin, hoping she looked bold. In truth, she was sure she'd burst any moment if he didn't make good on his wicked, sinfully exciting threat.

"Did no one e'er tell you that lasses who dance along the edge of a fire burn their skirts?" He leaned in, a scant breath away from her. "You, sweetness, just marched straight into the flames."

"Say you?" Catriona didn't flinch.

He glared at her. "I do. And"—he grasped her chin, lifting her face to his—"you're about to get the scalding of your life."

She met his gaze very directly. His words whipped through her, rippling along her skin and racing down her limbs, filling her with a delicious cascade of sensation.

"Hector, guard!" James glanced at the dog, nodding approval when the beast pushed to his feet and went to the archway back into the great hall.

Hector placed himself in the center of the entry, once

again lowering his rump carefully as he sat. But he held his head alert and proud, prepared to turn away anyone who might approach the stair tower.

"He listens well and heeds orders." James turned back to her, the look on his face making the world tilt and spin away, leaving only the two of them. He was close to her now, so near that she could feel the heat of his hard-muscled body warming her own.

"Hector knows what is good for him." His voice held silky menace. "A pity you are no' as wise."

Catriona bit her lip. To her way of looking at it, she was clever. He was about to kiss her, after all. This was her victory. Something she'd been yearning for since their first ill-fated encounter years before when he'd caught her in the hills above Castle Haven, searching for Grizel and Gorm, the Makers of Dreams.

Their recent meeting in the wood—and especially his taunt when he'd come to her on Blackshore's boat strand—only reawakened old feelings, leaving her no peace.

Now...

It was important that he made the first move.

But there could be no harm in taking just one deep breath, letting her lungs fill, and—she could scarce believe her brazenness—allowing her breasts to rise and brush ever so slightly against his chest.

"Ah, lass. You push me too far." He closed on her then, bringing his huge, iron-hard body so near to hers that her back bumped against the cold stone of the wall. Heat poured off him, scorching her, branding her forever. He made a sound low in his throat and braced his hands on either side of her head, trapping her within the circle of his arms. "Ne'er say I didn't warn you."

"I—"

"Save your words. I willnae believe a one of them. Only this..."

With masculine intent, he curled one hand about her neck and pulled her roughly against the unyielding wall of his chest. His arms were suddenly around her, and breath couldn't pass between them. Catriona grasped his shoulders, digging the fingers of one hand into his hair and clutching the coarse wool of his plaid with the other.

She gripped him fiercely, leaning into him. She could feel the entire length of him, granite hard and hot as flame, thrumming with a tightness that bespoke how much he wanted her. If she bore any doubt, the thick and rigid column of searing heat pressing into her hip proved his desire. Something inside her melted in response, releasing a spill of tingles almost too exquisite to bear.

"James..." She gasped his name against his shoulder, the heady male scent of him filling her senses, making her giddy with sensations more glorious than anything she'd imagined.

Before she could say more, or even think, he swept one hand down over her hip, splaying his fingers across her bottom. Even as he pulled her more intimately against him, he brought his other hand up to grasp the back of her neck, holding her firmly in place.

"You're a right pest," he snarled. "Ne'er has a lass vexed me more."

Then he lowered his head, slanting his mouth over hers in a hard, devouring kiss. He plundered her lips with a savage fierceness that stole her breath and made the floor dip beneath her feet. Her heart hammered wildly and the tingles whirling inside her spun faster now, concentrating in one intensely sensitive place, low by her thighs. As if he knew, he tightened his grip on her bottom, his strong, warm fingers kneading her flesh.

"O-o-oh..." She squirmed against him, clinging fast, desperate to prolong the startling pleasure.

He deepened the kiss, his mouth fierce and furious. He groaned—at least, she thought he did—and then his tongue was probing her lips, seeking entry. She welcomed that intrusion, the burning pleasure inside her increasing as his tongue slid into her mouth, curling intimately over hers. It was now a slow, languorous kind of kissing so wondrous that she felt her entire body softening with sweet, molten heat. She wound her arms more firmly around his neck, fearing he'd stop kissing her, ending her bliss.

But her pleasure only spiraled when he began stroking the sensitive skin beneath her ear, the side of her neck, and—she caught fire—when he moved his hand, letting his fingers drift over the top swells of her breasts. Somehow, her bodice came undone, the cloth gaping open so that her breasts spilled free. Cold air rushed across her nakedness. And then he was caressing her, roughly palming and kneading her fullness, circling his thumb over her nipple, teasing the taut peak with the tips of his fingers.

Catriona gasped, her heart tumbling. The pleasure was almost unbearable. Her breasts swelled and quivered, aching for more of his touch. As if he knew, he made a sound low in his throat and shoved the gown from her shoulders, exposing more of her.

"Sweet..." He bent his head to nuzzle her neck, flicking his tongue along her skin, nipping and tasting her.

"Don't stop kissing me." She reached for him, taking

his face in her hands, pulling him back to her. "Please, more kisses…"

"Aye, more…" He crushed her to him, holding her more fiercely than before. His kiss was a maddening fever now, the hot, silken strokes of his tongue against hers sending waves of desire rushing through her. Until— just when she was sure she'd break apart—a loud burst of manly laughter and a *thump* intruded. A crash and the splintering of pottery followed immediately, along with more hoots and howls of masculine ribaldry.

James's men in the hall, ale-headed and knocking into tables and benches, lurched ever nearer to the stair tower's archway.

"Drunken fools." He broke the kiss, dragging his mouth from hers. Swearing, he thrust her from him as swiftly as he'd seized her. He stepped back, breathing heavily. He also stared at her as if she'd grown two heads and cloven feet.

Catriona blinked, disbelieving.

He scowled.

"That, Lady Catriona"—he wiped his mouth with the back of his hand—"is why you need to stay safely behind Blackshore's walls. Take heed. If you attempt such foolery again, coming here to parade yourself beneath my nose, pushing me beyond any man's limits…

"Then be assured the next time I kiss you, we will no' be standing." His tone was cold and angry. "We shall be prone, my lady. That, I promise you!"

Pain, sharp and lancing, sliced into Catriona's heart. She could only stare at him, mortification—and fury— sweeping her as the shivery heat inside her whipped into a seething cauldron of fury.

"You bastard!" Eyes narrowing, she yanked up her gown and refastened her bodice with chilled, trembling fingers. "How dare you—"

But he'd already stalked away. Hector hobbled along behind him, the dog's tail no longer wagging but hanging between his legs.

Catriona glared after them, her pulse pounding wildly until they were swallowed by the boisterous crowd in the hall. Then, her face burning, she snatched up her skirts and followed them into the chaos.

But she didn't return directly to the high table.

She made certain that her path took her straight past the arrogant devil who'd dared to ravish her so heatedly only to shove her from him as if she'd turned into a writhing serpent in his arms.

So she took pleasure in bending a freezing stare on him when he glanced her way as she cut a swath through his long-nosed, gawping men.

He didn't gape, but his brows snapped together, darkly.

It was a look that suited her fine, as she'd only begun to annoy him.

Soon, he'd learn her measure.

And when he did, he'd discover he'd erred. The next time they kissed, they wouldn't be prone. But he would be on his knees, begging for the pleasure.

She'd make certain of it.

Chapter Ten

❦

Hours later, James followed Catriona up one of Castle Haven's winding turnpike stairs and then along a dimly lit passage. He took care to move silently and stay far enough behind her to remain unseen. But all his precautions couldn't chase the damning notion that he was creeping along on cloven hooves. It scarce mattered that he only hoped to ensure that Colin, Hugh, or some other besotted, ale-taken fool didn't accost her. He simply wished to see her safely to her guest quarters. Yet—he grimaced—each step of the way confirmed what he should've known.

If he wasn't already going to hell, he'd be on his way before the sun rose on the morrow.

His moony-eyed men weren't a threat to her.

He was.

He should turn around and take himself back down to the hall.

His honor burned inside him, roaring for him to leave before he was no longer fisting his hands at his sides, but reaching for her. She was the last woman he should touch and the very one he didn't dare to love. Every instinct screamed in protest, warning of trouble to come. Any moment she could pause, then swing about to face him.

To his horror, he kept on.

His heated awareness of her gave him no choice. Flickering light from the wall torches played over her gleaming, flame-bright hair, and his fingers itched to undo her braids so that her lustrous tresses would spill down her back to swing about her hips. The swaying of those hips stirred a throbbing heat in his loins, setting him like granite. And her light gillyflower scent drifted behind her, teasing and taunting him, heady as wine.

He scowled, wholly captivated.

She nipped around another curve in the passageway and he quickened his pace, not wanting to lose sight of her, wishing he could.

His need to keep up with her warned him of his fast-approaching fall.

Men didn't tumble the sisters of rival chieftains.

Most especially they didn't ravish such maids beneath their own roof. Certainly not in the ways he burned to pounce upon Catriona. It scarce mattered that he now knew she'd greet his passion gladly. Or that the notion of taking her set a whirl of tantalizing images rising before his mind's eye. She was a lady and a virgin, and—damn his honor again—he'd decided when he'd thrust her from him earlier that he wouldn't be the one to steal her innocence.

Yet, here he was...

Trailing after her like a rutting stag, trapped by her scent, and knowing she led him to a guest chamber where—were they at Blackshore—the strictures of hospitality would require that he strip before her maidenly eyes, allowing her, as lady of the keep, to bathe him.

Praise God this was Castle Haven.

He didn't think he could bear it otherwise.

Nae, he knew he couldn't.

He was close to bursting now. And the devil inside him clawed and twisted, straining to break free and scatter his restraint to the winds. Standing naked in front of her, stepping into a tub of steaming, scented water, and then feeling her hands soap and glide across his flesh—her questing fingers perhaps coming near or even grazing certain iron-set, aching flesh—was an agony no red-blooded, well-lusted man should be made to endure.

Setting his jaw, he pushed the stirring thoughts from his mind. But before he could recuperate, Catriona finally came to a halt.

James's eyes rounded as she reached for the latch of a heavy oak door, opening it wide to sail inside the handsome, well-appointed bedchamber beyond.

Unfortunately, the room wasn't meant for guests.

It was his.

And he had to tell her at once.

Castle Haven's guest quarters were elsewhere, and he needed to speed her there before seeing her so close to his bed dashed his restraint.

Though—his head was beginning to pound—what he most needed was to seize her, slide his hands down her back, over her hips, and then grasp her lush, well-rounded bottom so he could once again pull her hard against him. What he'd then do didn't bear consideration. But if someone pressed him, he might own that he wouldn't mind dragging his mouth over her smooth, silken nakedness, kissing her everywhere.

Such were his desires as he reached the open doorway and spotted her in the middle of his bedchamber, looking about the room.

Spotlessly clean, thanks to Isobel's householding skills and Beathag's fervor, the chamber boasted bright lime-washed walls with no less than three tall window arches, each one offering a sweeping view of the moon-silvered hills and the high moors beyond. Colorful tapestries were hung generously, lending warmth. And the pleasing scent of peat filled the air, blending nicely with whatever aromatic herbs simmered on the coals of a corner brazier.

Two heavily carved, age-blackened chairs and his large, iron-banded strongbox gave the room a bold, masculine feel. Wax candles glowed in the wall sconces. And someone, likely Beathag, had laid out a cold repast. Cheese, smoked mackerel, oatcakes, and sliced breast of capon winked from the small table near his bed.

But it wasn't his room's amenities that froze him where he was, staring.

It was how the corner of Catriona's mouth tilted up so amusedly when she turned to face him. "Somehow I don't think this is the guest quarters?"

"Nae, it isn't." He gave her a hard stare.

She might've mistaken the door, but the twinkle in her eyes said she knew he'd been following her.

"This, sweet"—he took a step closer—"is my bed-chamber."

Any other woman would have left then. Perhaps blushing pink and tripping over her skirts in her haste to be gone from a man's privy quarters.

But Catriona wasn't any woman.

Her chin came up and she did color a bit, but in a most provocative way.

"I see." She touched the ambers at her throat, her gaze going to his bed.

Massive, four-postered, and exquisitely carved, the great ancestral bed was dressed in plaid and could only be more magnificent if she were draped naked across its empty, waiting sheets.

"Perhaps it's as well I'm here?" She went to close the door behind them, making his insides knot when she slid the drawbar in place, locking them in. "In my experience—"

"You have none, save prancing onto thin ice. And I'll no' be giving you the other kind." James clenched his hands at his sides, unable to breathe. "No' even if there were ten bolts across the door."

She had the cheek to glance over him, head to toe. "I told you once that you think too highly of yourself. I only thought to offer you a *lady's courtesy.* Just as I would've done were we now at Blackshore."

Her gaze went to the far wall, and James felt the floor dip when he saw the bathing tub before the hearth.

"Such a service means nothing." She looked him in the eye. "All ladies are adept at it, and such baths are hardly matters of intimacy."

Thor's bollocks they are!

James kept the sentiment to himself.

The beast inside him roared, demanding he put an end to her long torment of him. For the sad truth was—he was loath to admit it—he'd wanted her for years, perhaps since the stormy encounter in their youth when he'd come upon her on the high moors and told her dreagans would eat her if she didn't run home to Blackshore.

She'd been a burr in his side ever since, though it near choked him to admit any such attachment. Just the thought sent heat crawling up his neck. He burned to storm across the room, seize her, and kiss her until he'd proved that it was only lust that he felt for her.

But he didn't move a muscle, because the fierce hammering of his heart said otherwise.

He didn't want to love her.

Nothing could be more disastrous.

So he wrapped his hands around his sword belt and pretended not to notice her lushly curved body or how much her boldness and spirit pleased him.

She lifted a brow. "The bath is to your liking? I heard you order one in the hall."

He had, but he'd intended to bathe alone.

He looked at her, unable to speak, for she was already removing her shawl. And then—the throbbing at his groin worsened—she began loosening her bodice, rolling up her gown's sleeves.

He knew why.

The reason was the great barrel tub, thoughtfully lined with linen, and—as always—possessed of a sitting bench to ensure his bathing comfort. Wafts of pine-scented steam rose from the tub's heated water, while a nearby stool held a small jar of soap and scrubbing cloths.

Drying linens warmed on a hook near the fire and—he actually gulped—he had no doubt whatsoever as to whose hands would rub his nakedness with those oh-so-innocent lengths of toweling.

Even as he resisted, he knew she'd win.

"Sweet Jesus." He was close to spilling, the tight pulsing at his loins making his eyes hurt. Apparently there was a god, for she didn't seem to have heard him.

Chin high, she stood beside the tub, waiting. "Well?"

He frowned. He wasn't going to undress before her.

She leaned down to ripple the water, sending up clouds of steam. "I've seen every man at Blackshore naked." She glanced at him, correctly guessing the reason for his hesitation. "And I've bathed most of them, at one time or another."

"That may be . . ." James felt his face flaming.

He was sure not a one of her bathing kinsmen had dropped his plaid to reveal what she'd see if he threw caution out the window and stripped to his own bare skin, presenting her with his urgent, rampant need.

She straightened, drying her fingers on one of the linen towels. "The bath is cooling."

"Lass"—he didn't budge—"it doesn't matter if the water's scalding or if there's ice on the surface. The truth is, if I climb into that barrel, we'll both be climbing into my bed when I'm done bathing."

He gave her one of his fiercest looks. "Dinnae say you weren't warned."

She smiled. "I'm not afraid."

And so she wasn't.

She loosened her bodice ties a bit more and then reached down to stir the bathwater again. Candlelight fell across her as she bent, and through the slight gaping of her gown's neckline, he could just see the dusky tip of one of her breasts. The nipple was taut, tight and thrusting, as if begging to be licked, nipped, and suckled.

He already knew the sweetness of her nipples. But he hadn't yet tasted them.

He groaned—and this time she heard him.

Straightening, she touched a hand to her breast, and he knew she knew what he'd seen.

He looked at her, sure he'd never seen a woman more beautiful, stirring, or incitingly sensual.

He'd almost kill a man for another peek at that one sweet nipple. He *would* kill a man to see both of them. And he'd face an army to rub his thumbs over them again, this time swirling his tongue round and round...

"There's pine-scented soap." Her voice shattered his lust haze. "It's quite fine. Very much like Alasdair uses."

James frowned. Hearing her brother's name made him feel like the worst sort of lecher.

He shuddered, certain he was.

"You do want me to bathe you, don't you?"

"I do, yes."

And he could hardly draw breath for wanting her.

He did wonder how a maid—an innocent, he was sure—could rouse him so thoroughly that just her glances, a peek at one pert nipple, had him as hard as if she'd curled her fingers around him, squeezing tight.

"You can't bathe in your plaid." She persisted, a faint smile curving her mouth, tempting him. "You have to get naked and—"

"Hellfire and damnation!" He strode a few paces, then swung back around, his reluctance to toss off his clothes vanishing beneath her boldness.

Her plainspoken words that carried such heat.

He looked at her, his heart thundering. "I didn't want this..."

But she'd pushed him too far.

The beast inside him broke free, and he could feel the

wickedest smile curving his own lips and knew his fingers were unclasping the large Celtic brooch at his shoulder, knew as well that his hands were whipping off his plaid, tossing it onto the bed.

He couldn't have held back now if his life depended on it. All he wanted was to hop in and out of the infernal washing tub and then sweep Catriona up in his arms and carry her to the bed, where he'd ravage her the whole night through, to hell with honor.

So his sword belt, shoes, and tunic went the way of his plaid. Then, no longer caring if she saw exactly what she did to him, he set his hands on his hips and simply stood before her, naked so that she could fill her eyes. And she did, staring at him in fascination, the awe on her face making him swell even larger.

Then, before he embarrassed himself, he strode across the room and swung a leg over the side of the bathing tub and eased himself into the steaming water.

"Ahhh..." He leaned back, resting his head against the tub's rim, closing his eyes. He'd fallen this far, sinned so badly, that he might as well enjoy himself.

Any moment, Catriona would begin soaping him, rubbing his shoulders and scrubbing his back, gliding her hands ever downward, tempting him anew...

But no such delights followed.

He did hear the rustle of her skirts as she stepped closer to the tub.

"I have to tell you something." Her tone prickled his nape.

He snapped open his eyes, peering up at her. "Unless you're about to say you'll be removing that gown and joining me in this bath, I dinnae think I care to hear."

"I knew this wasn't a guest room." She spoke anyway. "The door's grandness made me hope it was your bed-chamber."

"I see." He didn't at all. But somehow he wasn't surprised.

She nodded. "I needed to speak with you somewhere private. Guest chambers often have squints so that chiefs can hear what visitors say when they don't know that someone is listening."

James slanted a look up at her, amused.

Castle Haven did have one or two guest chambers with spy holes.

"And what is it that's so secret?" He wondered if she meant to confess that she'd come here to seduce him.

She peered down at him for a long moment. "It's more intriguing than secret." She dipped her fingers into the jar of soap and used a washing cloth to begin scrubbing his shoulders. Her touch sent shivers up and down his back. Hot desire, swift and sharp, so that it was all he could do not to pull her into the tub with him.

He closed his eyes when her hand slid around to the place where his heart pounded. Then she slipped lower, her fingers skimming across his abdomen, the pleasure becoming almost unbearable.

She leaned closer, soaping him. "See you, I—"

"Have a care, lass." His voice came rough, his need for her stirring in a way she'd soon discover if her questing fingers inched deeper.

"There's a ghost at Castle Haven." Her words hit him like ice. "I saw one in your hall. A maid who looks like your sister and—"

"You err." James shot to his feet, sending water

splashing everywhere. "You saw a curl o' peat smoke." He willed it so, not wanting Scandia and her doom anywhere near Catriona. "We've no bogles here."

He stared at her, amazed by her calm. "No' now, no' ever."

Cold dread sluicing him, he scrambled from the washing tub and grabbed a towel, rubbing himself vigorously. He threw the drying cloth aside, standing naked before the fire.

"You should no' have come here." He shoved both hands through his hair. If his clan's tragedy-bringer caused Catriona a shiver of sorrow, he'd singlehandedly tear down his castle's walls to banish the she-ghost.

"And"—he tried not to see how water from the bath had dampened her gown, making her bodice and the folds of her skirts cling to her shapeliness—"if you'd do what's best, you'll leave my chamber now."

Catriona shook her head. "I think not."

Her gaze dipped where it shouldn't. Her breath caught and her eyes widened. She could still feel the hard, muscled warmth of his skin beneath her fingers. Each sweep of her hand over his flesh had made her want him. Now, seeing his bold masculinity, stunning desire consumed her. She drew herself up, trying to tear her gaze away.

She couldn't.

She only stared, reliving how she'd just soaped him, feeling and caressing. If she'd touched him *there*...

Leaving was impossible.

As if he knew, his eyes darkened. "You're on the ice again."

His gaze lowered to her damp bodice and her breasts grew heavy, just as they had in the stair tower. Her nipples tightened, and sweet warmth spread where he was looking, making her ache.

He made no move to cover himself. But he did gesture to the door. "Go now, lass. Be gone while I can let you."

"And if I stay?" She lifted her chin, daring.

"Then the ice breaks." His gaze drifted over her now, making her tingle. "You plunge into the cold depths and drown."

She shivered, her insides melting. His dark, naked *readiness* excited her, making her dizzy. Just watching him look at her as if he were drinking in every inch of her, savoring her, pushed all other thought from her mind. She forgot his castle ghost, the centuries of clan feuding, even the King's trial by combat.

"MacDonalds never drown." She spoke boldly. Hot blood rushed through her veins, and the drumming of her heart demanded courage.

"And I"—she met his gaze, starting forward—"swim better than most."

She saw his hands clench, the beat of his pulse at his throat. "I hope that's true." His gaze strayed once again to the locked door. "Because if you cannae, it's too late. You're in the water already."

"Do you regret pushing me from you earlier? I do see"—she looked *there* again, feminine pride thrilling—"that you want me."

He made a sound low in his throat, almost a growl. "I'd shove you out the door now, if I could. Make no mistake, lass, you dinnae want this."

"Pah." She went over to him, sliding her arms around his waist, loving the feel of him warm and naked against her.

He frowned, not saying anything.

Taking his silence for encouragement, she rubbed her hands up and down his sides, reveling in the smooth, hard feel of his bare skin beneath her fingers, hoping her touch might persuade him to kiss her again.

But he only tossed back his still-damp hair.

She leaned in closer, the feel of him making her tremble. Giddy pleasure swept her, blurring everything, making her dizzy. Swaying, she grasped her necklace, curling her fingers around the ambers, seeking their strength. She knew she wasn't in danger, but she could feel the stones' heat, solid and scorching her fingers.

But she didn't understand why the ambers burned her hand when her necklace felt so cool at her throat. Her fingers were on fire, the stones' heat pulsing into them, insistent, thrumming, and—

"O-o-oh!" She leapt back, releasing James's male piece as if its fiery hardness had scalded her.

He had the gall to laugh. "I was waiting for you to notice. Though"—he stepped back and she could see what she'd done to him—"I was also hoping you might keep on. I did enjoy you holding and stroking me."

"Holding and stroking you?" She stared at him, her eyes so round he couldn't help but laugh again.

"There's no other way to call what you were doing." He grinned. "I vow I ought to be offended that you didn't realize where your hand had landed, but it felt so good, I couldn't bear to stop you."

"It felt good?" She cast a skeptical glance where, moments before, she'd been rubbing and squeezing him so rousingly. "My hand?"

He grinned. "Hands can feel wonderfully good." He

reached for hers, turning it upward and then using the edge of his thumb to lightly circle her palm. When she gasped, startled by the tingles that rippled all through her, his grin deepened and he pushed back her sleeve so he could use the tips of his other four fingers to trace circles up and down the inside of her wrist.

Catriona stared at him, unable to speak.

The pleasure curling through her, the delicious tingling, was almost too exquisite.

"Dear God..." She squirmed, unable to stand still.

"Those tingles"—he looked at her and she saw that he knew what she was feeling—"are nothing compared to how you made me feel when you rubbed me. I can show you how good that feels if you'll let me?"

"You made me feel good in the stair tower." Catriona couldn't lie. Her nipples had tightened, straining against her bodice, wanting his caress again. "I know what—"

"Nae, you dinnae." He shook his head, slowly. "You've only dipped your toe in the water. To *swim* is to feel me rub you where you rubbed me."

Catriona's world stopped, then spun madly.

She swallowed. "You want to touch me *there*?"

He nodded. "I want to touch you there, and everywhere. But only if you let me remove your clothes"—he reached for her bodice ties, undoing them—"and if you're able to trust me completely?"

"Ahhh..." She *did* desire him. That seemed justification enough.

And she had thrilled to his hands on her breasts earlier. The sensations he'd made ripple up and down her arm. She couldn't imagine such pleasure in the intimate place he meant to touch.

Or maybe she could, because the idea was stirring such tingles there now.

And they did feel good.

"You must tell me, Catriona." He'd finished unfastening her bodice. But rather than slip the gown down her shoulders, he reached for her hands, lacing their fingers. "Say the words. Tell me you want me to touch you."

"I do." She trembled with longing even now. "Aye, I do, James. Touch me, please. Just as you described, *there,* and everywhere."

"So be it." He pulled her to him, kissing her hard and swiftly. Then he lowered his head to nuzzle her neck, nibbling the sensitive skin there and sending shivers of excitement spilling all through her.

"O-o-oh..." Her knees went weak and she would've swayed, but then she felt a rush of cold air, and goose-flesh rose on her skin and she realized he'd stripped her as naked as he was.

"Come, lass, you'll soon be warm." He swept her up in his arms, carrying her across the room and lowering her gently onto her bed.

She waited, expecting him to lie down beside her, but he stepped back from the bed and stood looking down at her, the heat in his eyes making the tingling awareness between her legs almost maddeningly glorious.

As if he knew—that he could make her feel this way just by looking at her—a slow, very wicked smile curved his lips and he set his hands on his hips, unashamed of his own nakedness, which she could see quite well in the candlelight and the glow of the moon streaming through the windows.

"Now comes the good part, Catriona." He stepped

closer to the edge of the bed's high mattress. "I'm going to touch your breasts again."

And he did, letting his fingertips glide across her bared skin, skimming the upper swells, then tracing ever-smaller circles round and round until he reached her nipples. He looked down at her as he rubbed and toyed with her nipples, each touch sending jolts of intense pleasure streaking straight to the center of her.

"O-o-oh, don't stop." She squirmed on the bed coverings, wanting more, but not knowing what. "Please, don't stop, James. Please."

"So you like this?" He leaned down to kiss her, slow and leisurely this time. He slid one hand into her hair to grip the back of her head so that he could deepen their kiss, plumping and kneading her breasts with his other hand. "Open your mouth, lass," he breathed the words against her lips, then rewarded her with a bold sweep of his tongue, deep inside her mouth, when she did as he bade her. Again and again, he let his tongue twirl and tangle with hers, slowly, languorously, as they shared breath and sighs.

When he broke away, standing again, she felt bereft.

"Dear saints, don't stop kissing me." She reached for him, but he stepped back, just beyond her grasp. "It felt so good. You're right—all of it feels better than—"

"It feels good because I..." He shut his eyes, breathing deep. "It's good, lass," he began again, "because we're no' just in the water now. We've been swept into the ice floes." He looked at her again and his face was fierce, almost savage. "I've wanted you, *wanted this,* for years. You're mine now, feuds be damned. And, by God, I want to pleasure you from now into eternity."

"And you are." Catriona was sure she couldn't take

much more pleasuring. Her entire body was already aflame, quivering with the most wondrous sensations. Then James reached down to slide his hand along the side of her hip and she nearly shot off the bed.

He grinned, looking down at her. "That's my sweet lass, so responsive..."

She bit her lip, staring back up at him. Waves of deeper, more intense tingling began washing through her, each new crest seeming to pool low in her belly, near to her thighs. When she drew up her knees and started to rock her hips, his smile turned devilish.

"Open your knees for me, Catriona." He touched each knee lightly, gently urging them apart. "I want to look at you. And I can only do that if you let me. Will you? Can you open your legs wider? Just a bit more, so I can see all of you?"

"Oh, God!" Catriona writhed on the bed, his words making the pleasure almost so good it hurt. "I—I can't stand it, James, I can't..."

"You can, and beautifully." Locking his gaze on hers, he let his fingers glide up her inner thigh. "Just feel, lass, feel me touching you now."

And he did touch her then, teasing his fingertips oh-so-lightly across the soft curls of her femininity. Then—she cried out—tracing one finger right along the very center of her.

"Agggh!" She lifted her hips off the bed, sure she would burst apart any moment. "Oh, James, please..."

"I will please you, aye." Now he did stretch out beside her, rolling her gently onto her back but keeping her knees spread wide. "This is what you need." He let his fingers play over her, teasing and tantalizing. Then he touched a circling finger to a spot that sent bolts of intense pleasure spiraling everywhere.

She reached for him, but he'd moved down on the bed. Raising his head to look up at her, he licked the very place he'd been rubbing so exquisitely. He held her gaze and began flicking his tongue back and forth over that one little spot until she couldn't stand it anymore. The fiercest sensations yet crashed over her, sweeping her away in a maelstrom of delight that dimmed everything around her except James and the delicious intimacy.

"That's enough." His voice was harsh as he pulled away from her. "I'll no' be—"

"You will, too." Catriona reached for him, curling her fingers firmly around his still-hard need. Her own need still felt tender and swollen, the hot melting inside her banishing caution.

"I've wanted you longer than you know"—she guided him to her, thrusting her hips until he swore and began to push inside her—"and now I'm of a mind to show you how much."

And she did, seeking his lips, then sighing contentedly when he slanted his mouth over hers, kissing her fiercely. He reached down between them, stroking and rubbing her as he finally thrust deep.

"Odin's balls!" He stopped at once, dragging his mouth from hers, his entire body tensing above her.

"What?" Catriona froze, mortification sweeping her. "Am I...is it, not good?"

"No' good?" He stared down at her, his eyes dark with passion, his face set in tight, rigid lines. "Sweet lass, were it any better, you'd unman me."

Catriona relaxed, relief washing through her. She clung to his shoulders, shifting her hips against the stinging tightness inside her. But the pain wasn't as great as she'd heard, and the intimacy of it—feeling James's hardness so thick and hot inside her—sent rippling waves of pleasurable heat spreading through her.

"Don't stop now." She gripped him harder, digging her fingers into his shoulders. When he still didn't move, she lifted her hips, rocking against him until he swore again and began thrusting slowly in and out of her.

"Sweet Christ!" He grabbed her chin with one hand, cupping her face and kissing her roughly. He thrust his tongue deep into her mouth, matching the hot rhythm of his strokes. Faster and faster, each plunge of his body into hers rushed her closer to the hot, whirling pleasure that threatened to darken the world around them.

She started to slide, shattering as she slipped into the darkness. From somewhere distant, she heard him groan and call her name. "Catriona," he'd cried, then more fervently, *"his love,"* in Gaelic.

At least, she thought that's what he'd said.

Already, he'd pulled away from her. But just as he rolled onto his back and she would've snuggled against him, someone else called out for her.

"Catriona!" Alasdair's worried voice came from afar, muffled by the heavy oaken door.

"I know I saw her come this way." It was a female's voice this time—Isobel's—and drifting just past the bedchamber. "Perhaps she's gone to one of the other guest chambers and not the one I readied for her?"

"Could be." Alasdair was all reason, as always. "Aye, that'll be it. Where did you say..."

The voices faded, Alasdair's and Isobel's footsteps dimming as they moved down the corridor.

James had moved, too.

And he'd done so with such speed that Catriona hadn't even seen him leap from the bed. But he had, obviously, for he was dashing about the room, snatching up her clothes and throwing them onto the bed as quickly as he plucked the garments off the rush-strewn floor.

Catriona sat up, not liking the look on his face. "What are you doing?"

He glanced at her, the horror in his eyes chilling her. "I'm saving your good name, is what I'm about!"

She blinked. "My name?"

She'd believed he'd be offering her his.

After this, what they'd done together. She'd even been secretly practicing the sound of Catriona Cameron. She'd run it through her mind again and again on the long ride from Blackshore.

Now...

"Make haste, lass." James had her shoes now, waving them at her. "There's a secret passage behind thon tapestry." He gestured with her slipper. "It leads down to the corridor you already know but opens into the castle guest chambers on the way.

"Isobel prepared one for you." He dropped to his knees before her, grabbing one of her feet and shoving it into her shoe. "It's the third door you'll pass. I'll take you there now and no one will be the wiser. But we must—"

"Hurry, I know." Catriona yanked her other shoe from his hand and crammed her foot inside. "But I'll find the room on my own, thank you. And"—she snatched her gown from the bed, pulling it on as she marched for the door—"I'll go the same way I came.

"I, you see, am not shamed by what we've done."

Grabbing the drawbar, she yanked it free. "I *wanted* to be on those ice floes with you. And now..."

"Catriona!" James strode forward, reaching for her. "You dinnae understand. I only want to—"

"Have your pleasure"—Catriona whipped open the door, sweeping out and slamming it hard—"and now you have. But you won't again.

"Not ever." She fastened her bodice laces as she hurried down the corridor, blotting her ears to the angry curses coming from behind James's closed door.

He'd spoken of ice floes.

If he dared glance at her again, she'd teach him about blizzards.

Chapter Eleven

❖

Early the next day, James stood near Castle Haven's stables, wondering why the kinsmen he'd encountered since rising hadn't crossed themselves when he'd strode past them on his way to the bailey. There was surely a mad glint in his eye. His shirt and plaid were rumpled and his hair snarled into a tangled mess. After a night spent tossing, turning, and pacing his bedchamber, his temper had been too frayed to bother with his usual careful ablutions.

This morn—for the first time in all his days—he'd appeared before his men looking like a bog monster who'd just crawled up from a peat mire.

He also felt like one.

How could he not, after what he'd done?

But other than morning greetings, no one paid him any particular heed. The bailey bustled as always. Even the breaking of his fast had proved no different than any other. Catriona had passed the meal in suspiciously good spirits. Over bannocks and watered-down wine, she'd accepted Hugh's moony-eyed praise with smiles and easy banter.

She also looked more enchanting than any female should at such an unholy hour. And—he couldn't help but notice—she'd accoutered herself as if preparing for battle. James knew whose head she wanted on a pike.

And if she hoped to tempt him, she'd succeeded.

She'd plaited her hair into two shining braids that hung to her waist, even twining silk ribbons into the strands. Her rich green gown fit snugly to the hips and dipped low in the bodice, revealing the creamy swells of her breasts. James couldn't swear to it, but he was fairly sure that the crests of her nipples peeked above the gown's edge.

Fierce need had gripped him when he noticed. His mind had leapt from her pert rosy nipples to the swollen bud nestled beneath her soft and fragrant feminine curls. At once, he'd recalled the sleek flesh of her inner thighs, remembering how she'd parted her legs so he could stroke her there. And all that had happened afterward.

Then he'd sat at his own high table, making converse, while his vitals swelled and tightened so uncomfortably that he'd had to stifle a groan.

And if that wasn't enough to set him on his ear, her gillyflower perfume wafted around her like a delicately scented cloud, bewitching every masculine nose within ten paces and making him wonder if she'd soaked the gown in scent after she'd stormed from his bedchamber.

Worse, she'd granted him no more notice than a politely muttered "I bid you good morn."

She'd treated him like air.

Alasdair proved congenial as ever, not tossing a single narrow-eyed look his way.

And therein lay his problem.

The reason he'd spent a sleepless night. And why he now drew a tight breath and clenched his fists. His men and everyone else filling the bailey must've lost their sight. If they hadn't, they'd see a different man when they looked at him this morn.

He'd breached every code of honor he lived by.

Not just offending a guest beneath his roof, but insulting a woman. *A lady*. And one who was the well-esteemed sister of a feuding clan chieftain. Worse, he'd forced his kisses on her, however willfully she'd provoked them.

He'd stolen her innocence.

And wedding her to make it right would only unleash a worse calamity on her. She'd already seen the Doom of the Camerons. The specter's visitation could only mean Catriona was marked for tragedy. If—his gut seized unpleasantly—he forced nuptials on her.

He'd surely lost his senses.

Tipping back his head, he glowered at the low gray sky. Praise God the day was dark and overcast. The angry clouds suited his mood. As did the smell of cold, damp stone and the more pungent aroma of the nearby horses, standing patiently as they waited to be mounted.

Now wasn't the hour for brightness and light, the scent of spring meadows.

Not when he'd sinned so grievously he should be sprouting horns and a tail. And ravishing Catriona was only the beginning of his perfidy. The sad truth was, given the chance, he'd not change his behavior.

The only thing he regretted was his unexpected reaction to tumbling her.

He'd found heaven in the sinuous warmth of her sweet,

silken curves. And he could still feel the magnificent rounds of her breasts crushed to his chest, her nipples taut and thrusting against him. His fingers itched to again squeeze her deliciously plump bottom. And he knew he'd never lose the urge to run his hands over her naked flesh. Sinking into her, moving in and out of her tight, molten depths, had shook him with a force of passion more fierce than any he'd ever known.

"Damnation." He clamped his mouth in a hard, tight line and closed his eyes, willing the torrid thoughts to vanish from his mind.

But rather than fading, another wickedly vivid image of her parted thighs flashed before him. And this time when he recalled her triangle of glossy red curls, he could almost smell the rich tang of her womanhood, taste her muskiness on the back of his tongue...

Your opinion of yourself is grand.

Her taunt rang in his ears, shattering the rousing vision and minding him how much she'd erred.

He didn't see himself as grand. Not since yestere'en, anyway.

Now he wasn't wont to consider what he thought of himself. He certainly didn't wish to ponder how low he'd fallen. Or that she'd claimed to want him. He suspected she believed herself in love with him. He'd seen the starry look in her eyes. If so, she was on the path to sorrow. That rode him harder than all else. Feeling wretched, he left his post by the stables and paced to the castle well and back. If anyone noticed his agitation, so be it. His mood was foul for a reason.

It wasn't every day one of the proudest, most revered chieftains in the Highlands turned into a despicable, lust-crazed beast.

Yet he'd done the inconceivable.

He'd become the devil raging. A blackguard who'd hoisted the skirts of a highborn virgin, taking his pleasure and aching for her still. The lascivious, heated images were branded on him, whirling across his mind. Furious, he turned to pace again and—

He found himself facing her brother.

"MacDonald." James jerked a nod, guilt shafting through him. A strange buzzing roared in his ears as the bailey turned unnaturally quiet, as if the world narrowed to just him and Alasdair.

An annoyingly perceptive bugger whose eye he could scarce meet.

James swallowed hard, hoping his gulp wasn't audible.

Alasdair glanced at the hills beyond the curtain walls and then took a deep, lung-filling breath, surely enjoying the chill, pine-scented air.

"A fine day, it is." He returned James's nod amiably. His face bore no sign that he knew of James's disastrous encounter with his sister.

Even so, James could feel his face reddening.

The tops of his ears burned like fire.

It was a worse kind of shame than he'd felt when, as a young laddie, his father had caught him peering intently betwixt the wide-spread legs of a bonnie kitchen wench, his busy fingers exploring her mysteries.

Curiosity about women had sent him to the kitchens that day.

He *cared* about Catriona. A horrible voice deep inside him raged that he loved her.

Alasdair stood looking about, unaware of his turmoil.

James cleared his throat. "I trust your quarters were

comfortable? My sister, Lady Isobel, gave you our finest rooms. They would have been commandeered by Sir Walter and his worthies, but"—James threw a glance at the tower, a great hulk of wet, glistening stone on the other side of the bailey—"Isobel told them the last visitors to sleep there were lice-ridden mendicants.

"She swore the poor friars scratched all night." James hooked his thumbs beneath his sword belt, remembering. "The Lowlanders believed her when she claimed the chambers have been infested ever since, wholly uninhabitable."

"Hah—God save us! Your sister is resourceful." Alasdair grinned, looking for a moment as if he were a friend and not a foe.

A good friend, perhaps even one a man would want at his back in battle.

On the thought, James felt another twinge of guilt, wishing he hadn't mentioned sisters. But Alasdair hadn't blinked, his expression still showing no signs of suspicion.

"You've borne our visit well." Alasdair reached out and clasped James's arm, gripping tight. "My men and I thank you." He looked to where his escort already sat their mounts, a dozen sturdy Highland garrons. "I believe my sister has no complaints, either.

"Indeed"—he glanced toward the tower, clearly waiting for her to appear—"she's vowed to show you an even more lavish welcome if e'er you return to Blackshore. As I shall, as well, you can be sure."

Before James could frame an answer, a stir across the courtyard drew their attention. Catriona had just stepped through the hall's massive oaken door and was crossing the cobbles, head high and hips swaying. She cut a swath through the bustle, making for the little cluster of mounted MacDonald guardsmen.

James's heart began to pound.

She'd donned a voluminous cloak, its woolen folds hiding her lusciously curved body. But briskly as she walked, a fool could imagine how her breasts must be bouncing with each quick footstep.

James envisioned her naked. He knew how she looked walking toward him unclothed and with her breasts jigging delightfully, her braids undone so that her sun-bright tresses spilled over her shoulders to swirl about her hips with each provocative move she made.

The image made him hard, tightening his loins with an urgency he'd never felt for another woman. Furious, he tugged at his plaid before Alasdair—or anyone—could notice how she affected him.

Unfortunately, she chose that moment to look his way. She stared at him as if she'd sensed the moment his damnable body decided to add more smirch to his tarnished honor.

James glared at her.

She flashed him the most fleeting of smiles, then marched on toward her escort.

But as she went, she flipped one of her braids over her shoulder, and James was sure a tantalizing whiff of gillyflower sailed past his nose on the cold morning wind. When she glanced back over her shoulder, her deep blue eyes triumphant, he knew he wasn't mistaken.

She'd wanted him to scent her.

And he had, by God!

One of the older squires standing near James stared after her, his lips forming a low whistle.

James shot the lad a sharp glance. "She's a lady, you

lackwit. Mind your manners lest I have you scrubbing the cesspit rather than tending horses."

Alasdair's lips twitched. "I doubt she noticed him, Cameron. Her gaze was on you."

"Humph." James started forward, hot on that wafting drift of gillyflower.

"James, wait! She'll no' be thanking you—" Alasdair's warning was cut off by hoots of laughter from the gawking squires.

Even some of the older men, the patrol guards looking down from the wall-walk, loosed a chorus of their own guffaws and whistles.

James ignored them all.

Especially Alasdair, who'd obviously guessed his intent.

Not that James cared.

As her host—she was still within his castle gates— he'd be remiss in his hospitality if he didn't help her onto her garron. It'd be her fault entirely if, when doing so, he gripped her waist more intimately than if she hadn't once again provoked him.

"Catriona!" He quickened his strides, not missing that she'd increased her own at his approach. When he reached her, he bent a quick knee. "Let me assist you mount—"

"No need." She flashed him a blinding smile as she sailed past him, moving so quickly she must've fastened wings on her ankles.

Before he could blink—or even lower the arms he'd extended with such a flourish—she hitched her skirts and put her foot in the stirrup, swinging herself into the saddle, sitting astride like a man. As quickly, she tossed her head and then clicked her tongue, sending the horse trotting right through the open castle gates.

This time she didn't glance back.

Such an air wasn't necessary with the ramrod straightness of her back showing everyone what she thought of him.

James glared after her, livid.

He felt his face darkening, the hot color spreading under his skin. "Vexatious hell-cat."

"Aye, she can be."

James hadn't noticed Alasdair's approach but now whipped around to find him standing at his side.

"It matters no' a whit to me." James dusted his plaid, feigning indifference. "I couldn't know she'd leap onto the horse like a cloud-riding Valkyrie."

Alasdair shrugged, showing his perceptiveness at last.

When he spoke, his voice didn't hold a trace of mockery. Even more surprising, his clear blue eyes were sympathetic. "I tried to warn you. Our father taught her to ride before she could walk.

"Truth is"—he glanced after her, his words edged with pride—"she sits a horse better than any of us, though it pains me to admit it."

"Then let us join her before she rides through the Lowlanders' encampment on her own." James started for his own horse.

His concern was real.

In recent days, the number of the pitched tents crowded along the castle sward and beside the newly erected battling ground had swelled to the size of a large village. Some of the makeshift lodgings even encroached into the wood. And the scores of spectators pouring in from the south weren't all men of the noble class. Several that he'd seen even appeared to be shifty-eyed miscreants, come in the hopes of pinching a few coins, or worse.

Catriona riding alone through their midst was un-thinkable.

Her sire might have made her a fine horsewoman, but he intended to know her safe.

Even if the right wasn't his.

And that was a damnable shame, because, after last night, he couldn't imagine a life without her.

"Were my cook's honeyed bannocks no' enough to fill your belly this morn, or do you have a taste for fresh-off-the-griddle oatcakes?" James glanced at Alasdair, riding close beside him as they wound their way through the tents and cooking fires that covered every inch of ground between Castle Haven's curtain walls and the wood beyond.

"I do favor oatcakes." Alasdair kept his attention on a cook stall where a stout, red-faced woman shouted the tastiness of her griddled oatcakes.

James studied Alasdair's profile, noting the hard set of his jaw. Alasdair had hardly touched Cook's oatcakes, surely the finest in the land. A sudden fondness for them struck James as unlikely.

But he was curious.

Alasdair kept glancing at the traders' carts and food stalls set among the maze of colorful tents. His watchful eyes took in everything they passed. His gaze darted left and right, scanning the clusters of Lowlanders who filled the narrow spaces between the tenting or scurried about, some tending cooking pits, a few huddling near a supply wagon playing dice, while others hawked wares as if at a market fair.

An air of celebration hovered over the makeshift settle-ment, the jollity offensive, considering they'd gathered to witness men cut each other down.

Yet there was no disguising the festive mood.

And the deeper James and Alasdair led their party into the encampment, the more raucously their eyes, ears, and noses were assaulted by the revelry. The din was unceasing, a cacophony of voices, laughter, and shouting, spiced with the occasional barking of dogs or whinnying and snorts of horses. Smoke from the cook fires hung in the air, bringing the mouthwatering smell of roasting meat, while the steam rising from dozens of simmering cauldrons competed with the equally tempting aroma of well-seasoned stew.

Several tumblers and jugglers had drawn a crowd to their left, their antics reaping cheers. Closer by, a buxom young alewife with a quick laugh and merry eyes served ale from large earthen ewers to a handful of Lowland knights who appeared more interested in her boldly displayed charms than her frothy libations.

And—James noted with interest—all of them earned Alasdair's assessing stare.

Just now Alasdair slowed his garron to narrow his gaze on the red-cheeked, heavyset woman flipping oatcakes at her cook stall.

"We can stop if your belly's rumbling." James cast a look over his shoulder at the MacDonald men-at-arms riding in a tight column behind them. Catriona was wedged in the middle of them, a precaution insisted upon by her brother and one that—given the fierce glint in her eye—didn't suit her.

But as soon as she noticed James's stare, the annoyance vanished from her face and she assumed an air of ladylike calm, though she did lift an eyebrow at him. She did so quickly and subtly, before anyone else could see.

James let his own brows snap together, too irritated to care if she saw.

He saw more than he wished.

In the night, she'd taken his breath and his body. Here, in the open, and beneath the wild, roiling sky, she came near to capturing all of him. The morning breeze riffled her cloak, molding it to her curves. And her braids were beginning to loosen, the gleaming strands tumbling about her shoulders. It was a becoming dishevelment, more lovely than if she'd undone her plaits and arranged the glossy red curls with the sole intent of tempting him.

Almost, he believed she had.

Especially when he tore his gaze from her, only to find Alasdair no longer watching the stout woman at the cook stall, but eyeing him, with sympathy.

James scowled. He didn't want commiseration from a MacDonald. However much he was secretly coming to like and admire the lout.

So he did the only thing he could do, drawing rein beside his damnably congenial foe as Alasdair had already halted his own steed.

"Thon oatcakes you were eyeing do look good and"— James gestured to another cook stall a few paces beyond the stout woman's griddle offerings—"those sausages and meat pasties smell equally fine. I am no' in haste to return to my hall, if you wish to try something. Perhaps your sister will welcome a pause? She might appreciate refreshment before you ride on the Blackshore."

"You surprise me." Alasdair's lips twitched. "I'd think you've seen enough of her by now to know she'd sooner eat a bowl of salted peat than take one bite of Lowland food. Leastways"—his voice hardened—"victuals served up by Sir Walter's camp followers.

"Though I'll own she has a ravenous appetite." He

threw a glance at her, looking quickly back to James. "She hungers for many things. A few that are no' good for her."

James felt himself flush, gently reprimanded. "I'll no' be pressing my attentions on her if that's your concern."

"I'm glad to hear it." Alasdair's acceptance of his protestation stung. "She could tempt the devil with the crook of one finger. And I do know she favors you."

"I vow you mistake." James struggled against the urge to glance at his feet. He was sure he'd felt them turn into hooves in the stirrups.

"It scarce matters one way or the other." Alasdair signaled his men to halt and then swung down from his saddle. His smile flashed when he looked back at James. "You're a Cameron. And if that isn't a bad enough taint, chances are you'll also be a dead man very soon."

"And so will you." James jumped to ground, telling yet another lie.

He didn't know when or how it'd happened, but he was fairly certain that if it came to it, he wouldn't wield his steel on Alasdair.

To his surprise, Alasdair grinned. "I'd have words with you." He strode forward to grip James's arm. "There, in the trees beyond the food stalls."

"And the others, will they no' wonder what we're about?" James noted that Catriona and the guardsmen had already dismounted.

"We are men." Alasdair's voice held a spark of humor. "They'll no' wonder if we slip away for a moment. All men do when nature calls."

James wasn't so sure.

He glanced again at the MacDonalds, his body beginning to stir when his gaze lit on Catriona. Amid the men's jostling and leg-stretching, she stood cool as spring rain, lightly caressing the ambers circling her neck. The stones shone in the watery morning sun, a perfect complement for her richly burnished hair.

She caught him looking at her and dropped her hand as if the ambers burned her. Pink bloomed across her cheekbones, but then she turned away to bestow a dazzling smile on one of the guardsmen.

James felt a rush of annoyance that almost choked him.

But when a small group of Lowland knights strode past her and the MacDonald men-at-arms, her smile vanished, replaced at once by a look of disdain, a surge of admiration welled inside him.

"She is bold, too much so at times." Alasdair tugged on James's arm, urging him toward the nearest cook stall. "Come now, lest she turns her eye this way again. She's as quick-witted as she is daring, and I'd no' have her guess what I must tell you."

James jerked his arm from Alasdair's grasp. "I'll no' be dragged anywhere."

He did walk with Alasdair into the trees, keeping pace with him as they moved deeper into the wood. The trees were great Caledonian pines, thick-trunked and growing closely together, their red-barked girth and the soft morning mist hiding them from curious glances. But when Alasdair made no move to pause, James stepped around in front of him.

"We've gone far enough." He folded his arms. "If we stray any farther, no one will believe we had a natural reason for nipping into the wood."

He'd expected Alasdair to laugh—the lout had been in high fettle all morning—but now he pulled a hand down over his face, his levity gone.

"We can speak here, to be sure." Alasdair's voice was terse. "I wanted you to know that I wasn't fooled by Catriona's tale about Birkie. I knew the wee dog wasn't missing. I'd seen Maili, one of our laundresses, sneaking two bowls of rib meat and watered oats up to Catriona's bedchamber.

"I followed Maili and"—some of the twinkle returned to Alasdair's eyes—"I heard yipping behind the door. Birkie and his brother, Beadle, were both ensconced like fur-clad kinglets in Catriona's antechamber, their own maid seeing to their every whim."

"Yet you went along with Catriona's story?"

"I did." Alasdair swatted at a thread of mist sliding past them. "And at the cost of having you think she'd hoodwinked me again. I would've told you sooner, but there wasn't an opportunity."

James waved a hand. "I ne'er thought—"

"You did." Alasdair's gaze met James, good-naturedly. "It was writ all o'er your face, though I'll no' be holding that against you. I'd have thought the same. How could you know it served my own purpose to do as if I believed her?" He hooked his thumbs in his sword belt. "I wished to come to Castle Haven. Catriona gave me the chance."

He paused. "I also didn't want Sir Walter to suspect my reason for calling."

"That craven! What does he have to do with it?" James felt his nape prickle.

Alasdair rubbed the back of his own neck, looking uncomfortable. "I cannae say he's involved, though I have suspicions. See you, one of the kitchen laddies at Blackshore came to me upset that he'd seen a *monster* creeping along the lochshore just before sunrise. The boy claimed the apparition was slinking around our beached galleys.

"And"—his voice hardened—"those ships moored within wading distance to the shore."

"You think the boy saw Sir Walter?" James frowned. "He hasn't left my hall, save to prance about thon tents like a peacock. I've set men on him, good men who haven't let him from their sight."

"I expected no less." Alasdair glanced over his shoulder, as if the trees and mist had ears. "Nor would Sir Walter risk such foolery. Himself. Such men have minions to do their bidding. I believe it was one of them that young Scully saw at our galleys. When I pressed the lad for a description of the monster, I knew he'd seen a man. He spoke of a tall, dark-cloaked figure."

"Like the man I saw here, the morning I caught Catriona in the wood."

"So I wondered."

James drew a long breath. "The boy couldn't have erred? Perhaps he had a fearing dream or"—he didn't believe this himself—"saw bog mist?"

"Bog mist doesn't gouge holes in the hulls of galleys." Alasdair's voice was grim. "I, too, thought the lad might've conjured beasties from sea haar. Or that a bard's tale frightened him. But when I took a party of men to the lochside, we found a number of ships damaged."

James stared at him. "That bodes ill."

Alasdair nodded. "Now you see why I needed to speak with you. The man Scully saw knew what he was about. The holes were small and well hidden between the strakes. Yet their purpose was clear.

"Who'er the black-cloaked figure is"—he paced a few steps and then swung round—"he wanted us to board the galleys as e'er, and then—"

"Sink beneath your feet." James finished for him.

"Just so."

"Someone means ill with this glen."

"Or with us." Alasdair took a leather-wrapped flagon from beneath his plaid, pulling the wooden stopper before he handed the flask to James. "I'll ride to speak with Kendrew Mackintosh after Catriona is safely returned to Blackshore. Perhaps the Mackintoshes have seen a dark-cloaked stranger slipping about the dreagan stones beneath Castle Nought?"

James bit back a snort. "You think Kendrew would say if they have?"

"We have dealings now and then. But"—Alasdair rolled his shoulders, then cracked his knuckles—"if he isn't in a friendly mood, I'll persuade him, whatever."

James tipped the flagon to his lips, welcoming the burn of the *uisge beatha* as the fiery Highland spirits slid down his throat.

He thrust the flask back at Alasdair, then dragged his sleeve over his mouth before speaking.

"Could be Kendrew is behind this?" James didn't trust the man. "He's e'er at mischief. Perhaps the cloaked figure is his man?"

Alasdair shrugged. "My gut tells me otherwise."

James's did, too. But he loathed Kendrew Mackintosh enough not to admit it.

Mackintoshes were worse than MacDonalds.

And more worrying than either foe were the icy chills racing up and down his spine, the tight coil of alarm snaking around his chest. Memories flooded him of the night before, the brief bliss with Catriona, and how— even now—he wanted more of her. And it wasn't just the wonder of sinking into her tight, womanly heat, or the feel of her body naked and trembling beneath him. He'd kill a man for the pleasure of tangling his tongue with hers, sipping her breath. And he'd face an army if doing so would vanquish the dangers that would shadow her if he made her his own.

If other perils—a dark-cloaked man or a craven like Kendrew Mackintosh—threatened her, he'd break each one in pieces.

He shoved a hand through his hair, thinking.

"If no' those rock-climbing Mackintosh goat-men, then—" Trumpet blasts and the earthshaking thunder of many approaching hooves cut him off as the air filled with cheers and shouts, the scurry of running feet. The din— and the sharp reek of sweat-drenched leather and winded, hard-ridden horses—came from the encampment beyond the trees.

"God be good!" Alasdair froze, the flagon poised at his lips. "That can only be King Robert." He glanced at James, then started forward, his long strides carrying him back the way they'd come.

"We will speak of this later!" He glanced back over his shoulder.

James hurried after him, biting his tongue.

With the King's arrival, the trial by combat would take place on the morrow. And if the fighting proved as fierce as he suspected, it was doubtful he and Alasdair would ever share a word again.

How odd that the notion pained him.

Chapter Twelve

❧

About the same time, but in the coldest, darkest part of the Glen of Many Legends, a place where black mist often swirled and impassable, stone-filled corries kept unwanted intruders at bay, Grizel stood in the middle of her tidy, thick-walled cottage, *Tigh-na-Craig*—"House on the Rock"—and sent a silent prayer to the Auld Ones, humbly thanking them for the great powers they'd vested in her.

She resisted the temptation to laud them for their wisdom in recognizing that she, better than any other, knew how to best use such favor.

Some opinions should be kept to oneself.

And she knew well that such gifts as hers could be snatched away in a blink if a soul dared to be boastful. Or, Odin forfend, if one dared to misuse them. Though, admittedly, there were moments when she slipped, allowing her pride in her greatness to shine.

Most especially when Gorm annoyed her.

He wasn't the only Maker of Dreams. And if, now and then, he goaded her into flaunting her superiority, the blame was entirely his own.

But she never used her abilities to harm.

Though, given sufficient provocation, she had been known to needle those so deserving.

This was one of those times.

So she patted the snowy-white braids she wore wound artfully on either side of her head and then smoothed her black skirts. She took pleasure in the clean, freshening scent of cinnamon that rose from the heavy linen folds. The fragrance delighted her nose. For luck, she rubbed her knotty knuckles across the half-moon brooch of beaten silver that she always pinned at her shoulder.

Satisfied, she hitched her skirts just enough to ensure that her small black boots were spotlessly clean, no bits of heather or smears of peat clinging to the soles.

On finding no fault with her footgear—she did take care with such things—she allowed herself a deep, appreciative breath. Tigh-na-Craig was known for the earthy-sweet peat smoke that permeated the cottage's thick, white-washed walls. And the tantalizing food smells that always hovered in the air. This morn, a rich meat broth simmered in the heavy black cauldron that hung from a chain over her cook fire. The mouthwatering aroma almost tempted Grizel to forgo her duties.

Her diminutive stature—many likened her to a tiny, black-garbed bird—wouldn't let anyone guess, but she was fond of her victuals. And with good reason, for her skill with a ladle was nigh as formidable as her magical talents.

But her savory meat broth would have to wait.

Just now, more important matters needed her attention.

Eager to begin, she straightened her back as best she could and then hobbled to the door. She cracked it just enough to make certain that her special friend and helpmate, Rannoch, still guarded the cottage's entry. Her ancient heart warmed to see the white stag, for they'd been together beyond remembering and she loved him dearly. Also called *Laoigh Feigh Ban,* because of his remarkable coloring, the enchanted creature possessed powers to rival her own.

"Ahhh, you're a good lad," she crooned, pleased that he hadn't abandoned his post.

Looking most regal, for he was a magnificent beast, he rested in front of the door, his great white body curled like a dog's on the soft bed of heather and bracken that she'd prepared for him.

Ever alert, he peered up at her from his dark, velvety eyes. Behind him, billowy curtains of gray mist drifted across the high moor where the rest of the herd grazed in step. Their red-brown bodies moved like silent shapes in the fog, barely discernible. But when Rannoch turned his proud head to gaze in their direction, Grizel knew he wasn't drawing her attention to his hinds.

Rannoch focused his stare on the high peaks on the far side of the grazing ground. A sacred place where, were it not for the mist, a deep cleft in the fold of one of the hills would be visible. The black-jawed crevice that opened into Gorm's cave and where he'd now be hunched over his Pool of Truth, muttering spells of his own and scrying for the dreams he'd work with this day.

Leastways, Grizel hoped that's where he was.

When Rannoch twitched his ears, she wasn't so sure.

She did catch a movement—a dark smudge against the swirling gray—near the rocks that guarded the entrance to Gorm's sanctuary. He could've finished his dream making and decided he was for a dose.

Gorm relished napping as much as she loved to eat.

Grizel pursed her lips. She didn't need Gorm's trumpeting snores disrupting her concentration when she was about to indulge in a bit of wisewomanish mischief.

If the gods were kind, the dark blur had been nothing more than a shadow.

Even so, precautions were in order.

She peered down at Rannoch, seeing in the angle of his antlered head that he understood.

"That be the way of it, laddie." She eased the door wider, leaning out. "I'm trusting in you. If thon long-bearded he-goat comes loping back here before I'm done with my spelling, send him back to his cave.

"Better yet"—she scrunched her eyes, looking off toward where she knew the cave to be—"fuddle his mind for a bit. It would serve him well to wonder if he's gone addled, vain bugger that he is."

Rannoch snapped his head up even higher, antlers back now, as he bent his intelligent gaze on her. It was a look she knew well.

The white stag wouldn't let her down.

And if she plied her craft with as much skill as always, a certain craven named Sir Walter would soon take his pestiferous self from the castle of her beloved Camerons and find a bed elsewhere.

He'd plagued them long enough. Besides, his king was now in the glen and could provide a pallet in his royal tent. It'd already been decried that he'd bring his own lodgings, lest quartering in one of the glen's three castles showed an indication of court favor.

"We know better, eh, Rannoch?" Grizel clucked her tongue. "Thon *Stewart* fears sleeping beneath the roof of men he sees as wild-haired, bushy-bearded heathens. He'll worry he might waken with his kingly throat slit."

As if the pagan gods agreed, the wind rose just then. Cold and mighty, it raced round the cottage like a fury, tossing the bottom fringes of the roof thatch before howling away across the moor.

Pleased, Grizel closed the door and returned to her worktable, where she'd set out a small wooden bowl filled with tiny figures she'd been fashioning for days. The shapes were made of peat, oats, a few secret spelling herbs, the whole held together with newt spittle. They resembled rats, though one had the form of a man.

Reaching for the human figure, Grizel placed the tiny image in the center of a square of birch twigs. Then, with great glee, she cackled and began filling the enclosed space with the teeny rats.

She was just placing a generous handful of rats in the square, merrily using them to cover Sir Walter's miniature likeness, when the door opened quietly behind her.

"What are you about, woman?"

"Gah!" Grizel spun around, sending the peat rats flying through the air. Gorm stood just inside the threshold, his elfin face stern. His usually merry eyes were suspicious. And his splendid, near-to-his-knees beard riffled in an unseen wind, a sure sign that he was in a dangerous mood.

Grizel glared at him, peering past his shoulder at the now-empty door stoop. Even the fine bed of heather and bracken that she'd made for her four-legged friend had vanished. Everything was gone except the rocks and whirling mist.

"Glower all you wish, it'll change naught." Gorm's beard ends fluttered wildly. "As I've e'er been for trying to make you see."

"Where be Rannoch?" Grizel thrust out her chin, ignoring the beard-riffling.

"No' doing the fool *guarding* you ordered him to do, that's true." Gorm shut the door and came forward, bending to snatch up one of the peat rats as he crossed the stone-flagged floor. "Thon creature heeds me more than he does you, if ne'er you noticed."

"Say you."

"I don't need to be a-saying it. 'Tis true."

"And I'm a painted harlot at King Robert's court." Grizel put her hands on her hips. "Rannoch wouldn't have let you pass unless you bribed him with a treat. What did you conjure? Tender shoots of sweet spring grass? Or the succulent tips of pine and—"

"A basket of pine tips and a generous portion of tasty, buttery nuts, if you'd be knowing." Gorm stepped closer, his clear blue gaze piercing. "What I would hear is the meaning of this?"

He held out his hand, palm up to show the tiny peat rat. "What poor soul deserves an infestation of rats?"

"One who should be eaten by them and no' just visited by them." Grizel tightened her lips, annoyed that he'd guessed her purpose from a few teeny rat likenesses scattered across the floor.

But—she couldn't help it—her pride in her craft bit deep, so she moved away from the sturdy worktable, freeing the view of the birch twig square piled high with the little peat rats.

"Behold—Sir Walter!" She dug her fingers into the mound of tiny figures and retrieved the little man. "Asleep in his room at Castle Haven"—she indicated the birch twig enclosure, returning the image to the middle of the square— "and waking to find his chamber crawling with rats."

"And think you young James will appreciate such an infestation?" Gorm peered at her work, his beard tips no longer riffling. But his brows had snapped together to form a fearsome iron-gray bar. "We are here to guard this sacred place and look after Camerons, not make their lives more unpleasant than necessary."

"Think you I have bog cotton for a brain?" Grizel snatched the peat rat from his hand and dropped it into the twig square. "'Tis you who have your fool head on backward. Young James will see nary a single rat tail. My magic was cast so that only Sir Walter will see them."

"I'm still not for liking it." Gorm crossed the room and sat on a three-legged stool. "We have more earnest work to do than pester a fool Lowlander who"—he rubbed his knees as he spoke—"will soon be gone from this glen, after the trial by combat."

"Humph!" Grizel flicked a speck of lint from her sleeve. "There be some hereabouts who deem it fitting to salt the tails of those who bring grief—"

"I've already said that peace will return to the glen." Gorm stilled his hands, his tone annoyingly patient. "Have you forgotten my words? That all will be well when innocents pay the price of blood and gold covers the glen?"

Grizel snorted. "And the grief?"

"No man living reaches the end of his days without

knowing sorrow. If he does"—Gorm resumed his knee rubbing—"he is only half a man, because he hasn't learned that braving the worst storms brings the reward of a bright morrow. It is hardship that makes a man strong, not frivol.

"And"—he stretched his arms above his head, clearly hinting that he wished a nap—"happiness e'er tastes finer when it's first been seasoned with tears."

"You should have been a poet rather than a Maker of Dreams." Grizel knew he spoke wise words, but stubbornness wouldn't let her agree.

Instead, she went to her cauldron and busily stirred her meat broth. Gorm didn't need to see how much it peeved her that, while he'd revealed his prophecy about the battle's outcome to James—and to her—he'd kept silent as to the meaning of his cryptic words.

"I'm not for calling back my rats." She stirred her meat broth with particular vigor. "Don't be asking me, 'cause I won't."

"I want naught to do with your fool cantrips." Gorm pushed to his feet and came to stand beside her. "Though I will be hoping you'll spare a bit o' your skill for someone I saw outside my cave a while ago."

"A visitor?" Grizel almost dropped her ladle. The Bowing Stone always let them know when anyone approached the corrie that opened into their high moor.

As did Rannoch, unless he was distracted by one of his hinds and missed the stranger's approach.

Or...

If the visitor bypassed the standing stone and its secret entry.

And only souls no longer living could do that. Suchlike,

and—Grizel's regrettable peer envy made her bristle— other half-mythical beings like herself and Gorm.

"It wasn't the great Devorgilla of Doon if that's why you've gone all pinch-faced." Gorm leaned around her to sniff appreciatively of the steam rising from the meat broth.

Straightening, he took the ladle from Grizel's hand and dipped it into the cauldron, helping himself to a taste. "I didn't get a good look, though I've a fair notion who it was. Truth is, I've been expecting that soul's arrival for a good while now."

"And who might it be?" Grizel plucked the wooden spoon from his hand when he tried to dip it back into the broth. "I am for hearing."

"Mayhap I'll also be for telling you." Gorm snapped his fingers to conjure another long-handled spoon and, grinning triumphantly, helped himself to a second sampling of the meat broth.

"It was"—he smacked his lips—"someone who can bring much gladness to the glen."

"But who?"

"I daren't mention the name before I'm sure."

"You mean you won't be telling the name." Grizel glared at him, sure she'd burst from annoyance.

"I mean"—Gorm licked the back of his conjured spoon—"it would anger the Auld Ones who've allowed the soul to come here, if we speak the name before the soul comes to us asking for our help."

Grizel knew that was so.

But she didn't like it.

"I believe I saw the soul myself, I did." She lifted her chin, remembering the dark smudge she'd seen near the entrance to Gorm's cave.

"Then if you get a closer look, you can tell me if my suspicions are right." Gorm's answer wasn't the one she'd hoped to pry out of him.

But before she could prod further, he clicked his fingers to banish his drat spoon. Then, with the purpose of a man bent on vexing a curious woman, he marched across the room and lowered his bandy-legged self onto his heather-stuffed pallet. As deliberately, he turned onto his side and pulled the plaid covering over his head.

His snores soon filled the cottage.

Which was well and good.

If he slept, he wouldn't see Grizel slip out the door. If a soul was flitting about the high moor, desiring help, she meant to make herself available. From the sound of it, the soul's plight better suited her skills than Gorm's pesky truth mutterings.

It'd been a long time—many centuries—since she'd worked her magic twice in one day.

So she cast a last glance at Gorm's prone, noise-making form. Then she took her cloak off its peg by the door and hurried out into the mist.

She wouldn't mind finding the soul before Gorm.

If she did, he'd have to admit her talents were greater than his own. But above all, in her heart of hearts, she couldn't bear the thought of a soul in need.

Especially if—from Gorm's hints—the soul was who she thought it might be.

That would be glorious.

Very fine, indeed.

Several hours later, long after Grizel conceded defeat and returned to her still-simmering cauldron at Tigh-na-Craig,

Catriona, Alasdair, and their men-at-arms rode through the heart of Mackintosh country. It was a slow journey, because their horses had to pick a careful path through the maze of odd-shaped stones and outcroppings that crowded this northernmost end of the Glen of Many Legends.

Alasdair hardly spoke, his face grim as they pressed deeper and deeper into land held by a far greater foe to MacDonalds than Clan Cameron.

Catriona looked about with interest, having never been to this remote corner of the glen. Comparing this dark and stony place to Blackshore helped her keep her mind off James. So she sat up straighter and peered into the empty landscape.

Not that much could be seen.

Certainly no dreagans, though everyone knew this was where they were said to roam. But thick mist did swirl here, colder and denser than any she'd ever seen at Blackshore, nestled in the glen's less rugged southern bounds. Mackintosh territory couldn't be more different if it were a pebble on the moon. And the dark winds that blew mist everywhere roared angrily. At times, whipping past them like a riled, living thing. Then racing away to rush over and around the strange rock formations many claimed were all that remained of the dreagans' unfortunate victims.

Hapless souls who dared to pass through this way at times they shouldn't have, paying the price for their folly by being fire-blasted to stone.

Catriona drew her cloak tighter about her shoulders and shoved all thought of dreagans to the farthest reaches of her mind.

Since visiting Castle Haven and meeting Clan Cameron's raven-haired beauty ghost—*whoever she was*—she couldn't dismiss that such things did exist.

Perhaps even dreagans.

But despite the cloying fog, she could tell that nothing save bare rock and jagged, naked peaks surrounded them. She could feel the cold of the stones. And the horses' hooves rang hollowly on the broken ground, the sound echoing from the high, enclosing hills.

She tamped down a shudder, hoping no one noticed.

Her ambers were quiet, the stones cool against her skin. But once or twice, she thought she'd caught flickers of heat pricking her throat.

Imagined or not, the stirrings unsettled her.

She'd been raised on fireside tales about the Mackintoshes' fierceness. How they descended from Norse Berserkers, wild and ferocious warriors who lived to fight and knew no fear, ever. They were men who served as Odin's own, falling gladly into battle frenzy and even biting their shields when such bloodlust overcame them. Some even said they could take on the shape of an animal. Or turn themselves invisible, raging as unseen wraiths through the dark of night simply for the joy of terrifying their enemies.

Catriona wasn't sure how much of that might be true. Or even if the Mackintoshes did have blood ties to the Berserkers. She did know that even today, there were folk who swore Kendrew Mackintosh ate the babies and children of anyone who earned his displeasure.

Now that she was here, riding toward that chief's own Castle Nought, she understood how the storytellers came to spin such frightening tales.

Mackintosh territory *was* harsh and barren.

It was a place for men who thrived in thin air and chill, black wind.

Hard men and—she was sure—women who were equally toughened. No one else could hope to dwell here. And she could have done without visiting.

But because of James's tidings—Alasdair had finally told her of their damaged galleys and the tall, dark-cloaked figure James had chased that fateful day in the wood—Alasdair wished to speak with Kendrew Mackintosh before they returned to Blackshore.

Now, as they neared the soaring cliffs that supported the formidable Mackintosh stronghold, it seemed they'd made the tedious journey in vain.

Castle Nought appeared deserted.

Catriona craned her neck, straining to see the lofty castle through the billowing mist. From what she could make out, it did seem unnaturally still. As she'd heard, the walls were surely impregnable, hewn as they were from the living rock of the cliff. They were also thick and massive and rose to a dizzying height of at least thirty-five feet. Crenelated parapets ran the length of the walling, and only the narrowest slit windows broke the starkness.

But no men could be seen pacing the wall-walk.

And no matter how hard Catriona tried to see a flicker of life, nary a single candle flame shone in any of the darkened windows.

High on the bluff, a gatehouse loomed through the mist, apparently reached by a steep path cut into the cliff-side. If there were torches to light the way, or even to illuminate the gatehouse, no one had bothered to set flame to them. Most startling of all, the guardhouse's single arched entry lacked a sentry.

Catriona clutched her reins, not liking the thick silence that soaked the air.

She glanced at Alasdair, hoping he couldn't tell that icy prickles were racing up and down her spine. "I told you we needn't have bothered to come here. Either Kendrew and his men are sleeping or"—she suspected this was the truth—"they don't want visitors."

"No Highlander turns away guests." Alasdair scanned the cliff face as spoke. "If they wish to ignore us, it'll be because of the three Mackintoshes we killed in that skirmish last summer."

"They were stealing our cattle." Catriona frowned at the dark stronghold. "They could've run when we caught them, but they chose to stand and fight."

"They're no' fighting now!" One of the guardsmen hooted, slapping his thigh.

"Hiding beneath their beds, more like," another called from the rear of the column.

"I say the bastards took flight." One of the men urged his garron forward, trotting up alongside Catriona and Alasdair. "They're no' the spawn o' Berserkers. They're women!" He spat on the ground and then twisted in his saddle to glance at the other guardsmen. "They feared clashing swords with us and the Camerons."

His comment earned a chorus of guffaws from his fellow men-at-arms.

Alasdair said nothing.

But Catriona saw the tense set of his shoulders. She also noticed that he'd placed a hand oh-so-casually on the hilt of his sword. Nor did she miss the swift, almost imperceptible nod he gave to three of his most trusted men, silently ordering them to ride closer, flanking her in a well-practiced defensive formation.

Two took their places on either side of her, with one

riding at the rear, while Alasdair spurred ahead of her so that she was completely surrounded.

She wished James rode with them.

Even if she'd bite his tongue if he ever tried to kiss her again or if she wouldn't mind feeding his man parts to the ravens, she'd feel better if he were here, his sword drawn and ready.

She knew he'd protect her.

Just as she was certain that he cared for her, maybe even loved her, though—damn his eyes—he was much too thrawn to admit it.

Someday she'd make him eat his stubbornness. At the moment, she only wished he were near.

"Ho, Alasdair!" Egan, the youngest guard, rode up beside them then, pressing close. "Mayhap the dreagans ate them? There do be tales and"—he threw a glance at the stronghold, his eyes wide—"the gatehouse door is open. Could be the slavering beasties—"

"There's no such thing as a dreagan, slavering or otherwise." Alasdair made a dismissive gesture. "But I can't tell if the door is open." He narrowed his eyes, peering through the mist. "Are you sure?"

"Sure as I'm here." Egan nodded, importantly. "My eyes are sharp, or so I've always been told. Thon door is full wide, opened clear on its hinges. If it isn't, I'm lying in my bed, dreaming."

Impatient with their blether, Catriona clicked her tongue, sending her horse bolting from the little circle of men. She rode a few lengths ahead, only far enough to get a better view of the gatehouse.

The guardsman spoke true.

The door did stand open.

"Alasdair!" She glanced back. "His eyes are good. The door is wide. I can see it from here."

"God's curse!" Alasdair spurred forward to join her, his men following. "This cannae be good." He peered up at the gatehouse, concern all over him. "It bodes ill. For sure, no dreagan crawled up there to fill his belly with Mackintoshes. But"—his voice hardened—"it could be the work of the cloaked craven James and I discussed. He'll have henchmen helping him, that's certain.

"And that leaves us no choice but to climb up there and see what's amiss." He pulled a hand down over his chin, drew a long breath. "Could be the Mackintoshes have taken themselves elsewhere, but if they haven't..."

"You suspect they're up there bound, maimed, or worse." Catriona knew his mind. "And your honor would be forever tarnished if you hadn't gone to their rescue."

Alasdair's frown proved she'd guessed rightly. "That is the way of it."

His men grumbled and exchanged glances. But no one argued the need to have a look. Catriona wasn't surprised. Honor was everything to a MacDonald, and theirs would be stained if they rode from Castle Nought without seeing to the rights of the place.

Even she agreed, however grudgingly.

Castle Nought didn't please her.

But men—even if foes—could've suffered grievously up there behind the stronghold's cold, forbidding rock face and gloom.

Women, too, she knew.

Kendrew had a sister close to her age. Lady Marjory, Catriona recalled. A great beauty, it was said, but whose icy blue eyes could freeze a man at a hundred paces.

She was rumored so daunting that she'd earned the by-name Lady Norn after the three mythic Norse maidens, the Norns, who the Northmen believed ruled the destinies of men.

A curse and a loud *thump* returned Catriona to the present. She blinked to see they'd reached the base of Castle Nought's cliffs.

One of their men had already dismounted and stood near the stone-cut path up to Castle Nought. His face was flushed red and he was rubbing his backside. He'd clearly taken a tumble down the slippery, near vertical stair.

"Have a care on those steps!" Alasdair swung down from his own saddle, allowing the man his dignity. But he bent a warning glance on the others. "If aught is amiss at Nought, we'll need every hand.

"You, Catriona, will bide here." He turned her way, one foot already on the path's first step. "Egan will stay with you. And two others, as well. After we've had a look—"

"MacDonald—I greet you!" A booming laugh came from above them, where flaming torches now turned the mist red and a huge bear of a man almost filled the open door of the gatehouse. "If you've come to spill more Mackintosh blood, you'll be disappointed." Kendrew Mackintosh grinned, his teeth flashing white in the torchlight. "'Tis your own guts that'll slither to the ground this time, that I say you."

He strode to the top edge of the steps, clearly enjoying himself. Wind caught his wild mane of red hair, tossing the unruly strands about his face. And the silver Thor's hammer pendant hung about his neck made him look like a crazed-eyed denizen of Valhalla.

"My sword dances sweeter than a Glasgow whore,

MacDonald." He patted the great brand at his hip. "She'll slice you in two before you can blink."

"You're a madman, Mackintosh." Alasdair glared up at him, furious. "We come in peace, from Castle Haven. James Cameron and I—"

"That stoat! I'll have his head, too." Kendrew's grin widened. "On a pike o'er my curtain wall. Or, better yet, stuck on my own bedpost."

"Plague take you." Alasdair's voice rose with anger. "'Tis to your bed you can return. Or whate'er dark hole you've been hiding in. I erred to think a man could reason with you. We'll leave you be. But know this"—he set a hand to his sword, jerking it halfway from its sheath— "we shall meet again soon and—"

"I say we're meeting now." Kendrew whipped out his own sword and tossed it high in the air, laughing as the blade flipped brightly. "And you, MacDonald"—he caught the sword by its hilt as it fell—"are going nowhere this day, save taking a journey to hell!"

In the shadow of the cliff, Catriona's heart pounded fiercely.

Were she a man, she'd draw her own steel and charge up the stone steps, running the bastard through before he could loose another of his horrible bray-like laughs.

She shot a glance at Alasdair, the white around his lips and the hot glint in his eyes showing he burned to do the same. But he'd restrain himself because of her presence, a truth that galled her.

It was then that her necklace began to hum and burn.

"Alastair, my ambers—" She started to yell, but sudden shouts behind them made her twist around in her saddle. Men were running toward them, their war cries and the thunder of their pounding feet echoing from the hills as they streamed out from behind the odd rock formations and raced like wild-eyed demons through the rolling mist.

Mackintoshes, each man heavily armed, bristling with swords, axes, and spears. They bore no shields, as if they felt secure in their victory. And some—Catriona stared— had blackened their faces and slung terrifying-looking wolf pelts over their plaids.

"Bastards!" She leapt from her horse and ran to Alasdair, seizing his arm. "They've laid a trap for us!"

But he'd already seen. "So they have, but they'll no' have us without a fight."

Scowling fiercely, he grabbed her, dragging her round behind him as he whipped out his sword. The others acted as quickly, forming a wall of shields and horseflesh around her. All she heard was the screech of steel as they, too, jerked their blades from their scabbards.

Then, from behind and above her came an equally terrifying sound.

It was an inhuman bellow, followed at once by Kendrew Mackintosh's pounding footsteps as he charged down the steep stone stair.

Chapter Thirteen

❧

Hell everlasting, MacDonald!" Kendrew Mackintosh stood in the middle of his colorful, mead-reeking great hall and bellowed like a steer. "Have you lost your wits, man? Coming here with a woman? Your sister, no less! So easy"—he thrust a hand in the air, clenching his fist, swiftly—"and we could've snuffed out her life!"

"You would've lost your own, trying." Alasdair spoke hotly, his face dark.

"Ho!" Kendrew's deep voice shook the rafters. "Your blade couldn't find me if I were tied to a chair!"

Alasdair snorted. "A blind beggar could find you, loud and clumsy as you are."

"Nae, 'tis deadly I am." Kendrew drew himself up to his full, imposing height. "And just seeing you beneath my roof is making me itch to redden my sword."

"I've no' qualms to spill blood in your hall." Alasdair's words were harsh. "Mackintosh blood, no' my own!"

At his side, his men growled their agreement. They

also placed demonstrative hands to their sword hilts. One produced a wicked-looking, well-honed dirk and used its tip to clean his fingernails.

Kendrew raked them with a glare, his eyes glittering dangerously. Then he glanced at the man nearest him, one of his own warriors, a tall man nearly as burly and broad in the chest as himself. "Did you hear, Gare?" He thumped the man's shoulder, his gaze snapping back to Alasdair. "Beware, MacDonald, for we'll stuff your blades down your throats before you see a drop of our blood.

"Then"—he clasped his sword pommel, grinning now—"we'll dance on your corpses before we take our supper! Try and draw your steel and I'll prove it."

Catriona stood near one of the hall's narrow slit windows, watching. She almost expected Kendrew to turn into a bear any moment. There were tales said that he could. Stories that claimed the Berserker rage ran deep in his veins, slumbering and waiting to be roused. Those who believed in such things whispered that he most often became a bear when he was in a black temper.

She could well imagine it, big and fearsome as he was. Especially having seen him storm down the cliff stair, roaring like an enraged beast as he'd ordered his men to hold their steel. He'd taken the steps three at a time, his tangled red hair flying in the wind and his face wild-eyed and livid with rage.

He'd quite terrified her, though she'd sooner stick a needle in her eye than admit it.

She did feel her face coloring, the heated words making her pulse quicken. She also pretended to smooth her skirts, in truth seeking and resting her hand against the hilt of her lady's dagger.

Its hard shape against her thigh reassured her.

She might be a woman, but if a fight did erupt between her brother and Kendrew, she'd not stand by weeping. In a tightly packed hall, full of men and rows of long tables and benches, a short blade such as hers was handier than a man's great sword. She knew how to fight. And she wasn't squeamish. If she must, she'd seize her dagger and jump into the fray, stabbing and thrusting and doing whatever damage she could until someone stopped her.

Indeed, she burned to do so.

"You needn't prove aught, Mackintosh," Alasdair snarled then. "Your actions this day, ambushing good folk who came here in peace, speaks clear enough."

"I had reason." Kendrew's face set mulishly. "If you're getting forgetful, think back to last summer. We agreed that quarrel was over, vengeance served and accepted. Then you—"

"It was over." A muscle twitched in Alasdair's jaw, anger pouring off him. "I sent men with my condolences and, by God, I meant it!"

Kendrew laughed, coldly. "To be sure, you did. So much that you sneak onto my land, trying to kill me unawares. Think you—"

"I think only that you're crazed."

"That may be! Many say so. But you're overlooking one thing—"

Kendrew broke off to grab a horn of honey-mead from a passing squire. He tossed down the frothy brew in one long, guzzling swig.

"Mackintoshes dinnae make war on women." He thrust the silver-rimmed horn back into the lad's hand, flashing an outraged glance at Catriona. "We bed 'em, we do. We please and satisfy those who catch our eye, making them beg for our loving. And we honor the ones who give us life, and we protect the wee ones borne of our wives.

"Ne'er do we draw steel on them." He took a menacing step toward Alasdair. "I could split you for bringing thon lady here." He shot another look at Catriona, his blue eyes blazing like ice shards. "Had I no' seen her run to you, and called off my men, they'd have been all o'er the lot o' you in less than a beat."

"And did they no' see her before?" Alasdair seethed with equal fury. "It took us long enough to pick our way across your stony ground."

"Mackintosh land where your ilk isn't welcome." Turning his back on Alasdair, Kendrew elbowed his way through his sullen-eyed, black-faced men and went to stand by his hearth fire. Double-arched and massive, the fireplace could've roasted two oxen. Just now, huge logs blazed on the grates, the flames giving a hellish cast to the round, brightly painted shields adorning the wall above.

The shields, and an impressive array of weaponry, ran the length of that side of the hall. Boldly colored hangings and animal skins covered the other three walls, giving the vast chamber a masculine air. But the floor rushes were spread thick, clean, and had been recently freshened with meadowsweet. Catriona nudged the well-kept flooring with her toe, releasing a waft of springlike scent.

She also noted the polished sheen of the silver candelabrums set on the long tables. Each candle appeared to be of fine beeswax rather than inferior tallow. These were small but pleasing touches that, like the freshening herbs, indicated a woman's careful householding.

Curious, she edged away from Alasdair and their

guardsmen. They were sticking so close to her, she couldn't breathe. Her ambers had cooled, so she no longer felt threatened. And if she had to find herself at Castle Nought—however unpleasant the circumstances—she did hope to catch a glimpse of the famed Lady Norn.

But Marjory Mackintosh was nowhere to be seen.

Glowering men, MacDonald and Mackintosh, filled the smoky hall, their angry words beginning to make her head ache.

"That was no answer, Mackintosh." Alasdair was striding across the hall now, making for Kendrew. "I already know we're no' welcome. I'd hear why your men can't tell a wench with streaming, flame-bright braids and a bosom from a score of plaid-draped, ugly-faced men."

He reached the other chieftain, going toe to toe with him, crowding Kendrew against the shield-covered wall. "I'll have your explanation, or I'll be standing here till the end of all days, and so will you."

"Then who will lead your men onto King Robert's field of foolery?" a husky female voice queried from the door arch. "You'd both be here, gathering dust and doing no good, while your champions face trials no warrior should suffer without knowing his chief fights at the front of the affray."

"There speaks the bane of my life!" Kendrew's shout could've raised the dead, but admiration kindled in his eyes as he pushed past Alasdair to confront the young woman on the threshold. "MacDonalds—behold my fair and most wise sister, Lady Marjory!"

Catriona stared at Marjory Mackintosh, seeing at once why she was called Lady Norn.

Tall and generously made, Marjory had sparkling blue

eyes and a welter of curling red-gold hair every bit as wild as her brother's. Hair nothing like Catriona's own garnet-colored tresses, but sun-flashed curls with only a hint of red and shining with all the golden-blond brightness of a Nordic summer sun.

She wore a colorful gown in rich blue and gold tones, the bodice cut low and laced to highlight every ripe curve of her shapely body.

She could be a Viking goddess.

And—Catriona could scarce believe it—without even setting a foot in the hall, Marjory achieved what no other female had ever done: she'd rendered Alasdair speechless.

His face was still flushed with anger, but he'd un-clenched his fists and his eyes had gone just as wide as Catriona's. The look in them as he stared across the hall at Marjory would've made her laugh if they weren't all caught up in such a grim tangle.

But Alasdair recovered swiftly, crossing the hall to make Kendrew's sister a gallant bow. "Lady Marjory." He took her hand, kissing the air above her knuckles. "I am honored. Though"—he shot a dark look at Kendrew, who was grinning—"it grieves me to meet you under such circumstances."

"They are regrettable, I agree." Lady Marjory's blue eyes flashed, her hair glowing like sunfire in the torch-light.

Catriona almost choked. She couldn't guess the other woman's mind. But she knew it didn't pain Alasdair at all to meet Lady Norn.

He'd almost stumbled over his own feet hastening to bend his knee to her. Catriona squelched the urge to make a tart comment when he signaled for her to join him.

It wasn't easy.

But Marjory Mackintosh had warm, laughing eyes. And from the statement she'd made at the door, she also possessed spirit and wit, which were things Catriona admired.

"This is my sister." Alasdair turned to her when she stepped up to them. "Lady Catriona of Blackshore. She's with me because we'd been at Castle Haven earlier. There wasn't time to ride south to Blackshore and then hasten north again to Nought, so we made the journey directly. I had tidings to share with your brother."

Beside them, Kendrew snorted. "So you say."

His sister lifted a pale gold brow. "Do you have reason to doubt him?"

Kendrew glared at her. "Does a herring swim in the sea?"

"True enough." Lady Marjory shoved a sheaf of tumbled curls over her shoulder. "But sometimes they also land in hot, sizzling cooking fat and swim in the dark of a man's belly."

"See what I must listen to, every day o' my life?" Kendrew turned again to Alasdair. "I will sell her to you for the weight of a good barrel of ale in silver. If you think you could stomach her."

Marjory didn't look offended. "All you've done"—she fixed her blue gaze on her brother—"was demonstrate what I must tolerate, living with you."

Ignoring Kendrew's grumblings, she reached for Catriona's hand, her grip strong and firm. "Lady Catriona." Her voice was low-pitched and smooth, friendly. "I am sorry for how you were treated on arriving here. Perhaps I can make amends for my kinsmen's error—"

"We didn't err." Kendrew shot Alasdair a heated look.

"Thon bastard and his men should be fodder for carrion by now. They would be, no mistakes made, if he hadn't brought along his sister's skirts to hide behind."

"Have a care, Mackintosh." Alasdair took a step toward him, threatening. "I'll no' draw my sword in front of your sister, but if you dinnae cease insulting me, I'll gut you first chance I get. The fish in Loch Moidart can gorge on your flesh, and I'll order my squires to make rope out of your dried innards."

Catriona stifled a lip-twitch. Alasdair was so noble he gave any fallen foe a hero's burial, often tending the grisly task himself in honor of the dead warrior's bravery.

As if she suspected the same, Lady Norn watched him with interest.

Unaware, Alasdair balled his fists, his hot gaze on Kendrew. "That's only half of it. We'll use your ground bones to nourish our crops. And if there's anything left, we'll feed the remains to the crows."

"Hah!" Kendrew cut the air with a hand. "If you swing your blade as poorly as you shoot arrows, I won't be for fearing you overmuch."

"Arrows?" Alasdair glanced at his men. Then he looked back to Kendrew, frowning. "I ne'er shot an arrow at you. Nor did any of my men, that I vow."

"I say you did—or one o' your minions, whatever." Kendrew's eyes narrowed. "Who else would want me dead? Deny it all you will, your lies change naught." Striding to an aumbrey set deep in the wall near the hearth, he opened the cupboard's door and withdrew his evidence.

"Here it be!" Returning to Alasdair, he held out the arrow. A simple goose-feathered shaft tipped with a sharp steel head. *"This"*—he shook the thing beneath Alasdair's nose—"came whizzing past my ear when I stepped from the gate three days ago. Good for me, it thwacked into the curtain wall and no' into my skull.

"If your aim hadn't been two feet off"—he slapped the arrow onto a table and spread his hands, indicating the distance of the miss—"I'd no' be standing here tolerating your foul presence in my hall."

"I'm a man of the sword, no' a bow picker." Alasdair made a derisive sound. "But had I aimed an arrow at you, rest assured I wouldn't have missed. You have other enemies. Look to them, no' me."

Kendrew glared at him. "I did think of Cameron, that hound-lover, but"—he tossed his head, sending his wild red mane swinging about his face—"you're the one to come sneaking onto my land, no' James Cameron. So when my spies reported that you were riding through the mist, heading to Nought, I figured you were coming, with men, to finish the job you botched three days ago."

"Three days ago I was with Cameron." Alasdair went to examine the arrow, turning it in his hands. "There are no identifying marks. Whoe'er shot this"—he returned the arrow to the table—"went to pains to use an arrow that wouldn't reveal its owner."

Kendrew's face turned red. "Think you I'm a daftie? I know why the shaft doesn't show an ownership mark."

"And now you also know it wasn't me or James Cameron. We were together at Castle Haven. My sister"—Alasdair glanced at Catriona—"and my men will swear we were there for nearly a sennight. Cameron will tell you the same if e'er you ask him."

"Why should I believe either of you?" Kendrew started to pace, then wheeled around. "Come to think of it, what were you doing at Castle Haven? Or"—he thrust his red-bearded chin—"are the two o' you throwing your lots together to oust me from the glen?"

"I'm my own man." Alasdair didn't flinch. "But Cameron and I are of a mind about certain matters. That's why I came here. And now"—he glanced at his men—"hearing that someone tried to kill you—"

"Someone who shot his arrow from hiding and then rode off before anyone could see him. I heard his horse's hooves racing away, fast as night." Kendrew spat on the floor rushes, earning a sharp look from Lady Norn.

"Kendrew..." She went over to him, slipping her hand through his arm. "I've ordered a repast, victuals and good mead to soothe the wrong you've done—"

"I've done no wrong! Or have you been sticking your fingers in your ears as well as interfering in affairs that are none of your concern?" He jerked away from her just as a line of kitchen laddies marched into the hall bearing platters of ripe green cheese, freshly baked bread, smoked herring, and huge trays of steaming beef ribs.

"Thor's jumping hammer!" Kendrew's face turned purple.

"Nae." His sister angled her chin reprovingly. "Hospitality for guests as is custom in these hills, or have you forgotten?"

"Then I say we give them thon bandaging." Kendrew stalked to a table piled high with folded linens. "That will suit as courtesy. And save us the trouble of carrying them to the trial by combat."

"Kendrew!" Marjory hastened after him. "Now isn't the time to speak of such things. Not after what could've happened at the cliff stair."

"Humph." Kendrew set his mouth in a hard line.

"We do not need your wound linens." Alasdair looked from Kendrew to the folded cloths and back again to his foe. "We have enough—"

"Hah! You misheard me, you did." Kendrew barked a short, harsh laugh. Then he gave Alasdair the kind of look he might have worn if he'd just thrown open the gates to Niflheim, the Norsemen's frozen underworld realm of cold mist and unending darkness.

Viking hell.

His eyes still glinting, Kendrew folded his powerful arms. "The bandaging isn't for my warriors. We shall win the battle and leave the field unscathed. My sister and her women made the linens for *you*!

"A token courtesy we meant to deliver to you and Cameron on the day." He thrust his chin arrogantly. "That's my hospitality to you, no' my good victuals and mead."

"You're a snake." Alasdair clenched his fists, advancing on him.

Marjory stepped between them, flashing a furious glance at her brother, then touching Alasdair's arm. "He is riled. You can't know how much he reviles the mistreating of women. What happened at the stair has shamed him. That's why—"

"Hold your tongue." Kendrew pulled her away from Alasdair. "I'm angry, no' shamed," he roared, his deep voice rolling through the hall like trapped thunder.

Ignoring him, Marjory turned back to Alasdair. Her glance also flicked to Catriona and the MacDonald guardsmen. "When I learned what happened, I ordered rooms prepared for you. So you can recover and refresh yourselves before you leave in the morning. Besides." She cast a challenging look at Kendrew, as if she expected him to argue. "It isn't wise to ride through the dreagan rocks at night. Even we do not."

"Say you. I dance naked on top of the dreagan rocks when the mood takes me. Be it night or day." Kendrew stomped away, muttering into his beard.

Marjory glanced down the hall to where the kitchen boys were placing the food platters on the high table and then sailed after her brother. "Wait, you!" She caught up to him near the hearth, seizing the back of his plaid so he had no choice but to whip around. "It is enough." Her voice held the same thunder as Kendrew's, but her fury was controlled.

"Now"—she released her grip on him and stood back, hands on her hips—"lest good meat is refused, perhaps you'll finally tell the Lord of Blackshore why our men failed to see his sister in their party?"

"Dinnae goad me." Kendrew's angry blue gaze met her icy one. "I speak when it pleases me."

"If you do not tell them, I will." Marjory sent a look, a much warmer one, to Catriona. "At least let Lady Catriona know you've dealt with the scout who first spied their entourage. He is the one responsible."

Kendrew tipped back his head and blew out a breath before turning to Catriona. "I've punished the watchman. My sister speaks true. He should've seen you. The man swears the mist was too thick and that he only knew MacDonalds were crossing onto our land.

"We keep a man posted on our boundaries, always." He touched the Thor's amulet at his neck, his fingers gripping the silver. "It was his duty to report to me what he saw, or thought he did. Even so, I've ordered him to spend three nights in my dungeon, with only slaked oats and water, to ensure he looks closer next time."

"I hope he will." Catriona nodded, relieved.

She'd half expected him to say he'd have the poor man for his breakfast.

Alasdair wasn't as easily appeased. "What of them?" He jerked his head at the sullen-faced men gathered near two of the hall's narrow slit windows. They stared back, their faces still smeared with peat and their shoulders yet covered with wolf hides.

"They cannae be blamed." Kendrew bent a belligerent eye on Alasdair. "Odin's rage was upon them. Once they'd blackened their faces and donned the wolf skins, the battle frenzy blinded them to anything but their blood-lust. And"—he took a deep breath, as if any explanation burned like bile in his throat—"they had orders to stay hidden behind the dreagan stones until they heard you ride past and knew you'd have enough time to reach the cliff stair, where—"

"You meant to trap and slaughter us." Alasdair looked at him.

Kendrew glared back. "Would you have done otherwise?"

"No' if I thought you'd tried to kill me and were returning to finish a botched attempt on my life." Alasdair's voice was hard. "But I would've first made certain my suspicions held water, that you can be sure."

Kendrew flushed. "I only have two enemies. You and Cameron. No one else would dare to challenge me."

Alasdair lifted a hand, studying his knuckles. "Could be we all have an unknown foe? That"—he looked up sharply, fixing Kendrew with a stare—"is why I came here. To find out if you or anyone else at Nought has seen a tall, dark-cloaked man skulking about in shadow. James Cameron and I have seen such a dastard."

Casting a glance at his men, Alasdair arched a questioning brow. "Are you agreed we share what we know?"

When they nodded, he told Kendrew everything. He began with James's account of the figure he'd chased through the wood and ended with his own tale of the damaged galleys at Blackshore, leaving out no detail save Catriona's ploy with Birkie.

He also mentioned the suspicion that Sir Walter was somehow involved.

When he finished, the hall was silent.

Catriona and Marjory exchanged looks. The other woman had come to stand with her as Alasdair told his tale. Catriona couldn't help but notice that her scent was as vibrant as her looks. It was a seductive dusky rose, with a trace of something exotic Catriona couldn't place. Whatever it was, the result was pleasing. Perhaps later— unless Alasdair declined her offer of hospitality for the night—she'd ask her about the scent's ingredients.

Just now it was more interesting watching her listen to Alasdair. Marjory hadn't taken her gaze off him since he'd started speaking. She had a fiercely intent look on her face that was just as telling as Alasdair's charge across the hall to make her a gallant bow.

He hadn't bent his knee half that low to Isobel.

Catriona pushed the thought of James's sister from her mind. Thinking of Isobel or Castle Haven would remind her of James. And she needed her wits. Nothing would scatter them faster than remembering how she'd lain in his arms as if they'd been made for each other, despite their names.

And regardless of how rudely he'd jumped away from her.

She'd felt his passion.

Even now she could feel his mouth slanting over hers, kissing her fiercely. Or the incredible thrill that had ripped through her when she'd opened her lips to him and his tongue swept against her own. His hands smoothing over her, everywhere, then holding her fast against him. The surging pleasure when he'd slid into her—

"Lady Catriona…"

She started, blinking to find Marjory peering at her.

"I knew your brother would have a good reason for coming here." Marjory leaned close, her voice low. "He doesn't seem a rash man, not like Kendrew, who often lets his sword speak before he listens."

"Alasdair felt it was important to speak with your brother." Catriona ignored Marjory's other comment. She could've sung about Alasdair's hotheadedness. But seeing Marjory's face brighten when she spoke of him made it impossible not to hold her tongue.

She liked Lady Norn.

And she didn't want to disillusion her. Nor would she speak ill of Alasdair in front of a feuding clan.

MacDonald pride was strong, and she wasn't about to besmirch it.

But she would tease Alasdair mercilessly later. He could never again scold her for her attraction to James after he'd stood in the hall at Nought making moony eyes at his enemy's sister.

Just now he was looking at Kendrew, waiting. "Well?

I'm thinking your arrow-shooter may have been the dark-cloaked figure. Have you seen such a man?"

Kendrew drew a long breath and released it slowly. "Nae, I haven't done."

Alasdair nodded. "What of your men?"

"They would have told me." Kendrew shook his head. "They are loyal, true as stone."

But he glanced at them now. His warriors who stood so grimly over near the window slits. Sleety rain had just started to strike the windows' narrow stone ledges, and a cold, damp draught lifted the men's hair and beards, the fur of their wolf pelts.

One still had his huge battle ax slung over his shoulder. Several had kept their long swords, but they'd set aside their spears.

They all had glowering, hard-set faces.

Kendrew glared back at them, seeming a man who enjoyed scowling.

"You heard." He watched his men closely. "Any of you seen such a man? Note anything amiss? Besides"—his voice took on a sour note—"a party of MacDonalds?"

"Nothing, lord." The man with the war ax spoke for the group.

"Well, then." Kendrew's gaze met Alasdair's. "If such a man exists, and I am still no' convinced, perhaps we can all keep an eye out for him when we march to King Robert's fighting ground?

"If he's seen"—he drew a finger across his throat, grinning—"we put him out of his misery."

"I'm no' sure it'll be so easy." Alasdair frowned. "If he is Sir Walter, the King's man—"

Kendrew roared. "All the more reason!"

His warriors broke into a chorus of agreement, thumping balled fists on tables and rattling swords.

When Alasdair's men joined in, Marjory clapped her hands. "Come, let us take our meat." She raised her voice above the ruckus. "I'll not see the dogs snatching food from the tables while men work themselves into a frenzy that will bring no good to us."

Then she lifted her skirts and started forward, letting the others follow her to the raised dais and high table at the far end of the hall.

Catriona lingered behind, going instead to the nearest of the oh-so-narrowly cut window slits. She'd felt a need to stare out over the stony ground they'd ridden across—the dreagan rocks—and rid herself of the terrible prickles crawling up and down her back ever since the men spoke of Sir Walter and the hall had gone wild.

She'd hoped seeing the weird outcroppings without a band of screaming, black-faced warriors running and leaping through the stones would banish her chills.

The rocks were just that, after all, rocks.

And peat smeared on a face and a wolf skin thrown over shoulders didn't make a man a beast.

A Berserker, as Kendrew and his men seemed to believe.

But the view from the arrow slit proved disappointing. The day had turned dark. And she could only see cold mist, even thicker now, and the silvery sheen of ice rain, pelting the stronghold's walls.

Castle Nought *was* a forbidding place.

But not near as daunting a place as her heart had become.

Or as traitorous, for—God help her—each time she'd heard her brother or Kendrew mention Sir Walter's name and the coming carnage, it hadn't been Alasdair's face that had leapt into her mind.

Oh, she'd thought of him, to be sure. And every other MacDonald champion who would stride onto that field, ready to kill or be killed.

But her first thought was of James.

Imaging what could happen to him was worse than if a great iron fist burst into her chest, squeezing her heart until the world turned black and she couldn't breathe.

So she stared out Nought's ridiculous sliver of a window, seeing nothing and biting down on her lip, hard until she tasted blood.

Truth was...

If James fell, she didn't think she could bear it.

Much later, in the smallest hours of the night when Catriona slept comfortably in a chamber readied by Lady Norn's own hand, another maid of the glen found no rest at all. Even though, as many would point out, she'd been *at peace* for more centuries than she cared to remember.

Not that Scandia considered her ghostly existence tranquil.

And though she could have joined Catriona in her well-appointed guest quarters at Castle Nought, twinkling herself there in a blink, she preferred not to stray too far from Castle Haven.

It may have been long since she'd walked, rather than drifted, through her beloved home, but that didn't mean she felt any less attachment to the ancient stronghold.

She just regretted that the Camerons who came after her thought of her as a bringer of ill fortune.

The Doom of the Camerons.

In truth, she didn't feel like anyone's doom. She certainly never summoned the like. She simply took comfort in staying in the place she'd always loved so dearly. And she enjoyed being surrounded by the clan that shared her blood and still meant so much to her.

She was proud of each and every Cameron.

And although she'd met her own doom at Castle Haven, the tragedy hadn't changed her feelings about the place.

Even if she did do her best to avoid the Lady Tower, which wasn't named for any particular lady, but for the six window embrasures in its uppermost chamber. The alcoves were placed at intervals around the circular room and boasted unusually large windows, allowing splendid light throughout the day.

Ladies at Castle Haven favored the embrasure room to do their needlework.

The room also gave access to the battlements.

And that was the reason Scandia now hovered, shimmying agitatedly near the darkened entry to the Lady Tower's turnpike stair.

She didn't want to be reminded of a certain afternoon on the wall-walk.

A day that proved to be her last.

Her final *real* day, that was.

Her present existence didn't really qualify as such, although she did try to keep herself occupied, sometimes even enjoying herself.

It was pursuit of such diversions that brought her to the Lady Tower now. There'd been a terrified scream from one of the tower guest chambers. Cries, shouts, and much banging and bumping had followed the first ear-splitting howl, the noise sending James racing up the stair.

And, of course, Scandia floated after him.

She was grateful for any excitement, even if it meant entering the Lady Tower. But when James threw open the door of the room with the ruckus and burst inside, she hesitated to follow him. Instead, she stayed where she was, several paces from the door.

Now that she was so close, she recognized the yelling voice as Sir Walter's.

And he sounded very angry.

"I knew you Highlanders were naught but unwashed savages! Heathen barbarians! This is proof. Disgusting, vile—eeeeeie—" Sir Walter shrieked as a loud crashing noise came from inside the room.

"Sir, come down from the table." James's deep voice floated into the corridor, his words as calm as if he spoke to a child. "'Tis a fearing dream you're having, is all. A waking one that'll pass soon enough if you'll return to bed."

"Are you mad?" Sir Walter shrilled higher. "The bed is crawling with vermin! Rats! They're everywhere! I'm not getting down until you get rid of them."

Scandia floated to the doorway, peeking inside. She saw at once why the Lowland noble was so distressed.

The room was full of rats.

James stood in the midst of them, not seeming to see them. But Scandia felt her own eyes rounding as she stared into the room.

Huge rats scurried across the floor rushes, covered every inch of the bed, and were even climbing up the embroidered bed curtains. The wall tapestries were under similar siege. And even the sturdy table that now supported Sir Walter teemed with chittering, furry bodies.

Worst of all—to Scandia, anyway—Sir Walter was naked.

And he wasn't a comely man.

"Here"—James stepped closer to the table then, offering Sir Walter his hand—"let me help you down and—"

"Don't touch me!" Sir Walter jumped when one of the rats tried to scramble up his leg. "Just get the rodents out of here."

"There aren't any rats to remove." James grabbed Sir Walter's tunic from a chair and tossed it to him. "Get dressed and I'll take you to my chamber. You can sleep there, and I'll spend the rest of the night here."

Scandia blinked. She saw the rats, and plenty of them.

Puzzled, she knelt by the door and caught one as he raced past. The rat vanished in her hands, leaving a dusting of peat and other unidentifiable bits to trickle through her fingers to the floor.

She stared at her palms, understanding.

The rats were spelled.

And they'd clearly been sent to scare Sir Walter and no one else. That was why James couldn't see them. She had because, in her realm, she could see many such wonders. She also had a good idea who'd sent the scurrying creatures. But before she could wonder what Grizel was up to, Sir Walter gave another great shout.

"They're gone!" He'd pulled on his tunic and was glancing about, wild-eyed. "Where did they go?"

Scandia knew. She'd surely undone the charm by touching one of the rats.

But James only shrugged. "You were dreaming."

"I never dream. But"—Sir Walter sneered, his arrogance restored—"you'll soon wish I had been. I'm leaving here at first light. I'll not spend the remaining two days until the trial by combat in a rat-infested pile of stone. My men and I will take quarters in the King's tents. After I've had his ear, you'll regret—"

"What will you do?" James folded his arms, his calm making Scandia so proud. "Tell him you jumped onto a table for fear of rats that weren't there?"

"I will—" Sir Walter snapped his mouth shut, flushing deep red.

"Indeed." James grinned. Then he turned on his heel and strode from the room.

Scandia shimmered delightedly.

Then she drifted after him, eager to put the Lady Tower and its memories behind her.

Chapter Fourteen

✦

If ever you've helped me, do so now.

Catriona clutched her amber necklace, silently repeating the words as she stood at the edge of the battling field two days after returning home from Castle Nought. She'd scream her plea, shouting to God, the Auld Ones, and any others who might be listening, if only she didn't want anyone to see her dread.

MacDonalds were fearless, always.

And just now, every MacDonald in the glen pressed close to the wooden barricade separating them from the still-empty field on the other side of the barrier. Only early morning mist swirled there now, rippling threads of gray that slithered across the grass. But soon the vast open space would be slick with blood and covered with the bodies of dead and dying warriors. Yet not a single of her kinsmen showed a flicker of emotion except fierce pride.

Even Geordie, Alasdair's ancient dog, held his gray head high. He leaned into her, heavily, and she could feel the tremors that shook him now and then. His unblinking gaze was fixed on the field, as if he knew Alasdair would soon appear, taking his place in the battle line.

"Good lad." She reached down, curling her fingers into the rough fur at his shoulders. It worried her that he was there, but she welcomed the comfort he brought her. In earlier times, Geordie always accompanied Alasdair on warring forays, ever at his master's side. This morn, he'd joined the whole clan, trailing quietly after them, until one of her young cousins—a strapping lad, but too tender in years to fight—lifted the dog into his arms, carrying him the rest of the way.

"*Dia*, Geordie." The dog's devotion brought her close to doing what she never did, shedding tears. Instead, she drew a tight breath, willing calm. She moved her hand to Geordie's neck, stroking him gently, feeling the pulse of his terror and trying to soothe him. She prayed he wouldn't have to watch Alasdair die.

She blinked hard, hoping none of them would.

Hoped not a single MacDonald would fall.

She swallowed against the burning thickness in her throat, vowing that James would also leave the field whole. Not victorious, as she did want the MacDonalds to win. But she wished him alive and unharmed.

He couldn't die.

For now, she didn't want a single raven circling over him. She wanted only the chance to kiss him again. She refused to think of more. Doing so would steal her reason. Though if her wish was granted and he lived to kiss her, she might still bite his tongue.

She'd nip hard, if only to punish him for putting her through this agony.

She couldn't bear to see him slain.

And the waiting to find out if he would survive was killing her.

But already the eastern sky was beginning to lighten and the jostling crush of Lowland spectators was worsening by the moment. They were everywhere, pushing and shoving to reach the front of the barricades. The more privileged ones—the King's invited lofties—showed no more restraint, scrambling and crawling over each other as they fought for the best seats in the tiered viewing platforms.

Catriona raised her chin, glaring at them.

She might not allow herself to show fear, but she would show her contempt.

The Lowlanders' clamoring eagerness to see men die offended her.

As did the celebratory air that hung over the confusion, a chaos made worse by the hordes of roving hawkers, tumblers, and light-skirted women looking to turn a coin. The food and ale stalls from the tented encampment had been moved closer to the battling ground, each stand already doing a rousing trade even though the sun had barely crested the hills. Smoke from cooking pits drifted on the wind, stinging eyes and bringing the smell of whole roasted oxen. From somewhere came a waft of fresh-baked bread. And not far from where Catriona stood, a barrel of salt herring had burst open, spilling its reeking contents onto the ground.

She shuddered, wrinkling her nose. "A plague on the Lowlanders," she scolded, not caring who heard her. "They itch me worse than a thousand fleas."

"Here—drink this."

Catriona started. Maili stood at her side, offering her a beaker of *uisge beatha,* Highland water of life. The most-times cheerful laundress's usually saucy appearance was dimmed by her dark gray cloak and the angry jut of her chin, the fierce glint in her eye.

"I've had two gulps myself." Maili pressed the small wooden cup into Catriona's hand. "I'm thinking you'll not mind, not this morn."

"I wouldn't ever mind—you know that." Catriona took the whisky, gratefully draining the cup. "I just wish we could pour rivers of *uisge beatha* down the throats of the Lowlanders and then sink them into a bog as they slept. Though"—she wiped her mouth—"such an end would be too painless. I'd sooner see them skewered with an eel spear. Or gelded with a dull and rusted meat knife."

"Many of the men would have done it." Maili's eyes flashed as if she would've gladly helped. "Now it is too late. We can only hope our warriors' sword strength is great and that if fate is against them, their ends will be swift."

"I am hoping none will die." Catriona tossed aside the empty beaker and fisted her hands, willing it to be so. "I have heard the King is a fair man. He is also old." She paused, trying to recall his age. "I believe he is over fifty. And it is said that he is weak and ailing. Perhaps if our champions stand long enough, he will weary and call an end before too many men are cut down.

"Alasdair spent an hour on his knees in the chapel last night, praying. Then"—Catriona leaned close to her friend, lowering her voice—"he went up into the hills to ask the Auld Ones for their blessing, as well. He was gone until after midnight. I'm hoping he asked for a similar miracle and that the gods will grant us one."

"I wish it, too. But..." Maili tugged her cloak tighter against the wind. "Destiny is everything, my lady. If our men are to return to Blackshore with us, alive and hale, they shall. If it is their fate to do so."

Catriona glanced at the mist still rolling across the empty field. On the far side of the grass, Clan Cameron lined the barrier railing. The Mackintoshes were gathered not too far from them. Both clans already had a piper strutting up and down in front of their ranks.

Looking back at Maili, Catriona tried not to hear the challenging skirls of the other clans' pipes. Alasdair had vowed that no MacDonald pipes would scream until he and his men took the field.

"You think destiny has brought us here?" Catriona couldn't see the good of it, if so.

Maili shrugged. "I've always believed the like. That is why"—she glanced at her stubby-nailed, work-reddened fingers and then reached for one of Catriona's slender, smooth-white hands, lifting it in comparison—"I am a laundress and you are a great lady.

"We all walk the path the fates choose for us. But"—she released Catriona's hand—"we can decide how we travel that path. Either we make the journey with our head high, content and accepting. Or we are ever resentful and unhappy."

"Pshaw!" Catriona frowned.

Inside, she also believed destinies were writ long before a first breath was drawn. Just now, she didn't care for the notion.

She wanted to swim among the ice floes with James.

If fate meant to keep them from plunging into those cold, dark waters again, she needed to do some destiny-weaving of her own.

It was a reason she kept reaching for her ambers.

"Even if what you say is so"—she looked at Maili—"there's also Highland magic. Alasdair will be carrying his heirloom sword onto the field. Its amber pommel stone comes from the same treasure stash as the ambers of my necklace." She touched them again now, wondering at their coolness, hoping the stones' calm was a good portent. "The blade is charmed and will protect him."

Maili didn't look so sure. "The sword didn't save his grandfather when he was cut down wielding it."

Catriona tightened her lips. She'd forgotten that her grandsire had been killed in an affray with Mackintoshes, the amber-headed sword in his hand.

"The sword was good to my father." She felt better, remembering her father's affection for the sword called Mist-Chaser, so named because it was believed that even the mist drew back in respect when the sword's master swung the glittering blade.

"Your father's destiny was to die of a fever in his bed." Maili's voice was matter-of-fact. "You can't say the sword had anything to do with his death."

"I didn't." Catriona blew a curl off her forehead. Her friend was beginning to annoy her. "I said Mist-Chaser was good to him. And she was—"

A loud flourish of trumpets sounded, cutting her off as a great stir rose at the far end of the battling ground. Everywhere men fell to their knees, some even prostrating themselves on the cold, trampled grass. All cheered, the noise deafening as the trumpet blasts grew louder. Then a herald's voice rose above the din, commanding silence and obeisance as he announced the arrival of King Robert III and his son, Earl David, prince of the realm.

"All here, bow down before Robert, High King of Scots, by God's good grace, and his valiant and noble son, David, Earl of Carrick and High Steward of Scotland!"

There followed a lengthy rendering of praise as the King entered the field, Queen Annabella at his side, their son David with them. A train of richly dressed courtiers followed in their wake, each one more glittering than the other. Sir Walter strode in their midst, his nose higher than most. But the array made slow progress across the tourney ground, for the King was lame and walked with difficulty. Even so, he held himself with as much dignity as his frail body allowed. And although his face showed strain and weariness, he didn't look unkind.

Catriona stared. King Robert Stewart, great-grandson of Scotland's hero king Robert Bruce, wasn't anything like she'd expected, even having heard of his infirmities and melancholy disposition.

"He looks more like a priest than a king." She edged closer to Maili, whispering in her ear. "Stoop-backed and with all that white hair, the white beard—"

"But see his son." Maili was looking at Earl David, her gaze speculative.

Fair-haired and with remarkably beautiful eyes, the young prince walked proudly alongside his parents. Tall, slender, and as straight as his father was bent, he looked just as Catriona had always imagined the princes in the romantic chansons sung by minstrels.

He also looked so out of place against the backdrop of the Glen of Many Legends' wild and rugged hills that Catriona almost felt as if she were trapped in a dream.

That she might waken in her bed at Blackshore any moment and find the last few weeks hadn't happened.

That she'd dreamed everything.

She started to say so, but the trumpets gave another fanfare, signaling that the King's entourage was nearing the canopied royal loge. A brightly painted pavilion-like structure topped with streaming banners, most notably the King's own Lion Rampant of Scotland, red and gold against the dark morning sky. And his son's red-and-white standard of the earldom of Carrick. Other banners flew there, too, each one snapping in the wind, the colors brilliant.

The royal viewing platform held two tall, heavily carved thrones, meant for the King and Queen. Velvet-draped courtiers' benches flanked the high-backed, gold-enameled chairs. Earl David, it was known, would stand as he would umpire the trial of combat.

And seeing him and his royal parents now reach their loge set the earth to tilting beneath Catriona's feet. Because, she knew, as soon as the King and his party took their seats, the battle would begin.

At the prince's signal, horns would blast, summoning the three groups of champions. To the skirl of pipes, the warriors would march onto the field, each clan group shouting their war cries, beating weapons on their shields, and then drawing their steel, preparing to kill or die.

Again, James's face rose in her mind and she saw his dark eyes looking into hers, reaching deep inside her, ripping her soul bare so that the truth burned across her heart. If he fell, she'd never be the same.

For sure, she'd never let another man touch her.

How could she? Now that he'd ruined her for all others?

She lifted her chin, her pulse beating hard in her throat.

He'd surely run her mad. How else could she stand here, on such a day, thinking of him, when her mind should be on her fighting kinsmen and no one else?

Truth was, she could hardly breathe for worry what might happen to him now.

Any moment...

Maili grabbed Catriona's hand then, gripping hard. "They're sitting, look." Her voice was urgent, her gaze on the royal loge where King Robert and his queen claimed their golden chairs. Earl David and a gray-bearded, impressively tabarded man moved to the front of the platform. "That must be the King's senior herald."

"The Lyon King of Arms," Catriona agreed, watching Earl David incline his head to the man, signaling the herald to open the trial by arms.

At the prince's nod, the crowd hushed. Men stood on toes, heads craning to see the herald turn and make a deep bow to the King. When he straightened, trumpets blasted long and triumphantly until the Lyon King of Arms raised a hand, silencing the fanfare.

"The time is come." Catriona drew herself up straighter, lacing her fingers tight with her friend's. She lifted her other hand to touch her ambers, silently asking them to protect James, too. Then she released the stones and reached down to slip her hand around Geordie's neck, drawing the trembling dog closer against her. "I'm here, laddie. And Alasdair will be with you again soon. He'll be feeding you meat ribs before the sun sets this e'en."

Geordie glanced up at her, his rheumy eyes rimmed white.

She rubbed his ears when he returned his attention to the field. If the gods were Highlanders—she figured they could be, for no greater race lived—then she hadn't just lied to her brother's dog.

From the royal loge, the herald's voice rang loud. "All men, by the King's good grace and command, I inform you that a trial by arms between the Clans Donald, Cameron, and Mackintosh shall now commence. This contest of strength will resolve the long years of dispute and unrest amongst these clans, settling at last, and to the King's most fervent wishes, the troubling claims to possession of the Glen of Many Legends.

"Thirty champions from each of the three clans of the glen must face each other." He paused, lifting a hand when cheers rolled through the crowd. "These men shall fight with swords, dirks, and axes. A bow with three arrows per man is also granted. They may bear no shield larger than a targe, and no quarter may be given."

Beside Catriona, Geordie whined, startling her, as the old dog had rarely made a sound in years. She looked down at him, kneading his bony shoulders as he pressed harder into her legs. He was quiet again—she might have mistaken the wind for his whimper—but he trembled badly, as if he understood the herald's grim words.

"This is a combat to the death." The Lyon's voice swelled, exultant as he continued to shout the contest's rules. "The clan with the most men left standing will be pronounced as victors, unless"—he drew a long breath—"two of the clans cede defeat before the fighting has ended, thus forfeiting their claim to the glen.

"If any man, of any one of the three clan groups, leaves the field before the fighting has ended, all three clans shall be stripped of their land, titles, and rights. They shall be sent by the King's ships to the Isle of Lewis"—he raised his voice above the outcry from the clans—"where they will take up swords against the natives there, quelling the unrest and rebellion that trouble the King so sorely. If they are successful, they will be granted new lands and titles on Lewis, never to return to mainland Scotland."

"They can't do that." Maili's voice was an angry hiss.

"You know they can." Catriona didn't take her gaze off the herald. "But they won't have the chance." Pride swept her, heating her skin despite the cold wind. "No Highlander runs from a fight."

"If the King's rules and terms are not broken"—the Lyon looked out over the tourney ground, his voice booming—"the winning clan will hold sway over these lands from this day onward, the two defeated clans accepting their possession and authority without quarrel."

The words spoken, the herald turned to Earl David, who nodded to a solemn-faced guard standing at the edge of the canopied loge. This man bowed low to the King and then swept back a curtain, allowing Alasdair, James, and Kendrew to stride out before the platform.

Catriona's breath caught when James looked toward the MacDonalds at the railing, his gaze finding her at once, his dark eyes blazing with an emotion that sent hot shivers spilling all through her.

She didn't know what emotion it was, but she knew he was telling her something.

Before she could puzzle what it was, the herald droned on—she didn't catch his words for the loud roar of her blood in her ears—and then James was no longer staring at her, his full attention on the Lyon herald as he and the other two chieftains moved to stand directly beneath the King and Queen.

Hard-faced, proud, and already bearing their weapons, they made their bows to King Robert and Queen Annabella before turning to Earl David and the herald. Each chieftain stood tall, appearing as if carved of stone. They'd strapped their great swords at their backs rather than at their hips, and the hilts rose from behind their shoulders, so much quicker to grasp than at a man's side. Dirks and axes thrust beneath their belts. And their Highland shields, round leather-covered targes, were already in place on their left arms. They carried hunting crossbows in their right hands, the sight of them making Catriona's blood chill. The three arrows carried by each warrior would be the first weapons used, the first to taste blood. Or, she shivered, claim lives.

None of the chieftains wore body armor, and Kendrew Mackintosh was bare to the waist. Half naked, and with his wild red hair and beard, he looked more savage than Alasdair and James. And—Catriona stared—strange blue marks covered his powerfully muscled arms and chest.

"Dear God..." Catriona glanced at Maili. "Mackintosh has painted himself."

"Nae, my lady." Maili's gaze didn't leave the loge. "He bears those marks always." She leaned close, her voice low. "He etches them into his skin to celebrate each man he's killed in battle."

Catriona stared at her friend. "How do you know that?"

Maili glanced at her, a pink tinge blooming on her face. "He was once in Glasgow when I accompanied our men on a supply trip. He was supping in the common room of an inn where we'd stopped for the night. And—"

"I don't want to hear." Catriona shivered, remembering the man's ferocity. "He is—"

"…and you, Alasdair MacDonald, Lord of Black-shore?" The herald's mention of Alasdair's name drew Catriona's gaze back to the loge. The Lyon Herald stood looking down on the three chieftains, his hawklike gaze fixed on them, haughtily. "My lords"—he spoke the title as if the courtesy soured his tongue—"are you agreed to abide by the King's terms, accepting the consequences, however they fall?"

"We do." The three chiefs bowed, answering as one.

Once more, James's glance flickered to her.

Or, at least, she told herself he'd looked her way. But when she leaned over the railing, trying to make sure, he'd already glanced away.

On the loge, the herald nodded once, curtly. Then he looked to the King, before turning to Earl David. "These men have sworn to accept and keep the King's terms and wishes. Are you, my Lord Carrick, agreed that we may proceed?"

Earl David inclined his head. "I am."

Behind him, the King also nodded, his face showing no emotion. His arms rested on the heavily carved sides of his chair, and, on his acquiescence, Queen Annabella placed her hand over his.

Bowing to them, the Lyon herald turned again to face the crowd. He didn't even glance at the three chieftains, still standing side by side before the platform. But the guardsman who'd whipped back the curtain with such rel-ish moments before now stepped forward again. This time he ushered Alasdair, James, and Kendrew away from the loge.

"Good men, hear me!" The herald flung his arm in the air the instant the chieftains vanished behind the curtain. "By God's will and the King's grace, and before all these witnesses, I hereby declare the trial by combat to commence!"

A great roar went up from the crowd, the cheers and shouts deafening. The privileged Lowlanders in the long rows of tiered seating leapt to their feet. And along the barricades at the tourney ground's edge, common Lowland folk and the people of the clans surged forward, pressing close to the stout wooden railing as all vied for a better view.

"Dia!" Catriona's heart thundered wildly, her mouth suddenly ash dry.

Someone bumped hard against her, trying to shove between her and Geordie to get to the railing, and she whipped around to glare at the man. "Be gone," she scolded him—a Lowland hawker by the look of him—"lest you, too, wish to feel the bite of Highland steel!"

She whipped out her lady's dagger, meaning to frighten him by aiming its tip at his belly, or lower, but the man gave a shriek and spun about, disappearing into the crush as quickly as he'd appeared.

Then, even as she turned back to the railing, there was a commotion near the King's royal loge as the three groups of warriors took the field. Alasdair, James, and Kendrew marched forward together, striding side by side as they led their warriors to the center of the tourney ground. A score of pipers pranced and strutted before them, men from each clan, bound by the scream of their pipes. The pipers blew with gusto, the skirls and wails echoing across the hills in rousing, heart-stopping challenge.

The Auld Ones are on our side. A voice, very like the raven-haired beauty at Castle Haven, whispered the words at Catriona's ear.

But when she whipped around, it was Maili who hovered so near. "Look!" The laundress's eyes were round, the color draining from her face as she pointed to the middle of the field where the pipers were retreating. They now strutted toward their respective clans, where they'd parade back and forth along the railings, rallying their clanfolk during the fighting.

Maili's gaze wasn't on the pipers.

She was pointing at the warriors. "They're already drawing swords—"

"They can't be." Catriona stared, confused. "They have to use the crossbows first."

Yet Alasdair, James, and all the other champions were whipping out their blades. And they made grand flourishes with them, flashing their swords from side to side or windmilling them in showy figure-eight circles. Some men tossed their blades high in the air, letting them twirl and spin, before catching them by the hilts as they fell.

The bright steel of the blades glinted in the pale sun and made dreadful hissing sounds as the men slashed them through the cold morning air.

"Mother Alba save us if the King calls a breach of rules." Catriona felt her heart knocking against her ribs. "I heard the terms when Alasdair spoke of them with his men, often enough. The rules are that the three arrows were to be loosed before any sword cut flesh."

"I know..." Maili pressed a hand to her throat.

Catriona gripped the railing, leaning forward, trying to catch her brother's eye, or James', reminding them... "I can't believe Alasdair, James—"

"The Cameron?" Maili shot her a look.

A suspicious look.

Catriona stood straighter, brushing her skirts. "Alasdair, James, or any of them." She emphasized the last few words, not wanting her friend to know how James consumed her. "I can't believe they'd risk having the King—" She broke off when she saw Alasdair and the other two chieftains exchange a quick, fierce-eyed glance.

As one, they stilled their blades, lowering them.

Their men did the same; the sword-twirling, tossing, and mad, quick-as-lightning lunges stopped at once. But none of the warriors put away their swords. They kept them in their hands, tips pointed downward but still at the ready.

Catriona felt a thin trickle of cold sweat slip between her breasts.

"Dear saints, Maili." She glanced at her friend, keenly aware that her palms were damp against the cold, hard wood of the rail. "I think they're about to attack each other."

But when the warriors raised their steel again, it wasn't to swing them.

Shouting their war cries, they all thrust their swords high in the air and then lowered them, striking the hilts and steel blades against the wood of their targes. Then they began marching, slowly circling the field as they rhythmically beat their swords on the shields. The noise was terrible and frightening, worse than the screaming pipes. A nightmarish thunder that swelled and grew, striking terror into hearts, and all the more horrible because of the portent of the shield clashing.

When it stopped, the fighting would begin.

The warriors weren't breaking the King's terms.

They were readying themselves for battle.

*   *   *

On the field, about halfway between the royal loge and the shield-beating warriors, Scandia flittered along beside the Cameron champions, shimmying brightly. But it was so hard to keep pace with the marching men. From old habit, she hitched up her filmy skirts, determined to do her best. She also slid a curious glance at the MacDonald lass as the warriors neared the MacDonald spectators.

Scandia's heart squeezed, aching for her.

Catriona stood where she'd been all morning, gripping the barricade railing, surrounded by her kin. But she'd lost a good deal of her high color, and her eyes were troubled and stormy. She looked as if she knew someone were about to pull the world from under her, and she agonized because she couldn't stop them.

Scandia pressed a hand to her breast, wishing Catriona knew she understood, sympathized.

And she did, more than anyone knew.

She'd flit over to her—she'd stood with the girl earlier, trying to let her know there were some here this day who meant her well—but just now Scandia needed to march with her kinsmen. Even if her shimmying wasn't anything like a proper marching gait, it was important to her to show support.

She couldn't help the men, but she could do that.

She also cast another look in the MacDonalds' direction, hoping to catch a glimpse of the Maker of Dreams crone, Grizel, and her enchanted white stag, Rannoch. They were about there, Scandia knew. She'd seen them several times since daybreak, though none of the tournament spectators appeared to have noticed the pair's passing.

Even she couldn't see them now.

But the last time she had, Grizel was stroking the stag's neck and whispering into his ear. Then she'd stepped back, sending Rannoch alone into the thick of the MacDonalds lining their stretch of barricade. The MacDonalds parted for Rannoch, each man he neared stepping or jumping aside to clear the way. Though, Scandia knew, those men surely thought they were simply jostling about and had no idea they were freeing a path at Grizel's behest.

And for a powerfully magical creature they couldn't see.

Scandia had looked on excitedly, pleased when Rannoch reached the MacDonald maid and planted himself behind her and her dog.

Then Rannoch had vanished before her eyes, too. But she was certain he was still there. That even she could no longer see him had to mean that his magic would be particularly potent this morn.

She dearly hoped so.

Not just for the good of her clan and the weal of the glen, but because young James and the MacDonald maid were so passionately drawn to each other. Scandia could feel their attraction sizzle in the air each time their gazes met. And if they were close, she even sensed the rapid thunder of their hearts, the heat that would then sweep them, flooding them with awareness and quickening their pulses.

If they *touched,* the strength of their desire shook her, echoing through her wispy form until her heart also pounded with the wonder of it.

Unfortunately, like so many young lovers of feuding clans, they also thought they couldn't find happiness. At times, they even thought they despised each other.

But there was hope.

The maid fretted for James. Scandia could see her clutching her charmed amber necklace, holding the stones so tightly that her knuckles gleamed white. And—Scandia thrilled—Catriona's good wishes for James were so fervent, so desperate, that they poured out of her, vivid and shining, drenching the air around her.

Surely the ambers' magic wouldn't disappoint her.

Scandia shimmied faster, willing it so.

The maid cared for James, and mightily.

As he did for her, though he was much too thrawn to admit it.

Cameron men were among the most stubborn in the land.

Worse—Scandia shook her head sadly—when dusk fell that night, if James yet walked with the living, the young pair would forget that caring.

They'd return to thinking they reviled each other.

Such was the way of men.

Until—she sighed—they found themselves where she was and learned otherwise.

Wishing she could make them understand their folly, she twinkled closer to James. She flitted as near as she dared, for the ferocious thunder of the shield beating stirred the air, making it difficult to hover near the marching warriors without being tossed and whipped about like a curl of mist. Which, she supposed, she might as well be, given that she was quite insubstantial.

And if she used what energy she had to manifest properly, she'd surely give a good number of the champions a tremendous fright.

A frown marred Scandia's still-lovely brow. The last thing she wanted was to alarm anyone.

Every warrior on the field needed his wits about him. Being known as a doom bringer was a sad enough burden without giving truth to such a terrible by-name by shattering a man's battle concentration.

But James and his men were just now marching past the MacDonalds, and she caught him glancing at Catriona. The maid met his gaze and their eyes locked and held, fiercely. Scandia's breath caught, for she could see the path of their connection, the dazzling-bright band that stretched between them, glittering like the sun.

A *fate thread*, it was.

And Scandia hoped so fervently that nothing would sever it.

Men often did so. Knowing or unknowingly, they sliced such precious ties. Or, she knew, they allowed them to fray until the thread snapped on its own.

Scandia braced herself against the war music of the shield beating and fluttered closer to James. Near enough to see how firmly the fates had spun the shining thread tying him to Catriona. The thread looked like silken iron, the color of moonbeams.

She trembled, much in awe.

It would be difficult to damage such a noble bond. If it truly was spun as tightly as it appeared.

One could never be sure with such things, as she knew to her cost. Sometimes even the fate spinners made mistakes, dropping threads that should have held firm. Scandia shivered, the cold air around her darkening for a moment.

She was a dropped thread, she knew.

Catriona—she suspected, watching her follow James with her gaze—would yank back her thread if it fell from her hands.

She'd never become her family's doom.

Scandia hoped she *would* become Clan Cameron's joy.

Willing it so, she gathered her strength and whooshed herself higher in the air, where she circled brightly over the heads of the marching warriors. She knew they couldn't see her and would think her passing was just a cold breath of wind racing across the field.

But it made her feel good to make such a flourish, wishing each one strength and courage and willing that none among them were a dropped thread like her.

Men should die only when it was time.

Never a moment before.

Chapter Fifteen

❦

You have my oath, I will no' fell your brother. James kept his gaze on Catriona as he marched past her, willing her to hear his silent vow.

He'd shout the words if his cousin Colin weren't sticking so closely to his side that the lout may well have been a prickly burr.

Annoyed, James stepped faster. But Colin only increased his own pace, refusing to be shaken.

Ignoring him, James focused on Catriona. If he weren't striking his sword against his shield, he'd put his hand on his heart. Then she'd hopefully understand the assurance he'd been sending her ever since he'd strode out before the royal loge and spotted her in the crowd, staring at him with such dread in her eyes.

But now, as then, when she caught him looking at her, the fear vanished. Instead, her chin shot up and she blasted him with such a heated glare, he wondered the grass between them didn't catch fire.

"She hates you, she does." Colin long-nose proved once again how irksome he could be. "I've ne'er seen such loathing on a maid's face."

"She's fearful for her brother, you lackwit."

"Doesn't look like fear to me." Colin beat his shield with particular vigor. "I say she's hoping you'll soon be cut to ribbons."

"That may be." James hoped agreement would silence Colin's flapping tongue.

Some men grew quiet before a battle, some drank themselves senseless, quite a few bedded as many willing wenches as they could in a night, and scores knelt in prayer. Others were beset with a desire to talk incessantly.

Colin fell into the latter category.

And his blether was grating on James's nerves.

Wishing him on the moon, James again lengthened his stride. He also gave Catriona a hard stare, knowing it was surely best if she did hate him.

"She has a dog with her." Colin caught up with him, still thwacking his sword against his shield.

James struck his own targe harder than he'd intended. "I don't care if she brought a squirrel with wings. It changes nothing."

Or so he thought until the crowd around her shifted and he saw Colin was right. Alasdair's dog sat beside Catriona. The ratty-coated cur was leaning into her, cowering in terror. And the sight made James's gut clench. The dog—*Geordie?*—was one of those animals no man could look upon without feeling something twist inside him. The dog's frailties stirred sympathy. His fierce loyalty touched a man's soul, humbling him. Scowling, James beat his shield harder, tearing his gaze from the bony old beast.

Grinding his teeth, James bent an annoyed look on his cousin. "I'll wager two pins that Alasdair ordered his sister to bring the dog to the field. The bastard's that wily."

Colin shrugged. "We brought Skald."

"Skald isn't real." James prayed for patience. "He's embroidered on a banner. And he doesn't distract men from battle fury with frightened, milky-eyed gazes."

James clamped his mouth shut, determined to ignore his cousin and Alasdair's dog. It *did* trouble him to know the aged beast sat trembling at the field's edge. And it outraged him that Alasdair would stoop to such trickery. He wouldn't have thought it of the man.

Not that it mattered.

He'd already sworn not to kill the MacDonald chief. But if he hadn't, the old dog's presence would've made it impossible. Just as Camerons honored and protected women—regardless of blood or clan—there wasn't a man among them who'd inflict pain on a dog.

What would happen this day was bad enough.

Bile rising in his throat, he glanced across the field to where his own people pressed against the barricade. As Colin reminded him, the Banner of the Wind had been raised there, flying proudly. The streaming silk rippled in the wind, showing Skald's snarling head. And the beast's fiery eyes seemed to stare right at him, accusingly.

"Hellfire and damnation!" He looked quickly away.

Skald would chase him through eternity, tearing into his flesh and not an enemy's, if James let himself be cut down to spare the neck of a foe.

Skald knew no mercy.

But—James's chest tightened painfully—Alasdair's Geordie wasn't made of silk. The old dog was flesh, bone, and blood, and he loved his master as much as Hector worshipped James. Alasdair had even told him that the poor beast could no longer bark. And seeing Geordie so distressed now proved what James had known all along.

Geordie was Clan Donald's secret weapon.

Catriona and the dog sealed James's fate. So he aimed one last gaze their way, willing Catriona to grasp that he'd never bring her anguish. The haughty look on her face said he already had.

To her, he was the devil.

A cloven-footed, horn-headed jackal who'd sinned grievously against her.

That isn't the way of it. A soft, feminine voice came from somewhere above his left ear. *She doesn't want you to see her fear.*

Startled, he looked up, half expecting to see an angel. But there was nothing but mist and cloud, racing before the cold wind coming down from the hills. Even so, gooseflesh rippled his skin. Ignoring the chill, he crushed the urge to break rank and pound across the field, demanding a favor of Catriona. Something to bring him luck and perhaps give him the courage to yank her into his arms again, this time asking her forgiveness and telling her he wasn't the devil.

He was a man entranced by her, and he'd had good reason to push her from him that night in the stair tower. Just as he'd only wanted to guard her good name later, in his bedchamber. He'd thought to protect her.

Instead, he'd sullied her. A dark deed he'd committed because he was falling in love with her.

Nae, he already had.

God help him.

"God's mercy on us." Colin halted abruptly, his words echoing James's thoughts. But his cousin's oath had nothing to do with a woman.

James froze, seeing at once why Colin swore.

The shield beating had stopped.

Only James had kept on pounding his targe, though he ceased now, his ears filling with the roar of the crowd and the scream of the pipes, more shrill now than ever. The drones and wails competed against the sudden blaring of trumpets from the King's royal loge as a great commotion rose from the spectators gathered there.

Eager for blood, they clapped hands and stomped feet, shouting for the slaughter to begin.

Earl David and the Lyon herald stood at the edge of the King's viewing platform, their faces impervious. But their stares were trained on the three groups of warriors, more directly on James.

Or so it felt to him.

Certain they'd seen him striking his shield after all other champions had stopped, he straightened to his full height, shoulders back and standing proud. He also set his face as sternly as possible lest anyone in the crowd dare to smirk at him.

Then he flashed a glance at Alasdair, not surprised when that one merely nodded, grimly.

When he turned to the Mackintosh warriors, Kendrew patted his sword hilt and gave him a grin that would've shriveled the liver of a lesser man.

"Mackintosh is mad." Colin spat on the ground.

"His men are just as crazed." James dropped a hand to his sword, frowning at Kendrew and his men. Unlike their chief, naked to his waist, many of the Mackintosh warriors had thrown wolf pelts over their shoulders. "Long as they remember they're Highlanders and no' Odin's fools, they can fight naked for all I care."

Looking away from the demented cravens, James drew his sword and raised it high. The other two chieftains did the same, though Kendrew roared like an enraged bear as he did so, earning glares from James and Alasdair. He grinned back at them, his face almost feral.

Then, on a swift nod from James, they each brought their blades winging down to point at the ground.

But in the moment they all yelled, *"Archers!"* something drew James's eye to the royal loge, where a party of MacNaughton spectators stood nearby, sneering.

James blinked, suspicion chilling him, turning his heart to ice.

MacNaughtons weren't welcome in the glen. They dwelt in the next glen and were ever at odds with the Camerons, MacDonalds, and Mackintoshes.

But now wasn't the time to puzzle over their gloating presence.

Or that when James looked again, they'd vanished.

Already, the best bowmen of the three groups were loosing their shafts, the first two volleys of arrows whizzing over the warriors' raised shields. None found a mark, and James said a silent prayer.

He also risked a glance at Alasdair, catching him jerk a nod at the MacDonald archers.

Kendrew, damn the fool, was still grinning like a madman.

James scowled at him, but the jackal only threw back his head, laughing.

"Again!" James roared, glaring at his own archers,

hoping his shout would overtone the fool's braying. That his dark scowl would hide his own swelling relief that no arrow had yet pierced flesh.

"Launch!" Alasdair's cry also went up.

Kendrew's Berserkers answered to the crazed look on their leader's face, howling like demons as they sent their arrows hissing into the air. Wild-eyed as they were, they could have been the legended Berserkers of Norse myth. Odin's own bodyguards, ferocious fighters who craved battle lust more than they desired women.

All men fired now, the arrows darkening the sky, and—as if the gods indeed loved Highlandmen—some shafts sailed high over their targets while others glanced off the upraised shield wall of targes. Most of the arrows clattered together to fall harmlessly to the peaty ground.

"Damnation!" Colin jerked when one of them dinged his shield and another slammed into the ground near his ankle. He shot a furious look at James, the near misses sending a rush of cold down James's spine.

The two arrows had come after the others.

And the icy prickles creeping all over James's nape told him the shafts hadn't been loosed by one of Alasdair's men. Or even that wild-eyed fiend, Kendrew's.

But the arrows *had* been aimed.

He was sure of it. And he doubted they were meant for Colin.

He'd been standing right next to his cousin, and his every warrior's instinct warned him that the arrows had been launched at him.

And they'd come from the direction of the royal loge.

Fury slamming through him, James ripped one of the spent arrows from the ground. Not surprising, the shaft bore no ownership markings. James glared at the arrow, the rank stench of treachery almost choking him. He tightened his jaw, his blood heating as he broke the shaft in two and flung the pieces away from him.

He'd have thrust the two halves beneath his belt, keeping them to fret over later, but he wouldn't give the King—or the likes of Sir Walter and his ilk—the chance to accuse him of holding on to an arrow after the allowed quota of three shafts per man had been loosed.

They wouldn't care that the arrow was snapped and useless.

That he knew.

"They're no' ours, eh?" Colin kicked the arrow that had nicked his targe.

"They're no' any man's." James's head was beginning to pound. "The shaft was bare as a bairn's arse."

Colin's eyes glittered. "I say that's as telling as any mark etched on wood."

"I say it, too." James turned to scowl at the Mackintosh Berserkers, who were casting off their hunting crossbows, tossing aside the light weapons as they howled and leapt about like banshees.

"Heathens." James pretended not to see when Kendrew yanked his huge war ax from his belt and swung it in a vicious arc, saluting him. Kendrew's men roared approval, slapping their thighs or grabbing their own axes and waving them high above their heads, challenging.

"The bastards are starting with axes." Colin stared at them, gog-eyed.

"Thon Viking axes will do them no good." James rolled his shoulders, flexing his muscles. "No' when we slice through the hafts with our swords."

As if they heard, a round of hoots and rude taunts rose
from the Mackintoshes.

Wishing the earth would open and invite them into
hell, James threw down his crossbow, the signal for his
men to do the same.

Down the field, Alasdair's warriors were also rid-
ding themselves of their bows. Crossbows were useless
now. Dead weight none of them needed when fighting
face-to-face with the naked steel of great swords, dirks,
and axes.

Alasdair caught James's eye then—as did Catriona, for
the MacDonald warriors stood close to where their kinsmen clustered along the barricade—and James felt his
frustration clamp hard and tight around his chest. For an
agonizing moment, he couldn't breathe. Not with a fury
of kick-to-the-gut guilt slamming into him the longer he
stood there, Catriona's hot blue gaze locked with his.

Colin was right.

She did look like she hated him. Then, for the space of
an eye blink, her face cleared and she mouthed the words,
God save you.

At least, James thought she did.

Until it hit him that she must've been sending the well
wishes to Alasdair, who'd used the moment to make a
quick sword flourish to his kinsmen.

Ignoring Alasdair, James threw one more look at
Catriona and saw at once that he'd guessed rightly.

This time there was no mistaking that she was staring
at him. And the fury on her face scorched him.

If he'd thought she was angry before, her eyes blazed
like hellfire now. She'd flung a section of her cloak over
Geordie's head—James could see the dog's shaking

beneath the mantle's woolen folds—and she'd fisted her hands on top of the barricade railing. Her back was so straight it was a wonder the wind didn't snap her in two.

James couldn't look away from her.

Her rage was that terrible.

Alasdair was also staring at her, scowling fiercely. Then he whirled to face his men, thrusting his sword to the heavens as he turned.

"Arms!" Alasdair shouted the word, breaking the spell. His command unleashed chaos in the tiered viewing platforms as the crowd went wild. Closer by, the air filled with the shriek of steel as men on the field reached over their shoulders for the swords slung across their backs.

"Shields!" James yelled as hotly, bringing up his left arm to thrust his targe over the right edge of Colin's. "Shield wall, now!"

"Odin!" The Mackintosh Berserkers roared as one, surging forward like a tide, every man wild-eyed and howling. Some of them sent throwing axes winging through the air as they ran, their shouts and snarls blending with the unholy knocking of wood and iron as men from the other two clans locked their shields together.

Quickly grouping into a tight wedge, James and his men held their swords straight out before them, using the long blades as spears so that their shield wall bristled like a hedge of deadly steel. From the corner of his eye, James saw Alasdair urging his men into the same age-old battle formation. Then both groups of warriors began pacing forward, swiftly closing the distance between them.

Somewhere trumpets blared. And the pipes screamed louder than ever, the skirls earsplitting as the pipers dared to march closer, blowing gustily as they strutted back and forth along the outer edges of the shield wedges, each wail and drone meant to stir the blood.

"Hold tight!" James ordered when the man to his right let his targe slip.

"Valhalla!" Kendrew and his Berserkers gave another great shout and split in two, each group veering away from the center of the field. They whooped as they ran, clearly intending to circle round and attack from behind when the two shield wedges smashed into each other.

"Hah—look at them!" One of James's men yelled as the Mackintoshes raced across the grass. "They're turning tail. No stomach for a fight!"

"Shame, you!" Another man called after them. "Running off like the women you are!"

James adjusted his grip on the iron handle of his targe, knowing better.

Kendrew and his wild men weren't fleeing the field.

And they'd fight like demons.

But it was good for his men to shout taunts. The more they jeered, the less they'd think about dying.

Then Alasdair and his warriors slammed into them and the gates of hell opened as steel, iron, and men clashed fiercely together. The crash was terrible, loud as thunder and rocking the earth. Every man reeled, some men staggering backward, several falling to their knees.

Shock waves of pain shot through James's arms, flushing him with heat and jarring his bones. He set his jaw, blocking the teeth-rattling agony, the loud ringing in his ears as the horrible noise of splintering wood and steel scraping on steel echoed across the field.

"Push back!" James snarled the order, surging forward

into the press of the MacDonald shield wall. "Push hard now! Don't give!"

"Ottar, Ottar!" Several of James's men began chanting the name of the clan's most revered ancestor, Ottar the Fire-worshipper, whose famed standard sited Castle Haven and became known as the clan's Banner of the Wind.

Others took up the cry as men strained, shoving with all their might against the unmoving wall of shield-to-shield MacDonalds. "Ottar, Ottar!"

They lunged, panted, and pushed, gaining several feet only to have Alasdair and his men heave them back again, retaking the ground but gaining no more than the few feet they'd lost so briefly.

"Again!" James blinked the sweat from his eyes as they pressed heavily against the MacDonald line. Baring his teeth, he stabbed and thrashed with his sword, trying to plunge the blade into the hair-thin space between the MacDonald shields or knock aside one of them, freeing a gap in the wall.

But the round, leather-covered targes overlapped so snugly that not a breath could squeeze past them. And his blows, however huge, glanced off the sturdy Highland shields without so much as denting them.

His men fared no better, though Colin did cause one of the MacDonald shields to crack.

But the targe didn't spring apart, however fiercely Colin swung at it.

Cameron shields were proving equally invincible, and that was something, considering the force Alasdair and his men were putting into their blows.

Then the cracked MacDonald shield did split, but its

wielder didn't cast it aside, even though one half sagged dangerously, exposing the man's hip.

"Forward!" James urged his men to push again, not liking how close Alasdair stood to the man with the broken half-shield. Colin had succumbed to battle fever and was slashing at the MacDonald shield wall as viciously as if he were one of Kendrew's Berserkers.

"Push, I say!" James put all his lung power in the command. "Break their wall."

As long as they were straining to burst through the MacDonald resistance by brute force, his hotheaded, sword-swinging cousin would be too occupied to make a wild swipe at the man with the half-shield and lop off Alasdair's head in the by-doing.

Colin's aim suffered when he lost his wits.

James glared at Alasdair now, trying to send him a silent warning.

If the fool had any sense, he'd grab a shield from a man in the ranks behind him and thrust it into the hands of the broken-shield warrior before Colin or one of James's other men could thrust a blade past the damaged targe, piercing the gut of the shield wielder. And—very likely—also land a killing strike to Alasdair.

"Shove harder!" James cursed the lackwit as his men lunged mightily, gaining a yard.

"MacDonalds—hold fast!" Alasdair's voice rose above the din, greater than the clanging of swords and the men's grunts and curses.

Then, just as the two shield walls pressed so fiercely against each other that a shudder ripped through both sides, a sharp scream went up from the back of James's group. An ominous thud cut off the man's agonized wail.

Another yell—and more—followed quickly, all accompanied by the sickening glide of steel grating on bone.

"Odin!" Thirty deep voices bellowed the war cry.

The Berserkers were back.

And the bloodlust was on them. Shrieking like hell-hounds, they hurtled their light throwing axes at the men in the front of shield walls. They were even quicker to fall upon the men at the rear, slashing and hacking with larger Norse battle axes until the blades ran red.

In a blink, the shield hedges broke.

Men everywhere whirled to face the new threat, challenging the Mackintoshes with swords, dirks, and axes, the deadly thrusting edge of their targes. Some men even used their bare hands.

Chaos spread, the stench of death imminent.

And through the red haze of fury, James searched for Alasdair's flame-bright head. But the MacDonald chieftain was nowhere to be seen.

Unless—James leapt over the body of a fallen Mac-Donald, a sick feeling churning in his gut—Alasdair had been cut down before James could reach him.

He *had* seen the fool running straight for the Berserkers, sword drawn and fire in his eye.

"Aggggh…" A kinsman lurched at James, bloodied arms outstretched, his chest streaming red from an ax gash in his neck. The warrior—a bonny lad only a year younger than James and recently wed—crumpled to the ground before James could grab him.

Not that it mattered, as the man's sightless eyes stared up at James.

"Ottar!" James threw back his head, bellowing the cry.

Everything around him went black, the horror of battle-frenzied men hacking, slashing, and stabbing each other blotting all but the hammering thunder of his own pulse roaring in his ears.

A rush of hot, blood-drenched air hit him and he whirled, just blocking a vicious sword swipe that would have sliced him in two. The MacDonald warrior's blade stuck in James's shield, the vibrations of the blow storming up his arm. He jerked fast, yanking the sword from his assailant's hand. Tossing aside his impaled targe, he swung his own blade upward, slicing into the soft flesh beneath his foe's chin before the man could reach for his dirk or ax.

The man fell, spouting blood and surely dying, but James didn't wait to be sure.

Instead, he leaned down and helped himself to the warrior's targe, yanking the shield down and off the man's blood-slicked arm. Stinging sweat dripped into his eyes, almost blinding him, but instinct let him thrust his own left arm into the two leather straps on the shield's back. Then he straightened and glanced round, secretly grateful that the MacDonald wasn't anyone he recognized.

"Valhalla!" A Berserker ran at him, the wicked edge of the man's war ax arcing for James's head.

"Skald!" James bellowed back, leaping aside as the man charged. Whipping around, he swung hard, driving his blade deep into the Mackintosh's side. The man roared, toppling heavily to the ground, his ax still clutched in his hand.

Somewhere—in another world—the crowd cheered, their shouts of glee lifting above the furious blare of pipes. Rage, hot, swift, and terrible, swept James. He spun about again, this time glaring at the Lowland spectators. But his fury only earned more hoots and whistles as they jumped to their feet, yelling for more blood.

Utter silence came from the barricades where the clansfolk stood.

Above it all, the hellish din and the eerie quiet, the wild howling of the Berserkers went on without cease, piercing and terrible.

Panting, James gulped air. Blood, hot and thick, pulsed from a gash above his ankle. It was a wound he hadn't felt until now and likely took when a MacDonald in the shield wall stabbed beneath his targe, slicing at the only Cameron flesh he could reach.

Ignoring the pain—for he felt it now, sharply—he once again scanned the mass of fighting men for Alasdair. But he could hardly distinguish his own warriors. Blood reddened the faces of every man standing, even staining their plaids beyond recognition.

Only Kendrew's Berserkers stood out from the rest, their wild-eyed grins and ferocity setting them apart. And even they ran crimson, their tangled manes and wolf pelts blood-drenched and streaming red.

One of them raced at him again, roaring fury, his huge war ax whirling. James raised his targe, ready to take the ax swing, but the man tripped over a fallen MacDonald and slammed facedown onto the gore-slicked grass. Leaving him, James ran on, dodging swinging blades and lurching men, many of them dying on their feet, their lives spent before they could even open their mouths to scream.

"Come, bastards! Our hounds want your flesh!" Colin's cry came from James's left, and he wheeled about to see his cousin grinning devilishly, his great sword flashing in a deadly figure-of-eight motion as he taunted two ax-wielding Mackintoshes, their own expressions equally fiendish.

James sprinted forward, eager to help Colin send the men to Odin's corpse hall, but Colin's arcing steel sliced off his opponents' ax hands before James could reach his cousin's side. The two Berserkers screamed, reeling backward, blood spewing like a fountain from their naked wrists.

"Colin!" James hurried, jumping over the wounded and dying. He skirted the increasing number of men now fighting in single combat, warriors circling and hacking each other with dirks and axes.

Unaware of him, Colin leapt back as the two Berserkers charged, lashing at him with the iron-rimmed edges of their shields. But the blood gushing from their empty wrists pooled at their feet and they slipped, crashing to their knees even as Colin rushed in, lopping off their heads with one terrible sword swipe.

"Skald!" Colin thrust his red-smeared blade to the sky, shaking it fiercely.

James stared at him, his cousin's triumphant shout chilling him.

The horror of it iced his veins. The sharp metallic reek of blood—and the ghastly stench of other, worse things—froze him where he stood. He closed his eyes, only for a beat, to clear the burning scorch of sweat, and when he looked again, Colin was gone.

James shuddered, his own bloodlust draining away when he spotted Colin running across the field, making for one of the few clusters of still-fighting men.

Almost all fought one-on-one now. More littered the blood-red ground. Colin was just now cutting his way into the fiercest affray yet going and—praise God—James knew the brash-headed fool would emerge without a scratch.

James might be the devil.

But Colin had an angel on his shoulder, always.

Somewhere behind James, a Berserker howled again—the same mad wail he'd heard before—and James whipped around, his heart stopping when, across the emptying field, a dazzling flash of white caught his eye.

Rannoch stood at the MacDonald barricade.

The stag was staring at him, his antlered head high and his snowy coat shining with the brilliance of stars. But when James blinked, the creature disappeared, vanishing as quickly as he'd appeared.

And now...

Geordie stood with his paws on the railing, his grayed head tipped back as he howled and whined piteously. Terrible, gut-wrenching wails that—James knew—were the cries he'd mistaken for the Berserkers' worst howls.

To be sure, they'd bellowed like fiends, but the soul-splitting wails had been Geordie's.

The dog who—James knew from Alasdair—had hardly made a sound in years.

"God's mercy!" James gripped his sword, staring at the raggedy beast. His heart split, the soiled ground rolling beneath his feet.

Catriona was on her knees beside the dog. She'd wrapped her arms around him, her bright head buried against his shoulder, her face turned away from the slaughter.

"Mother Mary..." James dropped his sword, a hot, sick feeling sluicing him, squeezing his chest until he couldn't draw a breath.

"This is how you thank me, Mackintosh?"

Alasdair's furious voice came loud from James' right. "I risked all, even riding to Nought, your God-forsaken keep to warn you of treacheries—"

An outraged roar—Kendrew's?—cut off Alasdair even as James snatched up his blade and pounded off in the direction of the two chieftains' angry voices.

James ran blindly, knocking aside men and—only once, thank the saints—barreling right over a low mound of mangled and torn bodies. And when he reached Alasdair, he saw at once that he'd guessed rightly.

Alasdair and Kendrew were clashing steel. Though— James's gut clenched—it was Kendrew's huge Norse battle ax that the Mackintosh chief tossed from hand to hand as he stood grinning at Alasdair. Malice streamed off every inch of Kendrew's towering, bearlike body, while a gaping red wound in Alasdair's left arm showed why Kendrew smiled so wickedly.

Worse, Alasdair's injured arm wasn't just bleeding. It hung limply at his side, useless.

Men often fought with grievous cuts and slashes, wielding their blades on sheer will alone. If they could. Alasdair did still clutch his sword with his right hand. And his face was hard-set, his anger alive, seething. But his blade's swings were feeble, the blood pouring from his left arm draining any strength that was left in his sword arm.

"Hold!" Like a man possessed, James threw himself between them, sword raised. "Come at him again, Mackintosh, and you're a dead man."

Kendrew laughed. "Bluidy hell, I am, whoreson!"

Alasdair scowled. "Begone, Cameron. I dinnae need your help."

Ignoring them both, James let his blade flash, slicing cleanly through the haft of Kendrew's ax. Then, before either man could blink, he lunged closer to rend a groin-to-hem rip in Kendrew's kilt, exposing more than the bastard's thick, naked thighs.

Grinning wickedly himself now, James kicked aside the lout's fallen ax blade. Still smiling, he rammed the tip of his sword against Kendrew's belly.

"Say it's over." He pressed the blade into hard muscle, thrusting only enough to draw a bead of blood. "Say it now, or I'll slice down, unmanning you before you can wipe that mad grin off your poxy face."

"Odin!" Kendrew thrust his jaw, glaring.

"Fool!" James jabbed his sword tip deeper—and jerked down, ripping an inch of flesh. Blood welled, spilling down Kendrew's loins. "I'll no' kill you, see? I'd rather watch you tell your womenfolk that you've become one of them!"

"Bastard!" Kendrew hissed, the skin around his mouth turning white.

"Say it's over." James sliced lower, vaguely noting that a loud silence was spreading across the field. Even the pipes no longer skirled, and no cheers now came from the spectators, only thick, deep stillness.

"The words, Mackintosh." He eased the blade back a bit, risking mercy. "Now, or—"

"It is over, you arse!" Kendrew jerked away from him, clutching his stomach as he bent double, defeated. "Have you no' seen?" He turned his bearded head, glaring at James and Alasdair. "We're nigh the last men standing."

James stared at him, lowering his sword as trumpets blasted and the crowd roared. The pipers started strutting again, though now they played a mournful lament. Many of the spectators ran down from the tiered viewing platforms to race onto the field, their cheers deafening.

Throwing down his sword, James dragged his arm over his forehead. "It cannae be done so long as we're on our feet. No decision made until—"

Alasdair threw aside his own sword and leaned down to fetch James's blade from the grass, thrusting it at James. "Have done, Cameron. Make an end to it—one good turn for saving me from dying beneath a madman's ax."

James took his sword but retrieved Alasdair's and handed it back to him, forcing the lout to seize it. That done, he scowled and then yanked his own untouched battle ax from his belt, tossing it at Kendrew's feet.

"Then let's end it in proper Highland fashion!" He raised his sword high, waiting for Alasdair to bring up his blade and slam it against James's own.

When Alasdair did so, Kendrew swore and spat on the ground. But then he snatched James's ax off the grass and, perhaps a little too forcefully, thrust it against James's and Alasdair's raised swords.

And as they stood there, scowling darkly at each other, waiting for the King's trumpets to blare a final fanfare, somewhere in the crowd, a terrible howling eased to soft and quiet whimpers.

It was done.

Whatever came now, the three clans of the glen would decide their future on their own.

Chapter Sixteen

✤

God's mercy! That was as good a battle as any I've ever seen."

Earl David came hurrying across the blood-slicked ground to where James, Alasdair, and Kendrew held their weapons aloft, the blades touching. The smile splitting David's handsome face made James want to sweep his brand around and take off the young prince's head. Instead, he quelled the itch in his sword hand and raised his voice so that all men near—and some not so near—could hear him.

"It was the King's writ, lord. No' true warring." He bent a long stare on the prince. "And now our duty to the crown is served. It is done."

"And boldly, I say!" Earl David's grin widened, his eyes alive with excitement.

Jostling spectators pressed near, the sight of them making a muscle twitch in James's jaw. On and on they came, groups of Lowland nobles from the King's entourage, and commoners who'd left their tiered seats to race onto the field, eager to get a closer look at the steaming redness of Highland blood.

Just now they gave their prince cheering accord, clearly of a mind with him that the men of the glen had fought hard and well.

James squashed his contempt. All around them, the reek of slaughter was so powerful that the stench may well have been standing beside him, a living thing. Solid, terrible, and tainting the air.

"Never have I seen such boldness," Earl David enthused again, his eyes still shining. "So much hacking and stabbing, the clashing of swords..."

Several paces behind the prince, the guards in his escort said nothing. Big, hard-faced men in well-polished mail coats and bristling with arms, they stood silent. Their cold-eyed arrogance spoke louder than any words, their rigid stances showing disdain.

James ignored them.

It was the prince's glee that filled him with murderous rage. "All warriors are bold when faced with steel—if they are men! We have honor, lord." James looked straight into the prince's eyes. His tone was harsh, proud. "That is what you saw this day. That above all."

James secretly excluded Kendrew and his madmen from the ranks of the valorous. Men who ran around in wolf pelts and howled like demons deserved no such praise. But that opinion was his business and no one else's.

Not even the son of a king.

Against outsiders, Highlanders did stick together. That was just survival, however much the tradition could sour one's belly at times.

His own gut roiling now, he exchanged a look with Alasdair and Kendrew. Then he stepped back swiftly to slash his sword downward, plunging it into the ground. The other two chieftains did the same, thrusting their weapons into the glistening red grass so near to James's blade that the two swords and the ax raged from the earth as one.

"We are again our own arbiters." James turned to the prince, meeting his gaze squarely. "The Glen of Many Legends is ours, as ever it was."

Something, perhaps the devil inside him, made him put a hand to his sword's empty scabbard. His brand might be half buried in the ground, but his dirk—well honed and sharp enough to split a hair—still hung close by, within an easy and threatening hand grip.

The royal guardsmen noticed, edging nearer, their own hands dropping to the swords strapped low at their sides.

Alasdair and Kendrew moved to stand with him. Kendrew did so somewhat grudgingly, though he did turn one of his evil grins on the prince.

Oblivious, Earl David bobbed his bright head. "Aye, you shall be your own arbiters. You may retain your own Highland rule. And you will not be banished from your hills." He paused, some of the lightness disappearing from his tone. "So long as you honor and obey the King."

"We have ne'er done otherwise." James looked at him, anger still burning in his veins. "Your father agrees to such terms? He will take his men and their followers and leave the glen? Allow us our peace?"

"To be sure. He was much impressed." Earl David glanced over his shoulder toward the royal loge, but the masses of spectators blocked the canopied platform from iew. "His scribes are inking charters now, all you need to hold your own sway here."

"Charters?" James glanced at the other two chieftains. Alasdair's brows snapped down, and Kendrew raised his arms over his head, loudly cracking his knuckles.

"There is a grant for this glen." James flashed Kendrew a warning glare. "It is the ancient charter that, years ago, passed into the hands of Lady Edina, tied by blood or marriage to us all."

Earl David didn't appear to hear him, his gaze flicking over the carnage on the field. He seemed particularly interested in a slain MacDonald who'd been pinned to the ground, his spine pierced by a sword.

James stared at the prince, repelled.

Here, surrounded by a sea of blood, Earl David's clean, tidy hair and gleaming coat of mail made him look like a vision from another world. His fascination with the fallen was offensive. Bodies of the dead and dying covered the trampled grass, their reddened swords, axes, and shields strewn around them. Wounded men writhed in agony, though some lay quiet, their eyes deep pools of unblinking horror.

But if the prince noticed their agony, he gave no sign.

Instead, he glanced round, seeming unaffected by the thick, hot stench of battle, delighted by the gore.

Beaming again, he turned back to the three chieftains. "Bards will sing of this day for years to come." He glanced at his escort as if seeking agreement. "Highland men know how to fight!"

"Nae, lord"—Catriona appeared then, pushing her way through the wall of tightly packed spectators—"our men know how to die. They do so when they must, and always unafraid."

She started forward, Geordie trailing after her. The dog's tail hung low and he quivered badly—until he spotted Alasdair and ran to him as quickly as his stiff legs would carry him. The old dog barked and then jumped all over his master, swishing his tail and slathering Alasdair with kisses.

"Catriona!" Alasdair called to her, his cry almost drowned by Geordie's excited barking.

Or so James thought until he realized the voice had been his.

He turned away from Alasdair so the lout wouldn't see his face coloring. The fool had dropped to his knees, hugging his dog, but James didn't want to take any chances.

Alasdair was almost better at reading him than Colin, and—James knew—the perceptive bugger would take one look at his burning cheeks and know exactly why he'd called out Catriona's name.

James frowned, hoping anyone else would mistake his flush for anger.

Catriona glowed like a balefire, two slashes of pink staining her cheekbones, bright and vivid. His heart thumped as he watched her approach. She strode across the red-drenched grass like an avenging fury and looking so maddeningly beautiful, she took his breath.

He could almost see a flaming sword in her hand, wings of fire rising from her shoulders, so terrible—and glorious—did she look in her outrage.

Something very near to a smile tugged at his lips, but the icy blue glare she'd pinned on Earl David was so magnificent, so wondrous to behold, that he didn't want to risk banishing it by distracting her.

To his right—he caught the frenzied movement—

Kendrew spluttered and snatched at the torn edges of his kilt, yanking them together. James clamped his jaw, resentfully allowing Kendrew a jot more honor than he would have cared to give the wild-eyed bastard.

"Ho, James!" Colin burst through the throng then, hot on Catriona's heels. "I tried to head her off, I swear I did." He hurried forward, his face, plaid, all of him, streaming red, though—relief sluiced James—none of the blood appeared to be Colin's own.

As always in battle, Colin emerged unscathed.

But his dark eyes glinted with annoyance—irritation tinged with more than a touch of amusement as he skirted or leapt over the fallen, trying to keep pace with Catriona.

"I warned her that the field was no place for a lady." Colin paused near the prince's guard, panting. "She ran on, daring me to stop her."

James scarce heard his cousin's words.

He couldn't take his gaze off Catriona. The sight of her sent raw desire whipping through him. Searing awareness scalded him, tightening his loins and making his pulse thunder in his ears. She held him captive, dazzling him so thoroughly that everything else slipped away to nothingness and he saw only her.

"Highland men are proud and fearless." She looked at Earl David, but James knew her words were meant for him. "They are the hardest fighters in the land. They're also known to let their honor"—she took a breath, her eyes sparking—"drive them to commit acts of great foolishness."

Her outburst brought hoots and sniggers from the crowd.

Earl David's appreciative gaze traveled over her. "And Highland women—how are they?"

"We stand by our men, always." She shot James a look of pure challenge. "Even when they'd deny they need us!"

James held her gaze, taking some satisfaction when his stare caused her flush to deepen. He narrowed his eyes at her, hoping to make her acknowledge his triumph.

But she jerked her gaze away and marched closer, sweeping past the prince's guard, six tall men in well-polished armor and helmets, their long-bladed swords glinting brightly. Holding her skirts high, she stepped briskly, displaying crimson splashes on her legs, red smears that reached to her knees. The fierce sheen to her eyes showed how much it'd cost her to wade through the slaughter.

Her braids had come undone and her hair spilled over her shoulders, tumbling to her hips. Her amber necklace shone with a brilliance that hurt his eyes, and her breasts rose and fell with her agitation as she drew up before the prince.

"I will tell you of Highland women, lord." She'd stopped beside a fallen Berserker whose belly had been split wide, and she looked down at the man for a long moment before she spoke again. "We do not sit behind palace walls, listening to minstrels strum their lutes and praise our beauty while our men are bleeding. We do not sip wine and nibble on cream pastries as we wait for word of a battle.

"Truth is"—her voice thrummed with pride—"we'd fight alongside our men if they'd allow us. As is, we take the field after they redden the ground. We tend the wounded and comfort the dying, not that such heroes truly die."

She glanced again at the slain Berserker. "Our fallen become legends. We remember their valor in song and—"

"My lady, I have seen their bravery—and yours!" Earl

David looked amused. He threw a glance at his tight-lipped guardsmen. "Your champions could teach some of the men in my father's army to fight. And you"—he turned back to her, his tone speculative—"might give our court ladies a few much needed lessons in spirit."

He paused, rubbing his royal chin. "Perhaps—"

Geordie barked, cutting him off.

"My sister is to wed soon." Alasdair pushed to his feet, keeping his good hand resting on Geordie's head. "She is betrothed to Lore MacShade, chief of an allied sept."

"I am—" Catriona clamped her lips, her eyes flashing furiously.

"Ah, well. That is a shame." Earl David lost interest.

James was all ears.

He'd never heard of a betrothal between Catriona and a MacShade chieftain. But that didn't mean such an arrangement didn't exist.

The man's name *was* familiar.

And just the sound of it soured his gizzard.

Scowling, he curled his hands around his sword belt, gripping so hard he winced. Or he would have done, if he didn't want to show such weakness.

But it was hard not to grimace.

Every muscle in his body screamed, and his arm blazed from having held his blade pointed at the clouds for so long. He ignored the cut above his ankle, blocking his mind to the fiery bursts of pain shooting up his leg. The warm, sticky fug of blood in his cuaran, drenching the shoe's leather and quelling between his toes.

Alasdair and Kendrew bore worse gashes.

And he'd be damned if he'd be the first to attract Catriona's professed nurturing skills. Most especially not when—and the notion scalded him—she belonged to an arse named Lore.

Sir Walter strode into view at that moment, worsening his spleen. Several other courtiers accompanied him, each one more richly dressed than the other. Sir Walter, the most glittering of them all, held documents in his hand. Fresh red seals dangled from the parchments, the crimson wax gleaming like blood in the pale morning sun.

"The charters, lord." Sir Walter handed the scrolls to Earl David.

Sir Walter then turned to the three chieftains. "Sirs"—he nodded curtly—"King Robert sends his felicitations. With due regard for his queen's sensibilities, having witnessed such an affray, he's ordered an immediate departure from the glen. The charters grant you each—"

"We do not require parchments." James strode up to him, speaking into his face. "The land is ours, whatever. Our ancestors won it by sword centuries ago, and we retook it this day with our blood."

"You will accept the charters, and gladly." Sir Walter eyed him contemptuously. "The rules stated that the glen would be awarded to the clan of the last man standing at the end of the trial. You—"

"We're all standing—as you see!" James glared at him. "Blood was spilled, much blood." He swept out his arm, indicating the field, then toward Alasdair's limp left arm and Kendrew's bloodied kilt.

He didn't mention the gash above his ankle, knowing the bastard had seen. "It is enough, more than that!"

"So the King agreed." Sir Walter spoke the words as if they choked him. "And so"—he nodded at Earl David, who stepped forward with the parchments—"he's shown you the grace of granting each of you the title to your own portion of the glen. From this day onward, the lands are yours, lest you break his peace by returning to—"

Kendrew roared, thrusting between them. "The battle was for the whole of the glen, no' pieces of it!"

"Lady Edina's grant held all the land." Alasdair stayed with Geordie, but his words were harsh, ringing. "The glen was ne'er meant to be divided."

Sir Walter shrugged. "Then perhaps you wish to fight on?" There was malice in his words, a hint of triumph. "Earl David can act in his father's stead, burning two of the charters in favor of the remaining champion."

"I will do nothing the like." Earl David turned to James, pressing one of the scrolls into his hands. "They are all champions, I say! They shall hold their lands as ever they've done before this day. My father has decided the matter. So long as no unrest…"

James gripped the scroll, knowing he'd burn it as soon as he returned to his hall. He barely heard the rest of the prince's oh-so-convivial words, though he did catch Kendrew's mutterings and Alasdair's cold silence as they, too, had the parchments foisted upon them.

Frowning, he tightened his fingers even more, feeling the charter's heavy wax seal pressing into his palm.

His fury would surely melt it, or so he hoped.

He turned his head to look at Catriona, half expecting her to whip up her skirts and grab her lady's dagger, using its lethal blade to slash the charters to shreds.

But she no longer stood beside the fallen Berserker.

She'd gone out onto the field and was moving about among the slain, an armful of bloodied swords and axes clutched against her side.

James's heart split when he saw.

Sir Walter sneered. "Look there, lord!" He grabbed Earl David's arm, pointing. "If the chiefs will fight no more, their women are game. See her gathering arms—"

"Thon lady isn't collecting steel for a fight." Kendrew glowered at Sir Walter. "She's—"

"She's picking up weapons to place them in the hands of the fallen." James glared at Kendrew, annoyed that he'd dared to speak for Catriona. "It's a courtesy to the slain, allowing them to die in honor if they'd lost their sword as they fell."

"Or their ax," Kendrew snarled at James.

"That, too, aye." James kept his eye on Catriona, watching her until she disappeared behind a particularly high mound of bodies.

Then he turned on his heel and strode away, the prince's excited exclamations about heroic Highland women grating on his ears.

But he'd barely pushed through the worst of the milling crowd of spectators when he stopped short. Something lurched in his chest, and relief swept him, swift and hot.

He went taut, also recognizing a damnably frightening burst of elation.

He remembered where he'd heard of Lore.

The bastard didn't exist.

He was the scale-backed, claw-handed monster in a tale told to children of the glen when they misbehaved. A once-bonny laird whose every dark deed made him uglier until he turned into a shade, a night beast so horrible he couldn't bear to glimpse himself and so only roamed in darkness.

Have a care, laddie, mothers would warn, *lest you wish to turn as ugly as Lore.*

James tipped back his head and stared up at the heavens, stifling a grin, because this field of the dead was no place for smiles.

But he couldn't stop the gladness spearing him.

Catriona wasn't betrothed.

And—his lips did twitch a bit then—Alasdair was one clever bastard.

Lore MacShade, indeed.

James let out a long breath. Then he shoved both hands through his hair. He shouldn't care at all that Catriona was free. And even if he wasn't worried about turning into a shade, he wouldn't be surprised if lightning struck him for lusting after Catriona now, this hour.

But he did.

He couldn't put her from his mind.

The taste and touch of her haunted him. He burned to hold her in his arms again, quenching his need for her, making her his.

His chest tightened, cutting off his breath. He had but one choice if he wished to keep his honor.

He'd have to stay away from her. Because—the sad truth was—if he touched her again, he wasn't letting her go.

God help him.

Chapter Seventeen

✤

*L*ore *MacShade.*

The dread name echoed ominously in Catriona's mind as she knelt beside yet another fallen Mackintosh. But it wasn't the scaly-backed, foul-reeking Lore that plagued her. He was a bairn's nightmare demon and nothing else. Any other time, she would've spun her own tale about Lore as soon as the name sprang from Alasdair's tongue. She'd have faced the prince without a single eye blink, claiming her love and devotion to her future husband.

How excited she was by her pending marriage to such a paragon.

She *would* thank Alasdair for saving her from an invitation to court.

A proposal that—she shuddered—would have surely been made with the sole purpose of seeing her land in Earl David's bed. More like, she would've found herself in a royal dungeon, for she'd have sooner sliced off the prince's pride before she'd have let him touch her.

She'd almost favor Lore.

But just now, as she knelt on the wet and reddened grass, surrounded by horror, the monster's name reminded her more of the sad transformation of this ever-magnificent stretch of the glen than any childhood demon. As many swords, shields, dirks, arrows, and war axes covered the ground as rocks and heather, the sweet earth drenched with blood and the air reeking to the clouds.

Dark, lowering clouds racing in from the west, bringing wind and looking ready to send cold, icy rain spitting down onto the glen any moment. Catriona glanced up at them now, glad for their angry, roiling faces. A clean blue sky would've seemed an insult this day, considering.

Too many men lay unmoving on the field.

It served for the heavens to be angry.

She was livid, too. Her fury boiled so hotly that she barely noticed the increasing wind, or how the chill bit through her clothes, icing her skin. She did feel the spirit of the slain Berserker who lay sprawled so ignobly before her. The warrior's soul surely hovered near, looking on as she placed her armful of weapons on the ground and selected a suitable Norse ax to place in the man's empty hand, restoring his honor and dignity.

Someone had done grim work to him, but she could tell he'd been a good-looking man. Tall and well built, he had a curling beard and eyes the color of a summer sky. Peering down at him, Catriona was also fairly sure he was one of the men who'd stood so insolently in Kendrew's hall at Castle Nought, watching her and Alasdair as if he burned to sharpen his ax blade on their bones.

Had the day gone differently, he might have danced on Alasdair's corpse. James would've been such a prize—the

Berserker might've beheaded and quartered him, putting each piece on a pole along Castle Nought's stony ramparts. This man had been that ferocious, she knew.

Now...

She bit her lip, steeling herself. Then she pried open the man's bloodied fingers and placed one of the huge Norse war axes in his hand, carefully closing his fist around the red-smeared haft. She then swept her hand down from his forehead and shut his eyes.

"Good feasting in Valhalla." She gave him the farewell she knew he would've wished and pushed to her feet, pressing a weary hand to her hip. Her back ached from the weight of the weapons, and the cold numbed her fingers.

A hot bath when she returned to Blackshore would soothe her pains. And how she wished the steaming water would also undo the horrors of the day.

Yet that was impossible, so she took a deep breath and prepared to move on.

A flicker of movement caught her eye just as she reached to brush at her skirts. Glancing across the field, she spotted James's sister Isobel bending over a fallen Cameron. Many Camerons lay in that spot, near to a blood-splashed thicket of whin and broom, but Catriona hesitated to go there, not wanting to risk running into James if he went to pay his respects to his slain kin.

It'd been bad enough tolerating him in front of the odious prince.

The instant their eyes had met, she'd felt a sudden fierce rush of need and had almost forgotten to hasten to her brother, so great had been her sweeping relief to see James standing and whole. Uninjured save an ugly gash in his lower leg—a wound she hoped Isobel had already treated.

She'd have offered to do so herself—there and then, before the prince and all onlookers—if he hadn't scalded her with such a glare.

So she'd simply scowled back at him, hoping the heat of her stare roasted him to the bone.

He deserved no better.

Still...

She scrunched her eyes, scanning the far side of the field to see if he was anywhere near his sister. But no one moved there except Isobel. Catriona watched the other woman lean closer to her fallen kinsman, angling her dark head close to his. Likely, she was murmuring soft words of comfort in the dying man's ear.

If Isobel saw her looking, she gave no indication.

Not that Catriona wished to distract her. Isobel and other women, surely, would be performing the same grisly task as she'd been doing. Though she did intend to cross the field and join the Cameron women later.

If they needed her.

And once she'd seen to all the men who begged attention here, where most of the dead seemed to be MacDonalds and Mackintoshes.

Knowing there were still numerous empty hands awaiting her, she took a deep, back-strengthening breath. Then she bent to retrieve the swords and axes she'd left on the ground beside the Berserker, and she froze.

The weapons were gone.

"Dear saints!" Eyes rounding, she stared at the flattened patch of grass where the heavy swords and axes had lain. They *had* been there.

Straightening, she swung about—and saw the missing weapons at once. James stood frowning at her, the five-foot-long blades and huge war axes tucked lightly beneath his arm. He held them as if they weighed nothing. And the sight annoyed her beyond reason.

Catriona lifted her chin, bristling. "I didn't hear you coming."

"You weren't meant to." He stepped closer, and her pulse leapt because she was sure he meant to kiss her. Instead, he only caught her chin, tilting her face up to his. "If I couldn't move soundlessly, even when carrying weapons"—he shifted the swords and axes, without any discernible rattling—"I would've been dead years ago."

"So you thought I might've attacked you?" Too late, she remembered how she'd used her lady's dirk to slash his hand in the wood.

He leaned toward her, so near that his breath warmed her cheek. "These swords and axes"—he kept their sharp blades away from her—"are honed to kill. If you'd heard my approach, you might've grabbed one carelessly, hurting yourself in the by-doing."

"I know how to handle a weapon."

He gave her a look. "A wee blade a mouse could use to cut cheese."

So he was thinking of the morning in the wood.

She wondered if he knew their wild trek across the glen haunted her. That she'd dreamed about how closely he'd held her clutched to his side. And how she'd sometimes waken in the night, feeling all warm, tingly, and aching, wishing she were once again in his arms.

That she burned to lie with him on the ice...

If he shared any such yearnings, she couldn't tell.

His face could've been granite, and his grip on her chin was firm. Nothing at all that could be even halfway mistaken for a caress. His touch was cold, but the contact still flooded her with a rush of desire.

Furious, she tried to ignore the awareness crackling between them. "Even a *wee blade* can do much damage if used skillfully. A thrust in the eye, or..."

She let her gaze drift downward, meaningfully.

When he frowned, caught off guard that she'd look *there,* she jerked free.

"Those are mine." She reached for the weapons, but he captured her hands easily, clamping his strong fingers around her wrists in an iron-hard one-handed grip.

"They are no man's." He pulled her close, so near her breasts pressed into the solid wall of his plaid-covered chest. "These swords and axes have done the work for which they were crafted. They've earned their rest, just like the men who wielded them."

"That's not what I meant." She felt a shiver slip along her nerves. His heart thundered against her, the intimacy scalding. She swallowed, heat flaming her face, pooling low in her belly. "I need the arms to—"

"I know what you were doing." His gaze flicked to the dead Berserker, the war ax now resting in the man's clenched and bloodied fist.

"You've done enough." He looked back at her, his dark gaze piercing. "The swords and axes will find their way to Valhalla or God's heaven along with thon fallen champion and the other slain men. But"—he tightened his grip on her wrists, then released her, swiftly—"I will place the weapons in any remaining hands."

"I don't want your help." Catriona narrowed her eyes, struggling to accept the futility of arguing with a towering pillar of pure and stubborn Highland male.

She wasn't sure she could resist.

So she kept her chin angled, defiant. "Clan Donald women always do such honors. Your own sister is doing the same for your Cameron dead.

"She is there, see!" Catriona glanced across the field where, although Isobel held no weapons, she still moved among her clan's fallen. Watery sun shone on her raven-black hair, making the dark tresses shimmer. And she wore a cloak that looked much too fine and delicate for the cold. But the mantle must've been more substantial than it appeared, for its folds didn't catch in the wind.

James followed her gaze. "I see Beathag, our Cook's wife."

"You don't see—" Catriona blinked. A stout older woman was picking her way among the rocks and heather, a clutch of swords pressed against her ample hip.

Isobel was gone.

"I saw your sister kneeling beside a man." Frowning, Catriona turned back to James. "She was—"

"Isobel is tending the wounded." James looked at her strangely. "She's with the other women beyond yon cluster of whin and broom." He indicated a long thicket of the yellow-blooming bushes. "They're seeing to the men most grievously injured. Your own Blackshore laundress, Maili, is there with them.

"You should go to them." His eyes darkened, every hard, intensely masculine inch of him crowding her even though he hadn't moved. "I saw you press your hand to your hip when you straightened from thon Berserker. You winced and—"

"I did no such thing." Catriona wouldn't show him weakness. Not after all that had happened between them. "I'm as able to carry a few swords and axes as any woman.

And"—she didn't bother to tamp down the fury welling inside her—"there's nothing wrong with my eyes."

"I ne'er said there was." James set down the weapons he'd been holding and took a small leather-wrapped flagon from his sword belt. "Here"—he offered the flask to her—"have a sip of *uisge beatha*. Battles make people see odd things. Thon woman is Beathag and no one else."

"I can see that." Catriona waved away the whisky. *"Now.* But I know what I saw before."

"You didn't see my sister." He fastened the flagon back onto his belt.

"Perhaps not..." Catriona felt a chill. "Could be the woman was—"

"All Cameron women save Beathag are with the wounded." His harsh tone said more than his words. As did the sudden hard glint in his eye and the twitching muscle that leapt to life in his jaw.

She'd seen the Castle Haven ghost again.

And James knew it.

But for some reason, he didn't want to admit the lovely raven-haired spirit existed.

He also seemed bent on ignoring their night, no matter how hotly the memory beat around them, stirring the air. She couldn't deny the challenge sizzling between them, the storm of passion that seethed inside her whenever he was near. Since then, much of it was angry passion, but it still made her heart thunder and sent quivers of sensation all through her. A dizzy kind of madness that only worsened the longer he stood before her, so tall, dark, and irresistible.

Which meant it was time to be rid of him.

She glanced about as unobtrusively as she could,

searching for someone—anyone, or even anything—she could use as a reason to send him on his way.

But there was nothing.

This corner of the field stretched empty. Nothing stirred except the autumn wind, brisk, cold, and blowing ever-thickening curtains of mist across the rock and heather. An eerie creaking sound came from a nearby copse of pines, but the noise was only branches tossing in the wind.

If she wanted to be free of James, it fell to her to escape him.

So she flicked at her sleeve, pretending indifference.

Then...

Quickly, she darted around him, but she tripped over a sword hilt. James caught her before she could slam to her knees, flashing his arm around her waist in an iron-hard grip. But before he could right her, he also lost his footing and they tumbled into a springy patch of heather.

James landed on top of her, the long, hard weight of him pinning her to the ground. He'd tightened his arms around her as they'd toppled and he still held her fiercely, making it hard to breathe. Worse, his mouth was only a breath away from hers. And the desire in his eyes sent a jolt of pure feminine excitement racing through her.

"Get off me!" She squirmed, trying to wriggle out from beneath him.

But he only shot to his knees, straddling her with his powerful thighs, his hands braced on either side of her shoulders, caging her.

"Destiny, sweet, is everything. And"—he leaned down, bringing his face even closer to hers than before—"it seems my fate is to be plagued by you!"

Then he slanted his mouth across hers, stifling any

protest she might've made with a hard, rough kiss that was fierce, hot, and much more savage than their kiss in the stair tower. He swept one hand behind her neck, cupping her head with his strong fingers as he deepened the kiss, plunging his tongue between her lips to dance with hers as waves of pleasure began washing through her.

Her entire body tingled, arching against him as she slid her arms around his shoulders, clinging to him. She plunged her hands into his hair, tangling her fingers in the thick, silky strands.

"Ahhh..." Feeling dizzy, she let her tongue twirl and caress his, again and again, needing more. The taste and scent of him filled her senses, the heady thrill of his kiss blotting everything except the feel of powerful hard-muscled body pressed so intimately close to hers, the magic of his kiss, so impossibly seductive.

Then—just when she was sure the world had ended, leaving them alone in bliss—he broke away, leaping to his feet as if he'd been jabbed with a red-hot poker.

He threw his plaid back over his shoulder and shoved both hands through his hair. Hands that shook slightly, Catriona saw with much satisfaction.

She also heard voices—men's Lowland accents—and, following James's gaze, she saw Earl David, Sir Walter, and their guardsmen walking among the fallen, coming slowly in their direction.

"I'm sorry, lass, after the night of the bath, I'd sworn no' to come near you again." James glanced toward the approaching men, then back to her. "To be sure, I'd no' willfully cause you shame."

He reached to help her to her feet. "You bring out the worst in me."

"*Plagues* will do that!" Catriona ignored his outstretched hand and scrambled up on her own, brushing furiously at her skirts.

Then, before he could stop her, she snatched up the discarded swords and axes and strode away, leaving him to stand beside the crushed clump of heather.

He might think he'd just salvaged her honor.

But she knew the truth.

He thought she was a plague.

And that was a great shame. Because now, more than ever, she knew he was the only man she'd ever want. Worst of all, she was pretty sure she'd fallen in love with him. And, she knew, her chances of happiness with James Cameron were about as good as if she were betrothed to Lore MacShade.

She kicked a pebble as she marched along.

Just now, she'd almost prefer Lore.

Chapter Eighteen

❧

Hours later, at the Cameron end of the field, Catriona stepped beneath the shelter of two large sailcloths stretched across staked poles and was sure she'd entered the anteroom of hell.

"Dear saints." She paused just inside the door flap, pressing a hand to her breast.

The makeshift infirmary was worse than she'd dared to imagine.

Moans, groans, and worse sounds filled the air. Wounded men, the source of the terrible noises, lay on plaids and pallets. Women tended them, many looking almost as spent and ragged as the injured men. A light rain pattered on the sailcloth roof, and gusting mist blew in through the tent's opening flap each time someone hurried in or out, which appeared to happen often.

And because daylight was fading, scores of wax and tallow candles burned everywhere, casting a flickering reddish-orange glow on the shelter's linen walls. The flames from braziers and the fires beneath three steaming cauldrons added to the hellish scene, though the acrid woodsmoke from the kettle fires helped chase the stench of blood.

"Dinnae think to smear your owl droppings on me!" Kendrew's deep voice came from one of the pallets. "I'll slit you belly to gullet if you dare. I've ne'er laid a hand to a woman, so you'll be the first."

Turning, Catriona saw him at once. Purple-faced with outrage, he lay on a plaid, a folded wolf's pelt bolstering his burly shoulders. He'd pushed up on his elbows to glower at the stout woman kneeling over him. Her strong-looking hands held a small wooden bowl, the object of Kendrew's upset.

Catriona recognized the woman as Beathag, the Cook's wife from Castle Haven.

"'Tis gannet tallow and crushed elder leaves, naught else." Beathag's voice came as calm as Kendrew's was angry. "Even you must know that solan goose fat soothes wounded flesh." She dipped her fingers into the bowl, reaching to smooth the ointment onto Kendrew's stomach. "The crumbled elder leaves will do the rest, healing your cut before—"

"Are you blind as well as a pest?" Kendrew roared. "I've a scratch, no cut. You wasted good stitching thread on me, and I'll no' have your smelly goop—"

"He's been the worst of them all." Isobel appeared at Catriona's elbow, several lengths of clean linen bandaging draped over her arm. "The big ones always fuss the most, though he did take Beathag's needle pricks without a word. The cut to his groin was deeper than a scratch. It was wicked, reaching nearly to his man parts."

Isobel glanced his way, blushing.

"I heard James cut him." Catriona followed Isobel's gaze. Kendrew didn't see them looking at him, for he was too busy glaring at Beathag. But he was sitting upright now, and the reddish glow from the kettle fires fell across him, picking out the blue battle-kill marks he had carved on his massive chest and arms.

Catriona shuddered, recalling his ferocity.

Isobel appeared fascinated.

"The marks count each man he's felled in battle." Catriona saw no reason not to enlighten Isobel. She just didn't mention it was Maili who'd told her—or how Maili knew. "My brother might've been his next mark if James hadn't challenged Kendrew when he was hacking at Alasdair with his ax."

"Dear me—you've come to see your brother, and I've kept you." Isobel touched her arm, Kendrew and his blue kill-marks apparently forgotten. "He's over there, with his dog. They're just beyond the cauldrons…"

Isobel glanced toward the three fire kettles, where a red-faced woman twice the size of Beathag scooped dipperfuls of steaming water into pails held by a seemingly endless stream of harried, tired-looking women and a few wide-eyed boys who were clearly kitchen lads.

Alasdair was nowhere to be seen, though that wasn't surprising, as he was surely supine on a pallet, just like all the other men. And Geordie would be pressed against his side, sharing the ordeal.

Catriona did spot a woman's fair head, her hair as bright as a Nordic summer sun. The woman knelt behind the third cauldron, her back to the tent's opening flap, where Catriona and Isobel stood. Images from Catriona's night at Castle Nought flashed through her mind. Only one woman she knew had such shining golden tresses.

Or such a proud, commanding set to her shoulders.

Especially in such a hellish place, where most backs were hunched with exertion and even the most diligent shoulders sagged in weariness.

"Marjory Mackintosh is here?" Catriona wasn't surprised to see Lady Norn near Alasdair.

"That's her, aye." Isobel nodded, praise in her tone. "She's a wizard with a needle and seems to know as much of healing as Beathag. She tended your brother and she vows he'll regain full use of his arm. Your laundress, Maili, helped her, and"—Isobel leaned close, whispering—"Maili said Marjory murmured ancient Norse blessings over the stitching thread before she set to work."

Any other time, Catriona would've smiled.

She could well imagine Lady Norn promising to feed blood to Odin's ravens for all her days if the Norse god of battle helped her win Alasdair's heart.

The moony eyes they'd made at each other at Castle Nought had shown the way that wind blew.

Hopefully she hadn't made a similar fool of herself to James earlier. If he guessed how she felt about him, after what had happened between them, she'd never live down the shame. Just the thought set her blood to buzzing in her ears. Feeling almost dizzy, she forced herself to stand straighter and hold on to her nerves.

"Has anyone seen to James?" She blurted the question she hadn't planned to ask. "I'm good with a needle. If his ankle still needs care—"

She bit her tongue before any more such nonsense could escape her lips.

Something in the woodsmoke must be addling her wits. She was the last soul James would want tending him.

But Isobel just lifted a brow, giving her a woman-to-woman look. "He saw to the gash himself. He used to help Beathag when he was a lad. She has a son about James's age and the two of them followed her everywhere. I'd vow"—she stepped aside when someone threw back the door flap and hurried past them, into the tent—"James can sew a wound better than any woman here, save Beathag herself.

"He was here only moments ago if you"—Isobel's brow inched a bit higher—"wished to speak to him?"

She didn't.

If she did, she might stick a stitching needle in his eye.

She was that angry with him. Still.

"Shall I send someone to find him?" Isobel's gaze flickered to the kitchen laddies near the cauldrons.

"Nae." Catriona shook her head, no doubt too vigorously. She could also feel her face heating. "I came to help, that's all." She rolled back her sleeves, showing her well-scrubbed hands and arms. "I washed at the spring outside the tent. So if I can—"

"The worst is past us now, praise be." Isobel patted the bandaging on her arm. "I was just returning these linens to the bandage creels." She nodded toward the row of large wicker baskets running along one side of the tent, most of the creels empty.

"All of the injured men have been tended." She looked back to Catriona. "Most of us are just seeing to their comfort now. Plumping bolsters and making sure the pallets are as clean as we can keep them." She flipped her braids over her shoulders and then rubbed the back of her neck.

"There's wine and ale to be passed around to the men who are thirsty. And *uisge beatha* or draughts of Beathag's sleeping tisane for those who need something stronger.

"Anything you wish to do is welcome." Isobel glanced deeper into the smoky, stinking tent. "The men"—her voice hitched, roughly—"they are grateful, whatever."

Isobel frowned and lifted a hand, dashing at her cheek. "None of us should be here, doing this..." She spoke low, blinking hard against the sheen in her eyes.

And in that moment, Isobel looked so much like the beautiful, raven-haired haint that Catriona could only stare at her.

She touched her amber necklace, noting that the stones were chilled as ice. Almost as if the spirit of the ambers had withdrawn into some mysterious depths, hiding from the battle and its terrible aftermath.

But *she* was there.

And so was Isobel, along with every other woman of the glen. Including, she knew, one whom no one else had seen or acknowledged. It seemed a grievous slight, for Catriona was sure the raven-haired beauty felt the day's tragedy as deeply as the living women.

So she swallowed against the sudden thickness in her own throat. And then she drew a nerve-summoning breath, reaching to grip Isobel's arm.

"I must ask you..." Catriona's voice was amazingly firm. "Is there a ghost at Castle Haven? A lovely young woman with hair like yours and—"

"You've seen her?" Isobel's eyes flew wide.

Catriona nodded. "I believe so. Unless there is someone flitting about who looks very much like you but prefers to stay hidden."

Isobel's eyes went even rounder. "She's said to look like

me. Or"—she shook her head as if she couldn't believe her own words—"perhaps I should say that I am believed to resemble her, because she lived so very long ago."

Catriona's pulse quickened. "You know who she is, then?"

"To be sure." Isobel glanced round, dropping her voice. "But you mustn't tell anyone else you've seen her, for she is a bringer of bad tidings.

"She is Lady Scandia." Isobel leaned close, speaking the name against Catriona's ear. "She's known as—"

"The Doom of the Camerons," a deep voice finished behind them. "And to see her brings ill fortune and sorrow to all."

"James!" Catriona spun around, her heart beating madly. He stood just inside the tent flap, his damp-glistening hair and clean plaid showing that he must've bathed at the nearby spring.

He was also bending such a dark look on her that she forgot all about his spectral ancestress and wanted only to kick him in the shins.

"I will tell Lady Catriona of Scandia." He spoke to his sister, but his words brought the raven-haired beauty right back into Catriona's mind.

And—God help her—whatever the poor woman's tale, his harsh tone when he spoke of her made Catriona want to defend Scandia, regardless.

James had just tossed fat into the fire.

And this time she wasn't going to let him jump away from the flames.

Before Catriona could blink, James took her by the arm and pulled her through the tent flap and outside the makeshift infirmary. Cold wind slammed into them, whipping their hair and tearing at James's plaid and Catriona's cloak. A light drizzle still fell, and the air was thick with woodsmoke from the kettle fires. The acrid smoke stung Catriona's eyes, but when she slowed to knuckle them, James kept hurrying her along.

He slanted a look at her as they hastened past the spring where she'd washed earlier.

"We'll be there anon." He didn't say *where,* but she saw that he was leading her toward another tent. Colorful standards flew above this tent, and the banners were Lowland.

And when they reached the tent and he ushered her inside, she saw that it was a refreshment pavilion. Oak benches ranged around the walls, and several trestle tables stood in the tent's middle. Catriona could only stare at the rich variety of delicacies. Baskets of wheaten loaves were placed on the tables, and she even spotted bowls of oysters and whelks, though they didn't tempt her. There were also platters of cold spiced capon and trays of wild roast boar.

Heavy silver candelabrums should've illuminated the offerings, but the tapers had gutted, leaving the smoky tinge of melted wax to haze the air.

The tent was also empty.

Catriona dug in her heels just inside the door flap. "I'm not hungry, if that's why you brought me here."

He scowled at her. "I brought you here so we could be alone. The worthies who were using this tent rode away with the King. And the commoners yet remaining are too busy bending their necks to gawk at the slaughter to think of their bellies." His words held a fierce edge. "Our own people won't come here—"

"There's a flaw in your thinking." Catriona folded her arms. She ignored how her heart beat in her throat. How she'd responded—again—to his kisses in the heather, the feel of his hard-muscled body pressed against hers. "I have no wish to be alone with you. You could have told me about Lady Scandia outside the infirmary tent."

He took a step toward her. "Nae, I couldn't have done."

She lifted her chin, proudly. "I do not melt in rain and wind. Truth be told, I thrive in such weathers."

"So does every Highlander, last I heard." He glared at her. "This is no' about you. It's about my clan." He came closer, his voice hardening. "I'll no' have them hear the name Scandia. For sure, no' on such a dark day as this."

Catriona let her gaze pass over him, lingering on his broad, powerful shoulders and the sword at his hip. "I can't believe you're afraid of a young woman who's not just beautiful and your own kin, I'm thinking, but who is also as wispy as a moonbeam. However solid she might appear at times."

He flushed. "Scandia is a bogle. *A ghost.* She is no' a young woman."

"But she was."

"Aye, she lived—once. And I would that she'd ne'er been born. See you, each time she appears, tragedy befalls the clan. There are no exceptions to the blackness she brings."

"Perhaps she appears to help you?" Catriona liked that idea. "I've heard of such family bogles. They're always long-passed family members who show themselves to warn of ill things to come, not to cause them."

"Scandia is a doom bringer." He cut the air with a hand,

his eyes glinting in the dimness. "I'll grant she might no' have set out to be such a harbinger, but her death made her one. She jumped from the Lady Tower. Her death unleashed one of the worst disasters our clan has e'er seen."

"Dear saints." Catriona couldn't believe the ghost wished the clan ill. She'd seemed so proud of James the night he'd rallied his men. "Who was she?"

"If you knew her history, you wouldn't want to know."

"Then tell me." Catriona prodded.

For a moment, she thought James would push her aside and stride from the tent. He looked that angry. But he only rammed both hands through his hair and then heaved an annoyed sigh.

"Scandia lived hundreds of years ago." He took her by the shoulders then, looking down at her as if he was about to say something so terrifying she'd run from the tent. "She was the daughter of a Cameron warrior and a Viking woman, given to the warrior as a war prize. Those who have seen her say she has raven tresses and alabaster skin, and that she looks much like Isobel.

"I know that to be true, because I've seen her." He looked down at her, his gaze intense. "I also know you saw her on the field this morn. You mistook her for my sister."

"I think she wanted to stand with the other clans-women in support." Catriona was sure of it. "She looked sad when I saw her."

A muscle jerked in James's jaw, but he said nothing.

When he spoke, his words were harsh. "You are too kind to her. If she cared for our weal, she wouldn't have done what she did. See you"—he took a breath—"Scandia was betrothed to the son of a great Norse warlord. The marriage was to secure peace between her father and the Viking raiders who were her mother's people.

"They were a band of unruly Northmen who ne'er stopped harrying our coast. It was hoped that Scandia's hand would appease them. Her father also agreed to allow them to retain the land they'd seized and were beginning to settle, against the clan's will. But"—he paused when a gust of wind shook the door flap—"even such an alliance, so beneficial to the invaders, couldn't change that they were pagans and rough, bloodthirsty men.

"The Viking who would have been Scandia's husband, a young man called Donar Strong-Sword, was reputed to be especially fearsome. Clan legend tells that Scandia wept on her knees, begging her father not to give her to such a ruthless and savage man."

Catriona frowned, not liking the tale.

"Scandia's father refused to unsay the pledge he'd made to Donar. Such alliances between warring parties were known to bring peace if not happiness, and he had to think of the greater good." He spoke those words as if they soured his tongue. "So-o-o, when Scandia saw herself bound to a man she loathed and feared—"

"She sprang to her death," Catriona finished for him, the thought hurting her as if someone had rammed a blade through her ribs, piercing her heart.

"So it was, aye." James was watching her, carefully. "On the day Donar Strong-Sword and his entourage rode to Castle Haven to claim Scandia, she ran to the top of the Lady Tower to await his approach. Then, when Donar and his warriors appeared, she leapt from the battlements, dying at his feet rather than becoming his bride."

"Dear God…" Catriona blinked, stinging heat pricking

her eyes. She shuddered, the image flashing across her mind as if she'd seen Scandia's plunge. "I've never heard anything so horrible."

James arched a brow. "The worst came later when Scandia's father took vengeance on Donar and his people. He blamed them for her death, you see. And his rage was great, some say bottomless. He sent out the fiery cross, gathering his fiercest warriors and all that would rally to him from allied clans. Together, they set torch to the Norse settlement, burning every living soul, man and beast. They chased down those who tried to flee, slaying them where they stood and leaving their bodies for the ravens.

"When word reached Donar's homeland, the Norse-men's wrath was equally terrible and swift. They came at once, scores of their dragon-ships bringing their own best fighters. They raged along our shores for years, bringing death and destruction not just to Camerons, but to many innocent clans who had the ill fortune to dwell within striking distance of the coast. Before every such terror—"

"If you're going to say that Scandia appeared, I say she did so because she was appalled." Catriona straightened, bristling. "Not because she wished such horrors to happen."

"I ne'er said she desired such doom"—he took her chin in his hand, forcing her to meet his gaze—"only that she stirs the like."

"Because she took her own life?" Outrage whipped through Catriona.

"So it is believed." James proved his stubbornness. "All know such deaths leave darkness behind them."

"I know you're unfair." She wrenched away from him and grabbed the tent flap, flinging it wide. "I've known that for a while now. And I also know why Scandia is sad. The men of her clan blame her for their own hotheaded folly. She sought peace and took it the only way she could.

"You"—she threw a glare over her shoulder as she stepped out into the rain—"and your ancestors stole her rest. You are the Doom of the Camerons, not that poor, anguished maid whose name you blacken."

"Damn it all to hell!" James's roar echoed inside the pavilion. A shattering crash, perhaps a fallen wine ewer, underscored his wrath, his anger only making Catriona hurry faster from the tent.

But not because she feared his rage.

Her heart pounded, and the blood was roaring in her ears for a very different reason. A good reason. Because— she nipped around the edge of the infirmary tent, then stood, tipping back her head to let the drizzle cool her face—Scandia's tale gave her an idea.

And it was a wonderful plan, she decided, bending to pick a sprig of heather.

She held the blooms to her heart, feeling better than she had in weeks. She'd soon show James her mettle. And she had more in reserve, waiting for his next assault.

She'd not be cast aside again. She'd use her every womanly wile and her wits to ensure that no clan's strife and warring would ever again bring grief to the glen.

Men could be such fools.

But women desired only peace.

And a few other pleasantries that every female with blood in her veins desired. She certainly wouldn't be denying hers. Not after James had shown her how delicious carnal delights could be. She'd had only a brief taste, and she hungered for so much more.

How exciting if his kisses, and what she now knew followed them, might settle the glen feuding in ways a man's sword or ax never could.

If Isobel and Kendrew's sister, Lady Norn agreed, perhaps they could persuade the men of the glen to see things their way.

It *was* worth a try.

"An alliance?"

Isobel didn't hide her skepticism as she, Catriona, and Marjory stood in the shelter of an abandoned cook stall set in the trees behind the infirmary tent. "The three of us banding together to conspire against our men? I swear to you, the effort would only turn our hair gray and put worry-bags beneath our eyes. Cameron men wed only daughters of allied chieftains, friends. Not since Lady Edina—"

"Lady Edina was the last woman of a feuding clan to marry into the Mackintoshes, too." Marjory couldn't hold back a shiver of distaste. "Every chieftain since her long-suffering husband has vowed to never again wed a shrewish, unwilling wife. Kendrew would sooner—"

"I don't see it as conspiring." Catriona wasn't sure that was true, but she kept her doubt to herself. "And"—she turned to Marjory—"you're both overlooking one crucial key to the plan's success."

Lifting her chin—and wishing she'd just bathed and donned her finest raiments—Catriona held out her arms and turned in a slow circle. She forced herself to forget her mussed hair and rumpled, stained clothes and recall that she was a high-born daughter of a great and noble house, the sister of one of the most respected chieftains in all the Highlands and the Isles. As, she knew, were Isobel Cameron and Marjory—Lady Norn—Mackintosh.

When she'd turned full circle, she stopped, setting her hands on her hips. "Tell me true, ladies." She couldn't keep her lips from twitching. "Do I look like a shrew who'd go unwilling to her husband's bed?"

Isobel's face pinkened. "Nae..."

Lady Norn arched a golden brow, a spark of amusement in her eyes. "Anything but, by all the Valkyries."

"Exactly." Catriona nodded, smiling. "And"—her excitement was beginning to grow—"neither of you look like angry, shriveled-up stick women, either."

"But..." Isobel threw a glance over her shoulder, back toward the infirmary. "I'm still not sure it would work. Look what happened after the alliances with Lady Edina. The feuding only worsened, and Camerons have an even longer history with arranged marriages going wrong."

"I know." Catriona reached to squeeze Isobel's arm, knowing the other woman would understand that she meant Scandia's fatal match with Donar Strong-Sword. "But we are not those women of the past. We are our own selves and"—she glanced at Marjory, including her—"our marriages wouldn't be true arranged unions. We will make our future husbands want us.

"We'll seduce and beguile them until"—her heart sang with the brilliance of it—"they are so besotted that they think wedding us is their idea."

Silence greeted her.

Then Marjory's lips began curving in a smile. "I wouldn't mind considering such a plan."

"Then we shall!" Catriona could have hugged her.

Isobel still looked dubious. "They might become suspicious if we all—"

"We must start with just one of us." Marjory looked at Catriona as she spoke. "This was your idea, so perhaps you should be the first bride?"

Catriona swallowed. Ice floes came to mind. "I—"

"It might work if you plied your charms on Hugh." Isobel finally came around. "He would take you in a heartbeat and thank all the gods."

"Hugh?" Marjory looked from Isobel to Catriona, then back at Isobel. "I was thinking James might suit her better. He's chieftain, after all."

"James would never wed a woman from a feuding clan." Isobel shook her head. "He's too certain such unions bring nothing but doom."

Catriona felt her delight dimming.

"I will be the first, agreed. Though I have no wish to wed Hugh." She took a deep breath, knowing her happiness depended on being courageous. "I will persuade James to wed me."

There.

She'd said it.

"James?" Isobel's rounded eyes didn't inspire confidence.

But the sudden laughter in Marjory's did. "Odin's blessings on you, then!"

"Odin's blessings." Catriona repeated the wish, her heart thumping.

Then she held out the heather she'd picked earlier. "We must swear on it, vowing on these heather blooms, that we'll each seek to win forever peace in the glen by winning the heart of one of our enemy's men."

"I vow it." Marjory placed her hand over Catriona's,

closing her fingers around Catriona's fist so that they both held the heather.

"And I." Isobel did the same.

"Then we are agreed." Catriona stepped back, kissing the blooms and them tossing the sprig high in the air, letting the wind carry it away. "It is done."

The words spoken, she reached up to remove her amber necklace and placed it in Isobel's hands.

"Take this"—she closed Isobel's fingers around the precious stones—"back to Castle Haven tonight and show it to James. Tell him you found the necklace on the field and you know it is mine.

"He knows I always wear it, so he will believe you." Catriona raised her hands, palms outward, and backed away when Isobel tried to return the necklace. "Nae—you must keep it, for now."

"But how will a necklace help our plan?" Isobel frowned.

Catriona smiled, the idea seeming more perfect by the moment. "You must insist that James return the ambers to me at Blackshore. He will, I'm sure. And then—"

"You will seduce him." That was Marjory.

"Nae." Catriona shook her head, her whole body tingling with anticipation. "I will allow him to seduce me."

And this time she'd make sure nothing went wrong.

Chapter Nineteen

❧

Later that night, James entered his great hall and stopped almost as soon as he'd stepped from the entry arch into the vast room's smoke-hazed reaches. Something prickled his nape and breathed gooseflesh along his arms. But aside from fewer men lining the long tables—the slain had been washed and awaited burial in the chapel, and the injured rested in the solar and elsewhere, under Beathag's care—he couldn't see anything that would stir his warrior's instincts, warning him that something was afoot.

Beside him, Hector growled low in his throat, the dog's hackles rising.

Yet nothing appeared different than any other night.

Almost every torch blazed, and a well-doing fire chased the worst of the evening's chill. The tantalizing smell of roasting meats filled the air. Men crowded the trestle benches, eating and talking, and some had gathered in a corner, arguing loudly over a game of dice. And, as so often in autumn, windblown rain lashed at the walls, rattling shutters, lifting the edges of tapestries, and guttering candles on the tables near the embrasures.

Colin stood in one of the darker alcoves, his back to the hall and his hands braced on the window splay. He'd unlatched the shutters and appeared to be staring out at the cold, wet night. He was grimacing, for James could see the white of Colin's teeth in the dimness. Or so he thought until he looked deeper into the shadows and saw the plump kitchen lass on her knees before Colin.

"Damn fool!" James quickly turned away and started down the broad aisle between the long tables, the prickles at the back of his neck worsening the closer he came to the raised dais end of the hall.

Something was amiss there.

He could taste it on the back of his tongue.

Trickery or an ambush—he knew the feeling well. And the awareness-chills raced along his skin, wariness tightening his chest, humming in his veins. He saw why the instant he mounted the dais steps.

Catriona's amber necklace lay on the high table before his sister.

James froze on the top step, staring at the gleaming stones. The humming in his veins became a great roar. Narrowing his eyes, he started forward again, recognizing the serene look on Isobel's face. She always appeared most poised when she was up to something. And just now her calm signaled that she was as battle-ready as any warrior.

"Isobel." He stalked toward her, glaring.

"James. We wondered when you'd join us." She set down her eating knife and reached for a linen napkin, calmly dabbing at her lips as he came closer.

"Where did you get that?" He stopped before his laird's chair, gripping its high carved back. He didn't bother to say what he meant.

Everyone at the high table knew. The flurry of coughs, cleared throats, and reaching for bannocks or ale cups proved it. As did the averted gazes and, in some cases, the sudden attention to the castle dogs scrounging for scraps beneath the table.

Rarely had the beasts received so many prime bits of good meat.

"Isobel..." James ignored dogs and men, focusing on the soul he knew responsible. "That bit of frippery belongs to Catriona MacDonald."

"So it does, I do believe." Isobel gave him a sweet smile.

She set down her napkin, carefully folding it before she touched a finger to the necklace. The stones glowed like a living thing, gleaming brightly in the light cast by a wall sconce. For two pins, James would believe the hell-blasted ambers were heating, pulsing wickedly, catching fire beneath his eyes.

He tore his gaze away to glare at his sister. "Answer me. Where did you get the necklace? The last time I saw Lady Catriona it was around her neck."

"Then she must've lost it, mustn't she?" Isobel curled her fingers around the stones, all innocence. "I found the necklace outside the infirmary tent, long after the Mac-Donalds left for Blackshore."

"Far as I know, Catriona ne'er removes the necklace." James could almost see the word *liar* blazing on his sister's forehead. "She wouldn't have left without setting up a hue and cry to search for it."

Isobel dismissed his objection with an airy wave of one hand. "She would if she didn't realize she'd lost it. You know how fraught things were for us all." Her gaze met his, almost reproachful. "I dare say she had more on her mind than a necklace."

James scowled at her, not believing a word. "Where was it, then?"

Isobel, master mischief-maker that she was, didn't miss a beat. "It was caught in the heather near the spring. I spotted it when I went there to wash after we'd finished at the infirmary."

"I see." James took his seat, reaching immediately for his ale cup. He saw, indeed, though he wasn't sure where the two women's trickery was meant to lead him.

Nowhere good, he was certain.

"Looks to me, someone will have to return the necklace to her." Colin appeared then, claiming his seat with all the jaunty satisfaction of a man recently sated. "I've no' been down Blackshore way in ages." He plucked his eating knife from his belt and began piling his trencher with thick slabs of roasted meat. "I can ride there at first light—"

"We've men to bury on the morrow." James wasn't allowing his womanizing cousin anywhere near Catriona. He'd damaged her enough on his own. "If Catriona is distressed by the necklace's loss"—James almost choked on the words, for he doubted she'd truly lost the damty bauble—"she'll have to suffer her worry for a few days until—"

"I can go." At the far end of the table, Hugh put down his ale cup and wiped his mouth with the back of his hand. "I can compose my lays about the battle on the ride there. The journey will inspire me—"

"Nae." James was firm.

Just because, as clan storyteller, Hugh's work kept him from other duties didn't mean he was the right man to go riding off to Blackshore to return a necklace that—James was sure—was at the heart of some perfidious scheme.

Sure of it, James looked down the table at Hugh, not liking how his brows had drawn together in a stubborn frown. "You do your best tale spinning locked away in your turret. I'll vow a stroll across the battlefield will do more to inspire you than a trek across the glen, eh?"

He lifted his ale cup, waving it in Hugh's direction. "Aye, that is much better for your muse."

Hugh's face reddened, sourly. "You just want to deliver the necklace yourself."

"I—" James clamped his mouth shut, furious. The cold prickles that had danced up and down his nape earlier now felt like a white-hot iron band clamped tight around his neck, suffocating him.

"He's right, you know." Isobel sipped her wine delicately. "Who better than you to show our goodwill by returning what is surely an heirloom piece? The King did press us to maintain rapport with the MacDonalds and Mackintoshes. This is an excellent opportunity to prove we will abide by King Robert's wishes."

Colin grinned and slapped the table. "A splendid idea!"

James glared at them both.

He didn't bother to argue. It was true. And he'd known the moment he'd seen the necklace that this—him sallying off with the ambers tucked in his belt pouch, like a knight on a white charger—was Isobel's plan.

No doubt Catriona's, too.

For some nefarious reason, the two women were

plotting against him. A shame they'd overlooked that, as a battle-hardened warrior and chieftain, he knew a bit about tactical strategies himself.

Indeed, he was a master.

"You will go?" Isobel was eyeing him over the rim of her wine cup.

Colin made a business of spearing more slices of roasted meat onto his trencher, selecting the largest and most succulent-looking pieces. He slid a glance at James, his dark eyes glinting knowingly. "The maid will surely be overcome with gratitude."

James pretended not to hear him. His cousin knew him too well.

"So be it, then." James kept his face as expressionless as possible. "I will ride to Blackshore in a sennight, no' a day before."

"Seven days!" Isobel lost her calm. "Catriona will be beside herself by then."

James shrugged, pleased by the notion.

Then he applied himself to his trencher, plans of his own forming in his mind. And none of them had much to do with an amber necklace. Though they all revolved around the bauble's owner.

She'd pushed him too far this time.

And when they met again at Blackshore, he'd teach her at last that maids who didn't wish to get burned shouldn't tempt the devil.

"He's not coming."

Catriona cast a look over her shoulder at Maili, who sat on the edge of her bed. "I know it sure as you're perched on my bed." Wishing she felt otherwise, she turned back to her bedchamber window. Small flurries of rain splattered the stone ledge, but she didn't mind. The rain's light patter soothed her, and if she had to wait much longer for James's arrival, she was sure she'd turn raging mad.

She glanced again at her friend. "It's been nearly seven days."

Maili tucked her legs beneath the coverlets, yawning. "I thought you weren't counting?"

"I'm not." She wasn't minding the days. She'd been keeping the hours.

Now she leaned against the cold stone edge of the window arch, something close to fury simmering inside her. She'd been so sure her plan would work. In truth, she'd been henwitted to put such faith in James.

She blew a curl off her brow, all her annoyances bubbling up in her mind, demanding a voice. "Don't you see, Maili?" She could feel her face burning, the frustration making her heart pound. "If he intended to return my ambers, he would've done so by now."

"He'll come." Maili leaned back against the cushions. "I've seen how he looks at you when he thinks no one sees him." She stifled another yawn. "Such glances are always more telling than any direct looks."

Catriona wanted to believe it.

But...

"That may be." Catriona drew her night wrap closer against the cold. "But deeds count for something, too. His absence can't be good."

Maili didn't answer her.

Catriona turned back to the window, peering out into the chill, wet night. A half-moon sailed in and out of the clouds, spilling a narrow band of silver across the loch's black-glistening waters. And even at this late hour, she hoped to catch a glimpse of James riding over the crest of a hill. Or to see him suddenly come into view, torch in hand, on the far shore of the loch.

She'd counted on it until a short while ago.

As she'd been so sure he'd arrive on every other night that had passed since the trial by combat.

But he hadn't come.

And now her confidence was flagging.

She knew Isobel hadn't broken their pact. She felt that in her bones. James had her ambers, and he was deliberately keeping them, ignoring her. And that could mean only that he truly did think of her as a plague.

Frowning, she stepped closer to the window. The night wind helped her stay awake, and she did love the view. Her bedchamber was one of the highest in the tower, and the vista was sweeping, taking in much of Loch Moidart, the cliffs rising at the loch's edge, and even a bit of Blackshore's bailey. Just now, the moon cast a blue and silver sheen over the hills, and the night was silent save for the slap of wavelets on the rocks and the creaking of moored galleys.

Closer by, glimmers of red showed where guardsmen had lit braziers along the battlement's wall-walk, and now and then she caught flickers of light in the bailey. Wedges of yellow that spilled across the cobbles each time someone entered or left the gatehouse. And if she leaned out a bit and craned her neck, she could see that one or two of the other tower windows glowed from within, proving that she and Maili weren't the only ones yet awake.

Resting her knee on one of the window embrasure's padded benches, she took another breath of the cold night air, hoping to banish her sleepiness.

"I tell you, Maili"—she stretched, resisting the urge to sink down onto the bench—"if he doesn't come on the morrow, I'll have the guards bar the gate to him, whatever Alasdair says."

No, you won't, for you love him. Maili spoke from right behind her, the soft words breathing shivers down Catriona's spine.

She spun around, ready to deny any such feelings for the scoundrel, but the words lodged in her throat.

Maili hadn't left the bed.

And staring across the room at her, it was clear to see why she'd gone so silent.

Maili slept.

Catriona's two favorite dogs, Birkie and Beadle, were curled in tight balls close to her side, though all Catriona could see of them was one small black nose peeking out from the rumpled bed coverings. And—she almost overlooked it—a tiny white paw that was just visible beneath a mound of plush, embroidered cushions.

As Beadle and Birkie were litter mates and looked very much alike, she couldn't tell which dog's nose or paw revealed their sleeping presence.

Not that it mattered.

What did was that the three of them took up most of Catriona's large four-postered bed. Maili lay sprawled diagonally across the bed's high mattress. And the two under-the-covers lumps that were Birkie and Beadle occupied the remaining space.

And—Catriona frowned when Maili began to snore— she didn't have the heart to disturb any of them, even if they'd claimed her bed.

I loved him so...

Again, the softly spoken words came from behind Catriona. But this time the only thing behind her was the embrasure's open window.

And now she recognized the voice.

Heart thumping wildly, she swung back around, her breath catching to see Scandia standing at the window, luminescent and shimmering.

Catriona stared at her, frozen, unable to move. She tried to say something—she felt such sympathy for the ghost—but her lips wouldn't form the words.

The glowing raven-haired beauty didn't acknowledge Catriona, her gaze fixed on the darkness beyond the window arch. But she did drift closer to the broad stone splay, her lovely face lighting up, a wondrous smile curving her lips as she gripped the ledge.

Only...

Catriona's eyes rounded. The window splay was now a merlon. Scandia was gripping the solid part of a crenellated parapet that now stood where the tapestried wall of Catriona's bedchamber had been only moments before.

The dark, blustery night was also gone, replaced by a sun-washed blue sky stretching above an endless swath of deep purple heather and bog myrtle. Thick piney woods and great rolling hills, some with narrow gorges gushing with cold, sparkling cataracts, loomed where Loch Moidart's far shore should have been.

And—Catriona pressed a hand to her breast, her pulse racing—she recognized the magnificent stretch of glen, even though it'd been long since she'd seen the land around Castle Haven in summer.

It *was* summer, because the wind was warm. And the

air no longer smelled of cold rain and smoldering peat ash, but of whin, bracken, and wild thyme.

As if she relished the day, the sights and scents, Scandia touched a hand to her own shimmering breast and closed her eyes, breathing deep.

When she looked again, she gave a little cry, leaning forward in excitement.

Catriona edged nearer, too. She took only a step, for she was too awed to disturb Scandia and risk her vanishing, the glorious summer day with her.

The day and—Catriona's jaw slipped—the shining young Viking warrior who'd just emerged from the piney woods.

Tall, powerfully muscled, and with long fair hair and a curling golden beard, he was colorfully dressed in a brilliant blue tunic and sweeping red cloak. An enormous silver-and-gold brooch held the cloak fastened, and countless twisted gold rings adorned his arms. A golden hammer amulet hung from his neck, proclaiming his trust in Thor. And when he looked up at Scandia, flashing a smile, the love that shone in his eyes made Catriona's heart seize.

Donar!

Scandia cried his name when she saw him, leaning forward to wave both arms in the air, greeting him enthusiastically. *Donar, my love!*

Her smile was as dazzling as the young Norseman's.

Tears of joy glittered on her eyelashes, a few trickling down her happy, blushing cheeks. She cried and waved, jumping in her excitement, gripping the edge of the merlon with one hand so she could lean into the notched crenel space between and wave some more.

It was then that she fell.

The joy on her beautiful young face turned to horror when she realized she'd leaned out too far. She lost her balance, hurtling over the battlements.

Donaaaaaar...! Her cry ended abruptly.

Scandia...no-o-o! The young Viking's went on and on and on, unending.

Until Catriona felt a bump against her leg and then a small paw tapping at her knee. She came awake at once and looked down to see Birkie peering up at her, his round eyes filled with concern.

She understood why, for she lay slumped on one of the embrasure benches where she'd clearly fallen asleep. And the dampness on her cheeks proved what she already knew: she'd been crying in her dream.

If it'd even been a dream.

It'd felt so real.

Her heart still hurt. And her lungs pained her as if she'd screamed along with Scandia and Donar. Their cries did echo in her ears, horribly.

"Oh, Birkie..." She scooped the little brown-and-white dog into her arms, cradling him against her breast, grateful for his soft, warm weight. The sloppy wet kisses he gave her as he snuggled closer. "What am I going to do?"

She wasn't sure.

But she did know one thing.

Lady Scandia wasn't the Doom of the Camerons. She'd loved her betrothed with all her heart, and he'd loved her as passionately.

She hadn't taken her own life, she'd lost it.

And Catriona would set things right for her as soon as James arrived at Blackshore.

If he didn't come, she'd go to him.

But a short while later, just as pale gray light began to smudge the eastern horizon, sounds came to her from the loch shore, waking her again.

Someone was moving across the shingled strand, the crunch of stone unmistakable in the predawn stillness.

Careful not to disturb Birkie, Catriona slipped off the bench and peered out the window, her heart filling to see a small party of men just coming into view on the far side of the loch, near to the beached galleys.

James was coming at last.

And she couldn't wait to see him.

A short while later, though it may have been an hour, possibly two, James paced up and down Alasdair's lovely painted solar at Blackshore and wondered why he hadn't sent someone else to return Catriona's amber necklace.

The knocks and slams he'd taken in the battle had surely had a more lasting effect on him than he'd realized, for they'd addled his wits.

And here, in Alasdair's sumptuous solar—the well-appointed room was pleasingly warm with a crackling fire burning in the hearth—whatever might've remained of his good sense had flown out the window.

Catriona was to blame.

She had yet to show herself, and he knew she'd seen him arrive.

She'd waited for him on the little boat strand near Blackshore's postern gate where, so many weeks before, they'd exchanged such heated words. She'd stood at the water's edge, clutching both hands to her breast as she'd watched his approach, her heart in her eyes.

At least he'd thought so.

But he'd lost sight of her when he neared the curving wall of Blackshore's gatehouse. And it was then that her amber necklace started to pulse and burn, scorching his hip even through the leather of his belt pouch and the thick wool of his plaid.

Or so it'd seemed.

He'd credited the strangeness to his own nerves, for it wasn't every day he rode to an enemy keep to bare his heart before a female who might well slap his face for the effort. If her brother didn't first have him hauled from the castle and thrown onto his presumptuous arse.

Yet Alasdair had greeted him as courteously as ever, ushering him, as before, into his fit-for-a-king solar and ordering a fine repast of belly-filling victuals and jugs of good morning ale.

Only Catriona seemed determined to grind his nerves.

It wouldn't surprise him if she'd secreted herself in some hidey-hole in the thickness of the walling and now peered through a squint, watching him pace and fume.

And fume he did, for he wasn't a patient man.

But he was a prudent one—most times, anyway—and he wasn't going to shock Alasdair by professing his desire to wed Catriona until he'd seen her face-to-face. Only then could he assure himself that she'd greet such a union.

So he held his tongue and bided his time, content—or trying to be—that he'd had other important tidings to share with her brother.

Alasdair turned back to him then, dusting his hands, for he'd just thrown another log on the fire. "You're certain about this?" His face didn't show a muscle twitch of doubt, but his words were insulting. "I didn't see any MacNaughtons watching the battle."

"Then I vow you weren't looking in their direction."
James stopped pacing to stand before the brightly painted
mural of the sea god, Manannan Mac Lir, flying across
the foam in *Wave Sweeper*, the blue-robed deity's self-
sailing boat.

He glanced at Manannan's flowing beard, half wondering if he'd sprout such long whiskers before Alasdair
believed what James had told him.

"They were there." James spoke as patiently as he
could. "They stood near the royal loge one moment,
and"—he lifted a hand, snapping his fingers—"they were
gone the next. Vanished, as if I'd imagined them."

"Perhaps you did?" Alasdair looked at him, his rea-
sonable tone more than irksome.

"I'll own that's possible, given the day." The admission
cost James. "Men do see strange things on a field of battle.
But"—he started pacing again, careful not to stride too
near the table where Catriona's necklace lay in a shaft of
pale morning sunlight—"even if I only thought I saw the
buggers at the field, their missing plaids bode ill.

"I ne'er thought I'd defend a MacNaughton, but I'm
leaning toward taking their chief on his word." James
rubbed the back of his neck as he circled the room. "He
swears none of his men were at the battle. He told my
cousin six of their plaids had gone missing."

Alasdair frowned. "Your cousin believed him?"

"He did."

"Mundy MacNaughton is a known weasel." Alasdair
poured himself a cup of morning ale, his calm grating.
"He bends the truth every which way. I'd sooner have
heard your own opinion of his words than—"

"I sent Colin to question Mundy, because even when

the lies reek worse than a week-old barrel of fish, Colin can find the truth better than any."

"Your cousin strikes me as a man too intent on his pleasures to spend time pressing truths from a wriggly scoundrel like Mundy."

Alasdair took a swig of his ale. "Belike Colin spent more time tumbling MacNaughton's serving wenches than badgering Mundy."

For the first time since arriving at Blackshore, James felt a grin tug at his lips. "He enjoyed three of the lasses, aye. And each one sang the same tale as Mundy, claiming a creel of soiled plaids disappeared from right beside the wash kettles. The maids were laundresses and would know. Colin has a way with women, so I'm sure they told him true."

"H'mmm…" Alasdair set down his ale cup. "You think the missing plaids have something to do with the tall, dark-cloaked man we've all seen?"

"I do." James was sure of it. "When I saw the MacNaughtons at the battle, I wondered if they'd come to gloat at us. Later, it struck me that they might've sent one of their men among us to stir trouble. Poking holes in your galleys and shooting arrows at Kendrew Mackintosh. Because—"

"If we'd let ourselves be riled and caused more dissent, Sir Walter would have his grounds to urge the King to cancel the trial by combat and ship us all to the Isle of Lewis." Alasdair nodded grimly, speaking James's mind.

"So I thought, aye." James shot a glance at Catriona's ambers, her absence making him edgy. "I wondered if Sir Walter might've offered Mundy coin, bribing him to do his dirty work so Walter and his henchmen appeared blameless."

"And now?" Alasdair frowned again, blackly this time.

"Now..." James glanced at the door, willing Catriona's footsteps. "I cannae say. But I no longer think Mundy had a hand in any of it. No' after hearing about the six stolen plaids."

"The laundresses could've misplaced them." Alasdair's reason made James' head hurt.

"I considered that." James' hadn't, but he'd not have Alasdair think him less astute. "Until"—he looked at Alasdair directly—"I discovered several of my own spare plaids had also vanished."

Alasdair's brows lifted. "God's eyes! Someone must want to use the plaids as a guise."

"That could be the way of it." The thought chilled James to the marrow. "It's the reason I waited until now to return Catriona's necklace. Colin came back from Mundy's keep only late last night. I wanted to hear Colin's account of his meeting with Mundy before I rode to speak with you."

He kept silent about his other reasons.

But his heart did leap when the sound of light footsteps and a faint scratching noise came from behind the solar's closed door.

"Ahhh..." Alasdair glanced at him. "My long-sleeping sister has risen."

James didn't tell him he'd already seen her, beaming at him from the boat strand.

He did swallow hard, his mouth suddenly ash dry.

When the door swung open, he'd drop to one knee, making his plea before his damty nerves left him. He'd practiced his reasons—a strengthening of the greater good in the glen, a demonstration that the King's peace would be held, an end to long years of feuding—every mile of the way between Castle Haven and Blackshore.

It was a good, sound speech.

And now he couldn't recall a single word.

But he would tell Catriona he wanted her, even that he loved her, if it would help his cause. The saints knew he did love her, and badly. He knew he had to have her. He'd never again have any peace if he didn't. And making her his own was worth more than his pride.

Alasdair could laugh at him if he wished.

James would have her, and nothing else mattered to him.

Then the door opened a crack and Maili poked her dark head into the room, her bright smile fading when her gaze lit on James and Alasdair.

James stared at her, disappointment flooding him, hitting him like a steel-soled boot to the ribs.

"Where's my lady?" Maili looked to Alasdair, her pretty brow furrowed. "I came to see how things"—her gaze flickered to James—"were going?"

"She isn't abed?" Alasdair took a step toward the laundress.

Maili shook her head, her dark curls bouncing. "She left her room before sunrise. She saw you"—she glanced quickly at James—"riding in with your men and said she wanted to greet you at the gate."

James' heart stopped, all the blood draining from him. "I didn't ride in with an escort." He looked at Alasdair, seeing he'd blanched, too. "I came alone."

"But we saw you." Maili clapped a hand to her cheek. "I was sleeping, and my lady woke me. We watched you

ride out onto the far shore, about six men. Then I helped
Catriona dress and she hurried below stairs.

"I thought she'd be here." She looked from James to
Alasdair, then back at James. "She'd been waiting so long
for you to come."

And now she was gone.

"Damnation!" James flashed a look at Alasdair and
then hurried from the room, unsheathing his sword as he
ran. "She was outside the postern gate when I crossed the
causeway," he called over his shoulder, knowing Alasdair
was hard on his heels. "If she's no' there now . . ."

He didn't finish the sentence.

It was too horrible.

And when he and Alasdair raced through the great
hall, then pounded across the bailey to the wooden door
in the walling that was the postern gate, all the dread in
the world descended on him when Alasdair flung the door
wide and they burst out onto the empty boat strand.

Catriona wasn't there.

Chapter Twenty

❧

*S*pineless curs!"

Catriona glared at her captors, six of the most savage, rough-looking men she'd ever seen. Filthy, shaggy-haired, and with wild, unkempt beards, they stank of soured ale. And her disdain only earned their wrath as they scowled back at her, though several leered. The one who'd ran at her on Blackshore's boat strand, throwing a cloak over her head before he'd pushed her into one of Alasdair's smaller boats, gave her a forceful shove that sent her reeling backward onto the cold, peaty ground.

"You're a worm, not a man." She pinned him with a stare, knowing that was true.

In the boat, he'd stuffed a wad of rank cloth into her mouth. And after they'd rowed to the loch's far shore, he'd bound her wrists behind her back before rudely yanking her from the boat and hurrying her along the strand to where one of their men waited with horses behind a cluster of thorn trees. She'd had a brief moment of mercy when he'd swung himself into his saddle, but then he'd grunted for one of the other men to hurl her across his lap.

He'd held her clamped facedown across his thighs, gripping her so fiercely against him that she was sure her ribs were bruised.

She knew her dignity was—not that she'd show it.

Letting her eyes blaze, she recalled one of Alasdair's favorite slurs. "You're goat droppings, all of you. Though I vow your stink is worse!"

"Call us what you will." The man leaned close, crowding her against a large, lichen-speckled boulder. "While you still have a tongue in your head to use."

His comment brought hoots and sniggers from the others.

Catriona drew up her knees, sitting as straight as she could against the rock. She also lifted her chin, icing them with her frostiest stare.

"Goat droppings," she repeated, not recognizing any of them.

And if she chanced a guess, she'd say they were broken men. Outcasts who belonged to no clan and who were sworn only to roam the hills, living as they could and making trouble as it pleased them.

Most wore a motley assortment of plaids—she recognized the MacNaughton colors—though two were clad in mail. All were Highland, a truth that offended her almost more than being abducted in the first place. Well armed, they also bristled with swords, dirks, and war axes. Shields and helmets hung from their horses' saddles, as if they knew they wouldn't need the like against a mere woman.

But they *had* bound her hands. The scratchy piece of

rope rubbed and burned her skin, and she was sure her wrists would soon bleed.

Until moments ago, her greatest ordeal had been suffering the rancid cloth they'd shoved into her mouth. And they'd kept her wrapped so tight in the damp, smelly cloak they'd thrown over her that she'd nearly suffocated.

Now, after hours of what seemed like hard, fast riding, they'd finally halted. The same man who'd hurled her across her tormentor's saddle hauled her down with equal roughness, whipping the foul-reeking cloak off of her before her feet had even touched the ground.

Or so it'd seemed.

But—she wasn't about to let on—they'd made a grave mistake when they removed her gag.

Words could do as much damage as a sword if wielded with skill. So she settled herself against the rock, biding her time, assessing her options.

They'd paused in a birch wood, choked with bracken and large, moss-covered stones. Their horses grazed beside a nearby burn, and they must have believed they'd ridden far enough away from Blackshore to call a rest, for two of the men had thrown an old plaid on the ground and were setting out a repast of bannocks, cheese, and ale.

Catriona watched them closely, then focused on a huge, red-bearded man with a powerfully broad chest and arms so thickly muscled he looked like he could uproot trees with a flick of his fingers.

There was a tinge of dullness to the man's eyes. A slight slackening at his jaw, hinting that his wits weren't all too sharp.

So she took a deep, nerve-steeling breath and lifted her voice. "Sniveling cowards," she taunted, "hiding beneath an upturned boat and then leaping out of the shadows to throw a bit rag over a woman's head, rather than draw swords on men who can fight you."

"For cowards, we've plucked a ripe prize." One of them grinned, then bit into a chunk of cheese that looked older than time.

The others ogled her, the glints in their eyes turning lecherous.

Her worst tormentor—the cloak-and-gag bastard—only scowled. But when he took a whetstone from a pouch at his belt and used it to sharpen a wicked-looking dirk, his eyes not leaving hers, she did know true fear.

He had implied, after all, that they might cut out her tongue.

Hoping they meant to ransom her rather than slice her to bits, she tore her gaze from him and speared the others with the haughtiest glare she could summon.

"My brother will slit your gizzards." She kept her chin raised, trying desperately to twist her hands from the bonds behind her back. "James Cameron is with him. When they come for me, he'll do more than that. He'll empty you so this wood runs with your blood."

"He may do." The dirk-sharpener didn't sound concerned. "Unless Erc"—he glanced at the dull-eyed giant—"breaks his sword before he can try."

Catriona's breath snagged, her stomach tightening as a sick dread chilled her. They wouldn't speak a name if they thought to release her.

And Erc—she knew the name meant "battle boar"—looked more than able to have done with her, likely with the greatest pleasure. Meanness rolled off him, and she could almost see his fingers twitching in eagerness. He

was clearly a man who knew only brute strength and vio-
lence, killing gladly at a word from his leader.

But he wasn't going to touch her.

None of them would if she could get her hands on one
of their weapons.

Hoping to try, she swallowed her pride and assumed a
pained expression. "Sure of yourselves as you are, perhaps
you'll give me a few moments to myself?" She glanced
at the nearest birches, squirming a bit to make her point.
"It's been hours since you took me, and..."

She didn't need to finish, for the frowns the men
exchanged showed they understood.

But none of them spoke.

"Please." The word galled her. "One of you can go
with me if you're afraid I'll steal a horse and ride away.
It's no matter to me."

It was, but modesty wasn't important now.

Not that it would come to it if her ploy worked.

"I really must..." She tried to sound desperate.

"Ach, let her go." The man eating the ancient cheese
made an abrupt gesture at the others. "Her whines are
hurting my ears."

Her main tormentor looked annoyed but jerked a nod
at the giant. "Erc—take her into the trees. But dinnae lay
a hand on her. I'll have her fresh for myself afore any o'
you get a taste of her."

Erc stalked toward her then, his cold, expressionless
face more frightening than if he'd scowled. But when he
reached to haul her to her feet, Catriona summoned all
her courage and leaned away from him.

"I'll need my hands, if you please." She twisted round
on her knees, showing them her back, the tightly bound

wrists that would make her wish so awkward. "You can bind me again when I'm done."

She glanced over her shoulder, seeing Erc look to the others. Her heart pounded, the racing of her pulse so thunderous, she prayed they wouldn't hear.

No one gave any sign, much to her relief.

Then one of the older men, a grim-faced man who hadn't yet said much, spat on the ground. "Cut her free." His tone was as hard as his face. "Bind her again when she's done."

Erc grunted and took a dirk from his belt. Stepping closer, he leaned down to slice the rope. But the instant the bind fell away, she thrust her hand into a slit in her skirts, seizing her own dagger and wheeling round to sweep the blade right across his ankles.

"Whore!" Erc roared, and blood sprayed, but even as he jerked, Catriona lunged. With all her strength, she drove her lady's dirk upward, plunging the blade deep into the meaty flesh between his legs.

"Yeeeeeeow!" Erc screamed, reeling crazily as blood poured from his groin. Howling, he fell to one knee and then toppled to the ground, curling into a tight ball, a steaming pool of red spreading around him.

Catriona didn't waste a blink. Darting forward, she ignored her bloodied lady's dagger—its hilt thrusting obscenely from his privates—and snatched Erc's war ax. She gripped the long shaft at its middle, unprepared for its weight. But nerves gave her strength, and she whirled to face the others, swinging the ax left and right, her gaze never leaving her captors' shocked faces.

"Don't think I can't use this." She'd never held an ax in her life. But her blood was pumping, giving her courage.

'Come near me and I'll not just stick you"—she flashed a glance at the writhing, whimpering Erc—"I'll chop off that piece you hold dearest and stuff it down your throat!"

It was the wrong threat to make.

Barks of laughter, hoots, and guffaws met her challenge.

Her boldness didn't frighten—it amused.

"Oh—ho! A Valkyrie!" The man with the cheese feigned astonishment. Then he started toward her, drawing his sword as he came.

"Try and take this"—he whipped the blade free, slapping its broad side against his palm—"and I'll give you a much better ramming than you gave Erc, by God!"

Catriona's first tormentor snarled at him. "Sheath your steel, she's mine." He knocked the cheese-eater aside, his own blade already flashing in his hand. Grinning, he strolled in Catriona's direction, clearly not worried about her skills with an ax.

He'd almost reached her when the thunder of fast-approaching horses came from the wood, the pounding of hooves accompanied by men's angry shouts and jeers.

"Hell—" The man stared, his eyes flying wide. Then he turned to run, bolting for the far side of the clearing just as James, Alasdair, and others galloped out of the trees, each man couching his sword like a spear.

"Aye, it's hell for you!" James kicked his horse forward, spurring after the man to skewer him before he'd run more than a few frantic paces.

"James!" Catriona reeled, her tormentor's death cry echoing in her ears, shrill and terrible. Screaming, lathered horses and screeching steel filled her vision, the ground shaking beneath the fury of so many racing hooves. She stood frozen, dizzy as the earth tilted and the trees and rocks spun crazily, blurring everything.

Hell's gates crashed open, trapping her in a tide of whirling, red-tinged madness. Her skewered tormentor stared at her from where he'd fallen, his face a mask of terror, his grin no more.

His companions scrambled, tearing off in all directions, stumbling over rocks, and screaming like women. James and Alasdair rode them down, slashing with swords or swiping axes in deadly, hissing arcs. More MacDonald horsemen burst from the wood, one banking a long spear, which he used to make short work of the cheese-eater.

Only the tall, hard-faced man who'd ordered Erc to cut her wrist-binds stood firm, whipping his sword from side to side and even knocking the blade from the hand of one of the MacDonald horsemen.

Seeing him, James slewed his horse around, forcing the beast through the seething chaos until he reached the man. "Your name," he demanded, swinging down from his saddle, his own steel pointing at the man. "Now, if you'd no' have me carve it out of you."

The man spat in answer.

"He has no tongue!" James glanced at Alasdair, who, still mounted, had ridden near to watch. As were the other MacDonalds, for the steely-eyed sword-wielder was the only one of Catriona's captors yet on his feet. The others lay dead or dying, a menace no longer.

"Perhaps"—James spun fast, swinging his blade in a hissing arc that sliced through the man's sword arm before he could parry—"he'll find it now!"

And the man did, howling as he staggered backward,

lutching his severed wrist to his chest, blood streaming
hrough his fingers.

"Ah, so he does speak." James strode after him, prod-
ing the man with the tip of his reddened blade. "Your
ame, man. And dinnae tell me it's MacNaughton." He
icked the edge of the man's blood-drenched plaid. "For I
now this tartan isn't your own."

The man didn't answer, bending nearly double over his
leeding wrist.

"They've stolen more than MacNaughton plaids."
)ne of the MacDonalds came forward to fling a bulging
eather pouch at James's feet.

A score of plaids quelled from the bag's opening,
preading across the ground in a tangle of color. Cameron
laids, Mackenzie, Macpherson, and even a few Camp-
ell tartans blended together, proving their thievery.

As did a spill of silver coins, a bronze torque, two gem-
ncrusted chalices, a candleholder studded with almost
s many jewels as the wine cups, and—James's eyes nar-
)wed—even a battered golden crucifix.

James and Alasdair exchanged a look.

"Kill him now!" another of Alasdair's men growled.
)thers shouted agreement and started forward, each man
eaching for his sword.

"They came to rape and plunder." A burly, heavy-
earded man put all the men's thoughts to words. "No
natter this one's name, his life is forfeit!"

"That one was called Erc." Using both hands, Catriona
ointed her ax—she couldn't seem to unclench her fingers
rom the haft—at the fearsome giant now sprawled some
ards away, her lady's dagger still raging from his groin.
That's the only name I—"

"You stay where you are!" James flashed a look at her when she started forward. Anger blazed in his eyes, scorching her. "No' one step closer, I warn you. We'll speak when I have you alone."

To her surprise, none of her kinsmen challenged him for his boldness.

Alasdair hadn't seemed to hear, his own fierce gaze on the tall, stern-faced man who'd straightened again. The man was beginning to sway, weaving as he lurched from one foot to the other, trying to hold his balance.

"You have two choices." James snarled the words at him. "Die quickly, one sword strike and you're in hell. Or"—he whipped his sword again, letting the blade flash past the man's throat, missing his neck by a breath— "we kill you slowly, and we'll do it in ways so vile you'll remember the agony for all eternity.

"So-o-o." He leveled his sword at the man's belly. "Your name."

"Farlan." He glared at James, his tone surly.

James glowered back. "Farlan who?"

The man clamped his mouth, his face stony.

James's gaze flickered to the smelly cloak Catriona's tormentor had thrown over her head on Blackshore's boat strand. It lay discarded on the ground, near her captors' fretting horses.

When he turned back to Farlan, he gave him a look that would've jellied most men's knees. "Have you been skulking about the glen in a dark cloak?" Scorn tightened his voice. "Shooting unmarked arrows at men and"—he glanced at Alasdair—"jabbing holes in MacDonald galleys?"

Farlan said nothing.

James contemplated him, his silence deadly.

"You're a brave man." He finally stepped back, taking a few test swings with his sword. "Daring, or"—he ran his thumb slowly along the blade's edge, drawing a bead of red—"you're a fool."

"I'm no fool." Farlan found his voice.

"You thought to steal my sister and live?" Alasdair dismounted then and strode over to James, his expression fierce. He glanced at Catriona, a muscle jerking in his jaw. "No man touches—"

"We meant her no ill." Farlan jerked a glance at Catriona. "We're broken men. We needed coin and thought to ransom her, no more. Ask her, she will tell you."

Catriona started to deny it—they'd meant to kill her, she knew—but even as James and Alasdair turned to glance at her, Farlan rushed toward Alasdair, using his good hand to yank a dirk from his belt.

Raising the dagger, he lunged fast, aiming for Alasdair's back.

"Hah!" James whipped around so quickly, Catriona saw only a flash of steel and plaid. Alasdair spun about nearly as fast, but it was James's blade that sliced into Farlan's side, nearly cleaving him in two. "That trick is older than the hills, my friend."

James scowled at Farlan as the man twitched in the bracken, then went still. "Every beardless squire knows to watch for a feint."

"He was aiming at you, lord." One of Alasdair's men stepped forward and spat on Farlan's body. "It's been long since a MacDonald chief was cut down by a dagger in the back." The man glanced at James and then nodded tersely. "I ne'er thought I'd praise a Cameron, but I thank God this one is so quick with his steel."

Bending, the man snatched up one of the stolen plaids, handing it to James, who took it and began wiping the blood from his sword with a fold of tartan.

"Dinnae think I did it for you." James glanced at Alasdair, then flung down the soiled plaid and strode over to Catriona. "Truth is"—he sheathed his sword—"I cannae bide a woman's sorrow, and I know your sister would fill the glen with her keening if you died."

Alasdair grinned. "That may be, though I'm thinking you had other reasons, by God! Something I once said to you in Blackshore's bailey, eh? Could it be you mean to hold me to those words?"

"What words?" Catriona shot a gaze from her brother to James, then back again. She had a good idea what was meant—a possibility that flooded her with joy—when James's arm went about her and he pulled her close. He held her clutched tighter to his side than the day he'd caught her in his wood and dragged her across the glen.

And with all the passion of their night on the ice floes, but there was something else, too.

A fierce possessiveness—a sense of claiming—that made her mouth go dry and set her heart to knocking wildly against her ribs.

There could be only one reason he'd reached for her now, especially here before Alasdair and all their gawping, drop-jawed kinsmen.

When those men started to grin, not looking at all angry at James's seizing her, her pulse really began to race.

"I'm waiting to hear about the words?" She clutched his arm, hoping she'd guessed right.

"They were words I'll mind him he said, aye." James

pulled her closer, his arm about her waist as firm as banded iron. "Something about offering me your hand in marriage, it was. Were I of different blood."

The world dipped beneath Catriona's feet. Everything around her spun away except the promise she'd just heard, the hope that set her soul soaring.

She'd wanted to provoke him into seducing her again.

This was so much better.

She tilted her face up so that she could see his eyes, but he was looking at Alasdair, his dark gaze piercing. Her own eyes were beginning to burn, badly. And her heart knocked wildly against her ribs.

"So-o-o, MacDonald!" James's voice rang with challenge. "Are you a man of your word, or nae? I'll no' be minding you that I've saved your neck twice now. That alone should sway you, my blood be damned.

"And"—he reached into his plaid, withdrawing the amber necklace—"I've returned a MacDonald heirloom. 'Tis a great treasure, I hear. So wondrous, I vow, that I'm of a mind to demand something of even more value before I relinquish it to you."

Catriona's vision blurred. "Dear saints..." She could hardly speak past the hot thickness in her throat. But she did peer up at James, needing the truth. "I do think you must mean me?"

"Hah!" Alasdair threw back his head and laughed. "You see what a bold minx you're getting."

James grinned and pulled her harder against him. "I wouldn't have her any other way."

"What are you saying?" Catriona squirmed in his arms, twisting to peer up at him.

"Be still—or do you no' want me to fasten these stones

around your neck again?" James reached to do just that. The deed done, he turned back to her brother.

"There." He tightened his arm around her. "The ambers are returned. And now"—he bent his head to kiss her, hard and swift—"I'll be having my own prize."

"Dinnae make me regret it, Cameron." Alasdair came forward to thump James' shoulder. "You can have her, aye. If"—he glanced at Catriona—"she'll have you."

James laughed. "That's good, because I already know she will. And"—he glanced down at her, grinning—"I'd have made her mine with or without your consent."

"Make me yours?" Catriona touched her ambers, happiness welling inside her. Shivers of excitement raced through her, and it might have been her imagination, but she thought she felt her necklace thrumming sweetly.

She felt so giddy she could hardly stand. But James's arrogance did pinch her pride.

So she broke free of his grasp and stepped back, setting her hands on her hips. "I thought I was a plague?"

Behind her, Alasdair laughed again, his men quickly joining in.

"You are, the saints pity me!" Before she could reply, James pulled her roughly against him, his mouth claiming hers again.

He gripped her face in his hands, kissing her savagely until she cried out and slid her arms around his neck, clinging to him as she kissed him back with all the need and desperation inside her.

She was dizzy when he finally tore his mouth from hers and set her from him. Blinking, she peered up at him, her heart swelling with all the hope and pleasure she never thought she'd feel.

Ignoring Alasdair's grin and the hoots and whistles of her kinsmen, she blinked against the stinging heat pricking the backs of her eyes. "You *were* frightful to me." Her voice caught on the words and she blinked again, faster this time, for she hated tears.

"And"—she did her best not to sniff—"you did call me a plague."

He leaned close, kissing her softly this time. "So I did, right enough."

She held his gaze, her heart thundering. "And now you think differently?"

"No' at all." He looked down at her, a devilish grin curving his lips. "You're the worst sort of pest. And I hope you'll keep on plaguing me forever. Because"—he pulled her back into his arms—"I cannae live without you."

And as he kissed her again—much to the amusement of Alasdair and his men—a tall, colorfully arrayed figure watched silently from the shadows of the birch wood. Slightly transparent, for he wasn't of this world, the man's long fair hair shone like gold in the watery sun slipping through the canopy of trees. And those who might have seen him, if any present were so gifted, would have blinked against the brilliant blue of his tunic, the startling crimson of his fine, flowing cloak. His hand, as strong and well made now as ever, rested on the shimmering white flank of the magnificent stag standing beside him.

He looked on as the happy pair kissed, his own heart knocking painfully. But he ignored the hurtful pangs, as he'd learned so well to do, and relished instead the strong approval soaring through him.

And—if he didn't wish to draw attention to himself or

the enchanted beast who'd led him here—he would have lent his own whoops to the joyful cries of the MacDonald warriors.

He'd been a warrior himself, once.

In truth, he still was.

Such things stayed with a man, always. Though he knew, neither his sword nor his much-loved war ax would ever again taste the thrill of battle.

Those days were centuries gone, but his heart lived on. As did his pleasure in feasting and laughing, the joy he'd taken in being young, strong, and fearless. How he'd gloried in his journeys at sea. His exhilaration at standing at the steering oar of his high-prowed dragon-ship as she sped across the long swells, oars beating and sending up spumes of white spray to flash down her sides. And—he curled his fingers into the stag's snowy coat—the hope he'd once vested in these rugged, mist-drenched hills, the herring-filled waters of the sea loch, and the glen's verdant grazing land.

He'd loved the glen fiercely, though he'd only wanted a narrow slice of the rich coastal headlands. He'd yearned for no more than a fair place to settle, a haven where he could moor his ships and keep an eye on the horizon. And where those men who followed him could raise their families and cattle and grow their crops in peace.

He'd held such high hopes that his people would thrive here.

He'd thought to raise sons beneath the shoulders of these great hills and take them to sea from his own sheltering shores. Above all, he'd planned to spend his nights wrapped in his beloved's arms, keeping her safe from danger and sorrow, and loving her all their days.

It wasn't meant to be.

The spinners of fate had other plans.

But he was his own man now. As it were, all things considered. And much as he would've preferred to stride out from the trees and into the midst of the rowdy, jostling men, thumping backs, swigging ale, and whooping louder than any of them, he stayed where he stood.

The warriors were breaking up now, readying to return to their home, their duty done.

And the Cameron had just swung his bride up in his arms and was carrying her to his horse. He knew the pair would wed. The young chieftain grinned as if he held the greatest treasure.

To be sure, he did.

For a maid who loved a man truly, no matter his name or blood, was a prize worth more than all the world's gold, as he knew only too well.

If the spinners were kind, the Cameron and his lady would find happiness.

He wished them every joy.

And he desired himself back in Odin's mead hall, away from this place he'd once walked in the belief a part of it would be his.

Too many memories lingered here.

"Do not come for me again." He spoke to the white stag but kept his gaze on the departing warriors and the young pair. "I'll not go with you if you do."

He rubbed the beast's shoulders to soften the finality of his words, for the creature called for him often. And each time, as now, the returning only poured salt on old wounds, making them burn again as new.

Scandia walked here.

And each time he came, he'd seen her.

But always through a filmy veil that looked no thicker than air but proved impenetrable when he tried to pass through it. In the early years, he'd kick at the haze, pounding his fists on the shimmering, shifting wall as he yelled in fury. But no matter what a ruckus he caused—and he was a big man who knew how to be loud—Scandia never saw or heard him. Once he'd even swung at the barrier with his war ax, and the jolt that had shot up his arm on the impact had pained him for nearly a hundred years.

His frustration stayed with him longer.

This time he hadn't seen her or the wall of haze.

And, Thor help him, that was almost worse.

"This was the last time, Rannoch." He glanced down at the beast, his fingers freezing in midair, for he was no longer rubbing the stag's great shoulders.

The creature was gone.

Frowning, he glanced round, but the magical creature was nowhere to be seen. The only flash of white anywhere near was a shimmer of sun-sparkle glinting off one of the birches across the clearing.

Or so he thought, until the shimmer moved and he saw that it wasn't sun-sparkle, but the luminous skirts of Scandia's glittering gown.

She stood staring at him, more beautiful even than he remembered. Wind tossed her glossy black hair and tore at her pearly skirts. Her eyes were huge, startled and disbelieving. There could be no doubt that she saw him— this time—for she'd pressed a hand to her breast and tears brimmed in her eyes, then spilled, glistening like stars as they slipped down her cheeks.

And—his heart seized—he could see her so clearly.

No filmy veil stood between them.

"Scandia!" He ran from the birch wood, leaping over heather and rocks, racing across the clearing before the horrid barrier could appear, separating them. "Precious lass, I'm here! Come to me!"

But she didn't move, though he could see that her tears were streaming now, their silvery tracks dampening her face. She trembled, too, her entire sweet form quivering as if she'd never be still again.

Then he reached her and pulled her into his arms, holding her close until her trembling slowed.

"Donar!" She spoke at last, her voice a song in his heart. "I thought you were gone to me forever. That"—another great shudder wracked her—"you would turn from me if—"

"Turn from you?" Donar pulled back to look into her eyes. "Why ever would I do that? I've searched for you nearly every year since..." He didn't finish, for they both knew what had happened.

Then—

"By all the Valkyries!" A terrible dread swept him, letting him know why the haze wall had loomed so maddeningly between them. She'd put it there herself, however unwittingly. "Scandia, lass"—he took her face between his hands, his heart breaking—"tell me you didn't think I'd blame you for—"

She gulped, not looking at him. "It was my father who slaughtered your people. Even you—"

He cupped her chin, tilting her face so she was forced to meet his gaze. "He thought you'd taken your life to avoid wedding me. He only meant to avenge you."

"You are not angry?" She didn't sound convinced.

"I want only you." He pulled her closer, burying his face in her silky, raven tresses. "Now, and for all eternity, if you'll still have me."

She shivered and caught her breath, the sound giving him hope.

"So you still love me, too." He wasn't asking, he knew.

"I do." Her answer split him all the same. "I've loved you forever."

He grinned. Then he blinked back his own tears, quickly, before she could see.

Viking warriors weren't known for their soft sides.

But just now he didn't care.

"Then be mine, Scandia. We've waited long enough."

She smiled back at him, her eyes bright. "Aye, we have."

A true Norseman again, Donar grabbed her by the waist and lifted her high in the air, twirling her round and round, and whooping with all his lung power.

And when, at last, he could whirl no more, he did what he'd ached to do for so long.

He pulled her to him and kissed her.

Again and again, and masterfully, for that skill, too, stayed with a man.

Odin be praised.

Epilogue

❧

THE GLEN OF MANY LEGENDS
AT THE BOWING STONE
SPRING 1397

We must circle the stone three times and then drop to one knee, begging good fortune."

Catriona took care to stay away from the edge of the ravine where she stood with her two closest friends. Cloud and mist swirled around them, making it difficult to see. But a strange, low humming stroked the air, and the sound thrilled the three women.

It was the first indication that the towering jumble of broken stones before them truly was the hoary monument they'd hoped to find. They'd already climbed in vain to two other high corries. And while this one appeared no more than a deep and narrow defile, strewn with boulders, the shivering air made their efforts worthwhile.

This gorge felt different.

Catriona was sure that any moment the blowing mist would brighten and turn luminous with the sparkles said to hover near the enchanted standing stone. Even if—just now—the monolith looked no more sacred than an ordinary outcrop of quartz-shot granite.

Soon all would change...

Her pulse quickening, she touched the amber necklace at her throat and then withdrew a small leather pouch from beneath her cloak.

"Once we've honored the Auld Ones, you"—she glanced at the two women beside her—"must choose your heathers. The rest—"

"Makes my heart pound, it does." Her good-sister, Isobel, rubbed her arms against the predawn chill. "To think we're choosing our future husbands on the draw of a wee sprig of heather."

"Not all of us." Marjory, often called Lady Norn, slipped off her shawl and swirled its warmth around Catriona's shoulders. "One of us is very well wed and"—she smoothed the shawl's woolen folds over Catriona's cloak—"already increasing nicely, even if no one is yet supposed to comment on such barely there plumpness."

Catriona felt her cheeks color. "I'm not yet certain."

She was.

But she'd been waiting for the right moment to tell James. He'd been so busy making plans with Alasdair and, more grudgingly, Kendrew to erect a memorial cairn on the field where they'd fought the trial by combat.

"If you don't know, I do." Isobel's dark gaze dipped to Catriona's middle. She smiled then, her eyes twinkling. "I've seen you turn green each time Beathag sets smoked herring on the high table of a morn."

It was true. And at the mention of fish, Catriona had to

stifle a shudder. "Then pretend you don't notice, or you'll have lost interest in choosing a bloom."

"O-o-oh, nae." Isobel flicked her glossy black braid over one shoulder. "I want my heather."

"Lucky white heather, don't forget." Catriona loosened the ties of the leather pouch. "Unless you draw a red bloom and have to wed last."

Isobel's smile didn't fade. "The Bowing Stone is on Cameron land. It's sure to help me pick the right sprig." She slid a look at the third woman, a tall blonde with startling blue eyes. "Not wishing you ill fortune, Marjory."

"The Norse say destiny is everything." Lady Norn shrugged good-naturedly. "I shall meet my future husband when I am meant to do so, not a moment before."

"And if you already know who you wish him to be?" Isobel sounded breathless. She stepped closer to the outcrop, her face almost glowing in her excitement. "What will you do then, h'mmm?"

"I'll wait, of course." There was no question in Marjory's tone. "As will he, I'm sure."

"Then let's begin." Catriona glanced at the setting moon, just visible through the whirling mist. Mist that suddenly glowed as if lit from within by tiny glimmering lights. "Look! We were right. This is the high corrie of the Bowing Stone."

On her words, the outcrop shivered, and before the women could blink, the jagged rocks vanished and the legendary standing stone stood in their place.

Beautifully luminescent, the monolith speared heavenward, humming louder now, its runic-covered surface bright with the pearly sheen of ancient, much-blessed stone.

"Hurry!" Catriona started forward. "We must go deiseal, in the direction of the sun, if we hope for the Bowing Stone's blessing."

And so they went, holding hands and making three reverent circles around the benevolent stone. Tears shone on Isobel's cheeks when at last the women halted and dropped to their knees on the cold, dew-kissed grass. Catriona and Marjory exchanged a look, already guessing who would pull the sprig of lucky white heather.

Some things are meant to be.

"Now, while the magic is strong." Catriona rose, already opening her leather bag. "Who will draw first?" She offered the pouch to her friends, smiling when Marjory gave Isobel a nudge forward.

"Oh, dear!" Isobel bit her lip, her eyes worried and her fingers shaking as she reached inside the bag. But when she withdrew the precious white heather—the only such sprig in the pouch—her face lit with a smile brighter than the sun.

"Oh, dear!" she cried again, pressing the heather to her heart. "It is me! I shall be the next bride." Her tears spilled freely now. "Dare I tell you who I hope to persuade to marry me?"

Catriona and Marjory laughed.

"You don't have to tell us." Marjory spoke for them both. "Anyone who helped tend the men after the battle would know. We all saw how you looked at my brother.

"But I warn you"—Marjory's smile belied her stern tone—"Kendrew is a wild one. You won't have an easy time taming him. Though I do think you'll not have any difficulties turning his head."

"Does he really dance naked on your dreagan stones?"

Catriona glanced at Marjory. "I've always wanted to know
f that tale is true."

Isobel blushed. "Catriona! He isn't that crazed."

"He is, be prepared." Marjory glanced at Catriona.
"He does dance naked on the stones. All the stories you
hear about him are true, every one."

"Oh, my." Isobel's eyes widened. But somehow, she
didn't look alarmed.

Catriona and Marjory stepped forward together, hugging their friend. "If our blessing worked"—Catriona was
the first to pull back, for the Bowing Stone had already
turned again to its usual jumble of broken, lichened
stone—"we'll hope to celebrate another autumn wedding
in the glen."

"I shall do my best." Isobel tucked the white heather
inside her bodice.

"And I have something to help you." Catriona lifted
her hands to unfasten her amber necklace. "This"—she
slipped the ambers around Isobel's neck—"will protect
you if the dreagans around Castle Nought get too restless
and decide they want a bite of you."

"It will be my brother who'll be after supping on her."
Marjory pulled her cloak tighter against the wind. "I'd
suggest we return to Castle Haven now before all three of
our brothers come looking for us."

But before they started down the hill, Isobel grabbed
Catriona's arm. "You know I can't keep your necklace. I
know it's a clan heirloom and—"

"So it is, aye." Catriona patted her friend's hand. "But
you wear it in love and faith. James told me Gorm's prophecy about the battle. It was that peace shall come to the
glen when innocents die and gold covers the hills.

"Something like that, anyway." She spoke as they picked their way through rock and heather. "Innocents have already shed blood here, and James believes the autumn gold of whin and broom fulfills the rest of the riddle. We wed last October and you, then Marjory, must also be autumn brides.

"Until then, my ambers will keep you safe." She lowered her voice, not wanting Marjory to hear. "There are strange things around Castle Nought. You'll be glad for the protection of my charmed stones."

"Then I thank you. But—" Isobel started, pointing. "Oh, look! Here comes James."

Catriona turned, spotting her husband at once. Looking furious, he was just striding out of the thick wood where, so many months ago, they'd had their fateful encounter in the morning mist.

And he was heading straight for the hill where Catriona now stood alone.

Her friends—damn their faithless eyes—had dashed off in the other direction, leaving her alone to face James' anger.

"Odin's balls!" he roared when he reached her. "Aye, I knew you're headstrong, but what were you thinking coming out here before sunrise and"—his fierce gaze flashed to her aching breasts, then lower to her somewhat thicker middle—"putting our son in danger?"

"You knew?" Catriona blinked. Her heart split. The hot passion in his words filled her with more joy than the whole world could contain.

"To be sure, I know!" He swept her up in his arms, holding her hard against him. "Everyone in this glen knows, and we're all tired of waiting for you to tell us."

"But you've been so busy. I didn't want—"

"What I want is to shout my happiness from the battle-ments, you little vixen." He stopped, lowering his head to kiss her. "We'll have a celebratory feast this e'en to announce the news. It's a good time, with Alasdair and Kendrew at Castle Haven just now.

"But first, I'm of a mood to take you on a journey." He kissed her again, deeper this time, and so savagely that her toes curled. "Aye, we need to be on our way—quickly!"

Catriona pulled back to look at him. "A journey?"

He nodded, smiling. "So I said."

"But where?" Catriona puzzled.

"You cannae guess?" He lifted a brow, looking amused. "It's a place I vow you'll love."

"Then tell me." She slid her arms around his neck, wanting to know.

Something told her he had something very special in mind.

"I thought we might visit the north lands." He winked, the heat in his eyes melting her.

"The north lands?" Catriona's heart began to pound.

"Oh, aye, sweetness." He kissed her again. "I thought we'd explore a few ice floes. If you're of a mind?"

"I am!" She could hardly wait. "You know how much I love the cold."

"That I do," he agreed.

And then he set off for his castle, carrying his bride and grinning.

Life was good in the Glen of Many Legends.

And as the morning progressed, the soft spring air filled with frost . . .

THE DISH

Where authors give you the inside scoop!

♥ ♥ ♥ ♥ ♥ ♥ ♥ ♥ ♥ ♥ ♥ ♥ ♥ ♥ ♥ ♥

From the desk of Vicky Dreiling

Dear Reader,

The idea for HOW TO MARRY A DUKE came about purely by chance. One fateful evening while surfing 800+ channels on TV, I happened upon a reality show featuring a hunky bachelor and twenty-five beauties competing for his heart. As I watched the antics, a story idea popped into my head: the bachelor in Regency England (minus the hot tub and camera crew). The call to this writing adventure proved too irresistible to ignore.

During the planning stages of the book, I encountered numerous obstacles. Even the language presented challenges that meant creating substitutes such as *bridal candidates* for *bachelorettes*. Obviously, I needed to concoct alternatives to steamy smooching in the hot tub and overnight dates. But regardless of the century, some things never change. I figured catfights were fair game.

Before I could plunge into the writing, I had to figure out who the hero and heroine were. I picked up my imaginary remote control and surfed until I found Miss Tessa Mansfield, a wealthy, independent young woman with a penchant for matchmaking. In the short preview, she revealed that she only made love matches for all the ignored wallflowers. She, however, had no intention of ever marrying. By now I was on the edge of my seat. "Why?" I asked.

The preview ended, leaving me desperate to find out more. So I changed the metaphorical channel and nearly swooned at my first glimpse of Tristan Gatewick, the Duke of Shelbourne. England's Most Eligible Bachelor turned out to be the yummiest man I'd ever beheld. Evidently I wasn't alone in my ardent appreciation. Every eligible belle in the Beau Monde was vying to win his heart.

To my utter astonishment, Tristan slapped a newspaper on his desk and addressed me. "Madam, I am not amused with your ridiculous plot. Duty is the only reason I seek a wife, but you have made me the subject du jour in the scandal sheets. How the devil can I find a sensible bride when every witless female in Britain is chasing me?"

I smiled at him. "Actually, I know someone who can help you."

He scoffed.

I thought better of telling him he was about to meet his match.

Cheers!

Vicky Dreiling

www.vickydreiling.net

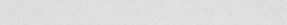

From the desk of Carolyn Jewel

Dear Reader,

Revenge, as they say, is a dish best served cold. If you wait a bit before getting your payback, if you're calm and rational, you'll be in a better position to enjoy that sweet revenge. The downside, of course, is what can happen to you while you spend all this time plotting and planning. Some emotions shouldn't be left to fester in your soul.

Gray Spencer is a woman looking to serve up revenge while the embers are still glowing. She has reason. She does. Her normal, everyday life got derailed by a mage—a human who can do magic. Christophe dit Menart is a powerful mage with a few hundred years of living on her. Because of him, her life has been destroyed. Not just *her* life, but also the lives of her sister and parents.

After she gets her freedom at a terrible cost, the only thing Gray wants is Christophe dit Menart dead for what he did—before he does the same horrific thing to someone else that he did to her.

I know what you're thinking and you're right. A normal, nonmagical human like Gray can't hope to go up against someone like Christophe. But Gray's not normal—not anymore. She escaped because a demon gave his life for her and in the process transferred his magic to her. If she had any idea how to use that magic, she might have a chance against Christophe. Maybe.

The demon warlord Nikodemus has negotiated a

shaky peace agreement between the magekind and the demonkind. (Did I mention them? They are fiends, a kind of demon. And they don't take kindly to the mages who kill them in order to extend their miserable magic-using human lives by stealing a demon's life force.) Because of the peace, demons in Nikodemus's territory have agreed not to harm the magekind. In return, the magekind aren't supposed to kill any more demons.

Basically the problem is this: Gray intends to kill Christophe, and the demon warlord's most feared assassin has to make sure that doesn't happen.

Uh-oh.

After all that, I have what may seem like a strange confession to make about my assassin hero who is, after all, a wee bit scary at times. He's been alive for a long, long time, and for much of that time, women lived very restricted lives. Sometimes he is completely flummoxed by these modern women. It was a lot of fun writing a hero like that, and I hope you enjoy reading about how Christophe learns to deal with Gray as much as I enjoyed writing about it.

Yours Sincerely,

Carolyn Jewel

http://www.carolynjewel.com

♥ ♥ ♥ ♥ ♥ ♥ ♥ ♥ ♥ ♥ ♥ ♥ ♥ ♥ ♥

From the desk of Sophie Gunn

Dear Reader,

After years of living in upstate New York, my husband got a new job and we moved back to my small hometown outside Philadelphia. I was thrilled to be near my parents, brothers, aunts, uncles, and cousins. (Hi, Aunt Lillian!) But I didn't anticipate how close I would be to quite a few of my former high school classmates. Didn't anyone ever leave this town? My life had turned into a nonstop high school reunion.

And I was definitely still wearing the wrong dress.

One by one, I encountered my former "enemies" from high school. They were at the gym, the grocery store, and the elementary school bake sale. It didn't take long to realize two things. First, we had a blast rehashing the past. What had really happened at that eleventh-grade dance? What had become of Joey, the handsome captain of the football team? (Surprise, there he is now. Yes, he's the one walking that tiny toy poodle on a pink, blinged-up leash!) Second, we were still terrifically different people, *and it didn't matter.* We were grown-ups, and what someone wore or whom they dated didn't feel so crucial anymore.

Cups of coffee led to glasses of wine, which led to true friendship. But friendship that was different from any I'd ever known, because while we shared a past, our presents were still radically different. My husband started to jokingly call us the Enemy Club, and it stuck.

That was what we writers call an *aha moment.*

The Enemy Club would make a great book. Actually, a great series . . .

The rest, as they say, is history. Each book of the Enemy Club series is set in small-town Galton, New York. Four friends who had been the worst of enemies are now the best of friends, struggling to help one another juggle jobs, kids, love, heartbreak, and triumph as seen from their very (very!) different points of view.

HOW SWEET IT IS is the first book in the series. It focuses on Lizzie, the good girl gone bad. She made one mistake her senior year of high school that changed her life forever. Now she and her teenage daughter get by just fine, thank you very much, with a little help from the Enemy Club. But then Lizzie's first love, the father who abandoned her daughter fourteen years before, decides to come back to town on Christmas Day. Lizzie imagines her life as seen through his eyes—and she doesn't like what she sees. She has the same job, same house, same everything as when he left fourteen years earlier. She vows to make a change. But how much is she willing to risk? And does the mysterious stranger, who shows up in town promising to grant her every wish, have the answers? Or is he just another of life's sweet, sweet mistakes?

I'm really excited about these books, because they're so close to my heart. Come visit me at www.sophiegunn.com to read an excerpt of HOW SWEET IT IS, to find out more about the Enemy Club, to see pictures of my cats, and to keep in touch. I'd love to hear from you!

Yours,

Sophie Gunn

♥ ♥ ♥ ♥ ♥ ♥ ♥ ♥ ♥ ♥ ♥ ♥ ♥ ♥ ♥ ♥ ♥ ♥

From the desk of Sue-Ellen Welfonder

Dear Reader,

Wild, heather-clad hills, empty glens, and the skirl of pipes stir the hearts of many. Female hearts beat fast at the flash of plaid. Yet I've seen grown men shed tears at the beauty of a Highland sunset. So many people love Scotland, and those of us who do know that our passion is a double-edged sword. We live with a constant ache to be there. It's a soul-deep yearning known as "the pull."

In SINS OF A HIGHLAND DEVIL, the first book in my new Highland Warriors trilogy, I wanted to explore the fierce attachment Highlanders feel for their home glen. Love that burns so hotly, they'll even lay down their lives to hold on to the hills so dear to them.

James Cameron and Catriona MacDonald, hero and heroine of SINS OF A HIGHLAND DEVIL, are bitter foes. Divided by centuries of clan feuds, strife, and rivalries, they share a fiery passion for the glen they each claim as their own. When a king's writ threatens banishment, long-held boundaries blur and forbidden desires are unleashed. James and Catriona soon discover there is much pleasure to be found in each other's embrace. But the price of their yearning must be paid in blood, and the battle facing them could shatter their world.

Fortunately, true love can prove a more powerful weapon than any warrior's sword.

There are a lot of swords in this story. And the fight

scenes are fierce. But passions flare when blood is spilled as James and Catriona showed me each day during the writing of their tale.

It was an exhilarating journey.

Catriona is a strong heroine who will brave any danger to protect her home and to win the heart of the man she never believed could be hers. James is a hardened warrior and proud clan leader, and he faces his greatest challenge when his beloved glen is threatened.

Because SINS OF A HIGHLAND DEVIL is a romance, James and Catriona are triumphant. Their ending is a happy one. Numberless Highlanders after them weren't as blessed. Later centuries saw the Clearances, while famine and other hardships did the rest. Clans were scattered, banished from their glens and hills as they were forced to sail to distant shores. Their hearts were irrevocably broken. But they kept their deep love of the land, their proud Celtic roots remaining true no matter where they settled.

Their forever yearning for home still beats in the heart of everyone with even a drop of Scottish blood. It's the reason we feel "the pull."

I hope you'll enjoy reading how James's and Catriona's passion for their glen rewards them with a love more wondrous than their wildest dreams.

With all good wishes,

Sue-Ellen Welfonder

www.welfonder.com

Read below for a preview of the next book in the
Highland Warriors trilogy,

TEMPTATION OF A
HIGHLAND SCOUNDREL

Available in mass market, August 2011.

The Legacy of the Dreagan Stones

Tales are told of a wild and untamed vale deep in the
Scottish Highlands. Protected by high, rocky crags,
blessed with rolling heather moors, and kissed by soft
mist and the silver sheen of the sea, this fair place is
known as the Glen of Many Legends.

Three clans—MacDonalds, Camerons, and Mackintoshes—call the glen home. These clans feuded
in the past but now bide a recent truce. Each clan
believes their corner of the glen is the finest. Clan
Mackintosh boasts that their holding is more. They
speak true, for their rugged, upland territory is home
to the dreagan stones; strange outcroppings that litter
the rough ground beneath Castle Nought, the forbidding Mackintosh stronghold that rises almost seamlessly from the cliffs that edge the glen's northernmost
boundary.

No one knows the true origin of the dreagan stones.

Odd things happen on Mackintosh land, especially on nights of dark, impenetrable mist, so many believe the unusual rock formations are sleeping dreagans. Dragons turned to stone, but able to waken and spread terror if they wish to do so.

Some tales are even more chilling.

Kendrew Mackintosh, clan chief, is proud of this legacy. Dreagans do lie beneath the dreagan rocks. He has seen them and knows.

And now they are stirring.

Kendrew suspects the dreagans resent the fragile peace that has descended on the glen. Clan Mackintosh has always been a warring tribe. Quiet living runs against their heated nature, so he welcomes the dreagans' unrest.

He, too, is restless. He'd rather stir trouble than pace his keep like a caged beast.

A man was born to fight, not lie idle.

He needn't worry, because tragedy is about to strike, giving him ample cause to swing Blood Drinker, his huge war ax. Along with sword-wielding foemen and stony-backed, fire-breathing dreagans, he'll be fighting a greater challenge than he would have believed.

His opponent is a woman.

And their battle begins in the shadow of the dreagan stones.